WEAPON OF BLOOD

By

CHRIS A JACKSON

ILLUSTRATIONS
BY
NOAH STACEY

This novel is dedicated to all the fans
who would not stop pestering me for a
sequel to *Weapon of Flesh*.

Without your support, this book would never
have been written.

Special thanks to Noah Stacey, once again, for the wonderful
cover art, and to my wife, Anne, for her editorial input and
tolerance of all of my foibles.

WEAPON OF BLOOD

WEAPON OF FLESH TRILOGY
BOOK 2

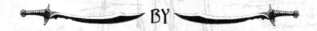 BY

CHRIS A JACKSON

ISBN-13 978-1-939837-06-6

JAXBOOKS.COM

PRELUDE

Murder weighed heavily on the noble's mind as he strolled through the beautiful gardens. Of course, as Grandmaster of the all the Assassins Guilds in the Empire of Tsing, murder was always on his mind. Death was his business. He took pleasure in his work, but more and more often that pleasure was tainted by unpleasantness.

Today's unpleasantness took the form of a garden party at the Imperial Palace. Dozens of overdressed courtiers strolled and chatted, strutting like peacocks dressed in plumage of silk and satin, frilled lace and powdered wigs.

More like a flock of carrion crows attending a corpse, cawing and flapping for a piece of the emperor's attention. He hid his sneer of contempt behind a placid smile and strolled on. They thought themselves superior, clever, truly *noble*, but he knew their secrets. He knew all their secrets, and their petty intrigues bored him, their blatant pandering a constant ache he could not ease, a rotten tooth he could not pull.

Politics.

Yet, as much as it disgusted him, he had to live the lie. He had to wear a mask of propriety to maintain his image and hide the assassin within.

A flash of darker color among the pastel hues drew the noble's eye. A man wound his way through the crowd, his simple crimson robe cinched with a silver chain around his waist, incongruous against the courtiers' finery. The golden

1

feather embroidered on the breast of his robe marked the man as a high priest of Demia, Keeper of the Slain, but he stood out from the gaudy courtiers in more than just his dress and calling. His fluid, purposeful steps and serious bearing gave him the look of a hawk amidst the peacocks. Sidelong glances and whispers followed in his wake. This priest of the death goddess disconcerted the courtiers, as if a shadow walked among them. They turned away, feigning disinterest, and gave him a wide berth.

A thrill of intrigue tickled the Grandmaster's stomach, heightening his senses and cutting through his boredom, for even though the priestly garb was no disguise, he knew what else this visitor was. He gestured, and the man smoothly shifted his trajectory, matching the noble's casual stride as he turned and made his way deep into the maze of flowering shrubs and groomed hedges, away from the inane banter and courtly laughter. Two bodyguards followed at a discreet distance, but he wasn't concerned with them overhearing the conversation. As blademaster monks of Kos Godslayer, they were constrained by spells of obedience, and had their tongues cut out to prevent unintentional slips.

When they were out of earshot, the man in crimson bowed and said, "Grandmaster, I bear news from Twailin."

He sighed. *Twailin again.* The subject of Twailin was beginning to irritate him. The news was never good.

"So, what news from our recalcitrant brothers and sisters, Hoseph?" He paused before a delicate topiary of jasmine and bent to inhale the heady aroma.

"The situation worsens, Grandmaster. They still have not appointed a guildmaster, the factions squabble amongst themselves like a gaggle of geese over breadcrumbs, and the Thieves Guild is moving in on their territories. Revenues continue to fall."

"A pity." The Grandmaster strolled over to a rose bush. Dew glinted on a spider web strung between two of the stems, and he smiled as he compared its complex architecture with his own situation. He was the spider, his network of Inquisitors the strands, feeding him information from assassins guilds in every city of the empire and beyond. When they told of something tasty, he pulled it in and feasted. Hoseph was his primary intermediary, his conduit to that web of information. The Grandmaster knew the players in this game as well as he knew the court fawners, though he did not know all of their secrets. Assassins were more circumspect.

Drawing a short, hooked knife from a fold of his robes, he snicked a blossom free from the bush with one deft stroke. The glistening petals shone dark and vibrant, the hue of fresh-spilled venous blood, and the aroma filled his head with a cloud of sweet remembrance.

Father's funeral...roses atop his casket...the satisfaction of putting that pretentious prig deep underground.

He thought about the dilemma as he methodically cut the thorns from the stem with quick twists of the blade, not unlike the motion he would use to sever a selected tendon to access the nerve beneath. Though he had been groomed from a tender age for the ultimate position of authority, as Grandmaster he rarely got the opportunity to practice the assassin's disciplines. He had a real knack and love for inquisition, however, even if his efforts were more recreational than professional.

"It's been five years since Saliez's death, and still we're feeling the repercussions. I'd hoped their attempts to operate without a guildmaster would not disrupt business, but that doesn't seem to be the case."

"Initial financial gains without the expenditures of a guildmaster's tithe were promising. Saliez *was* rather extravagant."

Hoseph's placating tone narrowed his master's eyes.

"Don't patronize!" He sliced the last thorn from the rose and brought the blossom to his nose. A deep breath, a slow exhale, and his ire eased. "Saliez may have been extravagant, and even egomaniacal, but at least he was ambitious and led with purpose. This intra-guild squabbling is detrimental. Tell them that they must appoint a new guildmaster from within their own ranks within two months, or I'll send them one."

"It *would* be best if someone familiar with Twailin filled that post, Grandmaster, but if you place someone of our own choosing in that position, it will work to your advantage." Hoseph's tone bespoke volumes, but he danced around the point as if it would burn him, and the Grandmaster fumed.

"People give me obsequious double talk all day long, Hoseph. If you wish to retain your position, speak plainly!" He inhaled the rose's heady aroma and leveled a stare straight into the man's eyes. "You obviously have someone in mind."

"Yes, Grandmaster. But the masters of the other factions may not agree with my choice."

"You need only concern yourself with *my* opinion, Hoseph. I don't give a bent copper for what these masters think! They may be skilled and powerful in their own little worlds, but the Assassins Guild is vast, and I'm the one who makes the decisions that benefit us all. Now, who do you think would best fit our needs in that post?"

Hoseph's face remained inscrutable, but his stance tensed under his master's rebuke. He cleared his throat before continuing. "Master Hunter Mya is ambitions and skilled, though young. Her revenues are higher than any of the other factions. She has potential."

Muscles writhed beneath the skin of the Grandmaster's jaw. "She was also involved in Saliez's death, wasn't she?"

"She *did* tell her fellow masters that she was there when Saliez died, but she wore a master's ring, so she couldn't have killed him." Hoseph swallowed and shrugged. "If you remember, the Royal Guard invaded Saliez's estate, so we had no way to find out *how* Saliez was killed. Mya managed to escape with his weapon."

4

"Yes. Saliez's weapon." The human weapon had managed to kill targets directly under the protection of the Twailin Royal Guard, an unprecedented feat. "She wields it still, does she not?"

"Yes, Grandmaster. She had been assigned by Saliez to its care, and after his death, she was the only one able to control it. She uses it as her personal bodyguard." Hoseph's mouth twisted into a smile. "It's kept her alive in spite of some serious attempts on her life from her fellow masters."

"The squabbling has gone that far?"

"Yes, Grandmaster. And she's returned the favor. You remember the report of the Master Inquisitor's death two years ago. That was rumored to be Mya's doing."

"Hmm...indeed." He dropped the rose to the groomed turf and crushed the delicate blossom under his boot. "She's dangerous. That weapon is the only creature in the Assassins Guild capable of harming me, and you think I should promote her to guildmaster?"

Hoseph tilted his head and pursed his mouth before answering. "Saliez promoted her to Master Hunter over many older and more experienced guild members. That suggests great trust. While it's true that the weapon has signed no blood contract, and is therefore not constrained from killing a wearer of a master's, guildmaster's or even the Grandmaster's ring, I think the key to controlling it is to control Mya. Elevate her to guildmaster and you put her securely in your debt, which might persuade her to wield her weapon at your command."

The Grandmaster's eyes narrowed. Yes, the thought had merit. Saliez's...*Mya's* weapon was an asset to be used properly, not wasted as a bodyguard. His trained mind skipped ahead to consider all the possibilities, plans, and plots that could benefit from the use of such a weapon, as well as the risks and opportunities for betrayal. The scales of risk versus potential gain tipped in his favor.

"Very well, make the offer, but make it directly to Mya."

"Yes, Grandmaster."

"Also, we must protect our investment. Instruct her to have a new ring forged, but insist that she doesn't tell the other masters about it until she actually wears the ring. If they learn of my offer before she has that protection, they'll go after her."

"Of course, Grandmaster."

"But we can't be sure the other masters don't have spies in her camp. If she dies, the weapon will be without a master. He'll run. I want Mya protected from the other masters until she wears the guildmaster's ring."

"She *is* protected, Grandmaster. The weapon—"

"Protect him, also."

"Protect the *weapon*? By all accounts, it's virtually invulnerable."

"*He* is human, and mortal, and as such, he must have weaknesses. The masters of the Twailin guild might be able to find those weaknesses and exploit them."

"I…suppose that's possible."

"And be subtle. Use resources outside the guild, someone familiar with Twailin. See to it." He waved dismissively.

"I will, Grandmaster." Hoseph bowed, took two steps back, and turned to go.

The Grandmaster smiled. He had spun a new strand for his web. His mind whirled with potential uses for the weapon once he had Mya under his thumb.

CHAPTER 1

Sereth stood at his master's elbow, hands clasped casually behind his back, fingers resting on the hilts of the daggers in his sleeves. *Watch nothing, see everything*, he thought, letting his vision slip into the attentive blankness that would best observe, even while appearing bored and inattentive.

He had plenty to keep his attention occupied.

The room itself was unremarkable, a wood-paneled office in the back of a brothel. The room's occupants, however, were among the most dangerous people in all of Twailin, master assassins and their bodyguards, the best of the best, or worst of the worst, depending on one's point of view.

Four of the five masters of the Twailin Assassins Guild were present for the meeting. Master Alchemist Neera sat stiffly, her rich robes drawn around her like armor. The eldest of the four, she seemed so frail that her ancient bones might shatter in a stiff breeze, her wrinkled skin dissolve to dust and blow away. Sereth knew better than to gauge her by her appearance. The alchemist wielded more magic than any other member of the Twailin guild. Her concoctions could heal, harm, kill or, rumor suggested, revive from the very brink of death. Her bodyguard, a slim fellow Sereth knew only by reputation, preferred envenomed darts, and rarely missed his target.

Master Enforcer Youtrin filled his seat like a side of beef fills a butcher's case. Huge hands, knuckles scarred by a thousand beatings, lay clasped on the table's varnished surface.

7

He might not be the sharpest dagger in the arsenal, but in a fight, he could receive and deal more hurt than any other two men in the room. A bodyguard seemed redundant, but he had one nonetheless, a huge brute with arms like tree trunks. His jutting lower jaw and olive-drab skin bespoke of ogre blood, but his eyes were sharp and cunning.

The newest member of the council, Master Inquisitor Patrice, lounged in her seat, clad in a comfortable array of silks and satins. She owned this particular brothel and a half dozen more like it, but Sereth knew that her greatest talents were not in the bedroom. She could flay the secrets from a person's mind like flesh from bone, and knew more about pain than Sereth ever wanted to learn. In his nightmares, he lay upon her table, his secrets laid bare as his skin peeled away.

Sereth repressed a shiver and focused on the Inquisitor's bodyguard. She was dressed like a trollop, but Sereth knew her vicious reputation, and did not allow the swell of pale flesh revealed by her loose bodice to distract him.

Sereth's own master, Horice, was head of the Blades faction, and probably the best swordsman in the city. That skill had served him well, clearing the path to the position he now held. Even so, he was not without adversaries, and not all attacks could be met with a blade, especially in this company.

Adversaries... The notion almost brought an ironic smile to Sereth's lips.

These three masters were supposed to be Horice's allies—had *been* allies not too long ago—but relations between the factions had become more than strained. Knowing an adversary's strengths and weaknesses kept you alive in this business. And while Sereth didn't know everything about these people, he knew enough. He supposed that they knew a great deal about him as well, but was certain they did not know everything.

If they did, he would be dead, or worse, strapped to Patrice's table.

A faint cry of passion drifted down from the rooms above, evidence of the quality services being offered. Everyone pretended not to hear, but like salt in a pot of water nearing a boil, the disruption served as a catalyst to action.

"I'm not waiting any longer!" Horice punctuated his remark with a fist to the tabletop. "That insolent upstart has kept us waiting long enough. I move we convene the meeting without her."

"Seconded." Neera's voice rasped from her withered throat, a consequence of age or a lifetime of inhaling the fumes of her noxious trade. Her fingernails, yellowed from the powders and acids of countless concoctions, tapped the table in an impatient staccato. "Mya must have been delayed with other business."

"She's ignoring us!" Horice hammered the table again for emphasis. "She's the one who suggested this council instead of appointing a new guildmaster, and she doesn't even attend the meetings! It's insulting!"

"The insolence of youth." Patrice flicked one manicured hand in a dismissive gesture. Though the youngest master present, she was near twice the age of the absent Master Hunter Mya.

"She may be young, but she is skilled. Her defenses are formidable and her revenge swift." Neera's wizened lips curved into a cruel smile directed at the Master Inquisitor. "As your predecessor learned."

Patrice's eyes shot daggers, but she didn't reply. Everyone in the room knew how the former Master Inquisitor had fallen; Mya's retaliation for an attempt on her life. The attempt wasn't the problem, but Patrice's predecessor had made the fatal mistake of leaving a trail that the Master Hunter could trace back to her.

"We'll *see* how skilled she is." Youtrin's scarred face stretched into a smug smile as he leaned back in his creaking chair.

"Shut up!" Horice fired a dirty look at the Master Enforcer.

Idiot, Sereth thought, then revised his assessment. *Twice idiot! Once for agreeing to help Youtrin kill Mya, and again for opening your mouth about it among the other masters.* Of course *he* knew what they were planning. It would have been difficult not to know, since he spent nearly every waking hour in Horice's shadow. And though they might not agree on much else, Horice and Youtrin shared a dislike of the young Master Hunter. Mya's dismissal of their condescending council had fostered that dislike, and it wasn't improved by her unconventional practices.

"Not another one!" Patrice's glossy lips tilted in a disapproving frown. "Don't you two ever get tired of trying to kill everyone who insults your fragile egos?"

"What I'm tired of is listening to *you* tell *me* what I should and shouldn't do!" Horice's hand shifted to the hilt of the rapier at his hip, and Sereth stiffened. Though the hilt was below the table, the movement of Horice's shoulder brought Patrice's bodyguard's attention to bear. Sereth gauged the angles between them. Though fetching, the deep V of her décolletage made an apt target.

Neera raised a wrinkled hand. "Enough of this bickering! I call this meeting to order. I suggested that we meet to discuss this very issue."

"Good!" Youtrin sat up in his chair, his brutish features intent. "It's about time we did something about that insolent whelp!"

"You misunderstand me, Master Youtrin." Eyes like pools of acid fixed the Master Enforcer with a pitiless gaze. "I speak of our continued inability to cooperate. This intra-guild squabbling makes us weak, and the Thieves Guild is pressing at every chink in our armor."

"That's the truth! A couple of my boys were roughed up on their rounds just yesterday." Youtrin cracked his knuckles, a sound like popping corn. "Our protection racket lost two more clients! Damned thieves undercut our rates, and they don't bluff about enforcing their new territory."

"It's not *their* territory; it's territory they *stole* from you!" Horice corrected. "They're pushing everywhere. It's got to stop!"

"So you two are diverting resources to attack a master in our own guild instead of focusing on the real enemy! *That* makes sense!" Patrice's sneer of contempt earned her a glare from the Master Blade.

"Slapping down that contemptuous little bitch isn't a matter of business, it's a matter of principle. She disrespects us, *all* of us."

"I disagree, Horice. It *is* a matter of business." Neera's calm tone juxtaposed his acerbic one, though Sereth could see her jaw muscles tense through her thin skin. "Resources allocated to one effort are necessarily diverted from others. We fight each other, so we have fewer resources to combat our true enemies. We *must* cooperate, or we will fall. We've lost a tenth of our territory south of the river in the last year, and revenues reflect that loss. Our lost income has surpassed the gains we enjoyed from not having to support a guildmaster."

"How can we cooperate when one of our own masters won't even come to council meetings?" Youtrin protested. "She refuses to lend her Hunters where they're needed, and won't even discuss issues that impact our operations. She's the one who suggested we could do without a guildmaster!"

"Yes, she did, and if you remember, it worked. Unfortunately, differences of opinion and refusals to compromise led to disagreements and this current lack of cooperation." Neera's tone had hardened, and her eyes flicked to all the others in turn, accusative and piercing. "The visit from the Grandmaster's representative to collect last quarter's revenues was not pleasant. She grilled me for a full hour about this situation, and I assume you all experienced the same. If this continues, we'll face sanction by the Grandmaster."

"Sanction?" Patrice's eyes widened. That word meant only one thing within the guild. "Kill us for squabbling? He wouldn't dare!"

"The Grandmaster has the authority to take any action he deems fit," Neera reminded her. "Our goal *should* be to make sure he does *not* see the necessity to replace us. We *must* cooperate!"

"And how do you propose we do that when we can't even make the youngest and most inexperienced of this council attend a meeting?" Horice shifted in his seat, and every bodyguard in the room tensed.

"This meeting is *not* about Master Hunter Mya!" Neera's lips constricted into a shriveled moue. "Her revenues are the highest among the guild factions. Instead of denouncing her youth and inexperience, perhaps you should consider emulating her success!"

"Success? She runs her Hunters like a band of peasants for hire! She takes contracts that do nothing to further the influence of the guild! She's even performed services for the thrice-damned Royal Guard!" Horice was in full rant mode now, and even the sternest glare from Neera could not quell his ire. "Sure, she makes more money than the rest of us! We're specialists, and Hunters are generalists, which means she suffers least from the lack of cooperation. She refuses to cooperate, thwarts us at every turn, and it makes *her* look good! She doesn't follow the tenants of the council *she* suggested we form! She votes against every initiative this council puts forth, all for her own gain! She's reckless and greedy!"

"And what does she do with her gains?" Youtrin put in, feeding off of Horice's temper. "She isn't even maintaining the image of her position as a master! She lives in that hovel of a pub!"

"Enough!" Neera's tone stifled their rants like a snuffed candle. "None of us are following the rules we all agreed to five years ago, Horice. I see only two options to help this situation, cooperate or appoint a new guildmaster."

"Fine! I move that we vote to pick a new leader of the Twailin Assassins Guild right now."

"*Another* vote?" Patrice slumped in her seat, obviously disgusted.

"Seconded!" Youtrin said.

Neera's eyes narrowed and her jaw muscles bunched and writhed until Sereth thought her teeth might shatter. There had been numerous such votes, and none had passed. The Master Alchemist always sided with Mya on this issue, and Patrice generally voted with Neera. Horice and Youtrin voted together as if joined at the hip. With Mya absent, the likely result was a stalemate.

"Very well. A quorum is present. All in favor of appointing a new guildmaster."

Horice and Youtrin raised their hands; no surprise there. The corner of Neera's mouth twitched in the hint of a smile.

"All opposed?" Neera raised her hand and looked to Patrice, but the Master Inquisitor did not raise her hand. "Patrice?"

The Inquisitor looked at her, then away. "I abstain."

Sereth cocked an eyebrow in surprise. This was a switch. Patrice wasn't exactly thwarting the Master Alchemist, but she wasn't supporting her either. Likewise, she wasn't supporting Horice and Youtrin. *What the hells is she up to?*

"The vote is two to one, Neera! The motion carries! We select a new guildmaster!"

"I nominate Master Alchemist Neera." Patrice glanced back to the older woman and smiled, then faltered when the Alchemist's lips remained pressed in a thin, hard line of displeasure.

Sereth squinted in confusion. *What just happened here?* But before he could fathom a plausible reason for the Patrice's actions or Neera's response, the Master Alchemist huffed and continued.

"*Before* we entertain nominations, we need a new guildmaster's ring."

Sereth shuddered. He remembered the previous guildmaster's ring all too well. Prior to becoming Horice's bodyguard, he had served as the Grandfather's assistant. The other journeymen had envied him for his position at the luxurious estate, currying the favor of the guildmaster. What they hadn't known was that every dawn he had wondered if he would survive until dusk. The Grandfather had taken lives at a whim, and tolerated no misstep or annoyance. Obsidian woven with gold and enchanted with powerful magics, the guildmaster's ring ensured the wearer's safety from all others in the Twailin Assassins Guild, just as the masters' rings protected their wearers from those within their factions. The rings were magically bound to the blood contracts that all assassins signed when they were accepted into the guild.

"We'll all share equally in the ring's cost."

"Agreed, but..." Youtrin's thick brow furrowed, as if thinking too deeply pained him. "I move that we don't inform Mya of this until after the new guildmaster is in place. She didn't help us make this decision; I see no reason to inform her until it's done."

"Seconded!" Horice flashed a wide grin and gave Youtrin a nod of approval. "At the least, it will prevent her from squawking about it until after the fact."

"All in favor?"

Surprisingly, in this if nothing else, all four masters agreed.

They fear Mya, Sereth thought, then amended his supposition, *or her weapon.*

"Very well. I'll contract a mage to forge the ring and contact you when it's finished." Neera raked the room with a sardonic glare. "Do try not to *kill* one another until it's done. Any more business for the council?"

There was none.

"Very well. This meeting is adjourned."

The masters stood, and their bodyguards moved to usher them out. Patrice and Neera disappeared through the door that led to the common room of the brothel, cheerful chatter and laughter reaching Sereth's ear's until the door shut behind them. Youtrin and Horice both turned toward the exit through the back hall to the alley where their carriages waited. Sereth took his time plucking his master's cloak from the rack beside the door and draping it over the man's shoulders. As he'd hoped, the Enforcers preceded them out the door. Despite the apparent camaraderie between Horice and Youtrin, he didn't trust the thugs as far as he could throw them. By the time the Blades reached the outer door, Youtrin's carriage had already pulled away into the rain-soaked darkness.

"Bloody rain!" Horice drew up the hood of his weather cloak as he squinted out the door. "My bones ache with this blasted weather!"

"Yes, Master."

Springtime in Twailin was a wet affair. Moist air rolled across the lowlands from the western ocean before slamming into the towering bluffs to the east, the high, steep walls of the ancient crater that contained the Bitter Sea. The result was rain. For three months, only shreds of pale sun eked through the constant covering of clouds, and the heavens opened up daily. It was not a cold rain—the lowlands were far enough south that the weather rarely, if ever, warranted a heavy cloak—but the constant dank weather chilled the soul. When summer finally arrived, the blistering heat was a welcome change.

As the carriage pulled to a stop in the alley, Horice started to step out into the rain, but Sereth put a restraining hand on his arm.

"Garrote weather, Master. Best let me check."

"Right. Thank you, Sereth. Don't know what I was thinking."

Sereth looked up and down the alley, then stepped out into the rain and turned to check above the doorway. He was well-

15

acquainted with the advantages of garrote weather, having used them himself. The constant hiss of rain on cobbles and the roar of deluges from downspouts prevented a mark from hearing an assassin's approach, and a heavy rain aided concealment. On the other hand, a downpour could ruin the trajectory of an arrow or bolt, darts or shuriken. Consequently, springtime was the season for close work, and garrote, dagger, and cudgel were the weapons of choice.

Tonight nothing lurked in the shadows above the door. Sereth crouched to peer under the carriage. Nothing. Lastly, he opened the carriage door and checked inside.

"Clear, Master."

"Very good." Horice hurried across the gap and boarded, shaking the rain from his cloak as Sereth ducked inside and took a seat. "Bloody rain!"

Settling back into the plush cushions, Horice doffed the hood of his cloak and propped his sheathed rapier against his knee. It seemed an extravagant weapon for an assassin, with an ornate silver basket-hilt and jewel-encrusted pommel, and was useless in the confined quarters of the carriage, but the blade never left Horice's side. Rumor was it was enchanted, but Sereth didn't know what its magic did, and Horice never volunteered the information. So be it; he'd take his sturdy short sword and slender daggers any day.

Sereth thumped the roof, and the carriage lurched into motion. He leaned back, rested one hand on a dagger hilt and the other on the latch to the carriage's door, tired, but attentive.

Horice shifted in his seat again, drawing his attention. The master often complained about the weather causing his bones to ache. Apparently, even the best swordsman in Twailin was not immune to the effects of age. Sereth didn't like Horice much, and didn't care for his assignment as the man's bodyguard, but the position had advantages, not having to fight in the inter-faction squabbles, fend off Thieves Guild advances into their territory, or serve a maniac like the Grandfather chief among them.

But there are disadvantages as well, he reminded himself. His position had attracted the attention of others, and Sereth was paying for it every day of his life. Even worse, he wasn't the only one paying for it.

The creak of an iron gate and the hail of guards snapped him out of his gloom; they had arrived at Horice's estate. The carriage lurched to a stop before the gaping double doors. A valet waited with a towel draped over one arm, a silver tray topped with a crystal tumbler and decanter in his other hand.

"Won't need you 'til morning, Sereth." Horice waited for Sereth to open the door and jump out before following and hurrying up the steps. As he toweled dry, he called back, "Good work today. Go home and get dry."

"Thank you, Master." Sereth strode across the courtyard and through the gates, nodding to the guards as he passed. He had much to do, and this weather was good for more than killing. With the aid of the rain, he could easily pass through the city without being noticed, and he had a long way to go—and another master to serve—before he could go to his own cold, empty home.

CHAPTER II

G arrote weather." Mya stepped out into the rain without even raising the hood of her cloak.

Lad followed without pause. He didn't wear a cloak. His old master's lesson rang in his mind: *Garments that impede movement hinder your abilities. Remember!* Discomfort was transient; a dagger in the heart was permanent.

Together, they walked through the rain. Mya didn't like carriages, preferring to walk regardless of the weather. He agreed with her; carriages were noisy, confining and slow, hindering both perception and mobility. May as well climb into a coffin, have it nailed shut, and be loaded onto a hearse. He scanned the street, the shadows, the surrounding rooftops and the storm grates. The rainy season always made him tense. His eyes penetrated the gloom easily, but the rain interfered with his hearing. Detecting a heartbeat or a knife leaving a sheath was impossible even for him in a downpour like this, and the rain masked the subtle scents of sweat, bad breath and flatulence that might betray a hidden assassin.

"Yes, Mya. Please, stay close. The rain—"

"Interferes with your perceptions. Yes, you've said that." She gave him a sidelong smile. "About a thousand times."

"Really?" He gave her a blank look. "You counted?"

"No, I didn't *count*, Lad." Mya rolled her eyes. "Sometimes I think that all the magic has damaged your brain a little."

Lad quelled a smile. Despite Mya's quick mind, she still hadn't caught on to his affectation. His understanding of subtle verbal interplay had vastly matured since his arrival in Twailin, but he found that people tended to underestimate him when they thought him naïve. *If your enemy is strong, feign weakness. If your enemy is weak, show your strength. Remember!* He would use every advantage he could to protect himself and his family, even in dealing with Mya.

"I hadn't considered that possibility." He glanced at her quizzically. "If my brain is damaged, could it be fixed?"

Motion low in the shadows...a rat. They passed the spot and the large rodent skittered away, a smaller rat screeching in its mouth. That was life in Twailin all wrapped up in one simple picture: the biggest rat wins. Despite that, Lad had not lost his love for the city; the teeming mass of humanity—each person struggling to be a just a bit too big for the next rat to eat—stimulated him as much now as it had the first day he walked through the city gate.

"Maybe. Magic can do amazing things, but without knowing what's wrong, it might be dangerous." She turned a corner and he scanned the narrow street carefully, every corner, every shadow, every niche. "Fixing a broken bone is one thing, but I don't know about letting a mage or priest into my head. I mean, what if they fix something that isn't broken?"

This, too, he understood, but the opportunity was just too juicy to pass up.

"How can you fix something that isn't broken?"

Mya sighed and rolled her eyes again. "You can't, Lad. What I *meant* was, if they go into your mind *looking* for something to fix, they might end up doing more damage than good. They could change what makes you who you are."

"Oh! Yes, that wouldn't be good." He had no intention of letting anyone into his head. He'd had more than enough magic controlling his thoughts, emotions and actions for a lifetime. "I think I'll stay like I am."

"That's fine with me."

They walked in companionable silence while traversing two narrow alleys and a broad avenue. It was late, so there were few people on the street, but Lad never relaxed his vigilance. The rain eased from downpour to shower, allowing him to pick up more sounds and scents again. *Metal clanking inside a second-floor apartment; just someone cooking. The scent of blood; only a butcher shop upwind. The creak of a window followed by a splash; someone emptying a chamber pot from a tenement window.* Mya finally broke the silence as they crossed from the South Dock district into Eastmarket.

"What did you think of the meeting with Jayse? Do you think he's sincere, or is there something else behind his request?"

Though Mya was very good at gauging people, and her tactical thinking was nothing short of brilliant, she often asked his opinion of their clients and colleagues, relying on his keen perceptions. People had tells, habits that betrayed their unease or nervousness, and Lad rarely missed fidgety fingers, pursed lips, or even the subtle tensing of muscles. Even Mya had tells, though she guarded her true emotions more closely than most. He would never admit to such an intimate knowledge of her body language, but he had learned much by watching her over the years.

"He didn't show signs of being evasive." He thought about it for a few steps, distracted by a sudden movement. *Just a flapping awning.* "I think he was sincere, but then, he runs a gambling house. He may be gambling that your help will be worth more than he'll have to pay you."

"That's kind of what I thought. He just seemed...I don't know...too nice. Almost like he was buttering me up."

"He seemed eager to tell you what he thought you wanted to hear. It could mean many things: he's trying to take advantage of you, he's afraid of you, he wants to have sex with you, or—"

"Sex?" She stopped cold, her eyes slashing at him through the rain. "You think he wanted sex from me?"

"His actions could be construed in that way." He looked at her curiously. Had she truly not considered that possibility? He had seen men's eyes follow her as she strode past, lingering on slim curves and snug trousers. He shrugged. "Why would that surprise you, Mya? You're an attractive, powerful young woman. Surely you've looked at men and thought—"

"Yes, Lad, I've looked at men and thought about having sex with them, but that's not the issue." Blood flushed to her face. The muscles of her jaw tensed and relaxed rhythmically, her teeth chirping against one another like tiny crickets. These were some of Mya's tells. His comment had struck a nerve.

"It's not?"

"No, it's not. If that's what Jayse wants from me, he's in for a big surprise!" She turned and continued on her way, her stride purposeful as she mounted High Bridge. Below, the rain-swollen river ran fast and dark, the roar of rushing water overwhelming the sounds of her steps. Lad matched Mya's pace, curious about what had set her off. He waited until they had descended from the arched bridge so he wouldn't have to shout his question.

"Why?"

"Because he's a businessman, and I'm a master in the guild!" Her voice sounded hard now. She crossed Broad Street, slowing as she entered the narrow alley that was the quickest path through the long block of shops lining the waterfront. Water still gurgled across the cobbles and through the gutters, but at least the rain had eased to a sprinkle. "I don't piss in my own bath, Lad. Relationships with business associates are a bad—"

The hiss of an indrawn breath from the shadows...

Lad moved before the sound of a puff of air through the dart gun reached his ears.

Hand on her shoulder, pull her out of the line of attack...

21

Mya yelped, but yielded as he thrust her out of the way.

...step around, acquire the target...

The dart that sped toward them was too small to cause much damage, and so, must be poisoned.

...palm sweep and pivot.

Lad's open palm slapped the dart aside without touching the barbed head, and he leapt toward its source. A blade sang from a sheath, another assassin in his path, sword arcing out of the night toward his throat.

Recognition of one's opponent, his weapons, his expertise, is vital for survival. Remember!

Katana. The information came to him instinctively, without any deliberation on his part. *Expert wielder, probably trained by a western blademaster. Lateral stroke meant to decapitate. Timing and execution perfect.*

Lad knew the fine, layered steel of a katana would not break as easily as a common tempered blade. He twisted in mid-air, arching his spine and flinging back his head. The edge of the blade passed a half inch from his nose, so close that he could see the glimmering reflection of his own eyes in its wavy luster. He clapped the flat of the blade between his palms and used the power behind the attacker's strike, as well as his own momentum, to pirouette around the sword.

As his heel met with the wielder's temple, Lad pulled back minutely, exerting enough force to knock the man senseless, but not enough to snap his neck.

I will not kill for you...

Lad had held to that tenant for five years. Not once had he killed in Mya's service, and tonight he would not break that vow.

Dropping to his feet, he released the blade in a flipping motion. As the braided sharkskin hilt slapped into his palm, he assessed his remaining opponents.

Three more.

The attacker with the blowgun stepped back even as the other two advanced. The nearest held two daggers low and ready to strike, but she had not anticipated Lad's theft of the first assailant's sword, which gave him a considerable advantage in reach. He parried her two thrusts, then swung the weapon in an arc. The flat of the blade met with her skull, and she fell like a poleaxed steer. Her partner dodged out of reach.

As the momentum of Lad's stroke turned him, he spied movement above and beyond Mya, two more assailants dropping from the rooftops. They would reach her before he could finish with these, but she was already turning to face them, her daggers out. Lad knew she was not without skill; he just hoped she survived until he could lend his aid.

The puff of air from the dart caster's second shot sounded like a hammer blow in his mind. Intuition and training brought the blade up into the path of the dart, and the envenomed tip shattered against the flat of the katana. He leapt, knocked the blowgun aside, and placed a careful kick into her chest. The blow broke ribs, and her head cracked against the brick wall. She fell in a wheezing heap, but she, too, would live.

The last assailant stood with two hooked axes at the ready, but hesitated. Lad brought the katana around and settled into a proper stance, ready for the man's attack.

It didn't come.

The axe wielder's gaze flicked past Lad, and then he simply backed away, turned and ran.

Lad whirled, ready to deal with the other two assailants, hoping that Mya had managed to stay alive. Unfortunately, he was too late.

Mya stood over two corpses, a bloody blade in each hand. One assassin's throat was slit from ear to ear, while the other bore a wound to her left eye which undoubtedly penetrated all the way to the back of her skull. Unlike Lad, Mya had no compunctions about killing.

"Did their blades touch you?" He dropped the katana and approached her, looking for signs of weakness or pain in her stance. "They were poisoned."

"No." She looked at the daggers in her hands as if surprised they were there. Her eyes shone white, wide in the dim light. He could see her pulse pounding in her throat. "No, they didn't even scratch me! HA!"

"You're sure?" He looked her over, but her clothes weren't torn or cut.

"Sure." She took a deep breath and grinned at him. "They made such a racket coming off of the roof, I was ready, and surprised them." She bent to clean her daggers on one of the fallen assassins' cloaks, then stood and indicated the three unconscious foes. "We should take one to question."

"Please. No, Mya." He gripped her shoulder. "We should go."

"Let me have a look at them, then." She rolled the swordsman over and snorted in disgust. "I know this one. Wu Jah; I think that's his name. Journeyman Blade. I should cut his head off and send it to Horice in a box!"

"Two deaths are enough for one night, and now you know who sent them. Come. Let's be off."

"If I send a message, maybe this bullshit will stop!"

"Or Horice will want revenge for the insult and try again." He turned her away from the prostrate forms. "Come on."

"Fine." She sheathed her daggers and followed him down the alley at an easy trot.

Four blocks later they slowed to a walk. Lad was on high alert, but his attentiveness was so intuitive, he managed to replay the attack in his mind as they travelled. Never before had they been attacked by more than two or three assassins. Mya had been lucky tonight; a scratch from a poisoned weapon was as lethal as a dagger to the heart. She was more proficient than he had thought if she could kill two attackers with no harm to herself. Even though they had initiated the attack, he regretted the deaths. They had only been following orders. He knew what it was like to have to follow orders, and he knew that someone would mourn them.

24

Family, friends, lovers…

The dead were beyond fear and pain; it was the living who would suffer.

"This attack could have been prevented, Mya."

"You're right." She cast him another vicious grin. "I should have killed Horice months ago."

"That's not what I meant!" He bit back his temper and forcibly calmed the tone of his voice. A deep breath returned his heart to a slow, easy cadence. "You ignore the council. They retaliate. If you paid them more heed…"

"They are old and irrelevant. They don't understand me, and I refuse to kowtow to their whims." She gave him an impatient glare; they'd had this discussion before. "I've tried to make the guild a less-brutal organization at *your* request, and I've succeeded with my own faction. By opposing the other masters, I'm trying to force them to change their ways. If I cooperate, the guild stays as bloody and brutal as always. You can't have it both ways, Lad."

"I know, but the violence is only worsening."

"There's no way to make lambs out of lions. Things change slowly or not at all, and change threatens the way they're used to doing business, which threatens their power."

"They wield enough power, Mya. If you cooperated on some things, they might—"

"You mean submit!" She gave him a short, humorless laugh. "No, Lad, if I give them a taste, they'll take the whole larder."

"Very well. You know these people better than I do." That was true enough. Lad understood human nature, and had even managed to grasp the intricacies of bantering speech patterns, irony, and humor, but the machinations of the Assassins Guild were beyond him. He knew one thing, however, and voiced it as plainly as he could. "They'll continue to try to kill you if you continue to alienate and ignore them."

"Ha! Let them try. That's what *you're* here for, my friend."

She gripped his shoulder, and he forced himself not to slap her hand away. He knew it wasn't an attack, but Mya's touch made him tense, which was odd, considering what they'd been through. She'd once cut a crossbow bolt out of his spleen, refusing his pleas to let him die. He'd never thanked her for that. Maybe he should have.

"We have the perfect relationship, Lad. You protect me…and I protect you."

Lad tensed again. *You protect me…and I protect you.* From Mya, it sounded more like a threat than a promise. He protected her from harm. In exchange, she kept guild Enforcers away from the *Tap and Kettle*, and kept his head out of a noose. Lad had blood on his hands, and as unwilling as his actions might have been, the Royal Guard would still hang him if they ever discovered he had killed more than a dozen nobles five years ago.

Their agreement was simple, but as with any agreement with Mya, it worked to her advantage. To Lad, it was a trap he couldn't escape without breaking his word twice over—his promise to Mya to protect her, as well as his promise to himself not to kill—for he knew she would never let him go until one of them lay dead in some back alley. He was too valuable to her, and she would never give up an advantage.

Finally, they approached the *Golden Cockerel*. Warm light glowed from the two large windows in the front of the bar's ground floor. Two men lounged on the porch, and one of them opened the door as Mya and Lad approached.

"Evening, Miss. Hell of a night for a stroll."

The two men were Hunters, and they were on duty. They didn't look like assassins, of course, but that didn't change what they were.

"Evening, Vic." Mya nodded in passing.

Warmth and light, laughter and the clatter of dice, the clink and clatter of cups and glasses, all met his senses at once. Lad's tension eased as he followed Mya into the pub's boisterous

26

common room.   Many of those present—barmaids and prostitutes, gamblers and drinkers—were Mya's Hunters. Here, if nowhere else in the city of Twailin, she was safe enough without his protection.

"Join me for some mulled wine, Lad?"   Mya handed her cloak to the elderly woman at the door and accepted a towel for her dripping hair.

He nodded to the cloak-check woman, who gave him a motherly smile and a wink.   As she hung up Mya's cloak, he noted the row of straight scars that crossed the underside of her forearm.   She, too, was one of Mya's people, and each scar, he knew, denoted a kill.

Fathers, brothers, daughters, friends...

"No, thank you. I should go."

"Well, be careful.   I don't want you to catch your death in this weather."

"Catch my..."   He automatically gave her a naïve look. "You mean catch a chill and become sick, right?"

"Very good, Lad."   She smiled and clapped him on the shoulder. He forced himself to not flinch.   "But there's more than one way to catch your death in garrote weather."

"Oh, right. Yes. I'll be careful."

"Do that. And thank you, Lad."   She squeezed his shoulder, and her sincere tone told him what she meant.   He'd saved her life again tonight.

"You're welcome, Mya."   He nodded, then turned and walked out into the rain and toward his other life.

CHAPTER III

Mya shivered, but not from any chill brought on by her damp hair or dripping clothes. Watching Lad's departure always felt like a warm blanket being pulled away, baring her to the cold night air. Mya knew she was safe here. Surrounded by her most reliable Hunters, she had nothing to fear. Besides, her performance tonight proved that physical dangers were less of a threat than they had once been. Still, after five years of having Lad at her side, Mya found herself comforted by his presence, and felt strangely exposed without him.

She shook off the feeling, dismissing it as post-fight tension. Her nerves still sang with adrenalin after their brush with Horice's assassins. She finished toweling her hair and returned the damp cloth. "Thanks, Jules."

"No problem, dear. Night like this isn't fit for a walk without a warm towel and a mug of wine to greet you home."

"Too true." She surveyed the boisterous common room. *Home.* Yes, it felt good to be home.

Mya breathed deep, savoring the scents, sights and sounds of her only refuge in the city. Paxal, her long-time landlord and self-appointed mother hen, stood behind the long teak-wood bar. Over his shoulder, the ridiculous portrait of a crowing golden rooster—the pub's namesake—glowed in the lamplight. As if sensing her gaze, Paxal looked up, gave her a nod and a gap-toothed smile. Mya smiled back. Aside from Lad, the barkeep was the person in the world she trusted most. More than a decade ago, he had taken in a frightened runaway, allowing her to sleep in the storeroom for the work she could do. After her sudden appointment to journeyman, then master, five years ago, he suggested she use the bar as her base of operations and had never asked for payment. She paid him, of course, but he had never once asked. She could never pay for his loyalty, she knew. That was something he had given her free of charge, that and one simple piece of advice one night years ago.

"There are two kinds of people in this world, Mya. People with power and people who live in fear. You have to decide which you are going to be."

"Which are you?" she'd asked, and he'd given her one of his rare smiles.

"Well, I'm the third type. The type that just doesn't give a shit anymore. But you're too young to be like that."

That axiom had been the single directing precept of her life from that point forward. She would be one of those with power, not one of those who lived in fear. The next day, she had sought out the Assassins Guild, submitted to their tests, and signed the blood contract.

Conversations rose from the bar and gaming tables. About half the people here were hers, and they had strict orders to maintain a festive air. The non-guild clientele remained blissfully unaware that the winsome young man on the next bar stool, or the buxom barmaid, might have just returned from casing a potential target, collecting a finder's fee for hunting down a fleeing debtor, or even slitting a throat.

A hearty laugh from one of the gaming tables told her someone had won a hand of cards or a roll of the dice. She encouraged her people to game; their contrived wins drew others to the tables. Guild member winnings were figured in as part of their pay, with Mya footing the expense. Everyone was happy, and the pub was always bustling.

Mya had once offered Paxal a formal appointment to the guild, complete with salary, but he'd just smiled his fatherly smile and shook his shaggy head. "Too old for that crap, Miss Mya. Barkeep's good enough for me. I'm my own boss and I drink for free." She'd let it drop without another word, but made sure his business thrived.

As Mya crossed the room, her nerves still jangling, she nodded to her people, one of the familiar barmaids, and a couple of regulars who knew her...or thought they knew her. Her pretense of being Paxal's rich niece allowed her to come and go at will. She strode down the short hall at the back of the common room, past the washrooms and storage chambers, to the thick oak door at the end. A heavy-set bouncer stood before the door, his huge arms crossed over a chest as broad and sturdy as an ale keg.

"Evening, Miss." One plate-sized hand closed on the door's latch and opened it for her.

"Thank you, Mika." She entered her office.

The tidy little room had been used to host private card games before Mya took it over. It was still set up as such in the unlikely chance that the pub was raided by the City Guard. But now no one entered except at Mya's express invitation, and she extended that to few. A fire crackling in the small hearth rendered the room warm and cozy. She pulled a chair nearer to the blaze, sat and worked at the wet laces of her soft black boots. Her fingers shook with pent-up energy, and she couldn't pick apart the knots. Laughing quietly to herself, she closed her eyes, took a deep breath and flexed her hands.

Memories of the attack flooded her mind.

Assassins falling out of the rain-soaked sky. Her heart beating like a hammer, her veins surging with heat, she could count the raindrops beading on their waxed cloaks. Plucking daggers from her sheaths, she was moving even before their feet touched the ground.

Duck-roll-parry-slash-flip-stab...and it was done. Two corpses lay at her feet.

Thank you, Lad...

30

The thought calmed her shaking hands enough that she could untie her boots. As she placed them on the hearth to dry, she heard a familiar clomp of boots, then the door opened and Paxal came in with a heavy platter. He was the only person who had an open invitation; anyone else would have knocked, or she would have heard Mika reducing them to a bloody pulp. The platter bore three items: a tankard of mulled wine, a plate of steaming stewed mutton with vegetables, and a cloth napkin rolled around polished silver eating utensils. Mya's mouth started watering even as he arranged the meal on the card table and laid out the silverware with precise motions.

"Thank you, Pax." She smiled at the nightly ritual and dragged her chair back to the table, facing the room and the door with the fire warm on her back.

"Bit damp out tonight, Miss, so I fortified the wine with some plum brandy."

"You're a godsend." Mya didn't know how he managed it, since the *Golden Cockerel* didn't have a kitchen, but every night he had her dinner ready and piping hot when she arrived, despite her irregular schedule. This was better than home had ever been, and Paxal was better family than she had ever had. Rumor had it that he'd lost a daughter long ago, and spent years inside a whiskey bottle, but he had never offered an explanation, and she had never demanded one. This was Pax, loyal without indebtedness or fear, exactly what she needed.

Mya raised the tankard to him, then took a swallow of wine. The hot spicy concoction set a tingling warmth in her stomach that radiated outward to infuse her limbs, and she sighed in contentment. "When I die, I'm leaving my entire fortune to you."

"Best not." He smiled and turned to go. "I'd just piss it all way on wine, women and song."

As the innkeeper left, her assistant, Dee, came in with a ledger, a stack of letters and a box of writing tools.

31

"Evening, Miss Mya." He placed the letters to the left of her plate, then sat across from her.

"Evening, Dee."

Dee was tall and lanky, and about her age. Though they apprenticed near the same time, she hadn't known him well, except as the butt of jokes about his rumored aversion to blood. His true talents, she had discovered, were an aptitude for numbers and organization, and his fine, elegant penmanship. Not one to try to fit a dagger into a sword's sheath, Mya made him her administrative assistant and lodged him in one of the rooms upstairs.

Mya took a bite of tender mutton, and tried not to let the meal distract her from business. This was another nightly ritual, and it calmed her nerves like the hot, spiced wine she sipped between bites. Her hands stopped shaking as she shuffled through the letters, dictated responses, and reported her activities of the day. She didn't mention the assassination attempt to Dee; it wasn't something he needed to know. She'd see to that bit of business herself.

Dee logged dates, amounts, and names in his ledger as she spoke, nodding with each notation, asking pertinent questions when they arose. By the time she was halfway through the letters, she had nearly forgotten that she'd killed two skilled assassins only an hour ago.

"Our meeting with Jayse went well, but I think he's hedging for a better deal than I offered. Send him a note thanking him for his hospitality, and quote him two gold crowns per day for our services, four if he requires personal protection away from his place of business."

"Got it." Dee looked up from his ledger. "Cordial or firm?"

This was a common question. Dee had a good grasp of language and could alter his prose and his penmanship to make a letter anything from friendly to downright threatening, an invaluable skill.

"Cordial, but no hints of personal friendship. He's a little too smooth for my taste."

"Right." The corners of Dee's mouth twitched in amusement, and she felt a twinge of irritation.

Forget it! Just nerves.

Mya went back to her letters; mostly reports from her Hunters on progress, or lack thereof, on their assignments. She fired off replies for Dee to jot down, later to be copied fair for her signature in the morning.

Only one more... Mya picked up an envelope of fine parchment sealed with black wax. Strangely, there was no imprint, just a blank oval impression in the wax.

"Personal correspondence." Dee nodded toward the envelope as he gathered up the rest of the letters. "I didn't want to get turned into something small and slimy."

Mya crooked a smile at Dee's exaggeration as she pressed the obsidian ring that encircled the third finger of her left hand—the ring that identified her as a master in the Assassins Guild—to the seal. A tingle ran up her arm, as if someone played their fingers gently over her skin. The tingle meant that if anyone besides the intended recipient opened the letter, the note inside would be destroyed. This simple magic ensured that private correspondence stayed private. Her own ring would impress the same enchantment upon a wax seal. A jolt of mild pain from her ring would have meant the presence of dangerous magic. Though a spell trap might not turn her into a slug, as Dee's little joke suggested, deadly magical traps were not impossible. Though he opened her guild correspondence, Dee left any personal or sealed letters for her.

She cracked the seal, removed the letter and unfolded it. The embossed crest in the corner caught her eye like a glint of moonlight on the blade of a dagger. She knew that crest like she knew her own name. Every member of the guild knew it...and feared it. All the tension and pent-up energy from the assassination attempt, quelled by her comforting routine, returned like a kick in the stomach.

She read the note.

Master Hunter Mya Ewlet
Twailin Assassins Guild

The increasing lack of cooperation within the Twailin Guild has resulted in an overall decline of revenues and a loss of guild influence in the region over the last six half-year cycles. This is unacceptable. Your own division, however, has not shown the same decline as others. Considering your success against the failures of your peers, and despite your youth, you show great promise.

Therefore, I am honoring you with the appointment to the position of Guildmaster of the Twailin Assassins Guild.

Since the previous guildmaster's ring was destroyed after the death of its owner, it is my wish that you contract the services of the guild crafter of magical implements in Twailin to forge a new guildmaster's ring. Upon its completion, don the ring, then convene a meeting of the other masters and show them this letter. From that day forward you will assume all the duties and responsibilities of Guildmaster of the Twailin Assassins Guild.

Sincerely,
Grandmaster

"Holy shit," she muttered as she re-read the note.

She shivered from a chill that the fire at her back had no power to dispel, quivering the paper in her hands so badly that she could barely focus on the elegant script. The illegible signature seemed to squirm as if it would writhe out of the page and bite her. Her office, so snug and secure only a moment ago, now felt claustrophobic, as if the walls were closing in around her. She couldn't breathe. Couldn't think.

"Something wrong, Miss Mya?"

Mya started and jerked her head up to look at Dee. She had completely forgotten that he was still here. She drew the parchment down into her lap, below the table's edge. Had he seen the Grandmaster's crest?

"No. Nothing wrong, Dee." She swallowed the lump in her throat. "Just a surprise, is all. Nothing important."

Godsdamned guildmaster… Her mind spun so fast she felt nauseous. It was one thing to fight with her fellow masters against appointing a new guildmaster. But the Grandmaster… No one but the guildmasters of each city and his secret cabal of representatives even knew who he was, but he wielded ultimate power in the guild. As nicely as the note was phrased, this wasn't a request; the Grandmaster expected her to assume the post.

You're a slave…

No!

Impulsively, Mya crumpled the note and pitched it into the fire. The fine parchment ignited instantly, and she watched it burn. She snatched up her tankard and gulped her wine. The drink warmed a path to her stomach, but did little to calm her suddenly singing nerves.

"Will you want to draft a reply?"

Dee's question snapped her out of her daze, and she forcibly focused her thoughts. "No."

All her life, Mya had relied on her quick mind. Now that mind, the mind of a trained Hunter and master assassin, whirred into motion. Like flipping through a deck of cards, relationships, causes, effects, dangers, and threats flashed by. Little more than an hour ago she'd survived the most organized and well-executed attempt on her life to date. Was it coincidence that she received a letter appointing her guildmaster that very night? If the other masters knew, they might take one last shot at her, knowing that once she wore the guildmaster's ring, she would be immune to attacks from anyone in the Twailin guild. She shook her head. The letter had been magically sealed; nobody could have read it. Nobody even knew she had received it except— Mya's eyes flicked up to her assistant.

"That's all for tonight, Dee. Write up those responses we discussed, and I'll sign them in the morning."

"Very good, Miss Mya."

She watched as he gathered his things, surreptitiously casting worried glances at both her and the fire.

Worried about me, or about my reaction to the letter?

Mya trusted her people, and Dee more than most, but news of this sort would be worth a lot to her enemies. She swallowed another gulp of the fortified wine and forced her voice into calm, sure tones.

"Goodnight, Dee. I'll see you first thing in the morning."

"Goodnight, Miss Mya." He looked relieved to see her acting normally again, gave her a casual smile, and left the room.

"Damn it! Suspecting Dee? You're being paranoid, Mya." But some niggling internal whisperer asked, *But are you being paranoid enough?* She sat back and sipped her wine, trying to force coherence into the whirl of suspicion in her mind.

Forge a new guildmaster's ring...

Mya held up her hand, gazing at the master's ring on her finger, reflected firelight dancing red on the polished obsidian. Each ring cost a small fortune to enchant, for they did more than seal letters and detect magical traps. Much more. Hers not only made it impossible for any of her Hunters to attack her, but also foiled any attempt to spy on or locate her using magic. But the ring's true power lay not in what it did for her, but what it did to her.

The magic of her ring bound her to the guild; she could neither leave, nor remove the ring. Lad had been right all those years ago. She had been a slave. The enchantments wouldn't even allow her to hack off her finger to release herself from its grip. And under the Grandfather's domination, she had learned what that slavery meant. Mya remembered the cold stone slab beneath her, the chill of the Grandfather's blades. The drug he had given her blunted the pain, but the real horror had been the elation on his face as he peeled her flesh from living bone.

My life was his to spend...

Ripples danced on the surface of her wine as she raised the cup to her lips.

...until Lad saved me.

Now, without a guildmaster, she was, to a certain extent, free. If she donned a guildmaster's ring and learned the identity of the Grandmaster, the shackles upon her soul would tighten again.

"Miss Mya?"

"Yes?" Her eyes snapped open, but it was just Paxal.

"Dee said you were finished, but..." His eyes settled onto her half-full plate. "Was the mutton not to your taste?"

"It was fine, Pax. I'm just not very hungry tonight. That's all." She forced a smile, finished her wine in one long swallow, and stood. "The wine was especially nice. Thank you."

"My pleasure, Miss." He piled everything on the tray. "Anything else tonight? Another cup of wine?"

"No wine, thank you, Pax, but..." Her mind spun ahead. She could trust Paxal, and he was subtle, a fixture everyone took for granted. "...a couple of favors."

"Name it, Miss."

"First, when the fire burns down, empty the ashes and scatter them in the rain. Do it yourself." Magic could do amazing things, and the last thing she wanted was for that letter to be resurrected from the ashes.

"I'll see to it personally."

"Good." She bit her lip. *Yes, he's the one to do this.* "Also, I need to know if Dee leaves the inn tonight. Let me know first thing in the morning, before he comes in with the letters."

"Of course, Miss." Not a hint of trepidation or worry, just simple, honest obedience.

Perfect.

"Thanks, Pax." She gave him a nod, and he left with the tray.

Mya paced the length of the room, looking into the dying flames of the fire with each pass, her mind a whirl of thoughts. *Godsdamned guildmaster... Why me? I'm too young! I'm more successful because the other masters need my help more than I need theirs. The Grandmaster has to know that!* Stopping before the fire, she leaned against the hearth and stared into the flames. The heat on her face matched the heat that rose in her blood. *Is this some ploy? Do the other masters already know? Is that why Horice tried to kill me tonight?* She knew she'd find no answers in the fire, but the mesmerizing dance of orange, yellow, blue and crimson drew her mind like a moth to the light. *Godsdamned guildmaster...*

"Stop it, Mya! You'll start talking to yourself next!"

Tearing her eyes away from the flames, she withdrew an ornate, three-sided brass key suspended on a chain around her neck, and inserted it into a depression in the third stone on the left of the hearth arch. Silently, the concealed door beside the fireplace swung open.

She stepped through the door, pushing it closed behind her and re-locking it. Although locks in a building full of assassins seemed superfluous, she felt assured by this one. The lock had three sets of tumblers, very difficult to pick, and only one other key to the door existed. It hung on a chain around Paxal's neck, which someone would have to break before the barkeep would give it up. Then, even if they had the key, an intruder would have to find the concealed lock, which looked like just another crack in the well-worn stone hearth. Finally, the door was set with a magical alarm to give her warning should some fool manage to break in. More likely, they'd be drawn to the little room that opened off of her office; a rumpled cot, small dresser, and a few personal items made this an apt decoy for her living quarters.

In reality, Mya lived underground.

Glow crystals set in silver sconces brightened to light her way down the stone steps to her apartments. Paxal had suggested she renovate the disused wine cellar, pointing out that it would be more secure than any above-ground dwelling. As Master Hunter, money flowed to her like water down a rain spout. She had spared no expense, hiring a foreign dwarven craftsman and paying him a fortune to ensure his silence. Here, hidden and surrounded by a veritable army of her Hunters, she felt safe.

At least, safe enough to sleep at night.

The stair emptied into a small living area paneled with wood and furnished with two comfortable chairs, a couch and an expansive rolltop desk. Her stocking-clad feet whispered across fine silk rugs. The hearth was cold, the firewood laid out, but unlit.

Knowing no fire could banish the chill she felt in her bones, she strode over to the map of Twailin that hung on the wall behind the desk. Pins crowded the map, each denoting an operation, their heads colored to indicate whose: green for her Hunters, blue for the other guild factions, yellow for non-guild. Picking up a red-headed pin, she drove it into the map where tonight's attack had occurred.

Mya backed up until her knees hit the edge of the couch, and sat. She squinted at the map, a mass of green centered on the *Golden Cockerel*, winding out through the city like the roots of a tree. Yellow pins—the Thieves Guild mostly—encroached on the patchy blue areas, less so when it neared her own. Red pins scattered across the city like drops of blood. She examined the map, looking for patterns, openings, weaknesses. Such analysis usually helped her focus her thoughts, but not tonight. She fidgeted, her mind skipping from the assassination attempt, to the other masters, to Dee, to the letter, to the Grandmaster... Lurching up from her seat, she paced around the room, perused the bookshelf that took up another entire wall, considered pouring herself a nightcap from one of the decanters on the sideboard.

This place was her refuge, her safe harbor, but tonight it felt like a cage.

You're a slave...

Mya shuddered when she realized how true Lad's words had been. She had always been a slave. She had spent her life trying to be safe, to be free from the things that could hurt her.

Memories... The stunning shock of a slap, blood in her mouth, shouting, ridicule, pain... More pain than any physical trauma could induce...pain that no child should endure.

"Mommy please, don't—"

"Don't call me that, you little rat! I should have rooted you out with a twig before you were born!"

Then, seeking safety, she had become a slave to the sadistic whims of the Grandfather. And now, scratching and clawing to keep what little freedom she imagined she had, she got that godsdamned letter. She found herself twisting the ring on her finger. In her youth, she had thought the ring would bring her power, and that power would keep her safe.

She had been wrong.

The only thing the ring on her finger had brought her was more slavery, more pain, more fear. She didn't know the Grandmaster, had no idea what being his direct underling would mean, and didn't want to find out. Lad had delivered her from her slavery by killing the Grandfather, and she wasn't about to put herself back under that kind of yoke.

Lad…

Mya went to a heavy oak door tucked away in the corner. Flinging it open, she stepped into her training room. Her eyes swept around the mirror-lined walls, the weapon racks, the smooth hardwood floor, and her heart slowed, the imagined bonds of slavery slipping away.

Over the last five years she had covertly trained with the finest instructors in armed and unarmed combat that money could buy. Here, every morning, she would practice what they taught her. They had filled her with their knowledge, tested and pushed her skills to the utter limit. A month had passed since she had sought their training. They no longer challenged her. Their skills were no longer a match for hers.

She slipped off her socks and unbuttoned her shirt. The dark wool rustled as she drew the shirt off her shoulders and flung it aside. Leather creaked as she loosed the belt of her trousers. The buckle clattered on the floor, and she kicked them away. Beneath her clothes, a layer of closely wrapped black cloth covered her from ankle to wrist to neck.

A subtle enchantment within the cloth kept her warm or cool regardless of temperature, invaluable in the rainy spring and sweltering summer. The other enchantment lay in the weave of the fabric itself. Any cut or rent would mend instantly, keeping her skin covered.

It kept her secret.

Slowly, in a ritual that had become as much a part of her as breathing, she unwound the supple wrappings. Her neck bared first, gooseflesh rising as the cool air of the cellar touched her skin. Inch by inch, she unwrapped the bindings until the entire length of cloth puddled at her feet.

In the mirrors, her bared flesh writhed with magic.

Her secret…her power.

Dark tattoos covered every bit of her skin save for face, neck and hands. Every night for five years, the runemage Vonlith had pressed his needles into her flesh, infusing her skin with his enchantments. Now she was complete, a dark tapestry of magic and flesh, woman and weapon. All of Lad's gifts were now hers: his strength, his speed, his prowess.

The runes squirmed before her eyes, as they would for anyone without a talent for magic. She could feel their power, *her* power.

Tonight, in the first real test of her skills, two assassins had died with the flick of effort she would have used to swat a fly.

She moved, smiling as her muscles rippled beneath the runes. Years of training had hardened her body and, along with the magic, made her into something more than she had been, something dangerous, something beautiful.

You are an attractive, powerful young woman…

The memory of Lad's words brought her up short. Mya had long ago abandoned any thoughts of a close, personal relationship with a man. She had never craved that kind of attachment, thinking it would only open her up to more pain. Besides, no one would look at her thus and think her attractive. Tracing her fingertips down her torso, she felt the raised flesh of her inked skin.

A memory stopped her movement.

Runes of emerald fire had burned beneath Lad's skin when she tested the bonds of his magic. Perhaps there was one man who might not think her secret so shocking or unsightly. She and Lad were the same, both etched with magic, both imbued with gifts no mortal could aspire to. He, if anyone, would understand her.

"Lad…"

Her own voice startled her, echoing off the four mirrored walls. She stood at an angle and looked into the infinite reflections of herself. *Are there really that many Myas? Am I really so much?*

Without thought, she began the dance of death.

Step, sweep, spin, punch…

This, too, she owed to Lad.

42

Block, step, turn, strike...

He had taught her the dance, the perfect form, the symphony of movement he had devised from the six formal styles of unarmed combat. In five years, with all her training, she had not been able to improve upon it.

Lunge, step, kick, spin...

Mya increased the cadence, flowing through the dance as effortlessly as the blood flowed through her veins. Heat flushed her skin as she moved faster and faster. To normal eyes, her movements would have been a blur, but Mya was not normal. She saw every lightning-fast strike of arm and leg with utter clarity, analyzed every nuance of motion and form. She *was* the dance, felt the rhythm, the grace, the perfection.

Thoughts of the Grandmaster's letter blinked into her mind, and just as fast blinked out. She nearly laughed; he didn't know who he was dealing with...

Step, turn, strike, block...

Blindingly fast now, each strike hammering the air with audible force, each step squeaking on the polished floor, each spin sending a shockwave of wind across the room, she was a deadly whirlwind.

No one can touch me.

Step, spin, strike, block...

No one can hurt me.

Kick, strike, block, sweep...

No one...except—

Mya halted the dance in the flick of a hummingbird's wing, staring at her reflection in the mirror, a faint sheen of sweat glistening over the ever-shifting runes, as she considered her last thought.

No one...except—

Closing her eyes, she pictured the day that Saliez died. In her mind's eye, she saw again a rune etched in the air, heard the gasps of pain and surprise as both Lad and the Grandfather lost their magic. One person knew her secret. One person held the magic that could snuff out her gift, rendering her helpless.

One last threat hung in the air like a blade ready to sever her spine.

Mya strode to the corner where she'd kicked her wrappings and picked them up. With an ease born of long practice, she rewound the cloth around her body, covering her secret from the eyes of those who would harm her if they knew. She tucked away the last flap of the wrappings and examined herself in the mirror again.

Tonight. It will have to be tonight.

She strode from the training room toward her bedchamber. From the dresser she chose a dark, slim-fitting shirt and trousers to don, then changed her mind. Vonlith's home was well protected. The man was almost as paranoid as an assassin. Breaking in would only alert him. No, she needed to play this differently. She donned a silk shirt of deep rose and tucked it into her pants. Soft leather boots laced tightly, pants tucked in and rolled over the tops. A slim stiletto slipped into the top of one boot, the rolled cuff hiding the hilt nicely.

In her bathing room, she brushed out her now-dry hair and added a touch of fragrance to mask the sweat of her exertion. Then, behind yet another mirror, she opened her secret egress and hurried out into the night.

The damp, chill air invigorated her as she slipped quickly through the shadows. Vonlith's home was more than halfway across Twailin. She had no time to waste.

CHAPTER IV

Lad walked away from the *Golden Cockerel* until the noise and lights faded, and shadows cloaked the roofs and alleyways. Stopping, he eased his mind into a light meditation, sharpening his senses until the hiss of light rain faded to distant white noise. He felt the patter of raindrops against his sodden hair and clothes, each one distinct, and through the background hiss, he heard just what he expected to hear: the scuff of a boot, the creak of leather, the click of a buckle against a hilt.

"Let the game begin."

The hiss of rain masked Lad's whisper, but he didn't really care if his stalkers overheard. They waited nearly every night to follow him as he left the inn. He'd never mentioned his dubious escort to Mya. If they weren't her own Hunters, she'd probably have them killed, and the last thing he wanted was more death on his hands.

Friends, wives, husbands, family...

So tonight, as he had every other night, he would evade them.

"Good practice..."

Smiling, Lad accepted the challenge. He bent to remove his shoes, unconcerned by his exposed back; these stalkers never tried to attack him, only follow. Tying the laces in a loop over his shoulders, he stretched the taut muscles of his neck, picked a direction at random, and vanished into the night.

Dashing from shadow to shadow, a silent wraith in the dark, Lad heard the patter of feet, the rustle of cloth, and the clatter of equipment behind him. *Four tonight,* he decided as he rounded a corner and doubled back through a courtyard. He lost two of the stalkers with that simple evasion. *They must be new.* He assumed his stalkers were apprentices—Hunters or of some other guild faction—assigned to follow him as a part of their training.

He heard the clatter of a loose cobble and a brush of leather against slate. The other two were more tenacious.

Good.

Lad lengthened his stride, exulting in the rhythm of his movement, the chill rain forgotten in the blazing heat of muscle and magic. Twists and turns, streets, alleys, and doors all flashed past him. He turned a corner and stopped to listen. *Still one left.*

He smiled, appreciating his stalker's persistence. The exertion was a pleasure after a long day spent following Mya from meeting to meeting. Despite his abhorrence for killing, he had been created for this, and loved to practice his skills.

Let's see how good he is.

Lad slipped into a narrow alley and bounded off a rough brick wall, converting his lateral momentum into vertical. A window ledge, a drainpipe, a clothesline hook, and his fingertips grasped the narrow eaves of the tenement's roof. A twist and a flip, and he landed atop.

Another moment's pause to listen. The creek of the drainpipe touched his ears. His last stalker was still with him.

Dashing across the roof, he leapt to another, his bare feet landing lightly on the wet slate shingles. He crouched behind a chimney and listened again. The faint patter of soft boots told him that his stalker had gained the roof and climbed to the crest, pausing there to look for his quarry. Whoever it was, they were very good.

How good?

Lad dashed into the open and over the next roof crest. Bounding like a cat, he landed with perfect precision, slid down the incline on the balls of his feet, and launched himself in a twisting leap into open air. Across the wide avenue, a balcony's iron rail arrested his fall, but only for a moment. He released in a flip, and his feet touched the cobbles of the street.

Dunworthy Avenue, just past Tony the baker's shop.

He knew every street, alley, nook and cranny of Twailin like he knew the scars on his own hands. The bakery's colorful awning was drawn down over the door for the night, and Lad melted into the darkness of the tiny space beside it.

Another pause to listen.

A faint patter, then the hiss of soft-soled boots sliding on slate shingles. Then...nothing. If it hadn't been raining, Lad might have heard the stalker's labored breathing or pounding heart, but not tonight. Slowly, he lifted his face and looked up. Across the avenue, a slim figure stood on the eaves high above: his stalker.

"Very good, indeed." Lad watched the figure's head sweep side to side, eyes scanning for movement. A minute passed, two—a stalemate of stealth against vigilance. Lad shifted his stance, considering his options. He had to leave his hiding place eventually, and his stalker knew it. When he did, the chase would resume.

A rat skittered beside his foot, and he shifted to avoid its teeth.

The slight movement must have caught his stalker's eye, and the figure acted without hesitation. Stepping back from the three-story drop, he ran and leapt for the balcony, but at the last instant, the sole of his leather boot slipped on a slick shingle.

He's not going to make it!

Even as the thought flashed through Lad's mind, he burst into motion, his lifetime of training—a thousand-thousand tumbling falls, desperate grasps, and twisting plummets—impelling him into action in the span of half a heartbeat. The

47

stalker's trajectory was off by several inches; his fingertips would miss the balcony's railing. The fall might not kill him, but Lad couldn't take that chance. Lad vaulted to the awning bracket above Tony's shop and launched himself at the balcony.

Midair, he saw the stalker's wide-eyed horror as he realized that he wasn't going to make his leap. His eyes snapped to Lad's and he twisted minutely, reaching not for the balcony rail, but instead toward his quarry's outstretched hand.

Lad snatched the stalker's hand and the balcony railing at the same moment, gripping both with fingers like an iron vise. Pain lanced through his shoulders as the weight of the falling body jerked hard on the tendons that held his arms in their sockets. The stalker's momentum swung him in a wide arc, but Lad kicked his legs and brought the two of them to a standstill, hanging there like an odd holiday ornament.

He pulled the stalker up—the weight was barely enough to challenge his magically enhanced strength—releasing the hand when the boy had a firm hold on the iron railing. For a boy he was, lanky and wiry, with barely a whisper of hair on his chin. Only inches separated their faces, the boy's panting breath hot on Lad's cheek.

"You're good," Lad told him, "but bare feet are always a better grip than leather. Remember!"

"I will." The boy gave him a startled grin. "You're bloody amazing!"

Lad released his grip on the railing and vanished before his stalker could move to follow. The boy's face, the eager grin and eyes full of wonder, haunted him all the way home. Lad had always thought of evading these stalkers as a valuable and entertaining means of maintaining his skills; never had he considered it a life-or-death struggle. One boy's clumsiness had changed all that. Imagining the boy's broken body on the cobbles beneath the balcony, he wondered how many corpses he had unknowingly left in his wake, how many mourners.

Friends, mothers, fathers, sisters...family.

48

The streets of Twailin flashed beneath his feet in a wet blur. His senses remained vigilant, but his mind drifted.

Family…

A block from home, Lad paused to listen. Certain that no more stalkers shadowed his trail, he strolled down the street and turned into the courtyard of the *Tap and Kettle*. The first time he had walked these cobblestones he had been no older than his stalker. Lad shook his head, dismissing his worries about the stalkers' safety. He could not control their decisions or actions any more than he could the assassins who had attacked him and Mya; they were only following orders. All he could do was try to keep them from dying. He remembered the two that Mya had killed only an hour ago. She, too, was someone over which he had no control.

There are things I can affect and things I can't affect. I can only worry about the things that matter.

Home, family…

Lad traversed the cobbled courtyard and slipped in through the kitchen door, bolting it behind him. The warm, cozy kitchen greeted him like a comforting embrace, the air still heavy with the smoky tang of roasted meat and the earthy scent of the taproom. At this late hour, all the guests were apt to be asleep. He smiled when he saw the towel and robe hung on the coat hooks beside the kitchen door.

Home.

Doffing his wet clothes, Lad scrubbed the towel over his skin. His shoulders ached from the wrenching pull, but that would pass with a good night's sleep and some light exercise. The soft towel brushed over the lacework of scars from the magical runes he had broken years ago. Breaking the binding enchantment had also broken the healing spells, and the ones that suppressed pain and his emotions. Though he still had strength, speed, and enhanced senses, his wounds healed no faster than any normal man's.

Well worth it, he thought as he considered what he had gained in the bargain.

Love, family, friends…

He caught his reflection in the shiny copper pots hanging overhead. He no longer looked much like the lanky youth Forbish had hired. He had filled out—his muscles were thicker and his face less angular—due mostly to maturing into a full-grown man, though Forbish's good cooking certainly helped. His unruly tangle of hair was longer now, braided in a simple queue down his back. He had cultivated these changes in his appearance, trying hard to leave behind the spellbound weapon, the assassin that he had been.

Dry, Lad slipped into the robe and went to the oven. A covered plate held his dinner, still hot. Retrieving it with a towel to keep from scorching his fingers, he put it on the counter, filled a small tankard from a keg of Highland Summerbrew in the taproom, and pulled a kitchen stool over to settle down and eat.

A faint noise from the common room caught his attention, a quiet slurp and grunt that he had come to know very well indeed. He wasn't the only one up. Smiling, he loaded his plate and cup onto a tray and eased through the door.

There, beside the glowing hearth, sat his two reasons for living.

Wiggen snuggled down into the cushions of a big chair, their daughter, Lissa, tucked into the crook of her arm, suckling. His wife looked up as he came in, her face lighting with pleasure, her smile tugging at the deep scar that marred her cheek. Putting the tray down on the hearth, Lad leaned down to her, the sweetness of her kiss worth every pain of his broken magic.

Who would have thought that a weapon could fall in love?

After Saliez's death, he'd avoided the inn during the day, slipping in through Wiggen's bedroom window late every night. Only two years later had he finally deemed it safe to openly court and wed the woman he loved. Forbish, by this time married to his barmaid, Josie, and guardian to her two nephews, had nearly keeled over when Lad revealed that he was still alive, though Josie accepted the news with her usual surly aplomb. Her twin nephews, Tika and Ponce, had taken to Lad immediately, treating him like an adored uncle. And just when Lad thought that his happiness was complete, Lissa had come along and stolen his heart just as her mother had. He had more than he ever hoped for, more than he ever dreamed possible.

"Hi." Wiggen's voice soothed him like a sweet balm, the mere sight of her an elixir that washed away his troubles.

"Hi." He ran the back of his fingers down her cheek, then reached down to brush a lock of hair from Lissa's brow. The babe, just less than a year old, barely stirred, so focused was she upon her late-night meal. His rumbling stomach reminded him of his own hunger, and he sat to eat.

"Busy night?"

"Yes." Lad held no secrets from Wiggen. "Another attack on Mya—unsuccessful, of course."

"Mmmm. Did you..."

"No," he answered, hearing the worry in her tone and knowing exactly what she was asking. "I didn't kill anyone, but Mya did. Two of them jumped her, and she did it before I could stop her." He shook his head in frustration.

"It's not your fault, Lad. You can't control her."

Lissa stopped suckling and started squirming, flailing her tiny hands through the air. Wiggen expertly shifted the baby up to her shoulder and began to pat her back, but she looked up at Lad with concerned eyes. "She scares me. I wish you would just quit and come work for father."

"Mya is a problem, but I gave her my word. Besides, you didn't marry the poor stableboy that Forbish took in, but the dedicated assistant to a successful businesswoman." Maintaining that false identity helped keep him safe from the Royal Guard. Though he doubted they still actively hunted him, they would never forget the lives he'd taken while under the Grandfather's control.

51

A resounding burp from Lissa drew his attention from his troubling thoughts, and a smile from his lips.

"Somebody's full."

"And ready for bed." Wiggen stood, then bent to give him another kiss. "Come in soon, Lad."

"I will." Watching her vanish down the hall to their rooms, he could hear her murmuring softly as she put the babe to her crib. Their own bed creaked as Wiggen laid herself to rest.

Lad resumed his dinner, leaning into the warmth of the hearth and listening to the ebb and flow of the world around him. The rain on the roof, the creaks and groans of the inn's timbers, the snores of sleeping guests, the stomp of a hoof from the barn across the courtyard. He loved this place, these people, the comfortable feeling of home. Only here did his worries melt away. Here he could be the man—father, lover, husband, friend—that he longed to be. Here he could be something other than a weapon. He knew that the sanctuary was temporary, that in the morning he would have to leave this safe haven and become the weapon once again.

But that's tomorrow.

His plate clean and his tankard empty, Lad took the dishes to the kitchen and put them in the wash barrel, then went to the room he shared with his family. A bare glow seeped from the lamp, but it was more than enough light for him to see. He bent over the crib where Lissa slept, and stroked a finger lightly over her pudgy pink cheek. He vowed silently to keep her from all harm, to give her the love and life that he had never known as a child.

Wiggen lay in their bed, the blankets tracing the smooth curve of her hip, her hair loose on the pillow. By her breathing, he knew she wasn't asleep yet, so he doffed the robe and slipped in beside her, pulling her close. She edged back into his embrace and sighed in sleepy contentment. Lad breathed in the scent of her hair, felt her heartbeat against his chest.

Wiggen...

With fingertips as light as feathers, he caressed her shoulder, tenderly kissing the back of her neck.

"Mmmm...that's nice, but I'm too tired tonight, Lad." She sighed and pulled away, just a tiny bit, but enough to get her point across. "Can't we just sleep?"

"Of course." After one more kiss, he ceased his amorous attentions and rolled onto his back. Since the baby, her interest in lovemaking had waned. He understood that, between her work at the inn and tending to Lissa, she didn't get much rest, and she had assured him that it was only temporary. Lad was content to wait. He missed their love-making, but knew there was more to love than sex. Closing his eyes, he meditated to calm his mind and aid his descent into sleep. It didn't work as well as making love to Wiggen, but it did work, and soon his thoughts settled into peace, on the verge of oblivion.

Just before sleep overtook him, a memory surfaced, his words to Mya earlier in the evening: *Don't you ever look at men and wonder...*

Why did I say that? Why would I care if Mya wonders about that?

CHAPTER V

D amnedest thing I ever seen, Captain." Sergeant Tamir stared down at the corpse with a look of stern puzzlement. "Can't figure out how he done it."

Captain Norwood joined his sergeant beside the thickly upholstered armchair and squinted down at the dead man. The corpse sat upright, a look of mild startlement on its face. A multi-hued ray of light shone upon the dead face, painting the pale features with bizarre rainbow colors. Norwood glanced up at the window in irritation, thinking to order Tamir to pull the shade, but there was no shade to pull. The mosaic of crystals set in the window's panes showered the room with wondrous colors, but Norwood was in no mood to enjoy the beauty. The window probably cost more than the captain earned in a month, and Norwood had been roused out of his home before he'd even eaten breakfast, all so he could come look at a dead rich man.

The rest of the room reflected the victim's affluent taste just as brilliantly as the window. The dark oak desk and its matching end tables and bookshelves, cunningly carved with abstract shapes and patterns, set with handles, latches and bookends of gleaming gold, ivory, silver and jade, were all obviously worth a fortune. In one corner stood a full-length oval mirror framed in silver, the gleaming metal decorated with spidery tracings that gave Norwood a headache when he tried to focus on them. The entire townhouse bespoke wealth. Wealth and magic.

The owner, however, would not be enjoying his wealth any longer.

The corpse's hands still gripped the arms of the chair, his eyes wide and fixed upon a spot straight across the low table at the matching chair, as if he'd been carrying on a conversation with someone seated there when he suddenly died. His legs were crossed, and a snifter of brandy sat on an end table at his elbow. In fact, the only clues that he was not still alive and paying close attention to that conversation were a slight fecal odor and a bloody stain on the collar of his expensive silk robe.

"It's a puzzle all right."

Norwood scanned the opulently appointed study for any clues to that puzzle, but his practiced eye found nothing obviously out of place. In fact, the room was immaculately tidy. According to Sergeant Tamir, the entire townhouse mirrored that condition, with nothing to indicate the master of the house sat dead in his study. Kneeling, the captain lifted the embroidered hem of the corpse's robe and peered beneath. The fecal odor wafted out stronger, and a broad stain marred the back of his nightshirt behind his crossed legs.

"Well, he died right here. Shat himself right in this chair." Norwood stood and glared down at the corpse again. "What did you say his name was?"

"Vonlith, sir." Tamir consulted his evidence log. "Housekeeper found him up here when he didn't come down for his breakfast. She went completely hysterical. Ran right out into the street screaming 'Murder' at the top of her lungs."

"Wonderful. Rumors will be flying all over Hightown by mid-morning."

"No doubt, sir. Anyway, she came in early this morning and made everything up just like she always did. She said he was a stickler for details, always wanted things just so. Part of bein' a wizard, I guess."

"Hmph. I guess wizarding pays well. This place is nicer than many of the nobles' homes I've been in." As Captain of the

Royal Guard, Norwood had considerable experience with nobility. He was less familiar with the habits of wizards, even though the Wizards Guild and many of its members resided in his jurisdiction, north of the river. To his mind, practitioners of magic tended to be quirky, arrogant, and more than a little annoying. "What other servants did he have?"

"Only a stablehand." Tamir flipped a page in his book. "But he just takes care of the outside of the house. Doesn't even have a key."

"Vonlith didn't employ any guards? Wealth like this attracts thieves like honey draws flies."

"None, sir, but I don't know many thieves foolish enough to rob a wizard's home. They're generally jealous of their privacy, and tend to have nasty magical doodahs to keep out the riffraff."

"Good point." He peered around the room again, wondering how much of what he saw was magical. The mirror, certainly. Hells, the carpet under his boots could be magical for all Norwood knew. "We better wait for Master Woefler to arrive before we poke into anything."

"Woefler's coming?" Tamir made a sour face. "That skinny git makes my teeth ache, sir."

"He might be a skinny git, but I'd rather have *him* burned to ashes by a wizard's trap than any of my guardsmen. Even you, Sergeant."

"Thanks, sir."

"We can, however, have a casual look around."

"Already done that, sir."

"Good. No windows or doors were broken or forced?"

"None that we've seen so far." Tamir gave a stiff shrug. "A few doors are locked, and I thought it best if we not go kicking any in."

Norwood bent closer to the corpse again, and placed his palm on the forehead. The flesh was cool; some hours had passed since death. He lifted one hand from the armrest, having to pull the rigid fingers away from the leather. The arm moved

56

with some resistance. The flesh was stiff, but not as unyielding as it would eventually become. The eyes were hazed and dry, but clear of blood. He opened the mouth with gentle pressure on the tip of the wizard's bearded chin, wary of what might issue forth. He'd seen some strange deaths in his time, and sometimes corpses didn't stay dead. There was no blood, and the man's tongue was not discolored or bloated.

"Rigor hasn't set in all the way yet. Maybe eight hours. No sign of blunt trauma to the skull." He looked at the back of the chair. "And no sign that something pierced him through the back of the chair, either."

Tamir's pencil scratched along the page of his log. "Got it."

"Also, note that there's no splash or spatter marks around the victim's head. His hair's mussed up, and he's wearing night clothes, like he might have gone to bed and then woken up to come down here." Norwood felt along the sides of the corpse's skull, but found nothing amiss. Finally, he gripped the man's hair and pulled his head forward. A wash of crimson painted the back of the dead wizard's neck. It had soaked his collar and wicked around both sides, but most of the blood had gone right down the back of his nightshirt.

"Not a lot of blood." He gingerly probed the back of the dead man's head with his fingers, ignoring the cool, congealed mess. "No sign of a busted skull but..." His fingertip found a small slit at the base of the skull. "Hmm. Yes. A stiletto or poniard, I think."

"Someone *pithed* him? Why go to that trouble?"

Norwood shrugged. A blade to the back of the skull was a tricky way to kill someone. The point of entry was small enough to require a narrow blade or pick. Without perfect precision, the strike would hit bone. Also, few people would sit still long enough to allow a killer such precision. It would be much easier and surer to cut the throat.

"I have no idea." Norwood tipped the wizard's head back against the chair and wiped his hand on his handkerchief. Too late, he realized that it was brand new, an impromptu gift from his wife. He'd catch hell from her for using it in such a manner. Maybe he'd just throw it away and claim he lost it. "It's a difficult kill, but it's tidy."

"So, the assassin piths him right here in this chair, then slips the dagger out and leans him back, just so he won't make a mess?" Tamir scratched notes in his log.

"Assassin?" Norwood gave his sergeant a curious look. "Why call him that?"

"Come on, sir. This has got 'professional hit' written all over it." He gestured around the room with the end of his pencil. "No sign of forced entry. No blood spatter or signs that the killer got all bloody doing the deed. All kinds of expensive knickknacks lying around, so he wasn't here to steal stuff. No mess, no fuss. He didn't even spill the man's brandy!" He gave a short, humorless laugh. "Someone's really proud of their skills here."

"Hmph." Norwood didn't like the idea of assassins or professional killings, preferring straight-forward crimes of passion, robbery, or revenge. Those were easier to solve. But Tamir was right; this looked far too neat to be any of those. "Well, we know how, so let's try to figure out who and why, shall we?"

"Yes, sir."

"We can assume he died right here. That means whoever did it stood beside or behind the chair when he put a blade in the wizard's skull." Norwood circled the chair, but the expensive western rugs gave no indication of where the killer might have stood while performing the deed. "The man was sipping a brandy, and he didn't have a book or anything, so maybe he was having a chat with the killer."

"So, it could have been someone he knew. Someone he'd let into his house for a late-night drink and conversation." Tamir picked up the snifter and passed it under his nose. "Doesn't

58

smell bad, but if the killer slipped him something, it would have made the pithing a lot easier."

"That's true." Norwood hadn't thought about poison. Tamir had a good mind for things like this. "Make sure we have a sample of that. Maybe we can figure out if it was doped. And check the other snifters. Our killer may have used one."

"Sure, sir." Tamir put the snifter back down and scratched a note in his book. "Seems like a lot of trouble when cutting his throat or hacking his head off with a sword would have been easier."

"But messier and not as elegant." Norwood pursed his lips. He couldn't remember a single killing so bereft of evidence.

"Elegant?" Tamir scratched something in his log, then looked up at his captain. "You think this was *elegant*?"

"Well, maybe that's the wrong word, but I think you were right about one thing. Whoever did this was very proud of their skills. They might have wanted to avoid making a mess to keep from tracking blood all over the place, but a dagger in the eye or the heart would have been easier than one in the back of the head, and just as sure. It's like someone's showing off here."

"Or sending a message?"

Messages...daggers...assassinations...

Norwood shuddered, remembering where he'd seen those three things together before; the worst string of murders Twailin had ever seen. *Those killings were nothing like this. The method is the message here. More subtle than a note around the hilt of a dagger thrust through someone's eye while they slept.*

"I don't know about a message, but whoever did this did it *like* this for a reason. Maybe as a signature or personal trademark. Whatever it is, I don't like it. Once you're finished here, search the archives for similar methods and circumstances."

"Yes, Captain." Tamir scratched more notes. "Professional, no doubt, but I've never heard of a wizard earning a visit from a pro. Can't even remember the last time a wizard got murdered.

They're dangerous targets, even for a pro. This one's a puzzle, all right."

"That's why we're here, Sergeant."

"That, and the fact that it happened on our side of the river." Tamir chuckled. "You know the joke; all the devils of the Nine Hells can rampage south of the river, and they just call the City Guard. But if a rich merchant or noble gets so much as a hangnail north of the river, the Royal Guard will be there with a bandage."

Norwood cast a withering glare at Tamir. "I despise that joke, Sergeant."

However true it might be, he resented the implication that the privileged classes received greater consideration from the duke's Royal Guard than the lesser got from the less prestigious City Guard. The river that forked in the center of Twailin split the city into three pieces. The portion north of that split included Hightown, the Bluff District, and the duke's palace, which sat right on the promontory overlooking the river's fork. The two southern portions made up the vast majority of the city's population, but only about a tenth of its wealth.

"Yes, sir." Tamir bit his lip and scratched more notes.

"Wait for Woefler and have a good look around, but if the killer was this careful with the body, I doubt you'll find much. If Vonlith let him in, that explains why there are no broken or jimmied locks. Tell Woefler to check with the Wizards Guild. I want to know more about Vonlith. I'll be in my office. You can both give me your initial reports there. Now, find out why this man's dead."

"Yes, Captain."

"And be careful! Wait for Woefler. That's an order."

"Don't worry, Captain. None of my people are dumb enough to poke into a wizard's stuff on their own."

"Good. He should be here soon."

"Very good, sir."

Norwood left Tamir to his business. He had other things to attend to, one of them his belated breakfast. But as he left Vonlith's opulent townhouse, he noticed a number of curious neighbors clustered along the street. Lords and ladies with their walking sticks and parasols paused to cast concerned glances and whisper behind their lace handkerchiefs. The rumors were already spreading.

ῤѴℲᾙᾶℲᾙ

Lad strode across the courtyard from the inn to the barn, leaving the aromas of blackbrew and oatcakes in his wake. After working out the stiffness in his strained shoulders with some quick morning exercises in the privacy of their room, and a hearty breakfast, he considered the chores ahead of him before he headed off to the *Golden Cockerel*.

He stepped into the quiet barn and stopped. Something was wrong.

The sun was up, and the entire inn's staff was awake and working. Tika and Ponce should have been busy with the barn chores, but they were nowhere in sight. Closing his eyes, Lad stretched out his senses: heart beats, shallow steady breathing, the rustle of straw from his right, a creak of rope overhead. Two assailants lay in wait for him. From their positions, he deduced that they would attack as soon as he ventured beyond the first horse stall. He quirked a quick smile, made a discreet noise to announce his presence, and walked into the trap.

Their timing was good.

Tika leapt from the stall to his right, vaulting over the railing to launch a flying kick right at Lad's head. At the same moment, his twin brother, Ponce, swung down from an overhead rafter, leading with the edge of his foot aimed at Lad's back. Either attack would have been a telling blow, painful or even incapacitating, but neither fell true.

The real trick for Lad was to deflect or evade the attacks without injuring either of Josie's nephews. This was getting harder as the two young men progressed in their training. When he started, they had been fourteen-year-old ruffians, no strangers to street fights and brawls, but without any true fighting skills. Now, three years later, they were dangerous.

Lad spun, ducking low under Tika's kick and blocking Ponce's lashing foot with his forearm—he'd have a bruise there later. Ponce released the rope he'd used to swing down, slid under his brother's flying kick, and snapped up into a fighting stance. Tika tucked into a roll and came up ready. Lad stood as if waiting on a street corner, relaxed and casual as they quickly moved to flank him.

"Good morning, Tika. Good morning, Ponce. Did you both sleep well?"

"Wonderfully," Tika said with a grin.

"Like a baby," Ponce added, mirroring his brother's mirth.

"Good." Lad smiled at their cockiness. The two young men loved to banter almost as much as they loved to fight. They claimed the non-stop quips set their foes off, taunting them into foolish or hasty action. That might be, but it was not a tactic Lad had been taught. He'd been made to kill, not to talk about it. Nevertheless, he indulged them. "I hope you had a good breakfast."

"Wiggen's oatcakes were delicious." Ponce's bare foot brushed the hay-strewn floor.

"Sublime in flavor, and so fluffy! A delightful meal." Tika's feet were nearly silent, but Lad detected a minute shifting in his stance.

"Good. Breakfast is the most important meal of—"

They struck simultaneously, one high, one low. Lad deflected and dodged the flurry of punches, kicks and foot sweeps, holding his ground and concentrating on their form, their mistakes, and their successes. He flexed his abdominal muscles to stave off a blow to his midriff, grasped Tika's wrist

62

Chris A. Jackson

and twisted. The youth flipped into a roll to avoid having his
arm wrenched, just as he'd been taught. Ponce lashed out at the
opening the move provided. Lad released Tika's wrist and
twisted around the kick, grasping Ponce's ankle to flip him onto
his back. He tapped Ponce on the chest, just hard enough to
leave a bruise.

"—the day. You're dead."

"I'm dead," Ponce agreed with a grimace.

"Well, I'm not!" Tika came up from his roll with the shaft
of a pitchfork in his hand. He'd obviously removed the tined
head earlier and set the shaft aside for easy access. Now he
squared off, flourishing the staff in preparation.

"You've been practicing, Tika. Good." Lad squared off
with him while Ponce propped himself up on one elbow to
watch. "Remember what I said about weapons, and show me
what you've learned."

Tika came in with a spinning attack, the hardwood shaft
whistling through the air. Lad bent back and let the strike that
would have broken his neck pass just beyond his chin. But, as
he'd hoped, the staff attack had been a distraction, and Tika's
food lashed out to sweep Lad's ankle. He let it strike true, but
flipped with the impact of the blow and kicked out, striking
Tika's hand on the staff with his other foot. Admirably, the
youth did not lose his grip, and continued his spin to attack
again, high with the staff and low with his other foot. Lad
evaded both, and the flourish ended with the two of them in
ready fighting stances.

"Very good! You need to—"

A scant instant before the blow landed, Lad heard Ponce's
whoosh of breath. He twisted, but the kick hit him hard in the
back, sending him right into the path of Tika's staff.

Reflex took over.

Lad's palm met the staff before it met with his temple, and
he brought his foot around to snap the shaft at its midpoint. The

broken end spun out of Tika's hand, and Lad caught it. He flipped both ends, caught them and thrust.

"Stop!"

Tika and Ponce froze, the two broken ends of the staff poised a half-inch from their chests.

"Now you're both dead. And you broke the rules, Ponce."

"I'm a zombie," he said with a grin and a shrug. "Sorry about the kick. I thought you'd block it."

"A good lesson for us both, then." Lad stood and took a deep breath. His back hurt where Ponce's foot had struck, though he didn't think the rib had cracked. "But please, both of you, pull your strikes, even if you think I'm going to dodge or block. Your training has progressed to the point that your blows could seriously injure or even kill. This is practice, remember. In a real fight, you strike as hard as you can, but here..."

"I'm sorry." Ponce looked duly abashed.

"Don't be. Just remember." He gave Ponce a grin. "And remember that we only use our skills...when?"

"When someone we love is in danger," they recited, nodding respectfully. "Only strike to defend. Only kill to prevent a death."

"Good! Now Tika, your staff technique is excellent, and you remembered what I said about weapons."

"That they often serve better as distractions than weapons? Yes. And it worked!"

"Yes." Lad flipped the broken ends of the staff and handed them to the twins. "Now, let's go through the fight one step at a time, slowly, and I'll tell you how it should have gone."

A half-hour later, Lad heard Wiggen's step outside, and turned from watching the twins spar together. She appeared at the barn door, Lissa on her hip.

"Yes, Wiggen?"

"The milking and the egging still need to be done, and the guests are starting to come down, so we're busy in the kitchen.

If my valiant warriors can find the time, we humble innkeepers could use some help."

The twins immediately backed away from one another under the weight of her stern gaze.

"Yes, ma'am," they said in perfect unison.

Lad just grinned. "We're done for now. I've got to go soon." He clapped the two young men on their shoulders. "I'll muck out the stalls for you."

"Thanks, Lad!"

The twins dashed out, and Lad looked fondly after them.

"You're turning them into dangerous weapons, you know."

The statement caught Lad off guard. Is that what Wiggen thought he was doing? Creating weapons for use against his enemies? Did she think he wanted to wield Tika and Ponce that way?

"No! I'm not!" The denial came out with more vehemence than he intended, and Lissa looked at him with wide, surprised eyes.

"Lad!" Wiggen cuddled Lissa close.

"I'm sorry." He shook his head. "I thought you meant...something else." He took a deep, calming breath. He went to her and brushed an errant lock of hair away from her face. "You know why I'm training Tika and Ponce. If anything happens to me, they will—"

"Nothing's going to happen to you!" Fear edged Wiggen's tone. He knew she didn't like this topic, but it was something that had to be said.

"Wiggen, no matter how careful I am, something *could* happen to me. Anyone can get hit by a carriage. But even so, I can't be here every day to protect you and the inn. If something should happen while I'm away, Tika and Ponce could be the difference between life and death. You *know* that."

"I know." Her lips tightened, and her hand strayed up to the scar on her cheek. "I know you mean the best for us, but it's *you*

I worry about—what you do, the people you associate with. It scares me, Lad."

"A little fear is healthy, Wiggen. You just can't let it paralyze you. You have to be ready." He took her hand in his and pressed it to his lips. The morning sun through the barn door glinted off her wedding ring, and he kissed that, too. "That's why we agreed that training Tika and Ponce would be a good thing. That's why I taught you how to use a dagger, and showed everyone what to do if there's trouble. You're safer now than you've ever been."

"I know." Wiggen hitched Lissa up on her hip and gave him a smile. "I remember what you told us. I know being prepared is important, and I'm less afraid now than I was before you came. It's not the fighting I hate, Lad, it's the necessity for it."

"That's something I can't change, Wiggen." He brushed Lissa's hair away from her ear, and the baby smiled and gurgled at him. "I would if I could."

"I know." She sighed and smiled. "I'm fine, Lad."

"Good." He bent down and kissed her. "Now, I've got some horse poop to shovel, so if you'll go back to the kitchen, I'll get to work."

"My brave warrior, shoveler of horse poop."

"That's me."

Lad watched his wife walk across the courtyard. He had long ago memorized everything about her—the sway of her hips, the way the morning light touched her hair—and it still amazed him how his heart leapt whenever he saw her.

Family…

Though he never let Wiggen see, his own fears often pressed at the fragile shell of his calm. *They're safer now*, he told himself. But still he feared for them. He had more now than he ever dreamed of, but that also meant he had more to lose.

CHAPTER VI

Y ou're sure?" Mya lifted her cup and took her first sip of Paxal's bracingly strong blackbrew. It woke her more effectively than a slap in the face, even though she'd already been up for more than an hour. She hadn't gotten much sleep with the night's activities, but her magic kept exhaustion at bay. She could go days without a full night's rest if need be.

"Positive, Miss Mya. Dee didn't leave the inn all night." Paxal gave her a wry look. "Seems he's got a thing going with that new Morrgrey barmaid, Moirin. Moirin's a talker, and Britty got an earful this morning. Evidently, Dee's *quite* the lover. I can tell you exactly what she said if you—"

"No, Pax. I believe you. Thanks." She put down her cup and wiped the dribble of blackbrew from her chin. His comment about Dee and Moirin had caught her off guard. Of course she knew that people had relationships, but it wasn't something discussed amongst colleagues, at least, not in her presence. But skinny, pale Dee with curvy, olive-skinned Moirin, a woman who made more in tips by flaunting her cleavage than she earned as salary? Mya tried to imagine the two of them together, then twitched her head in quick negation. It didn't matter. What people did with their own time wasn't her business. "I'll see you this evening."

"Very good, Miss Mya." The barkeep nodded and left the room.

Mya concentrated on her breakfast and thanked the gods that Paxal had discovered only Dee's little fling. She liked her assistant, and would hate to have to kill him. She'd do it if she had to, of course—quick and clean, just like last night—but she'd hate it all the same.

There was, however, the Grandmaster's letter to worry about. She considered her reply. "No, thank you," didn't seem adequate to express her feelings, and, "You can take your guildmaster's ring and stick it up your arse," might be too strong. But she had time. A messenger to Tsing took two weeks in good weather, longer with the spring rains. He couldn't expect a response before then.

Pushing that task to the back of her mind, she sipped blackbrew and took another bite of fried potatoes. *Horice tried to kill me last night.* That's *what I've got that to deal with today.*

A few minutes later, a knock sounded at the door, and Dee walked into the room carrying his papers and writing utensils.

"Good morning, Miss Mya."

Though he seemed as calm and relaxed as ever, Mya noted dark circles under his eyes and a slightly unsteady gait. A hint of flowery feminine perfume and a distinctive, musky odor wafted in with the breeze of the closing door, corroborating Paxal's report. She cocked her head, considering her assistant in a new light, until Lad's words from the previous evening—"Surely you've looked at men and thought..."—snapped her from her musing.

This is Dee, *godsdamnit! Stop thinking about him that way!*

"Morning, Dee." Her cup rattled into the saucer as he sat down and arranged the correspondence to sign. "Late night? You look tired." She continued eating, but watched his face, wondering if he knew that Moirin gossiped about him.

"No later than usual, Miss. There were only the five letters."

Not a hint of evasion or unease. *Either he doesn't know his own reputation, or he doesn't know I know it.* She watched his long, graceful fingers arrange the letters, inkwell and pen for her, and imagined them against Moirin's olive skin. *Focus, Mya!*

She speared her last bite of sausage, mopped up the dregs of egg with it and popped it into her mouth. She chased the last bite down with a sip of blackbrew and said, "Good. Let's get started then."

He slid the first letter across the table to her. "This is to Journeyman Keese."

Mya breathed in the flowery scent. *Got to be Moirin's.* She took up the pen and signed the letter.

"Next we've got the one for the master of the Teamsters Guild."

"Riley O'Lance. Right." She read the letter, noting his elegant hand and the cordial embellishments he'd added. "Perfect. Very good, Dee." She signed it and passed it back.

"Thank you." He gave her the next. "And the issue with the missing dues from the Westmarket brothels."

"Yes." This one was much more strongly worded, the hand firmer, the language plain and straightforward. "Excellent." She signed.

"And the moneylender on Serpent Avenue." He took the signed letter and handed her the next.

"Of course." She read, and tapped the text with a finger. "This phrase here, Dee. Do you think it sounds too soft?"

He stood and rounded the table, leaning over her shoulder to look at the phrase in question.

His proximity set Mya's nerves tingling, as if her tattoos writhed along her skin. She shifted in her chair, suddenly uncomfortable.

"I think it's adequate. Anything stronger might be misconstrued, and the Moneylenders Guild has strong connections with the Thieves Guild."

69

"Right you are." She breathed deep, and the tingling along her nerves coalesced into a warm quiver in the pit of her stomach. *Oh, stop it, Mya!* She signed the letter. "And the last one?"

"Here." He leaned across the table and grabbed the final letter, the one to Jayse. "The issue with that gang in the Sprawls bothering our friend."

"Right." She barely glanced at the letter before signing it. "Very good, Dee. Thank you."

"My pleasure, Miss Mya." He stepped back around the table and collected his things. "Anything else this morning?"

Best deal with this now. "Nothing to do with business, but I'd like to suggest something."

"Yes?" He stood there, attentive and open.

Mya gave him a canted smile. "Ask Moirin to wear a little less perfume when she visits you, and freshen up a bit before you bring the letters in."

"I…" His face flushed crimson. "I will, Miss Mya. My apologies."

A thrill of satisfaction banished the distracting tingles from her stomach. "Don't apologize, Dee." She stood and tugged her shirt straight. "No harm in taking what pleasure life offers you. Gods know it's a rare commodity in our business. But be careful. Relationships can be dangerous for people like us."

"I will be. Thank you, Miss Mya." He turned to go.

"And get some sleep."

"I will."

"Alone."

He blushed again, but could not suppress a grin. "Yes, Miss Mya."

The door closed, and she sat back down to pour herself one more cup of blackbrew. She worked the taut muscles of her neck and sighed. Lad would be there shortly, and they had a full day planned. She thought about Dee, happy for him, and glad that she hadn't needed to put a dagger in his skull. Her

70

thoughtful smile faded, however, as she remembered her last instruction.

"Alone..."

"Good morning, sir."

Hensen's eyes flicked up from the steaming scone he was buttering as his assistant entered the morning room. The morning sunshine lit up the woman's flaxen hair and porcelain features. *A rare beauty*, he thought before returning his attention to the scone. Her skills were as impressive as her beauty, of course, but Hensen loved to surround himself with pretty things. The elegant décor of his home, lavish furnishings, immaculate clothes, and beautiful assistant reflected that. As the head of the Thieves Guild, he could afford to indulge himself.

"Good morning, Kiesha." He scooped a lump of marmalade from a tiny crystal bowl with a silver spoon and spread it on his scone. "What news this morning?"

"A visit from Sereth last night, sir. More stirring in the Assassins Guild."

That perked his interest. They had worked long and hard to pressure the Master Blade's bodyguard into becoming their informant, and it had paid off handsomely. Hensen knew what the Blade faction would do before they did it, and received indirect news about the other masters' activities as well. Of all the fingers the Thieves Guild had stuck in pies throughout the city, Sereth was, by far, his most valuable spy at the moment.

"More infighting?" He took a bite of scone, chased it with a sip of tea, and dabbed the corner of his mouth with a gold-embroidered napkin.

"Yes, sir. Two deaths last night." She placed a single page at his elbow, her elegant, precise handwriting a pleasure to his eyes. "Youtrin and Horice teamed up to try to kill Master Hunter Mya. They failed."

"Blades and Enforcers teaming up against Hunters, hmm?" He bit into the scone, savoring the flavors. "Did Sereth say why?"

"Yes. Mya is ignoring the others, blocking their initiatives and refusing to come to meetings. She's been doing it for a while, but the situation seems to have reached a head. Youtrin and Horice are taking it personally."

"Temper, temper." He read the detailed report as he finished his scone. "Let that be a lesson to you, my dear. Never let emotion cloud your judgment."

"I never do, sir."

"Good. Now, what else?"

She placed another report beside his plate. "The Assassins Guild masters, minus Master Hunter Mya, of course, met last night and moved to choose a new guildmaster. They voted to have a new guildmaster's ring forged, and they're doing it *without* informing Mya."

"Wait! I thought they were trying to *kill* Mya."

"Only Youtrin and Horice, sir, at the moment, at least." She shrugged. "Their decision holds whether or not she survived the attempt. The details are in the report."

"Interesting." Hensen thought for a moment about the potential repercussions of this move. The infighting between the Assassins Guild factions had been good for the Thieves Guild, which had exploited the disorganization to advance its own interests throughout the city. A new Assassins Guild guildmaster would be bad for business. "Have they chosen someone yet?"

"No, sir. They'll forge the ring first, then choose."

"Hmm." He sipped his tea. "I assume Sereth will keep us apprised of the situation."

"Of course, sir. That brings up one more item: news from the *Golden Cockerel*." She laid a third report atop the other two. "Master Hunter Mya received a letter from the Grandmaster of the Assassins Guild instructing her to have a new guildmaster's ring forged and appoint *herself* guildmaster."

Hensen sat up straight. "Interesting indeed!" Reaching for another scone, he stopped, a troublesome thought interrupting his appetite. "I find it a disturbing coincidence that she should receive such a letter the very evening Youtrin and Horice tried to kill her. Any chance our informant at the *Cockerel* might be playing both sides of the street?"

"Anything is possible, but it's not likely, sir. Sereth would probably know if Horice received word of the letter. We have no way to know about Youtrin."

"Look into that possibility for me, Kiesha. We can't have our assets straying."

"Yes, sir."

"So, both Mya and the other masters are forging rings at the same time." Hensen reached for another scone, then frowned and picked up his tea cup instead. One of the downsides of being the boss, he'd found, was that he didn't get much meaningful exercise, and his expanding waistline showed it. "Do we know who they contract to craft these things?"

"No, sir, but the letter from the Grandmaster suggested that they only employ a single person to make the rings."

"Well, when he receives two identical orders, I imagine things are going to get even more violent." This could be very good; all they had to do was step back and watch the Assassins Guild destroy itself. "Kiesha, contact Sereth and find out exactly what those Assassins Guild rings do. I know they provide some kind of magical protection, but I want details. And keep an eye on this situation from all angles. If any of our informants' findings are contradictory, bring it to my attention immediately."

"Of course, sir."

"Anything else?"

"Yes, sir." She held out an envelope with a gold wax seal. "This came for you specifically, sir. It has a secure seal."

Hensen didn't recognize the seal, a stylized sunburst, but that meant nothing. He made no move to take it. One did not gain his status within the Thieves Guild without learning caution. "Has Master Tinto examined it?"

"Yes, sir. Just the usual enchantment to ensure that only the intended recipient opens it. No traces of poison or other spells."

"All right." Hensen took the envelope and broke the seal with his eating knife. He opened the letter and a second piece of paper fluttered out—a certified draft from an account with the Twailin Moneylenders Guild. He knew *that* seal intimately. Licking his lips gleefully, for the sum was considerable, he turned to the letter. As he read, he felt a tickle as the hairs on the back of his neck rose. Chuckling, he waved the letter at Kiesha. "The plot thickens! It appears that someone *else* has taken interest in Master Hunter Mya. They want to contract our services to protect both her and her bodyguard from harm."

"Her *bodyguard*?" The incredulity in her tone brought his eyes up to hers, and she continued in a more deferential tone. "Sir, that's…"

"Unprecedented?"

"To say the least, sir." She blinked and shrugged. "By all accounts she needs little protection other than him. Six assassins tried to kill her last night. Two are dead and three injured, and neither she nor the weapon got a scratch."

Hensen frowned. "The weapon. That's the term that Sereth uses for the young man, correct?"

"Yes, sir. He was trained as a weapon for the former guildmaster, but Mya took him on after Saliez's death. His name is Lad."

"Lad…" Hensen remembered the search that had ensued when this Lad had disappeared five years ago. Mya herself had given him a portrait when she enlisted Hensen's help. It was still in a drawer somewhere. *Such a lovely young man…*

He snapped his attention back to the matter at hand. "So, our solicitor seems to have a card in this game, and he wants

74

Mya to win. Well, for this amount of coin, we'll play along. He's paid half up front, the other half to be transferred in one month if the two of them are still alive." He handed the letter and the draft to Kiesha.

Her lovely eyes flicked over the note. "Baron Patino?"

"Nobody I'm familiar with, but there *must* be some connection to the Assassins Guild. Make it a priority to find out exactly who this person is. And write up a response indicating that we accept the contract."

"Yes, sir."

"Anything else?" Hensen snatched another scone and began the meticulous buttering process. Life was too fleeting to be wasted worrying about one's waistline, and this game had stimulated his appetite. He loved a challenge. It was what made him such a successful thief.

"Nothing pressing, sir."

"Good. Keep this contract on a need-to-know basis, my dear. Use our *best* people. Master Hunter Mya is no fool, and neither is her bodyguard, from what Sereth says. If either of them detects our interference, there could be repercussions."

"Of course, sir."

"Go on then, Kiesha, and do be careful out there."

"I always am, sir." She gave him a stunning smile and turned to go.

Hensen admired her beauty once more before the door closed behind her. After dabbing marmalade on his scone and pouring more tea, he sat back, intent on savoring the rest of his breakfast.

Yes, life is far too fleeting…

CHAPTER VII

Captain Norwood's stomach growled as Tamir and Woefler entered his office. He'd worked through lunchtime, and the two men brought scents of roast lamb, garlic and sautéed onions in with them. He rose from his desk to stretch the kinks out of his backside. He had not been able to escape his chair all morning, and looked forward to hearing about what they had discovered at Vonlith's.

The men were a mismatched duo if ever he saw one. Tamir stood tall and beefy, as were most of the Royal Guards, taciturn of face and smartly uniformed. The sergeant towered over the wizard, who darted about like a little dog exploring every new scent. For an important member of the Duke's court, Woefler was decidedly unassuming. His robes were well-made, but unadorned, his rings and amulets simple. His clean-shaven face didn't strike Norwood as particularly venerable or wise, but he'd been with the duke for even longer than the captain, and his proficiency was renowned. Unfortunately, Woefler also fancied himself a sleuth. His near-frantic enthusiasm grated against Tamir's stoic, methodical approach. But as much as Tamir might dislike the notion, the death of a wizard warranted Woefler's aid.

"Master Woefler, good to see you. I wish it was under different circumstances." He waved them to chairs, though he continued to stand, shifting from one foot to the other in a slow rocking motion to ease the pain in his back.

76

Chris A. Jackson

"Captain Norwood." The court wizard nodded and grinned, his angular face flushed with pleasure, unusual for the circumstance of a murder investigation, but not for the odd little man. "Good to see you as well, though we do only seem to reacquaint ourselves over dead bodies."

"We do at that." Norwood noted a sour expression on Tamir's face at the wizard's greeting. He had probably been listening to Woefler yammer on about the magical whatnots in Vonlith's home all morning. Stifling a grin, he waited until his visitors were seated, then got right to business. "What news of Master Vonlith? Tam, you first."

"It's probably a safe bet that the victim knew his killer. Though all the windows and the front door were locked, the—"

"The locks on the doors and windows were reinforced with magic, Captain," Woefler cut in. "If one were to pick one of the locks or try to force it open, an alarm would sound and the entire house would be sealed by a spell. All of these spells were intact when I arrived, except—"

Tamir's voice overrode the wizard's, and he continued. "— except the servants' entrance. When we questioned her again, the housekeeper admitted that she'd found it unlocked this morning. She absolutely swears that she locked it on her way out last night." Tamir consulted his notebook and checked something off with a pencil. "She's got the only other key besides the one we found in Vonlith's pocket. But..." The sergeant paused dramatically and grinned at the captain. "...remember the snifter on the table beside Vonlith? We found a matching one on the sideboard that still had a bit of brandy in the bottom. So, you were right about our victim having had a guest." He made another checkmark in his notebook, and sat back.

Norwood sank into his chair. "So, Vonlith probably knew his killer, let him in through the servant's entrance, and they had a drink..."

77

"Not a colleague, however. You would receive a colleague at the front door, not the servants' entrance."

Norwood nodded to the wizard; his reasoning made sense. "An acquaintance, then. Someone known, but not a peer."

"Someone known well enough to share a glass of brandy with, but not highfalutin enough to rate the front door." Tamir added.

"Or someone you didn't want your neighbors to see, perhaps." A thin smile spread across Master Woefler's lips.

"Or someone who didn't want to *be* seen…"

Quiet suffused the office for a long moment before Norwood waved to Tamir to continue. "What about the body?"

"The stab wound to the back of the skull was the only injury we found. We'll cut his head open later to see if there's anything odd about the death stroke, but I don't expect to find anything. It seems like a straightforward hit. There were plenty of valuables around, so robbery's not a likely motive."

"Unless the killer was after a specific item that we don't know about, Sergeant." Woefler wagged a skinny finger under Tamir's nose. "One does not recognize an item by its absence if one is not familiar with its presence."

"What the hells is that supposed to mean?" The look Tamir gave the wizard could have soured milk.

"It means, Sergeant Tamir, that something *could* have been taken. Perhaps something that Master Vonlith kept on his person, an amulet or ring, for instance, that required his death before it could be removed." Woefler smiled as if proud of his deductive reasoning. "One must not jump to unwarranted conclusions."

"Don't know why a thief would go to all the trouble of putting a knife in the man's head to take one thing and leave a whole pile of fancy stuff just sitting there." Tamir shook his head and turned back to Norwood. "*Also*, the method of the killing suggests a professional assassin, not a thief. My guess is that our victim pissed off the wrong people."

"Thanks, Tam. Let me know if anything new turns up." Norwood turned to the duke's wizard. "Anything from your perspective that stands out, Master Woefler?"

"Vonlith was a highly proficient runemage. Invading his home would have been impossible, even for a *skilled* intruder." He smiled pleasantly at Tamir. "The magic on the front door and the servant's entrance is substantial. Entry through either of those portals could *only* have been gained through use of one of the two existing keys, both of which bore subtle spells that would be recognized by the spells on the locks. Since both of those have been accounted for, the only logical conclusion is that Vonlith did, indeed, let someone in."

"We already figured that out," protested Tamir.

"But the locks *inside* the house were quite different. There were no keys to lose for those." Woefler's eye gleamed with secret satisfaction.

Tamir groaned as he cast the wizard a chagrined glance. "Yeah. Unfortunately, you're right about that."

"What about the locks inside the house?" Norwood looked from one man to the other.

"*Those* were mage-locked," Woefler explained, "designed to open only to Vonlith's touch."

"So, if they couldn't be opened by anyone but Vonlith, how did you open them?"

"I didn't say that Vonlith had to open them, Captain," Woefler said. "I said that opening them required Vonlith's *touch*."

"So how did you—" The look of disgust on Tamir's face told Norwood what they must have done. "Oh, you did not!"

"Yes, sir, we did. Master Woefler insisted that we parade around the house with the corpse, soiled nightshirt and all, touching its finger to every single locked door, cabinet, chest and bin. Like a bloody funeral procession it was."

"Well, it worked." Woefler grinned boyishly and shrugged. "And it was much quicker and more efficient than my trying to unravel every rune-spell. And as you have often said, Captain, time is of the essence in these investigations."

"Marvelous." Norwood rose from his chair and paced the floor, hoping that the Duke didn't hear of the grim spectacle. "Well, what about Vonlith? What did he do to earn a dagger in the brain?"

"He's got some nice stuff." Tamir shrugged. "We might look into who gets it all if he kicks the bucket."

"Have someone track down his next of kin. Start a list of suspects: relatives, or anyone else who might be in line to inherit. I assume he had a will, so let's get a look at it." He looked to Woefler again. "What about his guild affiliation?"

"He paid his dues on time, but was not politically active. His membership was in good standing, and has been for a very long time. Vonlith was quite a lot older than he looked."

"Lots of time to make enemies," Tamir noted.

Woefler wagged his head equitably. "He had few close friends, but he seemed to be on decent terms with his fellow guild members. I had met him several times socially at the guild lodge, and he was agreeable, though rather reserved. It's the way some of these fellows get, you know, when they practice in isolation for too long. For myself, well, I prefer—"

"Master Woefler." Norwood gently tried to steer the wizard back to the subject at hand. "You said he was a proficient runemage. Proficient enough to make other mages jealous?"

"Possibly. He's been practicing rune-magic at a level that I have not seen in many years. He was a specialist, and quite adept." Woefler made a face halfway between wistfulness and jealousy. "It is amazing what you can craft with the right arcane runes. Some of his things…"

"Like what?"

"Like a box in his study into which he could place items that he did not wish to be affected by time. It was empty when we found it, so we have no idea what he used it for. He also had a rune-etched knife in his laboratory that would cut through virtually any material, including diamond. Even his bed was magical. The runes inscribed in the headboard ensured calm, dreamless sleep. These things alone are quite valuable, and we still have not completed an inventory."

"Don't forget the wagon," Tamir put in.

"Wagon?" Norwood looked at them both again. "What wagon?"

"Vonlith had a wagon in the stable behind the townhouse." The wizard laughed heartily. "Your guardsmen were quite surprised to discover that it is a good deal larger on the inside than the outside."

"Really?" Norwood's eyebrows arched. "That would be handy."

"Indeed! It was quite impressive." Woefler looked around the expansive office. "This entire room would have fit nicely inside, with enough additional space to add a large closet. It's elaborately decorated, resembling a tinker's wagon more than a wizard's conveyance, but the decorations are all actually rune inscriptions."

Norwood raised an eyebrow. "Did it look like he was getting ready to take a trip?"

"Again, I have yet to identify and inventory everything, but the wagon contained wizardry implements, not a wardrobe or mundane supplies. His stableman said that he generally used the vehicle for short trips, but had not used it in some time."

"Interesting." Norwood continued to pace. Tamir and Woefler had provided him with many pieces to the puzzle, but he couldn't yet figure out how they fit together. "Anything else?"

"Somethin' about that wagon, sir." Tamir rubbed his eyes and sighed. "I never seen it before, but something about it seems familiar."

"There are lots of tinkers' wagons in Twailin, Sergeant."

"Yep, there are, sir, but something about runes and fancy wagons and mages is tryin' to work its way out of my skull. I can't quite get a handle on it."

"Well, let me know if you do. If there's one thing we need in this case, it's a handle. Anything more?"

"Nothing on my end." Tamir stifled a yawn as he stood. "I'll let you know if I find anything inside the wizard's skull. Maybe that's bigger on the inside, too."

Woefler chuckled. "I, too, will let you know what I find anything incriminating or warranting further investigation among Vonlith's things. There is a lot to look through. I'll also ask my guild associates about his relationships. He might have made a powerful enemy that we don't know about."

"Don't draw attention to yourself," Norwood warned. "A dagger in the brain puts a serious cramp in anyone's style, and the duke will have my head if anything happens to you while you're working on one of my cases."

"Thank you for your concern, Captain." Woefler stood and gave him an unassuming smile. "Rest assured, I'll be the portrait of discretion."

"Good. And let me know if you remember anything about that wagon, Tam."

"Yes, sir." Tamir saluted wearily as he followed the wizard out. Before the door could close, a girl wearing a bright green tabard slipped in, a scroll case in one hand.

"What is it?" The last thing Norwood wanted was another delay; he was already hours late for lunch.

"Message from Duke Mir, sir." The page handed over the scroll case and snapped into a textbook at-ease position, her hands clasped behind her back, her posture stiff as a board. Water dripped from her nose, eyelashes, and hair. It was obviously pouring rain out, which quashed his plan to run out for a quick bite to eat.

Norwood stifled a smile at the messenger's rigid propriety as she tried to hide her heaving breath. She'd undoubtedly run all the way from the palace. The young ones always took their duties so seriously. *She'll relax after a few years.*

Glowering at the scroll case in his hand, he popped free the leather cap. A red silk ribbon, the duke's trademark, bound the note inside. One glance confirmed his suspicion; he was summoned to the palace. *There goes lunch.* He'd hoped to have more time to analyze the evidence of Vonlith's death before reporting to the duke, but rumors among the courtiers flew faster than falcons on the hunt, and a murder north of the river was sure to attract the attention of Twailin's ruler.

"Reply, sir?" the page asked, bristling with pent-up energy. On a sadistic whim, Norwood decided to indulge that enthusiasm.

"Yes." Snatching up a pen, he scrawled an unnecessary reply on the bottom of the note. He sanded it to dry the ink, rolled it tight, and slipped the ribbon back over it. "Take this to the duke as quickly as you can. No lollygagging."

"No, sir! Er...yes, sir, I mean!" She snatched the case and dashed from the room, her neck flushing scarlet under her flying ponytail.

Norwood sat back down and sighed. "Oh, for the days of youth..." Memories of his own exuberance, long gone, fluttered through his mind. He'd been far too long without that kind of enthusiasm, plodding through life with grim resignation. He considered stopping for lunch before attending the duke's summons, but reconsidered. Meeting with Duke Mir always seemed to upset his stomach.

§∇϶⅄·϶ℨℌ

"Norwood! Thank you for coming so quickly. Have a seat." Duke Mir stood from behind his expansive desk and gestured to the leather-upholstered chair across from it. "Can I send for something? A drink? A bite to eat, perhaps?"

"Nothing for me, thank you, milord."

Norwood's stomach roiled at his lord's show of hospitality. This did not bode well. Mir was generally a direct and forthright man, straight to the point and clear in his instructions, which was one reason Norwood enjoyed working for him. The duke's overt cordiality meant that he was about to ask Norwood to do something that he expected the captain would not like. Waiting until the duke had seated himself once again, he decided to face the matter head on.

"The investigation into Master Vonlith's murder has only just begun, milord. We're still collecting evidence. The circumstances of his death suggest a professional assassination. As far as we know, theft does not seem to be the motive, but we can't yet rule it out. Master Woefler is helping us to identify and compile an inventory of the wizard's various magical items, and acting as our liaison with the Wizards' Guild. I'll provide you with updates as they come in."

Norwood felt a twinge of satisfaction as Duke Mir simply stared open-mouthed at him for a moment.

"I hadn't expected you to have *solved* it already, Norwood. I only *heard* about it two hours ago!"

"Of course not, milord. I just wanted to tell you up front what we've learned so far."

"Professional you say?"

"Yes, milord, we believe so."

Duke Mir's face turned as white as the parchments scattered across his desk. "What makes you think so?"

"The method indicated both skill and precision. In fact, more skill and precision than was probably necessary. The killing may have been meant to serve as a warning or a message."

The duke sat upright. "There was a message?"

"No, milord!" Norwood leaned forward and waved his hand. He knew exactly where the duke's thoughts had flown to. His own had done the same. "This showed no similarities to…those other killings. The method was different, the murder weapon was not left behind, the victim wasn't a noble, and there was no note or any indication that the killing was politically motivated."

"So, what type of message did you mean?"

"There are two types of professional killings, milord. One is meant to look like an accident or something other than a professional killing, the other is meant to tell everyone that it *was* professional as a warning or statement of some kind. This was the latter."

Mir heaved a sigh and pushed himself to his feet. Striding over to his sideboard, he poured a glass of pale wine from one of the artfully arranged crystal decanters and drank down half in one gulp. Norwood wished he hadn't declined the duke's offer of refreshment. His mouth was dry, and he would have welcomed a glass of wine, even on his empty stomach, but he wasn't about to ask for one now.

"The reason I summoned you, Norwood, isn't just about the Vonlith murder, though it has provided the proverbial straw that broke the camel's back." Mir topped off his glass and turned to regard the captain. "I know it's not your jurisdiction, but you undoubtedly have knowledge of the escalating violence south of the river: beatings, arson, some killings."

Norwood nodded cautiously, his guard up. "You mean the increasing gang violence, milord?" Mir nodded. "I'm aware of it, and in my opinion, the sooner these criminals kill each other off, the better. The more they fight each other, the less time they have to bother honest citizens."

"That is also the opinion of the captain of the City Guard and, while I understand that philosophy, Norwood, there is one problem with it."

"And what is that, milord?"

"Powerful members of my court who live *north* of the river have business interests *south* of the river. Violence hurts business, and not only is the violence escalating, but it now seems to have jumped the river into their own neighborhoods with this recent murder. They had already been complaining. Now they are beating down my door with demands to resolve this fiasco. The City Guard can't seem to prevent the violence or find the perpetrators, which makes it seem as if I do not have control of the situation."

"That's because you don't, milord."

"What?" Mir's hand shook, and the wine sloshed over the rim of his glass. "How *dare* you suggest that I don't have control of this city, Captain!"

"Milord, please. No insult was intended, but you, of all people, should understand that true control is impossible without an absolute police state. Not even the emperor has the funds to support that kind of oppression, and if he tried, the people would burn his shiny palace to the ground. He knows this, so he lets the lower classes continue to kill, maim, buy, sell and rob one another with minor supervision to ensure that his true supporters, the nobles, are not unduly affected." Norwood shrugged. "Besides, there's absolutely nothing to suggest that this murder has anything to do with the violence south of the river."

"Whether it does or does not isn't the issue here, Captain Norwood." Mir quaffed the remainder of his wine and glared. "The issue is perception. I need to be seen as trying to rectify this problem by assigning the Royal Guard to the investigation. What I need *you* to do is keep this situation from escalating."

Norwood didn't relish the prospect; the Royal Guard wasn't welcome south of the river. He couldn't expect much help from the City Guard. Still, there was one stipulation he had to get clear before he started treading on toes.

"What am I to keep from escalating, milord? The violence, or the worry of the nobles?"

It was a legitimate question, but Norwood immediately regretted his flippant tone as the duke's face flushed face and his eyes bulged. To stave off a tirade, the captain raised his hand in a gesture of calming.

"Please, milord, I ask that question because the two require very different amounts of effort and time. The murder investigation has barely begun, and it will take considerable time for all leads to be tracked down, especially if I must now split my efforts. Curbing the violence south of the river, if it can be done at all, will require a huge amount of manpower. However, quelling the worry of the nobles can be accomplished with much less effort."

"What do you *suggest*, then, Captain?" Mir's tone dripped sarcasm, but Norwood ignored it.

"That we continue working to solve Vonlith's murder, but in the meantime, round up a few thugs from south of the river, string them up, and tell your court that the problem is being dealt with, even though the violence will probably continue."

"You'd hang innocent men to quiet this situation down?"

"Innocent men? No, milord, but there are plenty of thugs out there who deserve hanging, and I'll happily put them on the gallows to keep this city under your governance. And if we pick the *right* thugs to hang, we might even send a message to the ones who are really behind all the violence." He regarded Duke Mir, keeping his face set in serious consternation. "I don't suggest you tell your moralistic court of my methods, milord, but I do get the job done. I thought that was why you hired me."

Muscles clenched in the duke's jaw. "Norwood, you are an insolent, overbearing, pain in the ass!"

"Yes, milord."

"Unfortunately, you are also right. That is *exactly* why I hired you." Mir put his glass back down on the sideboard and returned to his desk. "What will you need from me to get this done?"

Norwood considered a moment. "A copy of your orders sent to the captain of the City Guard. I want to make sure that everyone down there knows that this comes directly from you, milord. Also, I need a warrant giving me the authority to investigate the Wizards Guild. I've already asked Woefler to make some discreet inquiries, but I'd like to do some sniffing around myself. I'd like to review this wizard's activities, see what he's been up to lately, if he's perhaps made some enemies among his fellow wizards."

"That will cost me several favors, Captain. The Wizards Guild wields considerable power." Duke Mir raised his eyebrows in thought. "But I think I know which arms to twist. I'll have the documents delivered to your office within the hour."

"Thank you, milord."

The duke leaned heavily over his desk. "But be *polite* when you visit the Wizards Guild. I can't afford to aggravate them. They can disapprove contracts made by any guild wizard, and I don't relish doing without Master Woefler's services."

"Nor do I," Norwood admitted. He didn't want to consider investigating a wizard's death without the court mage's assistance. "I'll be cautious, milord."

"Just shut up and get to work."

"Yes, milord."

Norwood left the duke's palace vacillating between moods foul and fair. On the foul side, he had just been assigned a virtually impossible, and certainly thankless, task. On the other side, his favorite eatery was only a block away. He could enjoy a delicious lunch, and still get back to his office in time to hear Tamir's report on the inside of Vonlith's skull.

CHAPTER VIII

The scent of impending rain hung heavy in the air, and pedestrians scurried about like rats on a sinking ship. Lad and Mya were returning from a meeting in the Barleycorn Heights district, still a dozen blocks from the *Cockerel*, when the skies opened up, and the daily deluge began. It wasn't quite noon yet, but they had been trekking about the city for hours already, so he was grateful when she gestured toward a street-side eatery.

"We'll grab a bite and wait this out." She squinted up at the leaden sky and shook the water from her hair. "Maybe it'll pass."

Lad nodded, even though he didn't think it likely. In the shoulder-to-shoulder press of people, all with the same thought for getting out of the rain, he suddenly had much more than the weather to occupy his mind. As Mya ordered their lunch, Lad scanned the damp, jostling crowd, but felt his vigilance impaired. His back still ached from Ponce's kick the previous day, the hiss of the rain on the street cobbles dulled his hearing, and the smoke from the grill stung his eyes and masked any scents. A midday attack in such an open venue wasn't likely, but he couldn't discount an intrepid assassin trying to slip something lethal into Mya's food, or a knife into her back.

"Here." Mya handed him a hot wrap stuffed with steaming lamb, onions, peppers and dripping cheese, and followed as Lad opened a path through the crowd.

Weapon of Blood

Claiming a spot well away from the busy counter, Lad bit into his lunch, and his eyes welled with tears as the hot peppers lit his mouth on fire. Blinking to clear his vision, he felt Mya nudge him to make room for others, and stepped back until he stood at the edge of the waterfall cascading off the eatery's colorful awning. A laughing couple dashed in from the rain, and Mya bumped into him again, her shoulder pressed against his. Lad shifted anxiously. The rain, smoke, chatter of voices, and food were distracting enough; he didn't need Mya standing so close he could feel her heartbeat.

"Don't you *ever* relax, Lad?"

"What?" The question caught him off guard.

"You're as tense as a stallion with a mare in his sights." Mya poked him with her elbow, which only agitated him.

"I'm merely being vigilant."

"Vigilant is one thing, but you're wound up like a watch spring." She leaned closer and lowered her voice. "Frankly, you're stiff as a board, and you're starting to draw attention. Loosen up!"

Rain pattered on his shoulder as he edged away from her. She knew he could hear her even if she whispered. Why did she insist on standing so close that the scent of the soap on her skin competed with that of the food?

"Sorry." Lad tried to relax while maintaining his vigilance and eating his lunch, but found it difficult under Mya's scrutiny. "What? Am I not loose enough?"

"What's bothering you, Lad? You've always been a bit twitchy, but lately you jump at every shadow."

"It's my job to jump at shadows, Mya. The last shadow I jumped at was trying to cut off your head." He didn't recognize the expression on her face, and he couldn't tell if she was serious or not. Even though he provided her ample opportunity for jests with his continued semblance of naïveté, he didn't appreciate her making fun of him for her own entertainment.

"Yes, and you performed perfectly, but lately…" She took another bite of her sandwich and chewed, never taking her eye off of him. "I think being a father has made you edgy."

"Why would being a father make me edgy?" He didn't generally discuss his family with Mya or anyone else in the Assassins Guild. He knew she had Hunters watching the inn, so it was no surprise that she knew about Lissa. But he knew Mya did nothing without intent, which made him wonder about her motivation for discussing his home life.

"Oh, come on, Lad!" She laughed and nudged him again. "A crying baby in the middle of the night, and a nursing mother with post-birth doldrums. It can't be easy."

"Things have…changed a little, but…" He was hesitant to elaborate. *What does she want?*

"Relax, Lad. I won't tattle. After so many years together, don't you think you can trust me?"

"I trust you, Mya." That wasn't completely a lie. He trusted her not to slip a knife between his ribs, or turn him over to the Royal Guard. Neither would benefit her, and both would be dangerous. But trust her with his family? No, he didn't trust her or anyone else with that. He shifted away from her again, trying to be casual, but apparently not trying hard enough.

"Gods, is it *me* you're nervous about?" Mya barked a short laugh. "I don't bite, Lad."

Said the viper to the rat, he thought. Suddenly he realized that it *was* her making him edgy. She was acting strangely; this casual conversation about his family, her nudges and curious body language, made him nervous. *What is she up to?* The only way to find out was to play along. He purposefully relaxed his stance, muscle by muscle, and sidled out of the rain. Once again they were pressed against one another, Mya's shoulder brushing his chest, the scent of her damp hair right under his nose.

"That's better." She grinned and took another bite of her lunch, wiping the meat juice from her chin with her sleeve. "Has motherhood changed Wiggen, too?"

Another shiver of apprehension thrilled up his spine at her mention of Wiggen, but he forced it down. The twinkle in her eyes and wry smile, however, told him that she'd felt his reaction.

"So *that's* it!"

"That's what?"

"Why you're so uptight." She sighed, as if explaining something to a dull-witted child. "Motherhood changes women more than fatherhood changes men, Lad. Wiggen might not feel the same about...things for a while. Be patient."

He looked at her suspiciously. "What things?" Was she saying that Wiggen might not feel the same about him after having the baby? That was ridiculous!

"You know. *Physical* things."

"You mean sex?"

"Yes, that's exactly what I mean." She poked him in the stomach with her elbow. "I know men get tense when they don't get...those things."

"You think that's making me tense?"

"It might be. I could...help you with that, if you want."

"How could you—" He gaped at Mya as her intention came clear to him. A dozen assassins could have leapt out of the shadows at that moment and he wouldn't have noticed. "You...*what*?"

"I *am* a woman, Lad. And I'm not totally hideous to look at; you said so yourself just the other day." Her lips curved in a lascivious smile.

An all-too-familiar physical response thrilled through him before he could banish it. This was Mya. He didn't—he *couldn't* think about her that way!

"To tell you the truth, being Master Hunter isn't all it's cracked up to be. I don't get—"

"No, Mya." Lad clenched his jaw and leveled a stare at her. "I love Wiggen. She's my wife."

"All right. I understand." Mya turned away to take another bite of her sandwich, but not before he caught a flash of something in her eyes. Irritation? Anger? He wasn't sure. She brushed the hair back from her ear—one of her common tells when she was being evasive—and talked with her mouth full. "But sex and love are two different things, my friend, and if you don't find something to relax you soon, you're going to explode. Then where would I be?"

Lad didn't reply. He didn't know how to reply to that from her.

$\textit{ɣ⅁ʒ⅃ɘƧɭɣ}$

"Captain! I remembered!" Sergeant Tamir burst into Norwood's office without knocking. "I remembered that wagon!"

Norwood's eyes snapped up from his work at the interruption, but his tirade died on his lips. Tamir's face shone with excitement, and the man behind him, though he looked more frightened than excited, seemed familiar. He wore soft leathers and a cloak of deerskin, which was odd enough to see in the city, but the captain couldn't place his face. Norwood had hardly slept since meeting with the duke yesterday, and had spent the morning slogging through Master Woefler's voluminous report and pouring over the scant list of suspects, none of whom appeared to have the resources, motive, or nature to murder an accomplished wizard. Consequently, it took him a moment to realize what his sergeant was shouting about.

"Vonlith's wagon?"

"Yes, sir. The very same." He grabbed his companion by the arm and pulled him forward. "You remember my friend Poeter, right? He helped us out when we were investigating those assassinations a few years back. It ended up being that importer fella, Sleeze or something."

"Saliez. Yes, what about it?" Norwood felt like a cold hand had just clasped the back of his neck.

"Well, if you remember, Poeter here reconnoitered Saliez's mansion for us before we closed the trap, and he reported seeing a big, colorful wagon with gold and silver letters or designs on it."

"Yes, I remember." Norwood recognized the man now, and his heart skipped a beat. "You're saying that was Vonlith's wagon at Saliez's mansion?"

"That's right, sir!" Tamir grinned like he'd just won a week's pay on a bar bet. "I never seen the wagon myself, sir, for, as you know, it was gone by the time we busted in. So I took Poeter down to Vonlith's stable to see it, and damned if he didn't tell me 'Yep, that's the one I seen.'"

"You're sure of it?" Norwood fixed the man with a hard look. "There are lots of tinkers' wagons rambling the streets."

"Sure as a magistrate's warrant, Captain." Poeter braced his shoulders back and met Norwood's glare with surprising fortitude. "I remembered how a couple of them funny letters looked like snakes twisted up in a curlicue, and how the colors behind 'em seemed like a rainbow but in a spiral. There's no mistakin' it, sir. That's the same wagon."

Norwood leaned back in his chair with the memory of that horrific night: the fight in the courtyard, the torture chamber they'd found beneath the keep, the bloody corpse of Saliez with his throat crushed, his torso covered in arcane tattoos...*runes!* His mind snapped onto the thought like a mousetrap, and he shot up out of his chair.

"Vonlith was a runemage, and Saliez had runes tattooed all over his body!" He shook his head, cursing himself for not making the connection earlier. "Son of a..."

"Exactly, sir." Tamir grinned and stuck his thumbs into his belt. "So, if Vonlith was associatin' with scumbags like this Saliez, there's no wonder he ended up dead."

"And remember what that innkeeper's daughter said about Saliez? Master of the Assassins Guild." There was no physical evidence to support the relationship, but the presence of Vonlith's wagon at Saliez's suggested a link between the wizard and the Assassins Guild. With that in mind, Norwood could come up with all sorts of theories as to how the runemage might have earned a dagger in the brain. *So much for telling the duke that the cases were unrelated.*

"She did say that, didn't she, sir?"

"She did." Norwood rubbed his jaw. "And Vonlith was killed by a professional; neat and tidy."

"That he was, sir."

"Pull the records of that investigation, Tam. Everything! I want to know what the color of the godsdamned carpets were in Saliez's mansion. If we can link something we found there to this case, we might get some idea of who our assassin is."

"Right away, sir!" Tamir gave him another self-satisfied grin.

He's probably just happy that he was the one to get a lead, not Woefler, the captain thought, and that gave him an idea of where he might find another link between Vonlith's murder and that old case.

"I think it's time I paid a visit to the Wizards Guild lodge, Sergeant." Norwood rifled through the stacks of papers on his desk until he found the writ from the duke. It had a blackbrew stain on it, but was still legible. "We need to find out exactly who our dead wizard was doing business with."

$$\oint\!\beth\!\mathclose{}\!\beth\!\mathbin{}\!\beth\!\mathbin{}\!\beth\!\beth$$

The ledger must have weighed two stone. It hit the table with enough force that Norwood felt it through the stone floor of the Wizards Guild common room. He also felt the hair on the back on his neck prickle with the caustic stares of the mages sitting in leather-upholstered chairs all around him. They obviously did not appreciate his presence in their private domain. Only after examining the duke's writ with some disdain had the guild secretary finally allowed the captain access and brought out the guild log.

"Thank you." He gave the surly fellow a cordial smile.

"Damage a single page, smudge a single character, Captain, and you will be woefully sorry."

"I understand. I appreciate your help," Norwood said as politely as he could manage, remembering the duke's warning about alienating the guild.

With another glare, the guild secretary took two steps back, crossed his arms and set his feet, obviously intending to watch over Norwood's shoulder for as long as it took him to complete his task. The table upon which the logbook now sat had no accompanying chair, and one glance at the secretary's face told him that one would not be provided.

Marvelous. Suppressing a glare of his own, he opened the leather-bound tome with careful deliberation, stooped down, and began to read.

It took him a while to figure out how the massive logbook was organized. He'd be damned before he asked for help from the snooty secretary, and the man offered no assistance. His acerbic attitude seemed strange behavior to Norwood; one of their own had been killed, and the captain was here trying to solve the crime. Shouldn't they be more helpful?

The logbook turned out to be a linear chronology of every guild member's standing, activities and contracts, and as such, contained page after page of information Norwood didn't care about. He had had no idea there were so many wizards in Twailin, or that they were so busy. Flipping backward from the current date, Norwood found Vonlith's death noted in a precise, dispassionate reference.

Eighth day of Torith, year T-II-47: Master Vonlith, deceased. Wrongful death. Dues paid to end of the current month, balance to be forwarded to next of kin.

Next of kin.

That had been a disappointing avenue of investigation. Vonlith had left everything to his only living relative, a nephew who owned an unassuming bar in the Sprawls District. Tamir had interviewed the fellow, and reported that he didn't think the barkeep had either the financial or cognitive wherewithal to arrange—or commit—such a murder. Also, a dozen patrons were ready to swear that the man had been serving them drinks from late afternoon into the small hours of the morning on the night of Vonlith's death. The nephew would soon find himself embarrassingly rich. According to Woefler, the sale of Vonlith's personal effects alone would yield a fortune, and his fellow guild members were already gathering like crows to carrion.

The captain consulted his own notebook, then flipped backward through the ledger to the date five years ago when they had raided Saliez's estate. Nothing was noted for Vonlith on that date, but three days prior, the wizard had signed a contract to "scribe various runes." Half of the fee had been paid up front—a substantial amount—with the rest to be paid upon completion of the task. Two days after the date of the raid, however, another notation filled a line in the ledger. "Contract terminated prior to completion. Deposit retained."

Well, it's circumstantial, but it certainly suggests that Vonlith worked for Saliez. So it's no stretch to imagine that he knew the assassin who killed him. Norwood jotted the dates and notations into his notebook, cursing the Wizards Guild policy of confidentiality for patrons. There was no way to match names to these contacts.

He began flipping forward, one page at a time, searching the elegant script for Vonlith's name. Two weeks after the termination of the presumed contract with Saliez, he found another entry. "Contract to scribe various runes. Payments to be received monthly until completion."

Each month after that he found a notation that Vonlith had paid his guild dues in full, and that he had received payment for his ongoing contract. Norwood gaped at the amounts. *No wonder Vonlith lived in the lap of luxury.*

The captain continued flipping through the log's pages. Every month he found the exact same entry for Vonlith: dues paid, payment received. One year, two... *Two years of inscribing runes? Was he enchanting an entire estate or something?*

Finally swallowing his pride, Norwood crooked a finger to beckon the secretary over. "I find myself wasting your valuable time, sir. Perhaps you could help?"

The secretary glared at him, looking as if considering whether he should answer or not. He made a face, something between distaste and impatience. "If it will get you out of here quicker, I *suppose* I could help."

Pretentious twit! Norwood gritted his teeth and smiled pleasantly.

"Thank you. I'd like to know if there is a way to quickly determine if and when this contract was completed." He placed a fingertip on the recent notation. "It began almost two years prior to this date."

The secretary scowled at him, then stepped forward and placed his finger on the notation. He muttered under his breath, and his fingertip glowed briefly. Norwood stepped back, but the magic was apparently already done.

"Tenth day of Mirah, year T-II-47. About a month ago." The secretary waved a hand and the pages of the log flipped forward.

"One contract lasted almost five years?" Ignoring the secretary's condescending sneer, Norwood read the notation: "Contract completed, final payment received." The total sum of the money earned by the contract, noted in red, was staggering.

Five years earning a fortune, and a month after it's completed, he ends up dead... And the previous contract, presumably for Saliez, was cancelled because Saliez was killed. The connection between the two murders was still only circumstantial, but firming up.

He stepped back from the book and nodded to the secretary. "Thank you. That's all I need."

"Hmph." The man waved a hand and the heavy tome flipped closed with a thump.

Norwood didn't give the secretary the satisfaction of a response to his rudeness, but turned on his heel and strode from the guild lodge. The trail, it seemed, had led him back to events that he would rather not recall, events that had claimed the lives of more than a dozen of his guardsmen, not to mention as many nobles. He was beginning to have a very bad feeling about Vonlith's murder. But now, where else could he find information on a possible connection between Vonlith, Saliez, and the Assassins Guild? He only knew of one place.

"Where to, sir?"

The question from his driver jolted Norwood out of his musing. He was standing at the door of his carriage, the rain hammering unnoticed on the top of his head. Climbing aboard, he shook the rain from his cloak and wiped his wet face before pulling out his notebook once again. He flipped through the pages, found what he was looking for, and called up to the driver, "Westmarket. The *Tap and Kettle* on Beltway Street."

Chapter IX

The door to Norwood's carriage jerked open the instant the vehicle lurched to a stop. A bright-faced young man grinned up through the pouring rain and bowed.

"Welcome to the *Tap and Kettle*, milord." Stepping aside, he flourished an arm toward the inn. Golden light glowed from the windows, piercing some of the day's gloom. "My name's Ponce, sir. I apologize that I don't have a proper umbrella to keep the rain off. This weather's only fit for frogs and fishes, but we've got a warm hearth and hearty ale waitin' inside. Not every day we get a visit from the Royal Guard!"

"Thank you." Norwood stepped out of the carriage and dashed up the broad steps to the shelter of the covered porch.

Ponce matched his steps and hurried ahead open the door. "Anything for your driver while you're inside, milord? We've got a pot of blackbrew hot in the stable, and we can towel off your team so they don't take a chill."

"That would be fine. Thank you."

"My pleasure, milord." Ponce grinned, bowed and dashed off through the rain to guide the coach into the barn.

Norwood turned to enter the inn and stopped short, startled to find himself staring at the very same young man. At least, he looked the same, except that this one was dry and the other wet from the rain.

"Take your cloak, milord?" The new young man relieved him of his soaked weather cloak and hung it by the door. "My name's Tika. Welcome to the *Tap and Kettle*. I can see by the confusion on your face that you've already met my brother Ponce. We're easy enough to tell apart, really. I'm the handsome one, and he's the lout." He gestured to the bustling common room. "Will you be takin' a meal with us today, or just a pint and a seat by the fire?"

Norwood found himself taken aback for a moment by the welcome. Few inns in this part of town boasted both a groom and doorman, let alone manned by identical twins, and such mannerly ones at that. But the effect was not off-putting, and the captain found himself smiling. "Blackbrew will be fine. I'd like a see Mister Forbish when he has a moment. Tell him Captain Norwood of the Royal Guard wishes a word with him."

"Of course, milord. This way, please." Tika guided him through the busy common room to a cushioned chair by the fire. His uniform drew a few glances from other patrons, but that was to be expected south of the river. "Warm yourself here while I get your blackbrew and ask about the master of the house."

Norwood had no sooner sat down and propped his soaked boots on the hearth than Tika was back with a tray. A pot of blackbrew, a thick steaming mug, a pitcher of cream, a plate of cookies, and a silver honeypot vied for space on the tray. The young man handled the load expertly as he placed it on the small table beside the chair.

"Master Forbish'll be right with you, milord. He's up to his elbows in bread dough at the moment."

"That's fine."

The boy hurried off, and Norwood took a few moments to relax. Stretching his feet closer to the fire, he sipped the blackbrew and nibbled a few of the delicious almond cookies while he surveyed the inn's common room. Business, it seemed, was good. Customers sat at more than half of the tables. Most were merchants, some obviously locals taking time from their businesses to enjoy a hearty meal, others passing through the city, as evidenced by their foreign garb and travel-worn clothes.

One couple looked to be wealthy travelers, dressed in finery and eating and drinking in congenial company at a corner table, a pretty young wife attending to her older husband's every word and gesture. Two maids bustled about with tankards and trays of food, while Tika tended the door, occasionally stepping out onto the porch to shout for a coach to be brought around. The place seemed a well-run, clean hive of activity. Norwood vaguely recalled the inn as being much quieter when he visited five years ago. He was on his second cup of blackbrew and fourth cookie when Forbish bustled out from the kitchen, drying his hands on a towel and dusting the flour off of his apron.

"Captain Norwood!" Forbish gave him a quick bow, his smile a bit nervous, though not, Norwood conceded, more nervous than any innkeeper might be with an unexpected visit from the captain of the Royal Guard. The innkeeper wedged his considerable bulk into the other chair near the hearth. "Been quite a while since you've visited. Is this a social call or a matter of business?"

"Business, I'm afraid, but nothing to do directly with you." The captain swallowed the last of his blackbrew and put the cup aside. Looking around, he raised an appraising eyebrow. "It seems as if your own business is thriving."

"It is indeed. Best investment I ever made was to marry my barmaid Josie. She added womanly touches, like these comfortable seats for lounging by the fire." He patted the arm of his chair as if it was a pet, then gestured to the young man at the door. "And her nephews, Ponce and Tika, are like a couple of dervishes! Took to the business like ducks to water."

"I noticed. Congratulations on your marriage."

"Thank you, Captain." Forbish nodded gratefully, though his smile remained strained. "But you didn't come here just to look in on my business, I'll wager."

"You're right on that account." Norwood glanced around. Two tables of patrons were within hearing, so he kept the subject ambiguous for now. No need to start rumors flying by

Chris A. Jackson

mentioning a murder where others could hear. "I need to speak with both you and your daughter, in a private room if you have one available. A matter has come up that might be linked to that other affair she was involved with."

Forbish's eyes went wide for a moment, then he gestured to his guests. "We're very busy, Captain."

"It won't take long." Norwood kept his voice light, remembering how Forbish balked at a heavy hand. The last thing he wanted was for the man to clam up. "Only a few questions."

"I'd just as soon not bring Wiggen into this, Captain. We've put those happenings behind us and moved on. She's married now and has a little daughter of her own, you know."

"No, I didn't know. Congratulations again."

"Thank you, Captain."

"But I'm afraid I must insist that I speak with her." He edged his words with a bit more steel. "It won't take a moment, and I'll be happy to compensate you for your time."

Forbish bit his lip and finally nodded. "Very well, Captain." He stood and waved Tika over. The young man arrived with an eager grin on his face. "Show Captain Norwood to the small private room. I'll get Wiggen and join you shortly, Captain."

"I'll just bring along your blackbrew and biscuits, milord. It'd be a sin not to finish such delicious fare." Tika picked up the tray with all the aplomb of a high-class waiter and gestured toward a hall off the back of the common room. "Just this way if you please."

"Thank you, Forbish," Norwood said as he moved to follow the young man.

"You can thank me by not upsetting my daughter overmuch if you can avoid it, Captain." Forbish wrung his hands on his apron. "As I said, we've all moved on from those horrible times."

103

"I'll be as gentle as I can be, I assure you." He honestly didn't want to upset the girl, but he was going to get what he came for.

* ⸬𝓋𝕵𝕴𝕯𝟤𝕲 *

"What does *he* want?" Wiggen hitched Lissa up on her hip and continued stirring the huge pot of soup. The babe was fussy today, and every time Wiggen put her down, she rattled the dishes with her cries.

"He's just got a few questions for you, Wiggen."

Wiggen looked to her father and, despite the heat of the stove, felt a shiver of apprehension up her spine. She had hoped never to see Captain Norwood again.

"He said something's come up that might be related to that business with Lad a few years ago. Nothing to do with us, or so he says." As Forbish leaned past her to move the pot to the back of the stove, she noticed a slight tremble in his hands. He was nervous. "The soup'll be fine for a few minutes."

"I don't want to talk to him, Father." She lowered her voice to a whisper. "What if he asks about Lad?"

"As far as he knows, Lad's dead." He pulled gently on her arm. "Come on. I've already told him you'd give him a word. Putting it off will only make him mad."

"Oh, I'll give him a few *choice* words!" She didn't mean to snap at her father, but dealing with a fussy baby while attending to her work already had her nerves pinched so tight she felt like a bowstring ready to snap.

"Wiggen, try not to make him angry."

"I won't make him angry if he doesn't make me angry, Father."

"Fine, but keep in mind that if he makes you angry, *you* can't lock *him* up in a dungeon. He can, and has."

She scowled, but acknowledged his point. She had vivid memories of the dungeon beneath the headquarters of the Royal Guard. Reluctantly, she followed her father to the private room.

Captain Norwood sat close to the small stove, sipping a cup of blackbrew and munching on an almond cookie. At first glance, he looked unintimidating, merely a middle-aged man with a slight paunch and a receding hairline. His Royal Guard uniform and the long blade at his hip shattered that image.

He stood as they entered, brushing crumbs from his jacket with a sheepish smile. "Excuse me. I rarely eat sweets, and these are very good. Thank you for agreeing to speak with me, Wiggen."

"I'm glad you like the cookies, Captain." Wiggen nodded in acknowledgement instead of curtseying as she should to a man of Norwood's stature. Forbish shot a strained look at her, but she ignored him.

"And this must be the daughter I've heard about. She's adorable."

Wiggen softened for a moment, as she did whenever someone admired her baby, but then stiffened her resolve. He was just buttering her up with kind words, using Lissa to get her cooperation. She refused to rise to the bait. Instead, she bounced the baby on her hip, and brushed a hand over the silken little head as if to comfort the child.

"Yes, she's adorable, except when she's fussing and insists that I carry her around on my hip all day while we're dreadfully busy with a room full of guests, soup to stir, and biscuits still to be made for this evening." She sharpened her words with annoyance. She didn't want to anger him so much that he arrested her again, but she wasn't going to be intimidated.

His smile faded a trifle. "Yes, Forbish said you were busy, so I'll get right to the point. There's been a murder north of the river, a wizard named Vonlith."

He paused as if expecting some reaction or comment from her. She raised an eyebrow, wondering what this had to do with her. "I don't generally kill wizards, Captain, but I might make an exception if they interrupt me in the middle of work and taking care of a fussy baby."

He smiled tightly. "I wasn't suggesting that you had killed him, but I thought you might know the name."

"No, Captain. I've never heard the name before."

Norwood pulled a small book from the inside pocket of his jacket and flipped through the pages. "I'm asking you because we have evidence linking Vonlith to Saliez. That is a name I'm sure you remember."

Wiggen nodded and hitched Lissa farther up onto her hip. "Yes, I remember, Captain. But he's dead. Why should you care if this Vonlish had anything to do with him?"

"It's Vonlith, not Vonlish," he said with another tight-lipped smile. "A relationship with Saliez would suggest that he was working for the Assassins Guild, which might give us a hint why he was murdered. At the time, we thought that Saliez might have contracted a wizard to put the binding magic back on the boy you told us about"—he looked at his notebook—"Lad. Unfortunately, the wizard was gone when we raided Saliz's estate. We just found out that the wagon in Saliez's courtyard belonged to Master Vonlith."

Wiggen looked the captain straight in the eye, summoning the strength to steady her shaking knees at the mention of Lad. He had never told her the name of the wizard who had inked the neat row of runes down his chest. "So you already know that this Vonlith was involved with Saliez. Why ask me about it?"

"To determine if you knew why Saliez contracted the wizard."

"You just told me you already know that, too, Captain. I never heard the name Vonlith until you asked me. Frankly, if he worked for the Assassins Guild, it's no wonder he was killed."

"But our assumption came from what you told me about Lad." He flipped through pages in his notebook. "That a wizard put magic on him to make him kill those nobles."

"Yes, I did tell you that, Captain, but the only wizard Lad ever mentioned to me was the one who gave him the magic when he was a boy, and that wizard was apparently killed before Lad even arrived in Twailin."

"Yes, that is in my notes here."

"Then it should *also* be in your notes that I told you Lad was *dead*, and that I didn't mention a wizard named Vonlith." Wiggen took a deep breath, fighting to stay calm. "I'm sorry Captain, but I really can't help you. Forgive me if I'm upset. I've tried very hard to forget what happened back then, and you've just dredged it all up again."

"Now, Wiggen. Don't be like that." Forbish put a steadying hand on her shoulder. "He's just trying to solve a murder. He's not accusing you of anything."

"I'm sorry." Norwood at least had the decency to look chagrined as he tucked his notebook into a pocket. "Your father's right, I'm not accusing anyone here of anything. If you know nothing of Vonlith, I won't waste any more of your time. Thank you for your hospitality." He gulped a final swallow of his blackbrew, and plucked the last cookie from the plate as he reached into a pocket and pulled out a silver crown.

Forbish raised a hand to forestall the payment. "There's no need, Captain."

Norwood flipped the coin onto the tray anyway. "For your trouble, then."

Wiggen felt like screaming by the time her father ushered the captain out of the room. She dropped into the chair as her knees gave out, and hugged Lissa to her breast. They had thought themselves safe from the Royal Guard. If Norwood ever realized that Lad was alive, he wouldn't rest until they hanged him for the deaths of all those nobles. Fear for him, of losing him again, felt like a crushing weight on her chest. Closing her eyes, she forced herself to take deep breaths, to still her mind as Lad had taught her. Eventually, her heart slowed and her muddled thoughts cleared.

Once she was sure that her legs would support her, she stood, hitched her daughter up on her hip, and picked up the blackbrew tray with a practiced motion. "Well, we've certainly got something to tell your daddy tonight, don't we, Lissa?"

Lissa looked up at her mother with wide uncomprehending eyes, her father's eyes, and smiled. Wiggen kissed her cheek, wishing she could share the babe's blissful ignorance.

Hensen propped his feet upon the hearth, upon the very same stones where Captain Norwood's boots had rested only hours before. The master thief had been more than startled when his long-standing nemesis walked into the *Tap and Kettle*'s common room, but Puc, the God of luck, must have been smiling on him. The captain had barely spared him a glance before talking with Forbish, and then withdrew into a back room with the innkeeper and his scar-faced daughter. Hensen had been unable to overhear their conversation, but that was all right; his spies in the Royal Guard would let him know what the good captain was currently investigating. But that would come later.

Relaxing into the cushions, perversely pleased to be sitting where Norwood sat, Hensen basked in the warmth of the dying bed of coals. It felt good to be out of his house for a change, away from the damned account books, schedules, work assignments and contracts that took up all of his time and sapped his zeal for life. It had been years since he'd done any honest—dishonest, really—field work. Unable to resist the opportunity to stretch his legs and shake the dust off of his long-disused skills, he had slipped into all his old habits as easily as slipping into a pair of comfortable old shoes. He and Kiesha had checked into the inn that morning, a wealthy merchant in town for a few days with his young wife. Thanks to his subtle disguise, neither Forbish nor Norwood had shown a hint of recognition.

Now he sat alone in the common room—all the guests, and even the staff, had long since retired for the night—an old book of poems in his lap illuminated by the lamp beside his chair. Next to the lamp sat a glass of red wine, but he had not sipped it in hours. In fact, his whole posture was feigned; he wasn't reading, drinking, sleeping, or lost in thought.

Hensen was waiting for someone.

Just past midnight, when his spirits began to flag with the notion that his hunch might have been wrong, the kitchen door opened. Hensen's eyes flicked up even as he maintained his scholarly pose, his head bent over his book as if rapt in the verse.

A young man entered the common room wrapped in a robe. He strode across the floor, his movements as fluid as water on a sheet of glass, his steps utterly silent. If not for the creak of the door opening, Hensen might have missed his passage entirely.

It was him. The weapon.

A thrill of fear raced up Hensen's spine, an occurrence so unusual that it nearly broke his feigned composure. All his life, the thief had trod carefully around the Assassins Guild, reluctant to stir the ire of its cruel master. Yet this young man, or so the rumor ran according to Sereth, had managed to kill Saliez. The master thief would need all of his skills if he wanted to leave this chair alive.

Hensen flipped a page of his book and reached out to pick up his glass of wine, pretending not to notice the weapon's silent appearance. The wine didn't ripple in the glass, his false calm intact. Draining the small amount of liquid left, he looked up to set the glass aside, feigning surprise at the sight of his visitor. Hensen stifled a start of unease at the faintly luminous eyes, like a cat's, staring at him.

"Good evening." Hensen raised his glass in toast and smiled. *Calm, smooth, easy,* he thought.

"Sir." The young man nodded politely and stepped closer, so that the light from Hensen's lamp illuminated his face. The luminosity of his eyes faded. It must have been a reflection from the lamp.

Not quite the same as the portrait, but undeniably the same young man.

"Can I get you anything before I retire?"

"How kind of you to offer." The thief raised his glass. "Another spot of the grape would not go amiss. My insomnia is acting up, and wine, I'm afraid, is the only means I have to get to sleep."

"Of course." He vanished into the kitchen and returned with a chilled carafe of wine. "Here you are."

"You're a godsend, my boy." The young man—*the weapon*, Hensen reminded himself— leaned down to fill his glass, his motions smooth and sure. Hensen watched intently, memorizing every curve, every dimple and scar. He knew the weapon could kill him in an instant, yet still the wine in his glass did not ripple. His nerves tingled with the exhilaration of the danger. He felt more alive than he had in years. Hensen sipped, trying not to stare at the grace and beauty of the weapon as he placed the carafe on the table. "You must be Master Forbish's son-in-law."

"Yes." The weapon smiled, which was nearly as disturbing as his uncanny perfection. "My work keeps me out late, but it pays too well for me to quit."

"Difficult for a young father to be away from his bride and daughter, no doubt." Hensen sipped his wine again, examining the subtle changes from the illustration he'd kept all these years.

"It is hard, but I have little choice." The weapon—*he has a name*, Hensen remembered. *Lad*—smiled again and nodded. "We all do what we must. Goodnight, sir."

"Goodnight." Hensen watched him go, relishing that last glimpse of supple grace, and wondering if Lad's uncanny eyes had pierced his disguise. If they had, he could very well be dead by morning. He leaned back in the chair and closed his book. He had put himself in unwarranted danger here, and for what? To get a closer look at something far beyond his ken. Well, after tonight, he would consider his own safety above his curiosity. *I've operatives for this kind of thing, for the Gods' sake!* He would station them to watch over Lad, fulfilling the terms of the contract without risking his life again.

I should leave first thing in the morning, before he can see me again. But then Hensen remembered the look of Lad's light hazel eyes in the lamplight, so clear, so beautiful that they took his breath away. Perhaps leaving too early would draw attention. *We'll leave immediately after breakfast*, he decided, feeling sure that Lad would make an appearance. *Kiesha must see him as well*, he rationalized, sipping his wine and staring into the dying embers at his feet.

"Such a lovely young man…"

CHAPTER 8

"Good morning, sleepyhead." Lad handed Wiggen the cup of steaming blackbrew he had just poured. He had heard her shuffling across the common room before she entered the kitchen, and thought it best to greet her properly.

The sun had not yet risen outside the kitchen window, so it wasn't really morning yet, but the glow of the kitchen lamps seemed dimmer with the lightening sky. Lad had suggested they let Wiggen sleep an extra half hour, since he knew she'd been up twice feeding Lissa since he came home. Lissa gurgled and reached out for her mother, but Lad murmured sweet nothings into her ear to calm her down. Wiggen took the cup and rubbed her eyes, looking more tired than usual.

"What's good about it?" Wiggen sipped the strong brew and closed her eyes. "Ahh, that's good. I may just survive."

"Glad to hear it." Lad bounced the sleepy babe on his hip as he steered Wiggen to a stool. "Forbish said you had a visit from Captain Norwood yesterday."

"Yes." She sat down and took another sip of blackbrew, looking to her father. "Did you tell him everything?"

"No, I thought you should." Forbish shrugged and continued mixing dough for scones. "You were the one he wanted to talk to."

Lad sat quietly and waited for her to speak, hiding his impatience. Forbish's nervous demeanor had him worried. He had been incredibly tight-lipped about the guard captain's visit,

112

deferring to Wiggen. In fact, the Royal Guard showing up at the inn at all had Lad worried. He'd have to talk with Mya about keeping up her part of their deal. Wiggen seemed less nervous than her father, but she was also still half asleep.

"Norwood was investigating a murder. It wasn't anything to do with us. Not directly, anyway. I nearly died when he mentioned you by name, but—"

"He mentioned *me*?" Lad clenched his fist, but she put a calming hand on his arm.

"Only in passing. He thought the murder might have had something to do with the Assassins Guild."

"Well, that's not a stretch of imagination. Most of the murders in Twailin *can* be traced back to the guild one way or another. But why mention me, and why would he ask you about it?"

"Norwood thinks the murdered man, some wizard, had something to do with the Grandfather." She shook her head as if it would help dredge up the details of the conversation from her sleep-deprived mind. "He wanted to know if I had ever heard of him, but I hadn't."

Cold fingers of worry gripped the back of Lad's neck. He only knew of two wizards who had associated directly with the Grandfather. One had been his Master, and he was long dead. The other... "What was the wizard's name?"

"Vonlith. Was that who..." She waved her hand toward his chest, indicating the runes hidden beneath his shirt.

"Yes."

Vonlith dead.

Lad's mind spun. He touched his chest, rubbing the cloth of his shirt over the dark tattoos that Vonlith had etched there, the runes that would have once again enslaved him to the Grandfather. His feelings about Vonlith were conflicted, to say the least. The only reason the wizard hadn't completed his task was that Mya had helped Lad kill the Grandfather. He seethed a bit, then took a couple of deep breaths to calm himself,

113

remembering that Vonlith had only been doing his job, the same way that the assassins who attacked Mya, or the stalkers who tried to follow him home, were only doing their jobs. Besides, if not for Vonlith dispelling the power of the Grandfather's tattooed runes, Lad would never have been able to defeat the guildmaster. His help had not been altruistic by any means—rather to keep Mya's dagger out of his throat—but Vonlith *had* cast the spell, and then provided them a means of escape in his wagon.

"Lad?" Wiggen squeezed his arm, and he realized that she and Forbish were staring at him. "Are you okay?"

"I'm fine." He force a smile he didn't feel. "Yes, he's the one who gave me my tattoos, under orders from the Grandfather. He also saved my life…"

"He saved *your* life?" Forbish looked dubious.

Wiggen sat tight-lipped. Lad had told her most of what had happened that day, though he had never mentioned Vonlith by name, and she had kept her promise not to tell anyone, even her father.

Lad cracked a wry smile. "Only because Mya threatened to kill him if he didn't, but that doesn't matter." His mind skipped ahead to the real issue: who would kill Vonlith and why? He hadn't heard anything of the man in five years, but the wizard was one of two people who knew he'd killed Saliez. To murder a highly skilled wizard was a dangerous and rare undertaking. Someone must have wanted him dead very badly. "Did Norwood say how Vonlith died?"

"No. He only said it was murder. He's trying to find out who did it, and found out that Vonlith was working for the Grandfather. Since I was the one who told him about the Grandfather in the first place, he thought I might know what Vonlith was doing for him. I'd never heard of Vonlith and told him so, but as it turns out he had a pretty good idea…" Her voice trailed off, and she twisted a strand of her hair in agitation.

114

"Well, I'd like to know who killed Vonlith, too," Lad admitted. He handed Lissa over to Wiggen. "We better get to work. Don't worry about this. I'll look into it."

"It doesn't have anything to do with you." Wiggen put her cup down and propped the baby on her hip, giving him an admonishing look. "Why should you have to find out who killed him?"

"I'm just interested, that's all. I'm sure it has nothing to do with me, and it's probably not related to the Grandfather either."

"What if someone found out how Saliez died and is getting revenge?" He hated to hear the worry in Wiggen's voice.

"I doubt that's the case. It's been five years, after all, but I want to make sure, and I know who to ask for help."

"Mya?" Wiggen's eyes had narrowed, her voice scornful. She didn't like Mya, even though she had never met the Master Hunter. She understood that Lad had given his word to protect the woman, but she resented the danger it put him in.

"She was the only other person there when the Grandfather died." He gave her an easy smile, sure of his reasoning. "If someone's out for revenge, Mya will find out who it is." *Not because she wants to help me, but because it's in her best interest*, he thought, careful not to voice this opinion aloud.

"And she's also supposed to keep the Royal Guard away from us. Why don't you remind her about that?"

"I will. She has people who can get information from the Royal Guard, and she's spread a few rumors over the years to reinforce the notion that I'm dead, but something like this is probably a bit beyond her influence." Lad recognized the irony in defending Mya against charges that he, himself, had considered only a short while ago.

"Just be careful, Lad. I don't trust her."

"I'm always careful, Wiggen. You know that." He kissed her on the cheek and Lissa on the forehead. "I've got too much to lose not to be careful."

Mya ascended the stairs from her apartment, the cool air of the passage a sharp contrast to the warm hand clasped in her own. Unlocking the door at the top, she guided her guest into her office. He stumbled at the top step, and she reached back, quick as a striking snake, to steady him.

"I'm sorry. I should have told you—"

"No matter, milady." He smiled and squeezed her hand.

His was a nice smile, a very nice smile, and his hands... A warm shiver ran up Mya's spine as she recalled his fingers on her skin, teasing her with their feather-light touch. And that had just been the start. His patience, kindness, and consummate skill had proven him worthy of his reputation.

"Here. There's a chair for you, two steps." She led him to her chair, lamenting the loss of his touch as he released her hand, while at the same moment relishing the renewal of her solitude. "Wait here. I'll fetch your mistress."

"Thank you."

His voice touched her ears like stone-washed silk. The whispers, pleas, and promises of the night echoed in her mind, and she shivered again. Closing the door to her apartments, she strode to the door to the common room and opened it. Mika stood there like a monolith, arms crossed, face impassive. It was frightfully early, and yet he there he was. *Does he never leave that spot?* she wondered.

"Madam Jondeleth should be in the common room, Mika. Please fetch her."

"Yes, Miss Mya."

The door thudded closed, and Mya walked back to the young man seated complacently in her chair. His milky white eyes stared unseeingly past her, but the pale motes did not detract from his beauty. What did were the marks upon the flawless skin of his neck, marks that matched her teeth perfectly. She cringed when she considered the other marks she had left on him in the throes of her passion. She had nearly injured him badly before coming to her senses and reining in her enthusiasm, yet not one complaint or one admonishment had issued from his beautiful lips.

Mya went to him and lifted his collar to cover the marks, then combed her fingers through his tousled hair, smoothing it down. She remembered that hair between her fingers, her cries, his, and pulled her hand away. The long sleeve of her robe slipped up her forearm, exposing her lattice of tattooed runes; she had not yet donned her wrappings. Memories of his hands caressing her rune-etched skin flooded through her. For the first time she had exposed her secret to someone, and it was to a blind prostitute.

"Thank you." Again, that voice…

Gods, what's wrong with me?

The knock at the door sent her hand reaching for the dagger normally at her hip. Banishing the reflex, she straightened her robe and said, "Come in."

The door opened and Mika ushered Madam Jondeleth into the room. The woman had been quite a beauty in her youth, and still dressed like a courtesan, even though long past the age where she could ply that trade. Now she specialized in the supply side of the business, providing experts in the arts of physical pleasure to wealthy clients throughout Twailin, including royalty, clergy, and magistrates. Needless to say, she was accustomed to being discreet when it came to her clientele, a desire that Mya had emphasized. Mistress Jondeleth had only winked knowingly, a manner that set Mya's teeth on edge.

"Good morning, Mistress Mya. How was your evening?"

"Good morning." Mya hesitated, unsure of what to say about this type of transaction. She glanced at the young man. *Gods, I don't even know his name!* It felt so impersonal to discuss his performance while he sat right there, but Madam

117

Jondeleth waited with an expectant smile. "He was fine. Very good."

Her own words struck her like a kick in the stomach. She felt like she should have said something more, or nothing at all.

"Good. I'm glad you found him pleasing." The woman snapped her fingers several times in quick succession. The young man rose to follow the sound to where his employer held out her arm. Mya found the gesture insulting, as if the woman was summoning a pet. "If you wish his services again, please do not hesitate to call on me."

"I will." *When all Nine Hells freeze over*, she thought, clenching her fists until her nails bit into her palms. There was no pain, of course, but she felt the oozing blood slicken her grip.

The woman nodded, smiled, and turned to go. The young man followed dutifully, his hand resting lightly on the madam's arm. His blind eyes swept past Mya, and a sweet, secret smile touched his lips. Mya felt suddenly as if she owed him something beyond the gold she had paid for his services, some personal acknowledgement.

"I..." She stopped herself, but too late. Madam Jondeleth turned back, a question in her eyes. "I'll call on you again soon."

"Very good." The madam nodded again, and they left, Mika pulling the door closed behind them.

Mya breathed a sigh of relief, looked down at her bloody palms and wiped them clean on her robe. The tiny wounds were already closed. *What the hells is wrong with me? I go so far as to pay for someone's company, then can't wait to be alone again.* Anger and unease boiled up in equal portions. Fumbling with the key, she opened the door to her apartments and strode through, slamming it closed without relocking it. If someone skilled or stupid enough to get past Mika chose this moment to try to kill her, let them come. She'd welcome a fight.

I just need a bath, maybe some exercise. Yes... That'll set me right.

She hurried through her living room to her bedroom, and stopped short. The disheveled bed glared at her like a disapproving matron, condemnation plain in the rumpled sheets, the torn pillowcase, the dampness of sweat and blood on the coverlet. Mya had had few lovers in her life, and none for the past five years. No one had come close to giving her the physical pleasure that last night had provided, and still, she felt like she'd betrayed someone.

Sex and love are different, my friend... The words she had said to Lad felt like a slap in the face.

Lad! It would have been so easy for them to ease their tension together, so natural. Last night she had closed her eyes, imagining that it was Lad who caressed her. His refusal of her offer had hit her harder than she imagined it could, but she should have known better. He was completely besotted with that scar-faced tavern wench. How could he love someone like her, someone so weak?

Angry with Lad and angrier with herself, Mya turned away from the bed. She tore off her robe and flung it toward the clothes press on her way to the bathing room. The warmth of the thick stone walls greeted her like a welcome embrace. She'd spent a good bit of coin on this room, a refuge that nobody could invade. Simple magic warmed the floor and walls, and the water from the spigot high on the wall always came out at precisely the temperature she desired, whether she wanted a hot bath, a tepid rinse or a bracingly chilly deluge.

Scalding, she thought, turning the tap on full.

Water just short of boiling poured forth.

Steam billowed as Mya stepped under the torrent. Looking down, she watched blisters bubble up on her skin, but she felt no pain. The blisters healed, and rose again. Grabbing soap and a brush, Mya scrubbed her tattooed flesh, washing away every vestige of the previous night's lovemaking.

No, it wasn't lovemaking, it was sex, straightforward, simple sex. Nothing to be ashamed about! She scrubbed harder, wishing for the absent pain, anything to clear her mind of these plaguing thoughts.

When she finally felt clean, she closed the tap, grabbed a towel and scrubbed herself dry. Her blistered flesh healed once more, instantly and painlessly, resuming its seamless, scarless luster of dark runes. She cast the towel aside and strode through her bedroom without a glance at the incriminating bed, through the living room and into the training room.

On the floor in the corner lay her wrappings, her armor against prying eyes.

Mya held one end of the supple cloth against her ankle and began wrapping it up her leg, overlapping each successive layer. The cloth felt good against her skin, smooth and comforting. Her anonymity in physical form, it kept her secret from the rest of the world. With this simple layer of cloth, she looked normal, helpless, vulnerable—until someone tried to hurt her.

Halfway up one leg, she glanced up into one of the mirrors that lined the walls. She stopped and stared as her flesh writhed with magic, her beautiful gifts...

If you're so beautiful, why hide? Why pay a blind man to pleasure you?

Mya cursed at the nagging voice. She knew why. She had to keep her secret safe from her enemies.

Is that the only reason?

She stared into the mirror, barely recognizing herself, black tattoos against pale flesh, more magic than human. Who was she? *What* was she? Memories flashed into her mind of the Grandfather as he disrobed in his dreadful torture chamber, the dark, ancient runes revealed on his flesh as he prepared to fight Lad. Another memory, lying on his table as his blades sliced through her flesh, screaming as he laughed, realizing what she truly was. She had loathed the Grandfather, his domination over her and her fear of him. Now she had made herself into his likeness, his offspring.

Monster...

Mya stared at her tattoos. Before today they had always seemed to dance to unheard music before her eyes, they now writhed across her flesh like snakes. Lad had freed her from the Grandfather's slavery, and she had wrapped herself in her own dark chains. She would never have an honest lover, never be touched by someone who was not paid to pleasure her. She had thought being alone would make her safe, that relationships would only make her vulnerable. And Lad, the only man who had any chance of understanding her, any chance of being an honest lover, had spurned her.

With a surge of self-loathing, Mya lashed out. Her fist impacted the mirror, shattering her image into a thousand shards. Another mirror, another image, and her foot smashed it to splinters. Again and again she struck, spun, struck once more. Glass showered the floor, stained crimson beneath her feet. The wrappings trailed behind her, fluttering like a murder of crows in her wake as she spun and lashed out at herself, destroying every image, every semblance of what she was.

What she had made herself.

Monster...

Finally she slowed, and then stopped, gazing around. The room lay in ruins, blood spattered in decorative arcs where she had lacerated herself in her self-destruction. The black wrappings trailed away in a knotted tangle. Mya stood at the center, surrounded by splintered fragments of herself.

"What am I?" she whispered as she watched the cuts on her hands and feet heal painlessly.

"You're strong," she declared, though the timidity of her voice belied her words. "You're fast. You're deadly. You're safe!" Her last words boomed through the room, echoing off of the naked stone. Slowly, deliberately, she pulled the wrappings—her armor of anonymity—to her.

Untangling the knots and twists, she wrapped the cloth tightly around her limbs, her torso, her loins. Splinters of glass glittered like diamonds on the dark fabric, but she ignored them.

121

Tighter, she wrapped and wrapped, ignoring the painless prick of broken glass, ignoring the blood that seeped through, until she was covered in her blanket of painless pain.

Blood, but no pain.

Mya lifted a large shard of mirror and looked at herself. A mote in the reflection caught her attention. Tears, clean and pure, tracked down her cheeks. She wiped them away with the edge of the shard, ignoring the wetness that flowed in the wake of the razor-edged glass.

This is what she was; blood and pain that could never be felt. This was what she had made herself into.

Monster...

CHAPTER XI

The morning sounds of the *Golden Cockerel*'s common room faded behind Lad as he approached the door to Mya's office. Ahead, Mika stood like a granite statue at his post, a head taller than Lad and weighing twice as much. The two men had never spoken much, even though they had the same job: protect Mya. They nodded to one another, and Mika knocked upon, then opened, the door to the back room.

"Lad." Mya, eyebrows raised, stopped her fork halfway to her mouth, then lowered it to the plate with her half-eaten breakfast. "You're early."

"Yes. I need to speak with you." He glanced at Mya's assistant, Dee, who sat patiently across the table from her with a pen poised above a piece of parchment, then back to Mya. "In private."

Mya's eyes narrowed and her mouth twitched into an expression that Lad couldn't quite interpret, though after five years of watching her, he had become quite adept at reading her moods. *Worried, startled, tense, upset? Why?* He brought his vigilance up a notch.

His request to speak to her in private shouldn't have worried her. He had been in her office often enough, usually when she had a meeting with some nefarious sort and wanted protection. Today he needed to speak with her privately, before they started their rounds. It wouldn't do to have a curious shopkeeper or passerby overhear this discussion.

123

So why is she worried?

"All right." She made a shooing motion at Dee. "Go have a blackbrew. We'll finish this when I'm done with Lad."

"Yes, Miss Mya." Dee put down his pen and stood to go, glancing curiously at Lad in passing. Lad paid him scant attention, his senses attuned to Mya. When the door closed behind Dee, Lad settled into the chair the assistant had vacated.

"The captain of the Royal Guard came to the *Tap and Kettle* yesterday, Mya."

"I know. His name is Norwood. My people spotted him, and I received the report last night."

Of course. She already knows Norwood came to the inn. Is that why she's tense? Is she afraid of what I might do, or afraid of Norwood? "What are you going to do about it?"

"I haven't decided yet." She sipped her blackbrew and took a bite of toast slathered with preserves. "To do anything constructive, it would help to know *why* Norwood was there. My people only saw him arrive, go inside, and come out again a while later. Do *you* know why he was there?"

"Yes. He came to talk to Wiggin. He told her that Vonlith had been murdered."

"Vonlith? The runemage?" Her eyebrows raised in question, Mya put down her cup, dabbed her mouth with her napkin, and put it down beside her plate, her movements measured and precise.

Too measured and precise. Nothing causal about her motions. He'd seen this mannerism many times before. It was subtle, and most would have missed it. *She's straining for calm.*

"Do you know *another* Vonlith?" He didn't bother keeping the ire out of his voice.

"Relax, Lad." She leveled a stare at him intended to snuff his anger. "I need to know the details. Why would Norwood tell Wiggen about Vonlith's death?"

"Norwood somehow found out that Vonlith worked for the Grandfather. Since Wiggen was the one who told him about the

Grandfather in the first place, he thought she might also know something about Vonlith."

"And what did Wiggen tell him?"

"The truth; that she had never heard of a wizard named Vonlith."

"So, that's that," Mya said lightly as she picked up her blackbrew and sipped.

Lad was surprised by Mya's cavalier response, and wondered if perhaps he had read too much into the captain's inquiry. They hadn't seen Vonlith in five years. There was no way for Norwood to trace the wizard to them.

"Norwood hit a dead end and he won't be back," Mya continued. "End of problem." Then Mya brushed her hair away from her ear.

That stopped Lad cold. After five years, he knew that one tell better than any other. She only brushed her hair away like that when she was being evasive. Looking more closely, he noticed a slight quiver in her hands. The blackbrew rippled in the cup. She was uneasy.

Why?

He chose his words carefully, trying to think of the best way to provoke a reaction without letting her know that he was gauging her response.

"That's *not* the end of the problem!" Standing, he pulled up his shirt to expose the neat row of tattooed runes down his chest. "If Norwood finds out just *what* Vonlith was doing for the Grandfather, he might also figure out that I'm not dead."

Mya's eyes flicked over his chest, but this time he didn't recognize the expression in her eyes. He decided to push it farther. "And if he figures out that I'm not dead, he might think *I* killed Vonlith."

"Did you?" Mya's eyes snapped up to his, narrowing. Whatever emotion had been in them a moment before was gone, purged by a mien of pure calculation

Lad rocked back on his heels, shocked by the question. "I'm not a killer anymore, Mya. Besides, why would I kill Vonlith?"

"He was the only person outside the guild who knew what you are, Lad." Keeping her eyes locked to his, she placed her blackbrew on the table and raised her toast for another bite, her motions precise, exact. "I'd think you'd be relieved that he's dead, even if you didn't do it. Now he can't betray your secret."

"If he was going to betray me, I think he'd have done it by now. Killing him would only draw attention to me. I'm *not* stupid!"

Mya's eyes dilated and the tiny vessels under the skin of her face flushed with blood. The involuntary response faded, but not before Lad interpreted it. She was seriously upset. *But why?*

"No, you're *not* stupid, but sometimes you're a little naïve, my friend." Taking the last bite of toast into her mouth, she looked down at her plate as she chewed, then picked up her cup and sipped. By the time she looked back up to Lad, her features were calm; she was in complete control again.

He realized then what she'd done. Mya had put him on the defensive, turned the table so that this was about him, not her. She was a master of manipulation, but even she couldn't always control her reactions. He knew she was hiding something from him, but had no idea what it might be.

"Of course I don't think you had anything to do with Vonlith's death," she continued, "but it does neither of us any good for you to get angry with me over something I knew nothing about. As far as I know, the guild wasn't behind Vonlith's death, but I *have* missed a few meetings. I'll look into it and try to find out what's going on. I'd like to know who put a chill on Vonlith, too." She dabbed her mouth with her napkin, then brushed her hair back again. *Another evasion.* "We might even be able to pin it on Horice. That'd be a nice payback for the attack on us, wouldn't it?"

"His attack on *you*, you mean."

"In their eyes, we're inexorably linked, Lad." Mya dropped her napkin onto her plate. "I'll do everything in my power to keep you out from under Norwood's magnifying glass. Keeping you free is in my best interest, Lad. You've saved my life more times than I can remember. I don't take that lightly."

"I gave you my word, Mya. Did you expect me to break it?"

She laughed, a short, scornful sound. "You're just about the only person in this city that I *don't* expect to betray me. I just wish you'd trust me as much."

"I..." Lad stumbled over the words. This was the woman who had tricked him not once, but twice. In doing so, she had made him a slave and a murderer. But she had also released him and helped him kill the Grandfather. One thing remained certain: Mya would always do what she thought was best for herself. He hedged his response. "You always told me not to trust anyone completely, so I don't."

"What about Wiggen?"

Mya rose and stepped around the table, brushing a few crumbs from her lap. A speck of reflected light fell from her clothes, and Lad heard a faint chime as it met the floor. *Glass*, he thought automatically.

"You trust *her*, don't you?"

His mind snapped back to the question. "That's different. She's my wife."

"Wives betray husbands all the time, Lad. Just like husbands betray wives and siblings betray one another. Just because someone's married or related to you doesn't make them trustworthy. If it came down to a choice between your life and Wiggen's, who do you think Forbish would betray?"

"If you're trying to make me suspicious of my family, Mya, you're wasting your time."

"I'm not trying to *make* you anything but aware of the real world, Lad. You're going to get hurt if you don't open your eyes." She strode past him toward the door.

127

Bending quickly while her back was turned, he pressed a finger to the shard of glass that glinted on the floor. It stuck. Pinching it between finger and thumb to keep it hidden, he followed her to the door.

"I don't understand you, Mya. You tell me to trust you, then tell me *not* to trust my own family. How do you live like that?"

"There are different levels of trust, Lad. I trust no one implicitly, but you more than anyone else. There is no one in the world who wouldn't betray someone with the right incentive, my friend. The sooner you realize that, the better."

Lad nearly laughed with the irony. Mya had taught him that very fact. She had delivered him to the Grandfather for power and position, only to turn around and betray the Grandfather when she realized that her vaunted position was just a polished form of slavery.

She opened the door and sent Mika to fetch Dee, then turned back to Lad. "Wait for me in the common room, Lad, and try to relax. I'll look into this and see what I can find out."

"Tell me what you learn."

"I will." Her eyes flicked away from his for before she dismissed him with a nod.

Lad took a seat near the common room's front window and waved the morning barmaid away when she asked if he wanted anything. This early, the place was virtually deserted save for Mya's people. He watched the city through the window, but his thoughts remained focused on Mya.

Why was she being so evasive?

He felt the shard of glass from the floor between his fingers and examined it in the light. The splinter was perhaps as long as his fingernail, and silvered on one side.

A mirror. Looking closer, he noted a faint brown stain on one end. He scratched at it with his thumbnail, brought the residue to his nose, then his tongue. *Blood.*

Mya had broken a mirror and cut herself on some of the pieces. He thought about the old superstition about bad luck.

Could that be what had her upset this morning? He had not thought she was given to such silly notions, but he filed that bit of information away with the other innumerable details he had learned about her, and went back to pondering their conversation.

What was she hiding? There was no way to know, but he felt sure it had something to do with Vonlith's death. And if she was so determined to hide it from him, then it must be important.

Mya's right about one thing, he thought, *there are levels of trust.* And although Mya had not betrayed him once to his knowledge since the death of the Grandfather, that didn't mean she wouldn't if given the proper incentive.

Lad made a decision; he had to learn more about Vonlith's death. Unfortunately, he could only think of one source for that information.

༄༅༅༅༅

Lad flowed from shadow to shadow, silent and invisible, as he made his way through the elegant neighborhoods north of the river. He knew these streets as he knew the rest of Twailin, but in the past five years, he had avoided this area. The affluent neighborhoods of Hightown and The Bluff were where he had become the Grandfather's unwilling harbinger of death. Coming here brought visions of those assassinations, of victims five-years-dead, ghosting into his mind.

Lad had thought all day about this. On the one hand, Wiggen's question was valid; what did Vonlith's death have to do with him? And Mya was right, too; he should be pleased that there was now one less person alive who could betray him. Besides, Norwood thought Lad was dead. If Lad's curiosity changed that, would the guard captain renew the hunt for him?

But Mya's reaction that morning had disturbed him. She was hiding something, something to do with Vonlith. There was only one place he might find answers, and he had calculated that his need for those answers outweighed the risk of Norwood discovering his identity. Getting in to talk to the man, however, was not without problems. He could not afford to let anyone identify him. If they did...

I'm not here to kill anyone, he reminded himself. *I'm just here to talk.*

Part of the risk was his own fault. To placate Lad, Mya had posted Hunters to watch over the captain. He would have to avoid them to get into the townhouse unseen.

So where are they?

Ducking behind an ornate marble pillar, he examined the stately row of homes across the street. Though far more opulent than any neighborhood south of the river, the buildings in this area were a step down, both literally and figuratively, from the palatial mansions farther up the hill. The nobles of Twailin evidently wanted the captain of the Royal Guard to be near them, but not among them.

He crept closer, scanning the shadows and straining his senses, his bare feet silent against the slick cobbles. It was well past midnight, and the streets were deserted. The rains had slacked to a bare drizzle. The flickering street lamps barely penetrated the darkness, gleaming in well-defined halos of light.

Slowly, silently, he edged forward.

The faint, rhythmic thud of a heartbeat in the darkness a few steps ahead froze him in his tracks. He had found the first of Mya's watchers. A faint scent identified the watcher as a woman. Staring into the shadow of an elaborate topiary hedge, he resolved her outline; she was not completely invisible. She was good, though, utterly quiet and breathing slowly, her eyes sweeping back and forth, scanning the row of townhouses. He took a moment to admire her skill before slipping away to find another path toward his goal.

Gauging her angle of view, he guessed where the next watcher would be. He didn't know how many Mya had placed, but her resources were not so vast that she would dedicate more than two or three. The woman watched the front of the house from an angle. He assumed that there would be one more on this side, and found the man not far away, hunkered high up beneath the awning of a balcony.

The front was well watched.

The captain's townhouse stood in the middle of a row of buildings with shared sidewalls, so only the front and back were exposed. The block's inner courtyard had entrances at each corner. Lad slipped beneath an archway and scrutinized the courtyard from deep shadow. The flower beds, hedges, and trees were so pruned and manicured that they looked artificial. There he spotted a third Hunter pacing the rooftop of the building across the courtyard with a clear view of the back of Norwood's home.

Lad eased forward. If he could time his entry, he might be able to slip inside when the watcher made his turn. Movement in the shadows ahead froze him in mid-step. On the back doorstep lay an enormous mastiff, its collar linked by a heavy chain to the railing post. As if it sensed his gaze, the dog raised its head. Lad cursed silently. Dogs were a problem. He could evade the perceptions of any man or woman, and even an elf or gnome, but he could not hide his scent from a dog. Any closer and it would surely bark. Slowly, he retraced his steps.

Lad reconsidered the two Hunters watching the front. They were positioned well, but no eyes could watch everywhere at once. The Hunters were probably bored and not as vigilant as they should be. That was good. He slipped across the street again and analyzed the front of the townhouse.

The structure was built of quarried stone, polished smooth and set so close that the seams between the stones were too thin for any kind of climbing device. Tall bay windows protruded from each of the three stories, casting a narrow shadow from the nearest streetlight, though the light's hooded fixture cut the illumination just above the highest window. Entering through a window was out of the question; shuttered and no doubt locked, they were in plain view of Mya's Hunters.

Looking up, above where the hooded streetlight illuminated the structure, Lad finally found his point of entry. Each home in the row had a peaked roof with ornate eaves. Above the third story, the stone gave way to a low, triangular section of wooden shakes. Set among the shakes, directly above the center window, was a louvered ventilation grate. The grate wasn't made to open, but it could probably be removed with minor coaxing. With no moonlight from above, and none reaching up from the streetlight below, the grate was virtually invisible from the street.

Reaching back, Lad checked the small pouch of tools he had strapped to the small of his back, ensuring that they would not rattle.

Good.

A shadow among shadows, he eased back around the corner, out of view of the two Hunters, and made his move.

With a quick flip, he was over the wrought iron fence of the corner townhouse and back into the shadows. He froze and listened. Nothing had changed. His invisibility was intact.

He leapt to the sill of a ground-floor window and sprang up to the heavy metal brackets supporting the corner downspout. With a quick hop, he gripped the bottom sill of the second floor bay window. He scrambled up like a spider and launched himself again to grasp the downspout brackets, and gained the third floor window. Pulling himself up, he edged back into the shadows.

Pause. Breathe. Listen. He heard nothing out of the ordinary, and looked up to the ornate roof eaves. *Now for the tricky bit.*

The eaves were less than six feet from the top of the window, and the downspout, only four feet to his right, arched up to the corner of the building. The eaves jutted out about two feet. He would have to grasp the edge of the roof and flip himself up. Two things could cause problems: rotten wood and moss-covered shingles. Either one could send him plummeting three floors to the street.

Fear... It was there, niggling at him, reminding him of all he had to lose. For five years now he'd lived with his emotions freed from the magic that had made him a slave. He'd gained more than he'd lost, certainly, and had learned to deal with the fear.

All or nothing, he thought, committing his mind to the maneuver.

Lad launched himself into the night, grasped the outer rim of the eaves, and flipped up and over. No rotten wood and no slick moss. He landed like a dark bird upon the smooth slate shingles.

Stop. Breathe. Listen.

No sign that he had been spotted, and the light from the hooded street lamps didn't reach this high.

Perfect!

He moved along the edge of the roof, keeping low and watching to make sure he didn't silhouette himself against any lights for the Hunter across the courtyard. He reached Norwood's roof, climbed to the peak, stretched himself flat along the shingles, and edged out to peer down. He could not see the watcher on the balcony, for the awning blocked his view, and the woman at street level scanned only from side to side. Even if she looked up, she probably wouldn't see him.

Probably.

The attic vent was directly below, but still out of reach. The shakes around it looked too slick and thin to provide any grip or support, but he might be able to grasp the louvers of the grating itself. Lad gauged the distance from the edge—about four feet— and the timbers supporting the eaves—solid enough—and the angle between the two. Yes, this would work...if he didn't slip and fall to his death.

He looked down, and the fear edged up from his stomach. *Fear is a good thing*, he reminded himself. *Fear keeps you alive. Just don't let it paralyze you.*

Lad flipped up to sit on the peak of the roof with his back to the street, reached into the pack of tools, withdrew a wide-bladed chisel, and put it between his teeth. Positioning his fingers at the roof edge, he extended his legs out straight in front of him, and pressed himself up until only his fingertips and his heels touched the roof. Slowly, he moved his body out over the void, leaning in to keep his center of balance over his hands, his heels dragging along the roof until the backs of his knees were just above the edge of the roof. With one slow, steadying breath, he let himself fall.

His calves slapped hard against the roof, and his upper body swung down into empty space. His legs slid outward an inch, then his swing pulled him back toward the face of the townhouse and the grating. At the peak of his swing, Lad arched his back and reached backward to grasp the louvers of the grating. The wood creaked, but did not break.

Glancing down, he checked the Hunters, but neither had moved. Lad got to work.

As he'd hoped, the grate was decorative rather than secure, nothing but a thin wooden frame nailed to a stout timber casing. Thrusting the chisel into the tiny gap between the frame and the casing, he pried the grate away. A nail squeaked as it moved in its wooden sheath.

Slowly. Patience. Haste is your enemy. Remember!

Bit by bit, Lad loosened the louvered grate, pausing periodically to check the two watchers. Eventually, the grate came loose, and he swung free, hanging by his knees from the roof. Lad put the chisel between his teeth, and swung himself back to grasp the edge of the aperture. He craned his neck to peer into the space within. A dusty, dirty attic greeted him.

Perfect.

Making sure he had a good grip, he let go with his legs, swinging down and absorbing the impact against the side of the building on the balls of his feet. He pulled himself up, placed the grating inside, and slipped through.

The attic was a vast, empty space with only a framework of joists supporting the lath and plaster ceiling below. To Lad's right, he spied a trapdoor with a built-in folding ladder that would extend when the door was lowered. It was rigged with a counterweight so it could be easily closed from below.

Effortlessly balancing his way across the joists, Lad dropped flat and pressed his ear to the trapdoor. He heard nothing, but lack of sound didn't mean that someone wasn't there. He knew that trapdoors like this one generally opened into closets or hallways, so this one probably wouldn't open right over Captain Norwood's bed.

That would be a problem, he thought, envisioning himself hopping down to land right on top of the captain.

After securing the ladder to the hatch so it wouldn't noisily extend, he pushed down gently on the door. When nothing happened, he pushed harder. Still nothing. It was either stuck, or there was a latch or bolt on the other side.

Patience… Haste is your enemy.

Lad pulled a razor-thin blade from his tool pouch and slipped it in the crack between the door and the frame. As he worked it around the edge, it met with something metal in the middle, opposite the hinged end. A latch or bolt, surely. Picking a heavier blade, and working slowly to avoid noise, he cut away a four-inch section of the narrow wooden laths adjacent to latched end of the trapdoor. When the last of the wood came free, he went to work on the plaster, chipping away tiny bits at a time. Finally, the blade slipped all the way through, and he worked it around a square large enough to fit his hand. When he'd cut three sides of a square, he pried it up and lifted out the painted plaster in a single piece. Only a few tiny bits of dust and broken plaster fell into the darkness below.

Silence and darkness met his questing senses.

Good.

Reaching through, he eased open the simple barrel bolt, and pushed on the trapdoor with his other hand. It swung open into a large broom closet.

Lucky, lucky Lad. He smiled and dropped down, landing like a feather. Here, he stopped once again to listen.

A faint snort reached his ears. Someone was snoring.

Easing open the closet door, he peered straight down a dimly lit hallway. There was a door to his left, and one straight ahead, both rooms presumably overlooking the front of the house. Immediately to his right, a switchback staircase descended to the second floor. Another hallway ran alongside the stairway banister toward the back of the house, ending at a door. The snoring came from the door immediately to his left.

Perfect.

Lad tried the latch and smiled. It was unlocked. Predicting the cadence of snoring, he chose his moment and slipped into the room.

Well, damn!

The room extended across the front of the house far enough to encompass two of the bay windows. An ornate wardrobe dominated one wall, flanked by a full-length mirror and a vanity table. The cloying scent of perfume and talc hung heavily in the air. Unfortunately, only one person slept in the expansive four-post bed, and unless Captain Norwood was an obese, middle-aged woman—which didn't match Wiggen's description at all—this wasn't him. Disappointed, Lad slipped out and down the hall to listen at the other door. Nothing. He tried the latch, also unlocked, and slipped inside. The high canopy bed was empty.

Patience. One room left on this floor.

Lad didn't relish having to venture deeper into the house and farther from his escape route if this one proved empty. Creeping down the hall toward the back of the house, he put his ear against the door and listened.

A foot scuffed the floor just on the other side of the door. Heat surged through him as he heard a click, and the latch began to turn. He glanced over his shoulder; it was thirty feet to the broom closet—*too far*—and if he leapt the bannister onto the stairs, he ran the risk of making noise. He had nowhere to go.

Moving objects draw more attention than still ones. Remember!

Lad backed into the corner and froze.

The door swung into the room, and a man of perhaps fifty years with the build of a soldier gone somewhat soft stepped out, stifling a yawn. Aside from the nightclothes, he fit Wiggen's description to a tee. Captain Norwood took two steps, then stopped, tensed and started to turn toward Lad.

A lifetime of training kicked in.

Lad lunged out of his corner, passing behind Norwood, bounded off the opposite wall, and snaked an arm around the captain's neck faster than a single stroke of a bird's wing. A gasp was the only sound that escaped the man's lips before Lad tightened his hold and whispered into his ear.

"Silence, Captain! I didn't come here to kill you, but I can break your neck in an instant if you cry out." Norwood's body trembled, but to his credit, the captain didn't panic, struggle, or cry out.

"Good. Now, nod if you were alone in that room, and don't lie to me." Norwood's chin bobbed against his arm. "Excellent. Let's go in where we can talk undisturbed."

Lad urged the captain back into the room with gentle but inexorable pressure. Once they were inside the arc of the door, he closed it deftly with his foot. He looked around. The room spanned the entire width of the townhouse. Beyond the open drapes, the tops of the courtyard trees swayed in the night breeze. Mya's Hunter stood silently on the roof across the courtyard, invisible in the darkness to any eyes but Lad's. Thankfully, Norwood hadn't lit a lamp. The rumpled bed nearby was empty. A dagger lay on the nightstand, and a sheathed sword stood propped in the corner. Lad steered Norwood toward a sitting area at the opposite end of the room.

"All right, Captain, I'm going to release you." He felt the man tense in his grasp, and applied just enough pressure to the back of his skull to get his point across. "If you try to reach a weapon, I'll be forced to hurt you. I came here for information, not blood, but I'm more than a match for you. Trust me on that. If you agree to talk with me, I'll let you go. Nod if you agree."

The captain's chin wiggled up and down. Slowly, Lad released the pressure of his grip, then backed quickly into the dark corner before Norwood could turn around.

"Have a seat, Captain."

Norwood took a deep breath and rubbed his throat before he turned to glare into the shadows. "Do you mind if I stand? I think you scared the shit out of me." The man's voice had an acerbic edge, but his fear was controlled. Lad admired the captain's cool head.

"Stand if you like, Captain." *More flies with honey than with vinegar*, he thought, employing a tactic he'd learned from watching Mya. "I apologize for startling you, but I can't let you get a good look at my face. You have a reputation for taking your job seriously, and I know that, if you could identify me, you'd never stop searching."

"Who the hells are you?"

"You don't get to ask the questions, Captain. I came here to ask you about a murder you're investigating. A wizard named Vonlith. Tell me how he died."

"What's it to you?"

"I told you, I ask the questions, but if you must know, I'm with the Assassins Guild." Norwood's throat flexed as he swallowed, and his jaw muscles clenched briefly. *Fear. Good.* "It's come to our attention that you've linked Vonlith with Saliez, which makes this killing of interest to us."

Norwood's eyes narrowed. "How did you know that? It's not public knowledge."

Lad cringed. He couldn't afford to let Norwood make a connection to his conversation with Wiggen. He covered the mistake with a dry laugh. "We have eyes and ears throughout the city, Captain, even north of the river. You'd be surprised at what we know. What we *don't* know is how Vonlith died. Now tell me how he was killed."

"Fine." Norwood hesitated, as if considering how much information to give. "He was murdered in his study. We found him sitting in a high-backed leather chair with a stiletto wound to the back of the skull, right into the brain. Nothing was disturbed and, as far as we can tell, nothing was taken." Norwood gave him a snort of laughter. "Frankly, if you're with the *Assassins* Guild, I thought you'd know all this. It looked like a professional killing."

Lad's mind spun. Pithing was a difficult maneuver, really only feasible if you were standing right behind an unsuspecting target. It made sense that Norwood suspected a professional, and to Lad, that also meant a member of the Assassins Guild. Who besides him had the skill to pull this off, and why? He turned his attention back to Norwood.

"If I knew, I wouldn't be here, would I? What else?"

Norwood continued, though he sounded reluctant. "The entire residence was protected by magical locks and wards, but not a single one was broken or tripped. However, the servant's door was unlocked, and it looked as if Vonlith had been entertaining someone just prior to his death. There was a glass of brandy at his elbow, and another, recently emptied, on the sideboard. We presumed that someone was the killer, and that Vonlith had let him in."

A chill ran up Lad's spine. How many people had Vonlith known in the Assassins Guild? And who would he let into his home? Lad had no way to be sure, but knew that it had to be a short list. "That's useful, Captain. Thank you. How did you link Vonlith with Saliez?"

"I'm through answering questions without getting any answers," Norwood said, startling Lad with his brazenness. "But I'll make you a deal. I'll help you if you help me."

"I'm not here to solve your murder for you, Captain."

"I didn't say I wanted you to. I've got more interests in this city than one murder."

Lad paused for a moment, wondering if this was some ploy to put him at ease or catch him off guard. "I can't promise you anything, Captain, but I'll give you what I can. Now answer me, how did you link Vonlith with Saliez?"

"A wizard's wagon was spotted at Saliez's mansion before the raid five years ago, but it was gone by the time we arrived. After Vonlith's murder, someone recognized it in his stable."

"Do you have any suspects?"

Norwood laughed sharply, without humor. "Not anymore. We assumed it was someone in the Assassins Guild, but if you really don't know about this killing, I guess we need to rethink that assumption."

"I only deal with a single guild faction, Captain. Someone in one of the other factions might have had a reason to kill Vonlith, or taken a contract to do the job."

"There's more than one faction of assassins? Wonderful!" Norwood tossed his head irritably. "Then you have no idea who killed him?"

"Not yet. What else do you know about Vonlith and Saliez?"

"We're pretty sure that Vonlith did some type of work for Saliez. He was a runemage, and we found runes tattooed all over Saliez's body, so we thought maybe Vonlith was the one who did the tattooing. He also had a contract that ended without being completed right after Saliez was found dead." Even in the darkness Lad could see the muscles of Norwood's jaw clench. "My turn to ask a question."

Lad didn't like the idea of answering Norwood's questions, but he had agreed. "What do you want to know?"

"Do you know what Vonlith was doing for Saliez?"

"Yes, Captain." Lad chose his words carefully. "It had to do with a young man who was controlled by magic. You undoubtedly remember the assassinations of nobles some five years ago."

"I remember them. We were told about the boy, but frankly, I never really believed he existed. I was told he was killed."

"You were told the truth, Captain. Something happened to the magic controlling the boy, and Vonlith was contracted to renew it. The boy broke free during the process, and he and Saliez killed each other."

"We never found the boy's body." There was suspicion in Norwood's voice now, but Lad had expected this question, and had an answer ready.

"That's because there was no body to find. There were...fail-safe spells woven into the magic that had been placed on the boy. It may interest you to know that it took more than fifteen years to create that creature. He was more magic than flesh, really. The spells were designed to utterly destroy the evidence if he was killed while performing a mission. When he died, the body was completely consumed by the magic."

"You sound like you were there when it happened." The grudging acknowledgement in Norwood's voice suggested that he believed that Lad was dead.

Good.

"I was, Captain. Now, my turn again. What else have you found out about Vonlith?"

"Not much, really. Vonlith has had only one contract since Saliez's death. It began about a month after, and lasted until a month ago. It was lucrative enough to keep him in a very expensive lifestyle without taking any other contracts. It's more likely that his death is related to this recent contract than any work he did for Saliez, but we aren't ruling out either. Then again, it could be something else entirely. We just don't know."

Lad considered the information. Unfortunately, it provided no clue to the identity of Vonlith's killer. He agreed with the reasoning, but who would contract a runemage for five years and then kill him when the contract was done?

141

Suddenly he felt as if he'd been dipped in ice water. *Someone interested in making a weapon...a weapon like me. And they killed him to make sure no more were made, or that the one he'd just finished was kept a secret.* Lad had no idea how many in the Assassins Guild knew how he had been made. The Master Hunter, Targus, had known, but Lad had killed the man. Did the other masters know? In fact, Mya had led a wide-ranging manhunt for Lad, enlisting dozens in the search. Did they all know? His mind whirled at the prospect.

"Does that give you any ideas?"

Lad snapped from his thoughts back to Norwood. "I'm afraid, Captain, that the list of suspects could be very long."

"Then it's my turn again." Norwood shifted his stance, and his line of questions. "Why are so many people dying south of the river?"

"There's some squabbling going on within the Assassins Guild. The guild has no guildmaster, and the factions are vying for supremacy. Our...competition is trying to move in with the disruption, which has added to the violence."

"I don't suppose you'd name the leaders of these factions so I can stop the violence."

"Sorry, Captain. The violence will stop only when the factions learn to cooperate, or they appoint a new guildmaster. It's that simple. Now, I have to go."

"Wait!" Norwood held up a stalling hand. "Can I ask you one more thing?"

Lad saw no reason to deny the request. "You can ask, but I may not answer."

"How in the Nine Hells did you get in here? I have the best locks money can buy on all my doors and windows, and a guard dog on the back porch."

Lad smiled, though he knew Norwood couldn't see his face. "I came through the attic, Captain. No place is impregnable to a sufficiently skilled and determined..."—*assassin. Remember!* The words of his trainers were always with him, burned into his

mind, but that wasn't something Norwood needed to know—
"…person, Captain. And that's one thing that worries me about
Vonlith's death. Whoever put a dagger in his brain was very
skilled indeed."

"As skilled as you?"

"No one's as skilled as me," he said without a hint of hubris.
"That's what worries me. Now turn around please."

Norwood obeyed, turning slowly, and Lad saw him tense.

"Sleep well, Captain." Lad took careful hold of Norwood's
neck, pressing his fingers down on the arteries that supplied
blood to the brain. The captain had only enough time to reach up
and grab Lad's wrists before he went suddenly and completely
limp. The unconsciousness would only last a few seconds, but it
wouldn't hurt him, and gave Lad enough time to slip through the
door, down the hall, and out the attic window. Though the
conversation had been enlightening, he still had too many
questions and too few answers. But he knew where to look next.

Mya…

CHAPTER XII

T hanks for cleaning things up, Pax." Mya flashed the innkeeper a smile as she sat down to her breakfast. She'd come home the previous evening to find her quarters completely straightened up; fresh, crisp linens covered the bed, her robe had been washed and hung up, and every shard of broken glass had been removed from the sparring room. She felt guilty when she considered all the time and effort Paxal must have put into cleaning up the mess. Who knew what he thought—bloody glass and all—but she trusted him never to mention it to anyone. "I'm afraid things got a little…out of hand the other night."

"Nothing to fret about, Miss Mya." He shrugged, his round face utterly placid. "Every kettle's got to blow off a little steam now and then."

She chuckled. "Seriously, though, I appreciate your devotion. You know that."

"I know, Miss Mya." He shifted, obviously uncomfortable with her praise. "You want the mirrors replaced?"

"I don't think so, Pax. Having that many mirrors was making me vain. The one in the bathing chamber's enough for now."

"Very good, then." He turned to go. "I'll send Dee in."

"Thanks." She shook her head in calm wonder. *If only I had a hundred of him.*

Mya was well into her breakfast and second cup of blackbrew when a knock announced Dee's arrival. As usual, he bore a stack of correspondence, though he looked more rested today.

Maybe Moirin found someone else.

The report from the team she'd assigned to keep an eye on Captain Norwood lay on top of the stack of papers. She read eagerly, interested to see if Norwood had made any progress in the search for Vonlith's killer, though she certainly wasn't going to tell Lad everything she learned.

Damn him anyway! He had driven her crazy yesterday with his ceaseless questions about the runemage. It made her want to slit Norwood's throat for visiting the *Tap and Kettle* and bringing Vonlith's death to Lad's attention.

Reading the report, however, she was encouraged at how mundane the captain's routine had been yesterday. The day-crew noted the times at which he left his home, arrived at work, ate lunch with two colleagues at a nearby eatery, including the benign subjects of their conversation, and so on. She scanned the list of his afternoon meetings. Though she didn't have eyes inside the captain's office, and couldn't know who he spoke with or what they discussed, nothing hinted that the Royal Guard was anything but in the dark about the murder.

Mya flipped to the next page, the night-crew's report. The captain had arrived home at dusk. A light in a front second-story window had stayed on until nearly midnight, followed by one in the third-story rear windows, which was shortly after doused.

The next few lines brought her up short.

Just before dawn, Norwood had come out of his front door fully dressed and stood in the street, looking up at a square hole in the wall under the eaves above the highest center window. The other houses in the row all had louvered grates in the same spot. None of her Hunters had noticed the missing grate the evening before. Though his coach arrived at the usual hour, Norwood had delayed going to his office at the Royal Guard headquarters until after workmen had arrived to replace the missing grate with iron bars.

Godsdamnit! Fury rose in Mya, and she fought to maintain a disinterested mien in front of Dee. Someone had visited Norwood last night, and evaded her Hunters in doing so.

Lad... It had to be.

She couldn't think of anyone else capable of such a feat, but even he wouldn't be dumb enough to threaten Norwood, would he? *Or*—she felt a chill on the back of her neck—*did he have another motive for a late night visit?* If Lad suspected her of killing Vonlith, would he give her name to Norwood?

Her own words came back to her: *There is no one in the world who wouldn't betray someone with the right incentive, my friend.*

What might induce him to betray her? Had he already? The questions made her mind spin. She tossed the report negligently to the table and addressed Dee calmly.

"Draft a response to Journeyman Toki assigned to watch Captain Norwood. Continue surveillance and report everything, I repeat, *everything* that occurs. And tell her, good work."

"Got it." Dee's pen scratched across the parchment like a cockroach on a hot skillet. "That's all?"

"For now." She took a sip of blackbrew and reached for the next letter, but her mind lingered on the question in her mind.

Has he betrayed me? I've got to keep an eye on him.

That wouldn't be an easy task without him detecting her. But more than that, she somehow felt that she was wrong to suspect him. He had risked his life to save hers many times these last five years.

He doesn't trust me. He admitted as much.

Mya buried her worries by attacking both the pile of correspondence and her breakfast with a vengeance, but try as she might, she couldn't shake the fear that her friend—her *best* friend—might have betrayed her.

※⊃⅔⌐⊋⅔⅙

"It's useless." Neera's voice shook with rage as she dropped a beautifully wrought ring of obsidian and gold onto the table. "The spells to enchant the new guildmaster's ring have failed."

Every eye in the room stared at the ring. Sereth remembered an identical one on the hand of the Grandfather, and he didn't like the fear that memory evoked in him. Neera's anger was met with confusion, disbelief and contempt from her fellow masters.

"I don't understand." Horice had never tried to hide his dislike for Neera, and the disdain in his voice now showed it. "You told us that forging the new ring would take several weeks. It's only been four days, and now you're telling us it doesn't work?"

"That's exactly what I'm telling you, Horice." Neera's lip lifted from her potion-stained teeth in a contemptuous sneer. "Crafting the physical ring took three days. Casting the enchantments would have taken several weeks more. However, the very first spell Master Ronquin attempted to cast on the ring failed."

"So you're saying that the wizard who has been forging guild rings for sixty years, with no difficulty whatsoever, suddenly finds himself incompetent?"

"No, Horice. I am saying that the enchantment failed because, as you know, the Twailin guildmaster's ring, like *all* our rings, is unique. The enchantments are very specific, and can only function in one place at a time. This ensures that copies cannot be made to render someone outside the guild invulnerable to our assassins."

"So the original guildmaster's ring..." Patrice's voice trailed off, and Sereth watched understanding dawn on the masters' faces.

"...was never destroyed!" The back of Horice's neck flushed red with rage. "Mya *lied* to us!"

"Not only that, but she wears the guildmaster's ring." Neera pulled her lustrous robes close about her, a cocoon of shimmering satin, and sat down. "The enchantments only function when the ring surrounds living flesh, and enchanting a new ring would only be impeded by a functioning original, so she *must* wear it. The question is: what do we do now?"

"Kill the traitorous bitch, of course."

Sereth struggled to keep from rolling his eyes. Horice's solution to every problem was to kill someone. He didn't have a subtle bone in his body. The other masters didn't bother hiding their reactions to the Master Blade's suggestion.

"As your recent *failure* exemplifies, killing Mya is not as easy as you make it sound, Horice."

"At least now we know *why* our team failed," he countered with a glare at the Master Alchemist. "No Twailin guild assassin can attack Mya if she's wearing the guildmaster's ring."

"But our people did attack her!" Youtrin insisted. "Just because your Blades got themselves killed…"

Horice's hand drifted to the hilt of his rapier, and Sereth prepared himself. If his master did something stupid, he had no recourse but to try to save his life.

"Stop it!" Patrice's command caught everyone by surprise. Usually the least vocal of the masters, her comely features were now set in hard lines. "We need to deal in facts, not emotions. First, you have all said that you watched Mya command her bodyguard to destroy the old guildmaster's ring, and that this man was magically compelled to obey. Is this correct?"

The three nodded, and Patrice continued.

"Second, a new ring cannot be enchanted because the old one was *not* destroyed and is presumably on someone's finger. How can we explain the discrepancy?"

"Mya is nothing if not cunning." The contempt in Neera's tone had mutated into a kind of twisted admiration. She drew a ragged breath and coughed. Her face went suddenly ashen, and she gestured to her bodyguard as she continued. "*She* was the one who suggested we do without a guildmaster, and at our behest she commanded her bodyguard to destroy the ring." Her bodyguard took up one of the two bottles of wine that Youtrin had provided, drew the cork, and filled her glass. "We didn't see it destroyed, but foolishly assumed the task had been done when she produced a lump of melted gold and shattered obsidian." Neera's hand hovered over the wine for a moment, and a silvery powder drifted from her fingers into the crimson pool. Her hand trembled as she stirred the mixture with one claw-like fingernail and lifted the glass to sip. Color flushed to her wan features and her next breath came easier. "All she had to do was countermand the order after we had left, and take the ring for herself."

"All right. Next: at the last meeting she attended, Mya wore her master's ring. Can she wear both her master's ring *and* the guildmaster's ring at the same time?"

"Donning the guildmaster's ring would allow her to remove her master's ring, but it would not force her to do so," Neera said.

"All right," Patrice concluded after a moment's thought. "Why don't we go to the Grandmaster? We explain what's happened, and have him deal with Mya. If necessary, he could send an outside team to kill her. They wouldn't be bound by the Twailin guildmaster's ring."

"Are you crazy? Admit to the Grandmaster that we've been duped by a stripling girl! He'd likely have us all killed for incompetence!"

Patrice blinked at the three incredulous stares directed at her from her fellow masters. Even Sereth agreed with Horice on this one. *Though if the Grandmaster did kill them all, I'd be in the running for Master Blade. And with the Blades behind me, Hensen would have to—*

"Enlisting the Grandmaster's aid in this situation would not be a safe course of action." Neera finished her wine and put the glass firmly down, her tremor banished by either the potion or her own resolve. "We must take care of this ourselves."

"So, we kill her. But since she's wearing the ring—"

"She's *not* wearing the ring!" Youtrin rattled the bottles and glasses with a slap of his huge hand to the table top. "The ring *prevents* attack from any Twailin guildmember. An archer can't shoot, a swordsman can't thrust, a poisoner can't even put lethal toxins into food or drink. The ring won't let them even try. But our people *attacked*. They might have failed, but they *did* attack. She doesn't wear the ring."

"Youtrin." Horice put his hands flat on the table and stared at the Master Enforcer. "Did you even talk with the survivors of that attack?"

"Yes, I did! Mya killed two Blades assigned to a flanking attack, and her bodyguard took out three of the others. One escaped. So what?"

"The four on the frontal attack were ordered to draw her bodyguard out so the other two could get a clear shot at Mya. They attacked him, not her. None of them actually saw what happened with Mya. The only ones who attacked her were the two Blades who are now dead."

"What are you saying?" Suspicion put sting into Youtrin's question.

"I'm saying that *Mya* is not a *Blade*! Hells, she's only been a Hunter for barely ten years! There is no way she could get the drop on two of my best people before they could even mark her. Their weapons were poisoned; if they'd so much as scratched her, she'd be dead. No, the only way she could have killed them is if they just stood there like lambs waiting for the slaughter, which is exactly what would have happened if she wore the ring."

"So, I think we can all agree that Mya is wearing the guildmaster's ring. And that it will be a serious hindrance to killing her."

Youtrin sagged back in his chair at Patrice's proclamation, nodding reluctantly. "Even if she wasn't wearing the ring, we'd still have to get past her bodyguard, and he's godsdamned unstoppable!"

"That's not entirely true." Neera leaned forward, and her years seemed to melt away with her eagerness. "He *has* been bested before. Horice, you should remember!"

Horice sat up suddenly, as if the memory stung him. "Yes! Mya took some of my best Blades with her to capture him. I had forgotten."

Neera smiled slyly. "Yes, and it was poison that subdued him, or rather, a very potent drug, was it not?"

Horice craned his neck around to look at Sereth. "You saw Mya bring the weapon to Saliez, didn't you?"

Sereth's blood ran cold as the masters all turned toward him. The last thing he wanted was to be the center of attention. He walked a razor's edge between life and death every day, knowing that if his reports to the Thieves Guild were discovered, he would find himself manacled to Patrice's interrogation slab before he could draw another breath. But that fear had become such an integral part of his life that he had no difficulty answering in a calm, even tone.

"Yes, Master, I saw them, but only in passing. The weapon was unconscious. The rumor was that she wore a needle ring, and tricked him into shaking her hand."

"Yes, I heard the same rumor." Youtrin's thick brow knitted in thought.

"Wily bitch," Horice muttered.

"Perhaps we should learn from her cunning." Patrice's plucked eyebrows arched with a thoughtful look. "We've tried approaching him head-on, and he's met violence with violence. We cannot beat him that way. A successful attack would have to be subtle. If we could lure him in somehow, get someone close who he didn't suspect."

"How?" Horice looked at her dubiously. "He suspects everyone. It's his job."

"But he acts outside his job on occasion."

"He does?"

"Yes." Patrice pursed her sensuous lips and tapped them with a glossy fingernail. "And he shows compassion. I had wondered about this earlier, but was unsure what it meant. He saved one of my people from a lethal fall the other day."

"He *what*?" Yotrin's eyes widened in blatant disbelief.

"I occasionally have people try to follow him. Without the cooperation of Hunters or Blades, I've been trying to train my people in the skills of stealth and pursuit. They've been getting rather good, actually, and one young man shows amazing promise. He was following Mya's weapon the other night, and miscalculated a leap. The weapon intervened and saved his life. He even told him to be more careful."

"Unbelievable!" Horice leaned back in his seat and shook his head.

"But his compassion might give us a means to lure him in." Patrice looked to Neera with a raised eyebrow.

Neera's rheumy eyes swept around the table. "If we work together, we might have a chance."

"We may not be able to kill the snake, but we can pull her fangs." Horice chuckled at his symbolism. "Then we can bring in an outsider to deal with Mya."

"Agreed!" Youtrin stood and reached for the unopened bottle of wine. Wrenching the cork free, he filled the four glasses. "I move that we cooperate to eliminate Mya's bodyguard, and then her. We'll take the ring from her dead body and elect a new leader."

The masters all stood and raised their glasses.

"Agreed," they each said in turn, and the crystal chimed as the glasses touched.

Sereth watched the four drink to their plan while reviewing the meeting in his head and mentally preparing his report. *More fighting within the guild. Hensen will appreciate this.* He felt an uncharacteristic surge of hope. *Maybe it will even give me the leverage to get out from under his thumb.*

152

𝒦𝒟𝒵𝒶𝒵𝒴

Hensen admired the elegant drape of the cloth swatch in his hand, ran his fingers over the lovely silver embroidery in the black brocade, then frowned. Black was just so...dark. He let the swatch fall to the table and picked up another; gold, this one, with highlights in an elegant floral pattern. *Too gaudy.* It fell from his fingers atop the others he'd rejected. *Decorating is such a chore.*

A knock at the door interrupted his scrutiny of the fabrics.

"Yes?" He turned as his butler, a tall and utterly boring fellow, peered into the room. "What is it? I'm busy."

"My apologies, sir." His eyes widened when he saw what Hensen was busy with, and he stammered, "A...uh...visitor, sir. A man."

"At this hour?" Hensen picked up a swatch of red brocade and draped it over Kiesha's bare shoulder. *A nice contrast with her pale skin.* "Does this man have a name?"

"Sereth, sir. He seemed eager to see you."

"Sereth?" His eyes flicked up to Kiesha's, but she stood perfectly still, just as he'd ordered her to. With a considering look, Hensen said, "Show him up, Terrence, but make sure he's unarmed."

"Yes, sir." The butler left.

"Sir, I don't think—"

"Hush!" He glanced up to Kiesha's lovely blue eyes. *Perhaps something in a blue...* Perusing the vast array of swatches, he found a nice blue pattern with gold accents. "You should never admit to not thinking, Kiesha. One might think you vapid."

"Yes, sir." She stared straight ahead as he held the swatch against her skin.

Kiesha wore only a sheer chemise, and the rays of the morning sun shone through the fabric as clearly as they shone through the window behind her. Shifting to place the swatch against her other shoulder, Hensen's feet brushed the dull gray dress she had worn when she came in with her morning report. Wrinkling his nose—*That rag would offend anyone with the least sense of taste!*—he kicked the dress out of the way. Being decorated like a piece of furniture had seemed punishment enough for her offense of his senses, but it would be even better to have Sereth witness her humiliation.

"Do you like the blue?"

"Yes, sir." Kiesha hadn't even glanced at it.

"Hmph." Hensen dropped the swatch back with the others as another knock sounded at the door. "Come in!"

"Mister Sereth, sir." The butler bowed and ushered the assassin into the room.

Sereth took two steps and stopped, his eyes fixed upon Kiesha's backlit form. Hensen watched the muscles in the assassin's jaw tense as he dropped his eyes and gazed intently at the floor.

Ahhh, the thief considered, *perhaps a bit of discomfort will teach you a little humility, too, my headstrong spy.*

"Come in, Sereth. I'm doing a little decorating, and I'd appreciate your opinion, as you're such an observant fellow."

Sereth approached, eyes still averted, and spoke as soon as the door closed. "Something important has come up. The new guildmaster's ring doesn't work. The enchantment failed."

"Hmm. That must have been embarrassing." Hensen picked up another swatch, this one a darker blue. This wasn't the bit of news he'd expected. "Why would a failed enchantment warrant a visit from you at this hour? Aren't you going to be late for work?"

"It's important because it means the original ring was never destroyed. Apparently only one guildmaster's ring can exist at any given time. The masters think Mya wears it."

"That *is* interesting." And it explained why Mya had not requisitioned a new ring as she'd been instructed to. He held up the swatch in the light and admired the pattern embroidered with gold thread. *Yes, very nice.* "But if Mya wears the ring, why hasn't she claimed the guildmaster position?"

"The others would never support her claim, which means the Grandmaster would likely step in and have her removed. They think she put it on to protect herself from their assassins."

"Which seems to be working." *And makes our job that much easier.* Hensen could almost feel the gold they'd receive when the contract was fulfilled. With a happy sigh, he draped the cloth over Kiesha's shoulder. "Tell me, what do you think of this color? Does it accentuate her eyes well?"

Sereth's eyes barely grazed Kiesha before focusing on the pile of fabrics. He pointed to a swatch. "Not as well as the lighter blue. That one."

"Hmm." Hensen picked up the swatch Sereth had indicated. "And what will the masters of your guild do about this conundrum?"

"They plan to cooperate. They've devised a plan to kill Mya's bodyguard. If it works, they'll move against her with an outside contractor."

Years of controlling his emotions allowed Hensen to maintain an unruffled composure at this news. *There goes our easy money!* With a surge of pique, he took out his frustration on the only two others in the room. He slipped first one, then the other strap of Kiesha's chemise off her shoulders. The flimsy garment fell into a pale puddle at her feet, and he lifted the swatch to her bare breasts as if comparing the hues. To her credit, she didn't move a muscle.

"Attacking Mya and her bodyguard hasn't worked very well for them in the past." He picked up another swatch of darker blue and held them both up, brushing the fabrics—first one, then the other—over her breasts. "Tell me, Sereth, which do you think is Kiesha's color? Take a good look now. I want your honest opinion."

Sereth opened his mouth as if to protest, then snapped it shut and obediently looked up at Kiesha. Swallowing forcefully, he said, "The lighter blue."

"I agree." Hensen dropped the darker swatch, draped the lighter over her shoulder and took a step back to examine her. "So, how do your masters hope to succeed where they have failed before?"

"They're trying a new tactic. They spent half the night working up a plan. That's why I had time to come this morning; Horice won't be out of bed until noon."

Hensen reached up to adjust the cloth, and felt a warm drop on the back of his hand. Tears welled in Kiesha's eyes. She blinked, and another ran down her cheek, though she hadn't moved a hair's breadth. Mollified by the reactions he had provoked in them both, he turned and rummaged through the array of swatches, picking out another, still blue, but not so bright, richer in hue and beautifully accented. "So, how do they plan to do it?"

"Let me see my wife, and I'll tell you."

Hensen stopped short, dropped the swatch he held, and slowly turned to face the assassin. "Was that an *ultimatum*, Sereth?"

"No, that was an offer." The assassin met his gaze with more steel than he had yet shown. He swallowed again, and a drop of sweat glistened on his brow. "I want to see her."

Hensen ran his gaze over the assassin's clothing, wondering if Terrence had found all of his weapons. He had held Sereth's wife for three years now, but he kept her as healthy and happy as a captive could be, just as he had promised, and all at his own expense. Now this threat...

That's gratitude for you, he thought.

"Oh, very well. Tell me how they plan to kill Mya's bodyguard, and you can see your precious wife."

"Poison and trickery."

"Trickery?" Folding a few light blue swatches together, he handed them to Kiesha. "Have my seamstress make you a gown from each of these. Tell her: elegant, but not showy." He waved a hand in dismissal. "You can go."

"Thank you, sir." Kiesha quickly plucked her gray gown from the floor, clutching it to cover her breasts.

"I want that rag burned." Hensen's voice brooked no argument. "And *never* wear anything so ugly in my presence again."

"Yes, sir." Her lips clenched in a tight line, Kiesha nodded and strode from the room quickly, but calmly.

Hensen noted the hungry stare with which Sereth followed Kiesha's exit. The assassin's hands were clenched so hard that his knuckles shone white. *That might be of use*, he thought. *A man without his wife is a lonely man indeed.*

"So!" The master thief plopped into a well-cushioned chair, neglecting to offer Sereth a seat. "Tell me all about this assassination plot."

CHAPTER XIII

"It's been two days, Mya. You must have learned something by now." Lad kept his voice low enough that only Mya could hear as they entered the *Golden Cockerel*, not difficult with the evening din. He didn't leave immediately at seeing her in, as he usually did, but followed her toward the back room. "We traipsed around the entire city today, and you didn't ask a single one of your people to look into this like you promised."

Mya didn't answer until Mika shut the door behind them. "I told you I'd look into it, and I am. It's not that simple."

That was the same answer she'd given him all day. She must be tired of saying it. He was certainly tired of hearing it. Lad had thought that if he badgered her, Mya might get irate enough to drop her guard and say or do something that would reveal what she was hiding. He was convinced that she knew something about Vonlith's death. He had been reading her body language long enough to know when she was lying. Walking around the city, he had to be careful what he said, but here they could talk freely, and after today's trek she had to be tired. Fatigue might make her more likely to let something slip.

"What's not simple about it? We find Vonlith's killer, point Norwood at him, and we're done."

"It's not that simple because this was a professional assassination, Lad." Mya picked up a towel from the table and rubbed her hair dry. When she finished, her short crimson locks stuck up in all directions. "My people found out that much. I

158

also sent out some feelers, good journeymen who have contacts in the other factions, and nobody has heard this mentioned as a guild assassination. But if it *was* one of ours, outing the killer to the Royal Guard would be a breach of guild law. I've got to be careful. If the other masters suspect that I might rat out one of their people to protect one of my own, they'll kill me for it."

Lad had not spotted a single one of her tells. She seemed to be telling him the truth. His frustration grew. "How would that change things, Mya? They've already tried to kill you."

"They try to kill me *individually*. And to be honest, I return the favor occasionally. You don't think Patrice's predecessor really died of a heart attack, do you?" She smoothed down her hair, then picked up the mug of mulled wine from the table and took a gulp.

"You killed Calmarel?" The admission startled him. He had wondered about the Master Inquisitor's sudden death, but Mya had never said anything. Then again, he had never asked. *So why tell me now? Is she trying to show that she trusts me?*

"Not personally, but yes. She tried to have me killed, so I tracked her down and had someone slip foxglove extract into her tea." She draped the towel over a chair back and gave him a sardonic look. "Tell me honestly; does that surprise you?"

"Not really."

"Anyway, if they learned that I ratted out a guild member, all four of the masters would finally agree on something. They'd combine their resources, and my life wouldn't be worth spit." She took another draught of wine and sighed with pleasure. "This is very good, Lad. You should ask Pax for a cup on your way out. It'll keep you warm on the way home."

Lad almost smiled. He must be really getting on her nerves. She usually wanted him to stay.

"I have other things to keep me warm on my way home," he said, thinking of the impending game of chase. "Could we point Norwood at someone outside the guild to keep him away from the inn?"

159

"You mean frame someone?" Mya grinned at him. "I'm *proud* of you, Lad! You're starting to think like a proper assassin!" She moved to clap him on the shoulder, and he stepped back out of range. Her smile fell.

"I already think like an assassin, Mya. I've been one far longer than you."

"No, Lad," she said, her voice low and hard. "You were the *weapon* of an assassin. There's more to being one of us than knowing how to kill. I may be no match for you in a fight, but I'm *very* good at what I do, and that's *thinking*. The brain is the most dangerous weapon of all."

"Fine." Lad felt an uncharacteristic surge of anger at the implication that she was smarter than he. She wasn't, but he had to admit that her mind moved in devious ways that he couldn't match. "Use your brain and find some stooge to satisfy Norwood. Pick an old enemy or something. Gods know you have enough of them."

Mya opened her mouth to reply, but the door opened, and Paxal entered with her dinner.

"Evening, Pax." She stepped around the table and took her seat.

"Miss Mya." The innkeeper looked at Lad, then back at her. "If I'm interrupting something, I can come back."

"No. No, we're done." Mya looked pointedly at Lad. "Be careful on your way home, Lad. Garrote weather, you know."

"Yes, Mya." He gave her a short bow, playing his part as her dutiful bodyguard, and left the room, angry with himself. The verbal sparring had gotten him nowhere, and now she was on the defensive. Her reasons for her actions were sound and he had not detected a single one of her tells.

The brain is the most dangerous weapon of all. Remember!

This was not among the countless lessons he'd been taught, but he knew she was right. He had not been trained to think beyond immediate tactics, attack and defense. Mya, on the other

160

hand... The ways of her mind were darker and more labyrinthine than the back alleys of the Sprawls.

But Lad had learned a great deal in the last five years. He'd watched her run her Hunters like an efficient machine, building her business, and outwitting her competitors by anticipating their every move. Pitting himself against Mya with his usual tactics would be like beating a brick wall with his fists. The wall might break eventually, but his fists would break first.

So start thinking ahead. Lad walked through the common room, ignoring the din of laughter, the clatter of dice, and the flip of cards. *Why is Mya being evasive about Vonlith's death? What doesn't she want me to find out?*

He thought hard as he automatically sidestepped a busy barmaid carrying a heavy tray of drinks, posing and answering questions. *Why is Mya being evasive? She knows something about the killing. What might she know about it? Who the killer is. Why would she protect the killer? Because he or she is a friend. No, Mya has no friends. She considers me a friend, but other than that, her only friend is...herself.*

Lad stopped in the doorway. He hadn't considered that Mya may have killed the mage. He couldn't think of a reason why she would, then remembered what she had said to him. She thought he would be relieved that Vonlith was dead. One less person who knew his secret.

Did she kill Vonlith in a misguided attempt to protect me? Is this another death on my conscience? Mya knew Lad abhorred killing. Was she afraid of what he might do if he found out she had killed on his behalf? What *would* he do? Whatever else Mya had done, she had helped him escape his slavery and kill the Grandfather. Without her, he would have been the guildmaster's weapon forever.

But without her they might never have caught me in the first place. Did she have a choice in that assignment? Could she have rebelled? No. She was the Grandfather's slave. She'd had no choice, just as he'd had no choice.

Weapon of Blood

With too many questions and not enough answers, Lad walked out of the *Golden Cockerel* into the rain, and took a deep, steadying breath. A challenging chase through the streets of Twailin would clear his head. He stepped away from the pub and scanned the darkness with all of his senses.

Nothing.

These stalkers were getting good, apparently waiting for him to move to reveal themselves. Lad jogged slowly down the street, rounded a corner and stopped to listen. Still nothing. He squinted into the darkness, straining to hear, breathing deeply of the rain-washed air in hopes of catching a scent, all to no avail.

No stalkers tonight? He was disappointed. It wasn't unusual for them to skip a night or two, but he'd been perversely looking forward to the exercise.

Even so, Lad moved into the shadows and made his careful way up the street, listening and gauging the night. He thought for a moment that he might have heard the scuff of a soft boot against stone, but when he stopped again, he detected nothing. If someone was following him, they were very good indeed. The rain had slackened, but not stopped completely, so his senses weren't at their peak. He turned a corner, still not heading toward home, and finally heard something. He knew immediately, however, that this wasn't a stalker; they were too noisy for that.

A woman's laughter, a man's slurred reply cut through the hiss of rain. Lad cocked his head; they were in the alley just ahead, next to *The Silver Thistle*. The pub was a well-known rendezvous for the ladies and gents of the evening and their clients. Business was always booming and, from the giggles and grunts he heard, some of that business had spilled into the alley.

Not my business.

As he traversed the mouth of the alley, however, the man's voice raised in a shout.

"Filthy slut! Gimme that back!" The impact of a fist against yielding flesh and a cry of pain stopped Lad in his tracks. He peered down the alley to see a large man bending over a petite woman.

"Wait! I didn't—"

"I'll teach you to pinch a purse while a man's pants are down!" The man's fist fell again, and the woman's head jerked with the impact.

Maybe this is my business.

This pub was in Mya's territory, and she collected a percentage of the money made on the prostitution and gambling that took place there. The owner also paid her for protection. It seemed only right that Lad actually provide some protection.

Lad strode into the alley. "Stop!"

"What?" The main straightened and turned. "Who's that?"

"Who I am isn't your concern. Now walk away from her."

"If you're not a constable, and you're not one of Jonesy's boys, then *this* ain't *your* business." The man pointed down at the woman with one hand, the other fumbling to finish buttoning his codpiece. "She tried to lift my purse while we were conductin' a bit of business. I'm just teachin' her a lesson."

"She's learned her lesson, now walk away."

"She ain't learned half of what I aim to teach her, boy, so you best be on your way." The man reached down, grasped the front of the woman's dress, and lifted her easily. His other hand cocked back in a fist. The woman's piteous shriek split the rain-soaked night.

The scream dredged up a memory of the *Tap and Kettle* store room. The sight of four thugs threatening Wiggen and Forbish, Wiggen's wail of terror as a man's dagger rested against her throat, her dress torn, tears soaking her cheeks.

Lad moved.

He caught the man's fist before the blow fell and jerked two fingers out of joint. The man yelped and dropped the woman, swinging toward Lad with a roundhouse blow. Lad watched the fist come at him, ducked under it and planted a careful punch into the brute's solar plexus.

163

Weapon of Blood

Nerve clusters are targets of incapacitation when killing is to be avoided. Remember!

Lad didn't want to kill the man, just dissuade him, and his blow struck true. A spray of air and spittle left the man's mouth, but there was muscle under the fat, and he was stronger than he looked. His hand reached for his belt and came up with a pitted dagger.

"You picked the wrong fight, boy."

"No, I didn't." Lad stood easily within reach of the dagger. "Now walk away, or I'll break more of your fingers."

The thrust came at him with surprising speed and accuracy, but for Lad it moved like the flow of syrup on a cold morning. Grasping the man's wrist, Lad pirouetted around the thrust, and drove an elbow into the same spot he'd punched a moment before, harder this time. The man bent double with the blow, gasping feebly. Lad took the dagger away, cast it aside, and broke two more fingers. As the brute emitted a wheezing yelp, Lad twisted the man's mangled hand behind his back.

"Now walk away while you still can!" Lad shoved him toward the street, and was pleased when the man kept going, glaring back and holding his two injured hands over his stomach.

After the man rounded the corner, Lad turned to the sodden bundle of skirts behind him. "Are you all right?"

"I...think so." The woman sniffed wetly, and wiped blood from her face with the back of her hand. "Bastard would have killed me over a couple a' coins. Thank you, sir." She held out a hand. "A hand up, if you please."

Lad reached out. "I don't think he—"

The puff of air from a blowgun sounded from overhead and behind, barely louder than the hiss of rain.

Displacement is the only defense against a concealed missile attack. Remember!

Lad leapt and twisted, moving every portion of his body out of its former position in a desperate attempt to dodge the dart. He heard the missile strike flesh and waited for the pain to

164

indicate where it had hit. If he reacted quickly, he might be able to cut the dart out with the thug's dagger and draw out the poison before it killed him.

But there was no pain.

The woman at his feet gasped, blinked up at him, and collapsed.

Lad flattened himself against the wall and listened, wary of another shot. The patter of feet across the rooftop grew more distant by the second. Should he chase after the fleeing assailant? No, he should care for the woman. Looking down into the dead, open eyes staring up at him, he felt as if he'd been the one punched in the stomach. No amount of care could bring the woman back. The dart intended for him had hit her instead.

Kneeling beside her, Lad located the dart deep in the flesh of her throat. The fletching, oily black and trimmed at a steep angle, showed dark against her pale skin, though the shaft was completely embedded. The poison had been swift and, he hoped, painless. A wave of guilt washed over him, and he clenched his fists in frustration.

Some savior I am. If I had just passed by, she might be bruised, but she'd be alive.

The least he could do was take her body someplace dry where the constables would find her before the rats did. He owed her that much. But as he bent to pick her up, her arm fell flat on the cobbles, and he caught a glint of light on metal.

He froze, and slowly turned her hand palm up.

The faint light that stretched into the alley from the street gleamed on a ring that encircled her finger, a long, grooved needle extending from the underside. This was the hand she had reached up to him, the one he'd been about to take. He examined the needle closely and saw the dark stain in the groove. He bent low to sniff it, but the rain masked the scent. He touched the side of the needle with one finger, then touched the finger to his tongue. It had an oily, rancid flavor that piqued recognition from his early training. Poison certainly, a lethal venom. He spat, rinsed his mouth with rain water, and spat again.

"She was trying to kill me."

The fear in his own voice sounded strange to Lad. He had heard it often in others, but never his own. He had fallen prey to this very same trick once before, when Mya had captured him for the Grandfather. Envenomed rings were not an uncommon method of assassination, but he had missed the warning signs, had trusted a stranger in distress. He'd been inches from taking that hand, inches from death.

Wiggen... Lissa...

He had promised to be careful, assured Wiggen that he was in no serious danger, that it was Mya they were after. Lad had become accustomed to watching out for her, not himself. He had not been thinking like an assassin.

And the assailant from above had been no assailant after all, but his savior.

"Who?"

That was just one of the questions for which he had no answers. Who was the dead woman? He examined her face closely, but drew a blank. He thought of the man whose fingers he'd broken, and drew another blank. He didn't know all Mya's people, much less all the assassins in the other guild factions. Who had sent them? Who wanted him dead? Who had saved his life?

Lad looked up to the place from where his savior had shot.

Had this been an attempt by one of Mya's enemies to remove him, thus clearing the way to get to her? Was Mya even involved? She *had* seemed eager to get him to leave for home. Lad didn't like this train of thought, but he had to follow it through. Would Mya have him killed for his curiosity about Vonlith's murder? Had her watchers spotted him at Norwood's house, and Mya drawn the wrong conclusion? Or had she sent the stealthy marksman who saved his life? The potential answers were even more troublesome than the questions.

Lad dropped the dead woman's wrist and considered his options.

He dismissed the perverse desire to drag the corpse back to the *Golden Cockerel* and dump it on Mya's dinner table, though the action might finally rattle the truth out of her. He considered taking the dart and asking around to see if he could discover the owner, then thought about taking the ring for the same reason. Neither course seemed likely to yield success. Though part of their faction, Lad was not a Hunter trained in tracking down information. He couldn't show the dart and ring to Mya in case she was involved, and he certainly couldn't ask the other masters.

Turning on his heel, Lad left the woman where she lay. At the mouth of the alley, he looked both ways in the vain hope of spotting the man who had undoubtedly been her accomplice, but the street was empty. Should he hide and watch the corpse in the hope that he would return for her? *No.* His years among assassins had taught him that they didn't work that way. Returning to the scene of a crime was a sure way to get killed.

So Lad did what he did best; he vanished into the night.

He ran through the rain-streaked streets flat out, so fast that nobody could have followed him. He leapt to balconies, scaled drain pipes, and hurtled from rooftop to rooftop until he knew with absolute certainty that no stalker, no watcher, *no one*, could have tracked him. Then he dropped to street level and melted into the shadows to make his careful way home to his wife and daughter.

On the way, Lad girded his fears and considered his options. He could wait no longer; he had to *do* something. He would not risk losing all he had gained. He had never known love or a family until he came to Twailin, and now that he had them, he didn't know how he had lived without. He wanted to watch his daughter grow up. He wanted to be with Wiggen. He wanted to be the best father and husband he could be, but to do that, he had to stay alive. And if things continued as they were, he would end up like the woman tonight, in an alley, stone-cold dead.

ᛏᚱᛉᛉᚪᛉᛏᚴ

"Wiggen?" The whisper invaded her dreams, her wonderful, quiet, peaceful dreams.

Sleep...just a few more minutes...please.

"Wiggen?" A warm hand settled on her shoulder.

"Just a few more minutes...please."

"It's not morning yet, Wig. I need to talk to you."

She rolled over, still half asleep, and blinked at her husband. His beautiful, slightly luminous eyes shone in the dark. "Lad? Can't it wait until morning?"

"I don't think so, Wiggen. It's important. Someone tried to kill me tonight."

"You mean someone tried to kill Mya?" She settled back onto her pillow and closed her eyes. "Sometimes *I'd* like to kill Mya..."

"They didn't try to kill Mya, Wiggen. They tried to kill me...and they almost succeeded."

Wiggen lurched up, fully awake. "What? Who?" She reached for the lamp and turned it up. Lad sat on the side of the bed, looking as strong and beautiful as always, except for the lines around his eyes and mouth. There was a look there that unnerved her, and it took her a moment to realize why; she had seen many emotions in his face, but never such fear.

"I don't know who she was, but it was very professional, and nearly successful. If not for some...someone else, I'd probably have died."

"Oh, gods!" She flung her arms around him, and felt his encircle her. She had always felt safe here, wrapped in his strength, his body so warm against hers, the beat of his heart so powerful it overwhelmed the pounding of her own. The thought of losing him stabbed like a knife. "Gods, I hate this, Lad! I hate it!"

"I hate it, too, Wig. That's why I woke you. We need to make a decision."

"Decision?" She released him and wiped the sudden tears from her eyes. "What decision?"

"First let me tell you what's happening."

"Okay."

Wiggen sat and listened to every detail, all his suppositions, his fears, his theories of who and why and how. By the time he finished, her lip was clenched between her teeth to keep from screaming and waking the baby. She tried to calm her mind as Lad had taught her so long ago, and felt the panic subside, but it was a thin veneer. Someone had tried to take him from her.

"Mya is involved, but I don't know how. I thought that she might have tried to have me killed tonight, but it doesn't make sense. If she wanted me dead, she could have done it herself a dozen times."

"What? How could she kill you?"

"A pat on the back with a poisoned ring. Poison slipped into my food. Any number of ways." Wiggen's shock must have shown on her face, for Lad's features suddenly flushed with guilt. He pressed a hand to her cheek and said, "I'm sorry, Wiggen."

"I don't understand. Why would Mya want to kill you? You keep her safe!"

He shook his head. "The more I think about it, the more I think it's *not* her. It's not in her best interest to kill me. But I still don't trust her. I know she's being evasive about Vonlith's murder."

"Maybe *she* killed him." Wiggen had never met Mya, but that didn't keep her from loathing the woman. If not for Mya, Lad would be working at the inn, sitting down to meals with his family, and slipping into bed with her at a decent hour every night. But Mya had extracted a promise from Lad to protect her, and Lad was too honest to break his word. Wiggen knew that the same couldn't be said about Mya; Lad's stories of her deceptions and intrigues made her head whirl. It wouldn't surprise Wiggen in the slightest to discover that Mya had murdered the runemage.

"I thought about that, but it just doesn't make sense. As far as I know, she's had nothing to do with Vonlith for five years. And if she did it to try to protect me, to keep my identity a secret, it certainly didn't work. It only brought the captain of the Royal Guard to the inn." He rubbed his eyes with hands that were actually shaking. "I've either got to follow this through, find out who killed Vonlith, who just tried to kill me, *and* who saved my life, all of which will be dangerous, *or...*"

"Or what?" Wiggen didn't like the tone of his voice.

"Or we leave Twailin."

"Leave?" It felt like a kick in the stomach. "Leave father?"

"I know you'd hate it, Wiggen, but think." He took her hands in his and squeezed gently. "They're targeting me now, not just Mya. Someone killed Vonlith, and it looks like I might be next on the list. My first responsibility is to protect you and Lissa, and I can't do that if I'm dead."

"But...gods, Lad, do we have to *leave*?" The thought of leaving her father brought as much pain as the thought of losing Lad. Forbish had worked so hard to keep his family and this inn together. Now, just when everything was going well, they had to leave?

Lad grasped her shoulders. "I don't want to, Wiggen." He kissed her forehead and drew her into his arms. "But leaving might be the only answer."

"The only answer?" Wiggen nestled into Lad's shoulder, inhaled the scent that was uniquely him, and thought hard. She loved her father and Josie and the twins. She had been born and raised in the inn, and knew nothing else. Then she tried to imagine living here without Lad...and couldn't. There *was* only one answer.

"When?" She couldn't believe she had said it, but the decision brought a measure of peace. Everything would be all right. They'd get by. Wiggen pushed him back and wiped away her tears. "When will we leave?"

"Soon. I'll tell Mya tomorrow."

"You think you *should* tell her? Why not just go?"

"She's a Hunter, Wiggen. If we disappear, she'll set every Hunter in the guild after us, and, trust me, they'd find us eventually, no matter where we went. I need to make sure I leave on good terms with her. Losing my protection will scare her, and that's when she's most dangerous."

"Mya scared?" Wiggen didn't bother disguising her disbelief.

"She *always* scared," Lad said softly, his voice tinged with pity.

"So am I." Wiggen pulled him into her arms and held him as if she would never let go. Lad brushed her hair with his fingers and kissed her neck. His tenderness, his love for her, gave her strength.

"Okay, tell her." She raised her face to him and smiled through her tears. "But until morning, you're mine."

"I'm always yours, Wiggen." Lad pulled her into a deep, passionate kiss, his hands entwined in her hair.

"Yes," she murmured between their parted lips. "Always…"

ᛟᛝᛗᛟᛉᛝ

Bodies entwined in the lamplight, skin on skin, flesh on flesh…

So beautiful…

The rain dampened any sounds Mya might have heard through the thin pane of glass, but she could see clearly enough.

Keep an eye on Lad. It had seemed a reasonable precaution. Crouched on the back wall of the inn courtyard, hidden in the shadows of a moonless night and torrential rain, she watched.

She felt no discomfort, no chill, even though her clothes were soaked through. The wrappings beneath her clothes kept her comfortable, safe from the elements as they kept her secret safe from discovery.

"But not from this," she whispered, her gaze fixed upon the couple as they moved together: one body, one flesh. She could not pull her eyes away, could not feign disinterest or even disgust. But watching the only man she cared about making love to another woman felt like being slowly torn apart. This was a pain to which she was not immune.

This, she thought as she wiped the rain from her face, *this is what I want.*

This wasn't just sex. This was love exemplified in physical form. This was what her life lacked, what she longed for but never dared allow herself to feel. She watched every move, every kiss, every caress, and each one deepened her loneliness.

Only when Lad and Wiggen finally lay quiet in each other's arms, spent and sated, warm and safe, did Mya stir. Wiping the water from her face, she dropped from the wall and headed for home. Only later, after wiping the wetness away once again, did she realize that it had stopped raining some time ago.

# CHAPTER XIV

Sereth stared at Jud's broken fingers, crooked, bruised, and painful, if the sweat running down the assassin's face was any indication.

Gods, how I'd love to do that to Hensen! he thought. *Tie him down and break those delicate fingers of his one by one…*

Five minutes was all Sereth had been allowed with his beloved Jinny. Only five minutes to hold her soft hands, touch her hair, whisper how sorry he was. Not a single word of accusation passed her lips, but Sereth felt like he was drowning in guilt whenever he saw her. He was beginning to despair at ever breaking free from the master thief's control. He knew the trap he was in: the more information he brought Hensen, the more information Hensen wanted.

Jud winced as the guild healer straightened one of his broken fingers. To the man's credit, he didn't scream. His face streamed with sweat, but Sereth didn't think it was entirely due to the pain. Jud was an Enforcer; he probably knew pain better than he knew his own name. But the glares of four irate master assassins were enough to make anyone sweat.

"It went off like clockwork as far as I could tell. We had four teams set up around the *Golden Cockerel*, and got word when he stepped out the front door. He bought the whole 'damsel in distress' ploy hook, line, and sinker. He ran me off," Jud nodded toward his injured hands, "and I went straight to the rendezvous. But Bertie didn't show. He must have killed her."

173

"Perhaps Bertie succeeded, and he killed her before he died." Patrice cocked an eyebrow in Neera's direction.

"Possible. The toxin is swift, but doesn't kill instantly. He could have had time to kill her, given what we know of his abilities. Alternatively, if she failed, he may have taken her to Mya for questioning."

"We should send someone to have a look."

"We've already lost one person tonight," Youtrin countered with a derisive glance at Horice. "We've got people in the City Guard who'll tell us what happened. We'll just have to wait until morning." Turning to the healer, he said, "Take Jud out, and see that his hands heal well. I'd hate to lose a good man."

"Thank you, Master." Jud stood and followed the healer out of the room.

The masters seated themselves at the table in the center of the room, Horice at the head, since he was hosting the meeting. Sereth stepped over to the door and snapped his fingers at the apprentice Blade who waited in the corridor. The girl bore a tray with crystal glasses and two bottles of fine wine. Setting it on the table by Horice's elbow, she waited for Sereth's nod before scurrying out. Taking up his protective stance behind his master's chair, Sereth concentrated on the conversation.

Neera sat back in her chair and cocked her head in thought. "It intrigues me that this weapon shows such compassion. He used only non-lethal force to persuade Jud to leave. He could just as easily have killed him."

"Mya must have told him not to kill anyone unnecessarily," Horice hypothesized. "My people have told me that when she took over, Mya set new rules for her faction; more persuasion, less violence. Like that nonsense about *public opinion* she's always trying to foist onto the rest of us."

Youtrin laughed scornfully, and even his huge bodyguard smiled at the ridiculous notion of a gentle Assassins Guild. Enforcers lived by violence and intimidation, not goodwill.

"As much as I hate to work without all the facts," Patrice said, "I think that we need to assume that the attempt failed, and concentrate on the real problem here. Mya. Is she apt to retaliate for this attack on her bodyguard?"

"Against who?" asked Horice. "Even if she assumes one of us was behind it, she doesn't know which one."

"Unless she's got Bertie," Youtrin protested.

Neera waved her hand. "Worrying about retaliation is pointless until we know if Mya has Bertie, and we'll know that soon enough."

"So, Mya's protected from *us* because she's wearing the ring, and protected from anyone we might hire from outside the guild by a bodyguard who's not only seemingly invincible, but now also wary." Horice reached for a bottle of wine, wrenched the cork free, and filled his glass with the crimson liquid. "What now?"

"I say we tell Mya the truth."

They all looked at Patrice as if she'd just admitted to being a spy for the Royal Guard.

"Tell her we know she wears the guildmaster's ring?" Horice gave a snort of disbelief and quaffed half of his glass of wine. "She'd kill us all, and we'd be unable to touch her!"

"Not *that* much truth, Horice." The Master Inquisitor tapped her rouged lips, a behavior Sereth was beginning to recognize as habitual when the woman was deep in thought. "Tell her of our concerns that the guild is being destroyed by our seemingly intractable lack of cooperation. Even *she* can't disagree with that. Then tell her that we've decided to hold a vote to forge a new guildmaster's ring and elect a new leader."

"You want to bring her into a *meeting*?" Youtrin shifted in his seat. "Sit in a room with an assassin we can't fight, not to mention her unbeatable bodyguard? That's beyond dangerous. It's stupid!"

"Yes, it *is* dangerous, which is why we must placate her. We must hint, at the very least, that we'll back her bid for the guildmaster's position. She is, after all, the most successful of us."

Youtrin didn't seem convinced. "If she wears the ring, how can she allow us to forge a new one?"

"She can't," Patrice countered with a sly smile. "This is why we must give her the chance to destroy the ring."

"Destroy it? How can she do that if she can't even take it off?"

"Horice, please." Neera dismissed the Master Blade's concern with a wave. "She could order that bodyguard of hers to cut it off. He's not bound by a guild blood contract, so there would be no problem." She turned to Patrice with a nod of affirmation. "If she knows we plan to forge a ring, not destroying hers would bring her deceit out into the open. Then she would have to answer to the Grandmaster, who is the one force she cannot flout with impunity."

"Exactly." Patrice smiled like a viper. "And once the ring is destroyed, she'll be vulnerable to a concerted attack."

Sereth's opinion of Patrice rose. Even Neera was following the Master Inquisitor's lead. *But she'd better not try to force her hand*, he thought. *Mya is no fool. If she gets wind of this plot, all her talk of goodwill will be so much dust in the wind, and she'll send her weapon to kill them all.*

"It will be interesting to see how far she is willing to go to avoid forging a new ring." Neera swept her ancient gaze from face to face. "So, if no one is opposed to this course of action…" Youtrin looked least comfortable with the plan, but no one dissented. "It's agreed then."

The Master Alchemist turned to her bodyguard. "Have a message drafted. Master Hunter Mya's presence is required for a meeting of the masters of the guild at—where is the next location?" At Yotrin's raised hand, she continued. "At Youtrin's warehouse, two hours past noon tomorrow—actually, it's past midnight, so make that today. The matter is vital to the future of the guild. Attendance is not optional."

ꮭꓱꭾꓱꮭꮭ

"This one better be worth being dragged all the way down here," Norwood mumbled to Sergeant Tamir as they approached the City Guard captain.

He got only a grunt in reply. Neither of them was happy about being summoned to the Westmarket District at this hour of the morning. The Royal Guard had already been called to six wild-goose chases in the past four days. Suspicious deaths, it seemed, were more common south of the river than the captain had expected when he requested notification of professional or peculiar killings.

The captain of the City Guard didn't look any happier. A half dozen of his guardsmen stood in the shadowed alley behind him. The morning sun lighting the rooftops was warm enough to raise steam from the shingles, but was not yet high enough to illuminate the streets. A guardsman guided a distraught woman from the alley, pointed her toward the nearby pub, and stopped to report to his supervisor.

"The victim certainly looks like a trollop, sir, but not one of the regulars here. Betsy there worked last night 'til closing, and she's never seen her around here."

Norwood stopped short, directing his rising ire at the captain. "What's a dead prostitute got to do with the Royal Guard?"

"A dead prostitute and a dead *guardsman*, Captain Norwood." He turned on his heel and entered the alley, and the cordon of city guardsmen parted to let them pass. The captain stopped and pointed down at an odd scene. "When one of my men falls dead with no discernible cause, I call it *mighty* peculiar."

The prostitute in question lay on her side, her eyes open and staring up at the sky, an expression of surprise frozen on her pale face. Only a step away, a city guardsman was stretched out, face down, his arms at his sides.

177

"Well, it's peculiar, I'll give you that." Norwood peered at the woman's face. Her nose was bent, probably broken, and her lip was split. "Looks like your man picked a fight with the wrong trollop,"

"My *man*, Captain, did nothing of the kind!" He gestured irritably to a glowering guardsman nearby. "Tell him what happened, Corporal Nix."

"Yes, sir." The corporal cleared his throat and began his recitation, obviously not for the first time that morning. "We arrived about two hours ago, after we was called by the pub owner. One of his maids found the body when she was takin' out the night waste. We found the victim layin' just like she is. It was still pretty dark, but we seen enough like this to think she'd been raped and beaten to death. Alan reached down to check how stiff she was, then yelped, turned, took one step and fell over. I never seen anythin' like it. I thought it might be magic, a curse of some kind, so I sent a runner to fetch the captain."

Norwood's anger abated at the tremor in the guardsman's voice. He'd just lost his partner, probably a close friend. And if the man's account was accurate, his friend may have died from some kind of curse. Corporal Nix was rightfully shaken, but Norwood needed more details.

"Nobody's touched the bodies since?"

"No, sir! We just blocked off the alley and sent for the captain."

"And when I learned the details, and that there might be magic involved, I sent messengers for you and the duke's wizard."

"Rightly so, Captain."

Norwood stepped closer and peered down at the woman. There was no blood, or at least, none that the rain hadn't washed away. The split lip was not scabbed, and there was no bruising, so she'd probably been beaten right before she died. But had the beating killed her? Most beating victims were found curled up, trying to protect themselves from their assailants, but this woman seemed to have been staring straight up at her attacker, with a wide-eyed expression of surprise on her face rather than a grimace of pain. In his experience, these elements didn't support the idea that she'd been beaten to death.

"So, Corporal, your partner approached, reached down to touch the victim, then died."

"Well, first he poked her with his stick, sir," the corporal said. "To make sure she wasn't...um...well, to make sure she was dead-dead, you know."

Norwood nodded absently. Legends of the walking dead were still alive among Twailin's superstitious lower classes, even though it had been decades since the last of the necromancers had been rooted out and put to the torch.

"Give me your truncheon, Sergeant."

Tamir lifted the two-foot length of hardwood from his belt and handed it over. The stick was heavy, weighted with lead to give it more stopping power.

"Shouldn't we wait for the duke's wizard?" the City Guard captain asked.

"It'll take Master Woefler hours to get here. Don't worry, Captain. If I drop dead, you can tell the duke I said it was my own fault."

"You bet your sweet pension I will, Captain Norwood." The man folded his arms and took a long step back, glowering his disapproval.

Warily, Norwood tried to turn the woman's head with the tip of the stick, and found that rigor mortis had stiffened her neck enough that he couldn't. *More than a few hours dead*, he thought. He had noted only one rat bite on the corpse, and assumed that she had died not too long ago. Curious now, he looked her over carefully. A fleck of black on her neck contrasted starkly with her pale, waxy skin. He'd thought was a bit of detritus or soot until he considered her sodden clothing.

Odd that the rain didn't wash that away. Norwood leaned in for a closer look.

"Ah, sir, do you think that's wise?"

Ignoring Tamir's warning, Norwood saw that the fleck wasn't dirt at all, but a tiny tuft of feathers. He drew his dagger and poked the tuft with the tip, but it remained stuck to the woman's neck. Delicately, trying to not touch the woman's bare skin in case she did bear some kind of curse, he pinched the tuft between thumb and finger and pulled. A dart the length of the last two joints of his index finger slid out of the sheath of flesh. The dart's shaft shone black in the dim morning light, its tip beveled and hollow.

"Well, I don't know how your man died, Captain, but this woman was poisoned, or I'm a court jester." He held up the dart for them to see. "Got an evidence bottle, Tam?"

"Right here, sir." Tamir held out a small glass jar. Norwood dropped the dart into it, and the sergeant stoppered it and sealed it with a smear of soft wax.

"That goes to Woefler. He knows every alchemist in the city. Depending on what kind of poison was used, we could potentially track down the supplier and maybe find out who killed her. It may not put a dent in the violence, but it's a start. The duke has been pressing for progress on this." He turned back to the corporal. "So, your partner poked her with his stick. What next?"

"He reached down and lifted her arm to see how stiff she was. Then, like I said, he gave a little yelp, like, and snatched his hand back. Then he turned to me with a strange look on his face, took one step, gasped, and fell flat, just like you see him."

"Which hand did he touch her with?"

"Uh, his right, I think, sir."

The man had collapsed without even trying to break his fall, sprawled with his hands palm up at his sides. Norwood examined his right hand, moving the fingers with the tip of his dagger, still wary of some type of magic. The constable had died less than two hours ago, so his fingers were still pliant. In the center of his palm, a single spot of blood caught the captain's eye. It had not yet rained this morning, so the hand hadn't been washed clean. Norwood scraped the edge of his dagger across the man's palm, shaving away the clotted blood. There, barely visible, a tiny pinprick marred the tough callus.

"Well, I'll be damned." Norwood stood and sheathed his dagger. "Where did he grab her?"

"I don't really remember, sir. I think he just grabbed her hand to see if her fingers had gone stiff."

Norwood peered at the dead woman's hand, and spied a ring on her index finger. Using Tamir's truncheon to lift her thumb out of the way, he saw the long needle set into the underside of the ring.

"Have a look, Captain. Your man was murdered by a dead woman. The ring on her finger has a needle on the underside that was undoubtedly poisoned. Whoever killed her with that dart also used poison. It seems pretty clear that we're dealing with professionals here."

"Professionals. You mean assassins."

The captain's tone was hard, but Norwood could hear the underlying fear, and couldn't blame the man. He considered telling him what he had learned from his midnight visitor about the source of the violence, but didn't want the entire City Guard to know. No, he'd keep that information to himself for the time being. Better to stick with hints for now.

"Yes, I mean assassins, Captain. This murder is a puzzle, more sophisticated than most, and poses some interesting questions. Who killed the killer, and who was the killer supposed to kill? Either she didn't succeed, or someone took that body away." He scratched his stubbled jaw and sighed. "I'll be interested to hear what Master Woefler thinks of this scene."

"But you said they were both poisoned. Do we still need to bring the wizard in?"

181

"As I said, Master Woefler knows every alchemist in the city. Besides, just because they were poisoned doesn't mean magic is out of the question." Norwood gave the captain a thin smile.

"Master Woefler's welcome to look all he wants, Captain Norwood, and good luck to him." The City Guard captain nodded to his men. "We'll share anything we find out from the pub owner and his staff, of course."

"Thank you, Captain." Norwood turned and headed out of the alley, Tamir at his side. Pointing to the bottle containing the dart, he said, "Give that to Master Woefler first thing, Tam, and don't forget to tell him about the poisoned ring. I'd hate to have him drop dead, too."

"You want me to stay here and help him, I suppose." Tamir didn't sound happy about the arrangement.

"Is there a problem with that, Sergeant?"

"No problem, sir."

"Good."

"I just wonder why you hate me so much."

Norwood couldn't suppress a smile as he boarded his carriage and ordered the driver to take him to his office.

ᛉⅎℲⅉⅇⅉⅉⅈ

Hensen looked up as the door to the breakfast room opened, smiling at his assistant as she strode gracefully in, blue dress glittering in the morning sun, ledger in hand. A complex coif left tendrils of hair curling down the nape of her exquisite neck.

Lovely…

"Since you are alive and looking quite beautiful this morning, I venture a guess that last night's operation was a success." He speared a tiny bit of sausage and popped it into his mouth.

"Yes, sir. Lad is still alive." She curtsied at his compliment in a manner that showed off her new dress nicely. "I had to

182

intervene, so he undoubtedly knows someone is protecting him, but he lives."

"So, Sereth's information was accurate?"

"Perfectly accurate. My people located the teams of assassins before Lad even left the inn. I waited until he came out, saw which direction he took, then made sure I got there before him."

"So, he knows someone is protecting him." Hensen sipped his tea and narrowed his eyes at her. "Did he see you?"

"No, sir. I stayed behind the roof edge, and left immediately after I shot the assassin."

"How do you know you were successful if you didn't stay around?"

Kiesha shrugged away his concern. "I don't miss, sir. Besides, I couldn't tarry and risk a chase. I'd have lost. Our operatives watching the *Tap and Kettle* reported that Lad returned home safe, and all was quiet for the rest of the night."

Hensen smiled, picturing the puzzled expression that must have crossed that sweet young man's face after Kiesha's life-saving intervention. "Good. Let him wonder who his mysterious guardian is."

"Yes, sir."

Hensen sipped his tea and smiled at his beautiful assistant. "You've done quite well."

"Thank you, sir."

"And this confirms that Sereth is being forthright with us, despite his recent obstinacy."

"It does, sir."

"And the dress is quite lovely."

"Thank you, sir."

"Continue to keep both Mya and Lad under observation and alive, but keep our people hidden. If any of our operatives feel that they have been spotted, they are to retreat, and under *no* circumstances are they to allow themselves to be captured. We can't allow anyone to track them back to us."

"Of course, sir."

Hensen sipped his tea and ate a few more bites of breakfast while he considered the next step. Kiesha stood and waited patiently; she was well-trained.

"Send a message to Sereth. Thank him for this information, and tell him to inform us immediately of any other plots against Master Hunter Mya or her bodyguard."

"Yes, sir."

"Also, contact our operative at the *Golden Cockerel*. I'd like to know if Mya has sent any letters to Tsing yet."

"Yes, sir." Kiesha made a note in her ledger.

"Excellent." Hensen ate the last of his sausage and wiped his mouth with his silk-embroidered napkin. "So, what else is on the agenda for today?"

"We received a report from our operatives assigned to investigate Baron Patino." Kiesha placed a single sheet of parchment beside his plate. "It would appear that our benefactor is who and what he says he is."

"Hmm, yes." Hensen read the document carefully. "Third generation nobility, ample funds, and three country estates. Well, he can certainly *afford* to contract us."

"Yes, sir."

The report also stated that the baron paid his taxes, liked to socialize, had two mistresses who didn't know about one another, though his wife knew about both of them, and had no known affiliation with any element of organized crime. This meant one of two things: either he was extremely subtle in his underworld business transactions, or he was a front for some yet unknown person interested in the Assassins Guild.

"I want him kept under surveillance, but at a distance. And find out who handles his correspondence. If Patino is indeed as innocent as he appears to be, it could be an underling sending out letters and embezzling funds under the good baron's nose without his knowledge."

"Very good, sir." Kiesha scratched another note in her ledger, then handed him an envelope. "This for you specifically, sir. It's been examined."

"Thank you." He cracked the seal with his eating knife, flipped open the letter and read.

Hensen had always prided himself on maintaining his poise. *You must be like a swan*, his old master had told him when he was but a boy. *Beautiful, regal, and calm above the surface where people can see. Only beneath, where they cannot see, are you allowed to paddle like there is an alligator ready to bite you in the ass.*

Hensen didn't react to the letter's content, but he felt like he should check his hind quarters for tooth marks.

"Sir? Are you all right?"

The thief chided himself; staring wide-eyed at the letter without so much as a twitch was a reaction in itself. Dropping the letter, he reached for his tea.

"I'm fine, my dear." He took a careful sip and returned the cup to the saucer without so much as a tremor. Proud of his achievement, he considered the letter again. "We do, however, have a concern." He passed the letter to her. "Baron Patino has thanked us for our acceptance of his contract, and also appreciates our interest in his affairs. He asks if we wish to know any additional details about his personal life, lovers or associations."

"But how could he *know*?" Her eyes, wide with shock, scanned the letter.

She's even more beautiful when she's terrified, Hensen thought, *though she really should learn to be a swan.* "Possibilities come to mind, none particularly pleasant. Either his people are better than ours, which I find hard to fathom, or he has eyes in our camp."

"A *spy*?" Kiesha swallowed, the smooth muscles of her throat moving in waves. "A spy *inside* the Thieves Guild?"

185

"So it would seem, my dear. But that's not the half of it." Hensen withdrew a tiny silver flask from his waistcoat and unscrewed the lid, then poured half the contents into his tea and stirred it. Tucking the flask back into his pocket, he sipped the mixture of dark tea and spiced rum. As the warmth seeped from his stomach outward, calming his jangling nerves, he sighed and explained. "By sending this letter, he has told us two things: he knows we are watching him, and he does not care."

"So...what do we do, sir?"

"Other than sit and drink spiked tea, you mean?" He gave her a little smile, which seemed to reduce her state of terror to a simple case of dread.

"Yes, sir, besides that."

"We do exactly as our contract states, my dear." He sipped the brew again, enjoying the mixture of flavors, the heat easing down his throat, and the feeling of exhilaration brought on by danger.

"Should we pull our surveillance on Baron Patino?"

"Oh, by no means, my dear! If we do that, we show fear." *We must be swans*, he thought, *but we must be vigilant for hungry reptiles*. "We play the game, my dear. And we play it very, very carefully."

CHAPTER XV

A rare break in the rain left Twailin looking as fresh as a newly minted coin. Her cobbled streets shone as if they'd been freshly scrubbed, and the sun-glittered minarets of the Duke's Palace thrust into the sky like golden spears high atop the bluff. The beautiful spring day drew the city's populace out of their homes in a bustle of life that Lad had not seen in months. Vendors hawked wares from their carts, tinkers hammered on pots or turned their wrenches at the backs of their colorful wagons, and couples strolled arm in arm, smiling at the bright, beautiful day. Even Mya wore brighter colors today, though to Lad she still looked like an assassin. Her blousy purple shirt fluttered in the breeze, but couldn't hide the daggers at her hips, and his practiced eye caught the glint of another beneath the fold of her right trouser leg where it was tucked into her high, soft boot.

The bustle, the colors, the voices and clatter, all brought back memories of Lad's first day in the city. He recalled how it had seemed like such a wonder, such a miracle. It still did.

Leave Twailin…

He loved this city; his life revolved around it. In reality, this was the place of his birth, the place where he became a human being. Twailin was the mother and father he had never known. Leaving it would be like leaving his family. However, the choice looming over his head—leave Twailin or risk losing everyone he loved—was no choice. He didn't want Lissa to grow up without a father, as he had. Every street, alley, pub and

187

shop of this miraculous place would be forever etched in his memory, but in the end, Twailin was just a city. There were other cities, other places they could live.

There's only one Wiggen, one Lissa...

Mya stopped her brisk pace at a fruit vendor and picked out two ripe mangoes. She tossed one to Lad, flipped a penny to the shopkeeper, and continued on their way. She produced a tiny knife from her belt and started to peel the tough skin from the fruit in strips, holding it to avoid the dripping juice. Lad simply stripped the rind back with his teeth and bit into the flesh, ignoring the sweet, sticky nectar that escaped his lips.

As he followed her stiff back, he realized that Mya had been strangely quiet all morning. Usually she chatted, telling him their schedule, which people they would meet with, what to watch for, but today she had a distant, almost brusque manner.

Is she angry about last night's argument? They had argued before, and she had never held a grudge. Was it about the assassination attempt? He still didn't think that Mya had tried to have him killed. It was more likely that his savior had been one of her Hunters watching out for him. *She hasn't mentioned it, but that could be why she's acting strangely.* He decided not to mention it. At least not yet. He had more important things to tell her.

Lad watched everything as they walked, even more vigilant than usual with the memory of his brush with death so fresh. Still, his mind spun away on his real dilemma. *I've got to tell her I'm leaving, but how will she react?* It didn't bode well that she already seemed upset.

A clattering wagon approached, the canvas sides rolled up to display copper pots and pans, all jingling and jangling in a musical cacophony. The vendor sang out his jaunty rhyme to the crowds: "Copper, copper, pots! Copper, copper pans! Better'n tin. Better'n gold! Best in all the lands!"

Tuppence Way was narrow, so pedestrians, Lad and Mya included, crowded to the side to avoid the wagon. As the noisy vehicle passed, one of its wheels dropped into the hole where a cobble was missing, pitching the wagon to one side. The mule snorted, the vendor shouted, and several pots clattered to the cobbles. In an instant, Lad observed it all and dismissed it as harmless...until a figure darted toward them.

On such a bright, sunny day, amid bustling happy crowds, the threat of assassins seemed remote. A good killer would know this, however, and might hope that the festive atmosphere would lower their guard. Lad certainly knew this, and his partially eaten mango plopped to the street.

Lad moved... *Step, turn, pivot.*

When an attack is imminent, position yourself to greatest advantage. Remember!

His position, between the commotion and Mya, might not be to *his* best advantage, but it was to hers. His job was to protect her life, and he was far better able than she to meet an assassin's assault.

Assess the threat at hand, but do not commit until the appropriate action is determined. Remember!

The figure, a small boy, dashed toward the wagon, grabbed a fallen pot and scurried away; a clumsy bit of thievery...or a distraction.

Noise and motion are often used to hide an attack. Remember!

Lad spun, his eyes scanning the crowd, the buildings, the roofs. Beside him, he saw Mya mirror his motion, her drawn dagger glinting in the sun. They ended up back to back, Mya's shoulder blades pressed against his. They stood poised for several heartbeats, waiting for an attack.

Nothing happened. No assassin struck from the shadows, no arrows flew from the rooftops.

"It's nothing, Mya." Lad stepped away and turned toward her, glimpsing her swift resheathing of her dagger. *She's fast!* The thought prompted a memory of her performance in the alley days ago. Killing two trained assassins without getting a scratch was no easy task. His eyebrows drew together thoughtfully.

Mya straightened and noticed Lad looking at her. Nudging her fallen fruit with her toe, she gave a bark of nervous laughter. "Little bastard ruined a perfectly good mango. Come on, we need to get out of here."

They turned away from the ranting pot maker as he recovered his fallen wears. A small crowd of onlookers had stopped to gawk, and a few eyes lingered on them. Lad could hear the whispered suppositions, as he led the way up the street, still scanning, listening, feeling the city around them.

Satisfied that no trouble followed, he glanced back at Mya. "You're very quick."

"I've been training a little." Her defensive glare took him aback, but she quickly looked away. "I've got to spend my money on *something*, don't I?"

"More than a little." He nodded back up the street. "Back there, you did exactly as I did, scanning for threats, ready to meet them. That's more than a little training."

"Yes, well..." She shrugged casually. "I've been training a lot. It kept me alive the other night, didn't it?"

"You're right." Lad saw the opening to broach the subject of his leaving, and took it. "You'll be fine without me."

"What?" Mya stopped so suddenly that he took two paces before he realized that he no longer heard her footsteps behind him. When he turned back to look at her, the astonishment in her eyes almost made him smile. For once, he had truly caught her off guard. "What did you say?"

"I'm leaving, Mya."

"No." He watched her face transform, tried to read the fleeting emotions there and failed. Finally, her features hardened, her lips pressed in a thin line. *That* he could read; she was angry. "No, you're not leaving, Lad. Our agreement—"

"Our agreement was made almost five *years* ago, Mya. You're safer now. You've been training and your skills are very

190

good, as you just demonstrated. Besides, you now have dozens of trustworthy Hunters to protect you. You don't need me."

"Safer now? Are you *insane*?" Her shrill question drew a few glances from passersby. She noticed the attention and resumed walking, her pace faster, her strides stiff. "How do you figure I'm *safer* now than before, Lad? The last attack was the worst yet! Were you not *there*?"

"I was there, Mya, but two good Hunters could have protected you as well as I did." He wasn't going to back down. If he wanted a life for his family, they had to leave. He countered with the argument he'd been rehearsing all morning, and hoped she'd buy it. "The issue is not my protection of you, but yours of me. You can't control Norwood, and you can't keep him from investigating Vonlith's death. Vonlith worked for the Grandfather. Eventually, Norwood's going to find me."

"So what? We can beat anyone he sends after you, and I've got enough people watching to know when he's going to try it. Hells, I can tell you what he had for his godsdamned breakfast! Norwood's no danger to you, Lad. You've got to trust me on that!"

"It's not just that, Mya." Lad grasped her arm and pulled her into an adjacent alley for a measure of privacy. The pounding of her heart sounded loud and fast in his ears, and her face was flushed. He had never seen her so agitated. She was even more upset than he had expected. It was clear that his Norwood argument wasn't working, so he decided on another tack. Watching her reaction closely, he said, "Someone tried to kill me last night."

"What? When?"

Her surprise seemed genuine, which in turn surprised him. But if Mya didn't know about last night's assassination attempt, then who tried to kill him, and who saved his life?

"Last night, about three blocks from the *Golden Cockerel*." Still, her astonishment seemed authentic.

"Tell me what happened. Everything. *Right now!*"

"I thought you might already know…" A quick shake of her head in denial, no guile or deception in her eyes, only something he couldn't quite identify. *Worry? For me?* He continued. "A man was beating a prostitute, and I stopped him. She held out a hand for me to help her up, but before I could, someone shot her with a poisoned dart."

"Shot her, or shot at you and hit her?"

"At first I thought it was intended for me, but it hit her right in the neck, too accurate for chance. When I looked more closely, I found a poisoned ring on her finger…on the hand she had offered to me. Whoever shot her saved my life."

"That's…" Her voice trailed off, questions in her eyes.

"I thought maybe you sent one of your Hunters to look out for me."

Mya shook her head slowly. "Who would *do* that?"

"Kill me or save me?"

"A poisoned ring…" She glanced down at her own hand, and shot him a quick look of irony, "That's professional. I'd be willing to bet that one of the other masters is behind the attack, but who's looking out for you?"

"If it wasn't you, I don't know, Mya, but it's really not the issue." He gritted his teeth and reaffirmed his resolve. "I'm leaving because I want a life for my family, a life where my daughter won't wake up every morning wondering if her father was killed last night, or if it's safe to step out her front door."

"I can protect them! I can put people—"

"No, Mya! I don't want your Hunters standing guard over my family."

"I don't understand you, Lad! What in the Nine Hells did you expect?" There was scorn in her tone now. "People like us don't *have* families!"

"No, Mya. People like *you* don't have families. I am a husband and a father. I am *not* like you."

Rage contorted her features, and he knew she would threaten him before she opened her mouth.

"You think you can just walk away from this? Away from *me*? You think I'll *let* you walk away?"

He smiled at her, but there was no amusement in it. "Don't, Mya."

"Don't what? Try to convince you that if you leave, I'm as good as dead?"

Her quick change of attack caught him off guard, but he recovered. "No, I mean don't threaten me. You can't stop me from leaving. Your skills are good, but not that good. If you threaten my family, I *will* kill you."

Her eyes flashed with shock.

"After *years* of protecting me, you'd do that?" Behind her disbelief, something else, something he couldn't read, added a tremor to her voice. "You'd *kill* me?"

"I love my family more than anything else in the world, Mya." He thrust his words at her low and hard. "Don't test me. You'll lose."

"Godsdamnit, Lad, I *need* you! I..." Mya bit her lip, one of her minor tells; she was holding back. "There's nobody else I can *trust* like you!"

"You're wrong, Mya. Your Hunters are loyal. Trust them. They surround you at the *Golden Cockerel*. You're safe there."

"Not like I'm safe with you! If you go, I'm dead."

The desperation in her eyes sent a pang of guilt through him, but he forced it aside. *Wiggen... Lissa...* He couldn't let her change his mind.

"No you're not, Mya. You're an expert at survival. You'll be fine. And you can't stop me from leaving."

Mya turned away and stood with her back to him for a long moment, her fists clenched, her whole body as tense as an over-wound spring. Finally she strode away, flinging her words back at him.

"All *right*, for the gods' sake! But give me some time, a few days to put together a network of bodyguards to take over your

193

job. If you leave before I get them in place, you may as well kill me yourself on your way out the door."

Lad thought about it as he fell in behind her. A few more days wouldn't hurt; he could give her that. It wasn't a matter of him trusting her to keep her word, but simple logic. He'd warned her, and she knew he was serious. If she dared to threaten his family, he *would* kill her on his way out the door.

"Five days, Mya, then I leave."

"Fine."

He followed her for a time, maintaining his vigilance and girding his worries. Not until they reached the looming warehouses of the South Docks District did Lad finally realize where they were headed and break the uncomfortable silence.

"We're going to Youtrin's warehouse? There's a meeting of the masters?"

"Figured that out, did you?" Anger and scorn edged her words, but he'd expected it. Mya didn't like to lose an argument.

"Yes, but you usually warn me. I didn't think you were attending meetings anymore."

"Then you didn't *think* of everything, did you? The summons I received made it clear that attendance wasn't optional." She glanced back at him. The desperation and fear in her expression had been replaced by anger and resentment. "Just do your job and keep your mouth shut."

"Yes, Mya." Lad stepped up his vigilance. If they were walking into a nest of vipers, he had to be at the top of his game.

𝅘𝅥 ⅃⅄ ⅌ 𝅘

Master Woefler tilted the tiny crystal vial back and forth in the light from the window, smiling as it cast a flurry of rainbows around Norwood's office. The annoyed captain would have snatched the vial away had he not been so daunted by the light brown liquid inside.

194

Sergeant Tamir nodded at the glittering vial. "We found that tucked in the dead woman's dress, sir."

"It really is the most deadly toxin I've ever encountered. No more than a tenth of an ounce, and it's enough to kill every member of the Royal Guard twice over." Woefler seemed elated by the lethality of the substance. He placed the vial carefully on Norwood's desk. "An alchemist colleague of mine identified it."

"After we visited four *other* alchemist shops first," Tamir added with a note of annoyance.

Woefler ignored the sergeant's comment and continued his speech. "It comes from the spines of a small tropical fish, the two-step stonefish. It's so named because if you step on one, you can take about two more steps before you fall dead."

Tamir rolled his eyes. He'd obviously been listening to Woefler prattle on all morning.

Wizards! Norwood thought. *Give them a spot of mold to look at, and a band of ogres could tromp through the room without drawing attention.* "That's very interesting, Master Woefler, but it provides me with absolutely no information to help solve this murder."

"Oh, but it *does*!" Woefler picked up the vial and turned it in the sunlight again. "This is rare, Captain. Very rare! Consequently, we should be able to find out who supplied it."

"Which means more visits to *more* alchemist shops," Tamir muttered.

"The intended method of delivery was rather mundane, just a grooved needle, but quite sufficient when combined with the high potency of the stonefish toxin." Woefler withdrew from a pocket the dart Norwood had extracted from the dead woman's neck. "Then we have this little toy!"

"Careful with that! I didn't know you'd taken it out of the jar!"

"Relax, Sergeant. It's been cleaned." The mage turned back to Norwood. "The toxin in this was not so rare, but still very potent. The mechanism of this dart, however, is astounding. Look!"

Woefler held the lethal little projectile beneath Norwood's nose and twisted it between his fingers. Something clicked, and a tiny port opened in the side of the dart's shaft. "The poison is loaded here, and the click you heard was a spring being cocked back." He withdrew another little vial from a pocket and used a tiny glass pipette to transfer several drops of green liquid into the port. "Don't worry, this is just colored water. Now you twist it back, the port closes, and the dart is ready."

Woefler tossed the little black dart in a high arc.

"Hey! Watch it!" Tamir stumbled back, his eyes fixed on the tiny missile.

The dart's fletching righted the projectile as it fell to the captain's desk. The beveled needle stuck into the polished wood with a thud and a faint click. Green liquid squirted out of the needle, staining the papers that littered the desk's surface.

"Oh, sorry." Woefler drew a kerchief from yet another pocket and dabbed up the spill. "But you can see how effective it is at delivering a lethal dose of venom. Much more effective than the simple coating of a grooved needle. The dart was filled with white scorpion venom, a potent neurotoxin that is deadly at a mere one one-hundredth of the dose that was injected into the woman you found. Whoever used it wanted to make sure that the target died instantly."

"Good gods." Norwood was getting the picture; great expense had been taken both in the woman's attempt to kill someone, and in the second assassin's strike.

"Obviously professionals, sir, both of 'em," Tamir said.

"I see that." The captain rubbed his eyes; the wizard's enthusiasm was not infectious enough to overcome his fatigue. Sleep had been as elusive as Vonlith's killer since his late-night visit from the assassin. All the security in the world would not protect him from someone like that, and worrying about it had ruined his ability to relax. That, in turn, impaired his ability to think. Twailin seemed suddenly full of assassins, and all of his efforts felt futile. "Any chance of tracking down who sold any of these items?"

"I can work on the dart and the ring, sir," Tamir offered. "I know a few crafters. There's an old gnome on Ironmonger Street who makes clocks and such, intricate kinds of stuff. He might recognize the work."

"An excellent idea!" Woefler looked at Tamir as if the man had just surprised him with his investigative prowess. "I, of course, will look into the origin of the venoms."

"Good. Concentrate on the rare items, the maker of the dart and the supplier of the stonefish poison. We want to know who these items were sold to."

"People who sell poisons and spring-loaded darts aren't likely to want to talk, sir. It's more likely they'll just clam up.

"Give them some inducement to be forthcoming, then."

Tamir grinned. "I can do that."

"*Without* breaking any bones, Sergeant. Mention that the duke himself has an interest in the activity of professional assassins in the city, and anyone helping us discover who is behind these killings will receive a reward."

"There's a reward?"

"No, but a carrot might work where a stick won't."

"I agree, Captain. Threatening an alchemist is unlikely to produce the desired cooperation."

Norwood nodded respectfully, as if he cared what the wizard thought of his tactics. Tamir simply rolled his eyes again.

"Any theories as to what exactly happened in that alley, Sergeant?" Norwood had his own theories, but he wanted Tamir's opinion. The sergeant might be thinking more clearly than he was at this point, and had a good mind for things like this. He was the one who discovered the significance of Vonlith's wagon, after all.

"The dead woman was dressed like a trollop, and the ring on her finger was already poisoned. Just wearing that ring would be dangerous, so she was ready to kill someone." Tamir rubbed his jaw. "Don't know why she'd been beat up though. Maybe whoever killed her tried to knock the truth out of her before they shot her, but that'd be dangerous, too."

"What if someone interrupted the attempted assassination with another assassination?" Woefler asked.

"What?" Norwood looked at him as if he'd made a bad joke. "What do you mean?"

"The dart was shot from a distance, correct?"

"That's true, sir." Tamir looked at the wizard and cocked an eyebrow. "We figured that the angle, assuming she was sitting up or standing, would have put the shooter on the rooftop."

"So, perhaps the dead woman was going to kill someone, and whoever shot her did so to prevent the killing." Woefler looked pleased with his inference.

"That seems reasonable." Norwood looked to his sergeant. "Tam?"

"Yep, that works. And we've already know that both were professional killers."

"Guild war." Norwood had wondered how much of what the assassin had told him was the truth. His assessment of the violence, it seemed, was spot on, though he had called it squabbling between the factions. It meant the same regardless of the exact words.

"Seems like it, sir."

"Well, sergeant, see if you can find out who made that dart, and who they sold it to."

"Yes, sir." Tamir saluted and left the office.

"And I'll investigate the poisons," Woefler offered, grinning like a kid with a new toy.

"Do that. And be careful. You might walk into the wrong apothecary and find yourself in the company of assassins."

"Ah, but they will find themselves in the company of an accomplished worker of magic!" He pulled a pinch of something from his pocket and snapped his fingers. A shimmer of sparkling motes drifted down, and a dark space opened in the air. "I'll be in

198

Chris A. Jackson

touch, Captain." Woefler stepped into the dark space and the shimmer vanished, taking the wizard with it.

"Son of a..." Norwood blinked and stared at the spot where the wizard had disappeared. "Marvelous! Now I'm going to have an even harder time getting to sleep tonight."

CHAPTER XVI

T*his day is going from bad to worse*, thought Mya as she entered the dingy office. She'd never liked this room. The bare wooden walls and drab stick furnishings seemed to suck all the color out of the bright sunny day outside. Lamps on the walls barely lit the space to the brightness of a rainy day. Of course, it was inside a warehouse, and Youtrin's warehouse to boot, so she didn't expect elegance. In fact, the gloom matched her mood, which wasn't made any better by Neera's attempt at congeniality.

"You're dressed festively today, Mya."

"It's a beautiful spring day outside, Neera." She took a seat at the table. "If I wore anything less *festive*, I'd stick out like a sore thumb."

After last night's soul-crushing misery, she had hoped a bright color might lighten her mood, but with Lad's ultimatum, the beautiful spring day only seemed to mock her. She could feel his solid presence behind her, the heat that radiated from his body warming her back like the summer sun. How cold it would feel when he was gone...

He's leaving me!

Mya forced her panic aside, struggling through the rising maelstrom of emotions that threatened to pull her down into darkness. If the other masters detected her mood, they would think she feared them, and fear to an assassin was like blood to a shark. They would eat her alive.

Focus! Here and now are all that matter!

Forcing her voice into a calm, bantering tone, she smiled at Neera. "In this neighborhood that gown of yours is like an invitation to get robbed. Don't you ever find that it draws unwanted attention?"

"When people look at me, Mya, they see a rich, successful woman, which is precisely the image I want to project. What image are *you* trying to project?" Neera smiled back, but something poisonous lurked beneath the superficial pleasantry.

Strange, Mya thought. *Neera's usually the least abrasive of the other masters.*

"Well, we're all here, so let's begin. Gentlemen, if you please."

Horice and Youtrin, who had been talking quietly in the corner, approached. The Master Blade claimed the seat across from Mya. Youtrin scowled and cracked his huge knuckles, then took the only empty seat, to Mya's right. Patrice, silent and beautiful, sat between Neera and Horice.

Neera looked each of her fellow masters in the eye before beginning. "The Twailin Assassins Guild is at a crossroads. All of us, or nearly all," she glanced sidelong at Mya, her rheumy eyes sharp as daggers, "received quite a dressing down from the Grandmaster's representative last quarter about fallen revenues. Personally, I never want to experience such a humiliation again. But revenues continue to fall. We *must* change how we operate. I see two paths we can take: we must either cooperate, or elect a guildmaster."

A surge of adrenalin ignited Mya's nerves. Her skin tingled as if her tattoos were writhing. Once again, the specter of the Grandfather loomed over her, his blades parting her flesh as he laughed at her pain.

Never again.

It had been barely a week since she'd received the Grandmaster's letter. Since then, she had deliberately refused to deal with the issue. She knew that eventually she would have to decide what to do, but not yet. Even if she had sent an immediate response, it wouldn't have reached Tsing yet, so he couldn't be disappointed by her silence. She still had time. But now this…

"Cooperation isn't working." Horice's hard, angry voice wrenched her attention back to the present, stretching her nerves so taut she thought they might snap.

The bastard who just sent people to kill me has the gall to say that cooperation isn't working? Mya fantasized about putting a dagger between his eyes to quell his scowl. *Do it!* the voice of her temper screamed in her mind. *He deserves it! You could do it! You could kill them all before any of them could stop you! Then you'd be safe! Then it wouldn't matter if Lad left you. You'd be safe!*

Mya's fingers twitched, itching for her dagger. She clenched her fist in frustration. It wasn't true. She *could* kill them, but it wouldn't make her safe. As the only surviving master, it would only precipitate her promotion to guildmaster. And it wouldn't make up for losing Lad.

"It's no mystery why we don't cooperate," Patrice said. "None of us has all the resources we need to function properly, we don't trust each other, and we won't share power."

"When Saliez was guildmaster, we exchanged expertise much more readily." Neera shot a significant glance at Mya that raised the Master Hunter's hackles.

Feigning indifference, she shrugged. "I've always been willing to cooperate. If you remember, I was the one who suggested we could function without a guildmaster. My Hunters are always available to you, if you just agree to my terms…"

"Your terms!" Youtrin sneered. "How are my people supposed to enforce compliance without violence? All your crap about *public opinion!*"

He deserves a knife in the brain, too.

"We need a new leader!"

Horice's pronouncement caught Mya's attention quicker than the sound of a sword being drawn would have. Panic threatened again, and she turned an incredulous gaze on her peers.

"Does any one of you *really* want to work under another Saliez? The man was a nightmare!"

"He made *you* Master Hunter!" Patrice shot back, her full lips set in a tight pucker.

"Right after he allowed Master Targus to be killed when he could have prevented his death with a single word! He murdered him on a *whim*! He killed his own valet right in front of me, for the gods' sake!"

"He had…strange predilections, but—"

"The man was a sadistic freak! Did any of you see the torture chamber beneath that keep of his? I did. I felt his blades part my flesh for no reason other than to lay me out as bait for a trap!"

The masters stared at her in shock. They undoubtedly had knowledge of Saliez's perversions, but apparently no personal experience. *Lucky you*, she thought as she looked around from face to face. Mya caught a spasm of sympathy on the face of Horice's bodyguard. She thought it curious until she remembered that Sereth, too, had worked directly with Saliez. *He knows…*

"None of us is Saliez," Neera countered.

"Power can change people, Neera." *Gods know it's changed me.* Mya could easily see how the woman could become another Saliez. Her elixirs had made her aged yet ageless, as Saliez's runic tattoos had done, and cruelty aplenty lurked behind the woman's ancient eyes. "I don't relish the thought of calling *you* Grandmother."

"I did *not* suggest that I take the Grandfather's place, Mya, I merely—"

"Neera, Mya, please." Patrice's calm tone snapped Neera's ire like a shorn thread, which caught Mya off guard. The Master

Alchemist did not usually back down so readily. "This bickering is getting us nowhere, and is the *exact* reason why cooperation is an unviable strategy. We lack leadership. We need a guildmaster, but who it will be is academic until we forge a new ring. I move that we use combined funds to do so at our earliest convenience."

"Seconded," Youtrin said triumphantly.

A warm hand gripped Mya's shoulder, and Lad's breath brushed her ear. "I need to speak to you! Now!"

Mya tensed at his touch, then immediately became wary. Why would Lad interrupt in the middle of this catastrophe? Some threat to her life? She scanned the room and saw nothing. Four masters, each with a bodyguard, so eight people who could oppose them. Not a problem; she and Lad could kill them all in a heartbeat. Wary of hidden assailants outside the room, she cocked her head to listen. No creaking boards, shuffling feet, sounds of breathing, creaking leather... Nothing...

"Be quiet, Lad. We'll talk later."

His grip tightened on her shoulder. "It's *important*, Mya!"

"I said *later*! Now shut up!" As he took his hand away, she felt a tremble...his or hers, she couldn't tell. A chill fell over her that wasn't entirely due to this new insistence on a guildmaster. *What could frighten Lad?* She couldn't deal with that right now; larger issues were in play.

Adopting a conciliatory tone, she turned to the others. "Forging a new ring is an unnecessary expense if we choose to remain our own masters."

"A motion has been put forth and seconded. A vote is called for."

"Not without discussion!" Mya looked at the hard faces staring at her. Any one of them could become like Saliez, and she would be at their mercy. She could *not* allow them to make her a slave.

Never again!

But how could she persuade them?

204

Cooperation... This was Lad's fault. He had pushed her to make the guild less violent, which had led to her falling out with the other masters. From there the situation had spiraled ever downwards. Cold anger replaced hot panic as she forcefully ordered her thoughts. *With Lad leaving, I can do as I damned well please. To hell with a less brutal Assassins Guild. To hell with Lad and his high ideals. To hell with everything that doesn't get me what I want!* With new resolve and a controlled voice, she put forth her proposal.

"Our problem stems *not* from a lack of leadership, but from a lack of cooperation. I agree that much of it is my fault. My Hunters have more diverse skills, so I've enjoyed relative success, and haven't fully recognized the adverse impact on the rest of you."

Eyebrows raised around the table. This was a Mya they had never met. But she wasn't done yet.

"To show my willingness to cooperate, I'll offer *each* of you the services of one of my senior journeymen and all those under them to use as you see fit, with no preconditions and no cost."

"Even if I use them to enforce my protection racket?" Youtrin asked, his expression disbelieving. "What about your terms?"

"Forget my terms. Use them however you wish! Dress them up as doxies and parade them into the Duke's Palace for all I care."

"What do you want for this new-found cooperation?" Horice's suspicion was thick enough to spread on toast.

"What do I *want*?" Mya gave him a short, hard laugh. "I've already *told* you. It's not what I want, it's what I *don't* want, and that is someone leering over my shoulder and dictating my every move. We were slaves under Saliez. We're free now. Do you want to forge your own gold and obsidian shackles and hand them over to a new master? I *don't*!"

"We're all subservient to the Grandmaster," Patrice reminded her, biting her lip in consternation.

"But he's not *here*!" Mya punctuated her statement with a finger to the table top, hitting it harder than she intended. "He doesn't meddle in our day-to-day affairs like a guildmaster would."

Silence reigned for a long moment, and Mya was encouraged by the considered looks on the masters' faces. *This can work*! she exulted as she realized that the plan might solve more than one problem. *I can write to the Grandmaster that there's no need for a new guildmaster, that with our new approach to cooperation, we'll be even more profitable than we were under Saliez.*

"Would you change your mind if we promised to support *your* bid for guildmaster?"

"What?" Mya stared at Patrice in shock. *Where the hells did that come from?*

"I said, would you change your mind if we promised to back you for guildmaster?" The Master Inquisitor glanced around the table. "You're the most successful among us. You must be doing something right."

Mya's eyes raked the room as dread surged up from her gut. Not one of the other masters met Patrice's suggestion with the scorn she'd expected. *They've tried to kill me! Why would they now support me?* But there it was, the chance to take the power for herself...

Godsdamned guildmaster...

First the Grandmaster, now the rest of the Twailin masters. It seemed her destiny to become guildmaster. A younger Mya would have rejoiced, but now she just saw it as a trap pulling her deeper into slavery. There would always be someone in charge, someone ready to spend her life on a whim. The higher the position, the worse that someone would be.

"No."

Confusion and shock swept around the table, as she'd expected, and she tried to explain.

206

"I don't *want* to be guildmaster, because that would be the same as appointing one of *you* guildmaster. It would make me a slave again, answering directly to the Grandmaster, subject to his every whim and command. I won't live like that again."

"That ring," Horice nodded to the circle of obsidian on her finger, "means you have responsibilities to this guild. If you didn't want that responsibility, you shouldn't have put it on."

"I didn't have a *choice!*" Mya protested, but she could see she had lost the argument. She had given them all she could. *Why are they so insistent about electing a guildmaster?*

If they chose to forge a new ring, they would be in for a big surprise, because she would ride to the Nine Hells on a flaming horse before she would let one of them become her master. If it came down to the last resort—become guildmaster or suffer under the lash of one of these four—she would choose the lesser of two evils and take the position. She found herself wishing she hadn't burned the Grandmaster's letter. None of them would have argued with the Grandmaster's edict.

"A motion has been put forth," Neera announced. "All those in favor of forging a new guildmaster's ring?"

Neera and Horice immediately raised their hands.

"Opposed?"

Mya raised her hand, and for a long moment no other mirrored her action. She stabbed Youtrin and Patrice with her eyes, all but pleading for their support. Slowly, the Master Inquisitor also raised her hand.

"Youtrin?" Neera's voice virtually dripped acid.

Mya tensed; Youtrin could swing the vote either way.

"I—"

"Youtrin!" Mya fixed her eyes on the man and leaned in earnestly. "I don't *care* what you think about me, and I don't care about what you've done to oppose me. Just think about whether you want to be a slave, or your own master."

A thin smile crossed the Master Enforcer's lips, but something else registered in his eyes. She could hear his heart racing in his chest, smell the sweat beading on his brow.

He's afraid of me! she realized. *Or more likely, afraid of Lad.* She flicked a glance over her shoulder toward her bodyguard, then looked back at Youtrin.

"I abstain."

Mya allowed herself to breathe.

Neera's sandpaper voice broke the moment of silence.

"The motion fails in a deadlock, so we are left with the only other option. We must cooperate. Master Hunter Mya has pledged her Hunters to aid our endeavors with no preconditions and at no cost. What additional matters can be addressed with shifts of manpower?"

Her tension finally easing, Mya sat back and let them haggle over manpower and resources. Though it had cost her dearly, she had won the battle.

"What in all Nine Hells was *that* about?" Neera snapped, glaring at Youtrin and Patrice. Mya had left the meeting, and their failed plan hung like a pall over the four masters. "We were *supposed* to vote to forge a new ring!"

"She would have killed us." Youtrin snatched up one of the bottles that his steward had just brought in and pulled the cork. The wine sloshed onto the table as he filled his glass. "I could see it in her eyes. If I'd voted against her, she would have told that *weapon* of hers to cut our throats!" He quaffed the glass of wine as if it were cheap ale. "Hells, she could have slit my throat *herself*, and I couldn't have done a damn thing to stop her!"

And what would I have done if Mya and her weapon had attacked the masters? Sereth wondered. *Would I die trying to protect Horice, knowing that I'd fail?* Personally, he had found

208

Mya's argument accurate and persuasive. Having worked directly under the Grandfather, Sereth knew better than most what a maniac the man had been. He was best gone. *Maybe she would make a good guildmaster.* And the weapon—*Lad*, he thought—intrigued him. Lad was always around, but such an enigma, always calm, collected, and quiet, but intense in a manner hard to identify. *Why the hells does Hensen care so much about those two?*

"You're *afraid* of her." Neera's voice dripped with scorn.

"Godsdamned right, I am, and you would be, too, if you had half a brain!" Youtrin cast aside his wineglass, and it shattered against the wall.

"And what about you?" Neera turned her gaze to Patrice, unfazed by Youtrin's temper. "Did you vote with her out of fear, too?"

"No." Patrice filled her own glass and sipped, her face contemplative. "I voted with her because I was paying attention."

"Paying attention?" Neera's eyes widened. "Paying attention to *what*?"

"To the discourse between Mya and her weapon, Neera."

What? Sereth tried to recall what they said to each other. *Lad told Mya he needed to speak to her, and she told him to shut up. Was there more?*

"What are you talking about? They barely said three words to each other!"

"More than twenty, actually, but I won't quibble about the number. The point is, Neera, I think I've discovered a chink in Mya's armor." Patrice sipped her wine and smiled like a cat that had just eaten a piece of raw meat.

"What chink?" Horice asked.

"The weapon disobeyed her," Patrice said.

"What?" Neera lurched forward in her seat. "When?"

"Didn't you see when he interrupted her?"

209

"Interruption is independent action, not disobedience," Neera argued.

"Correct, but after his initial interruption, Mya told him to be quiet. That was a direct command. But then he interrupted her *again*!"

"He did!" Horice slapped the table with his palm, rattling the glasses. "Ha! Mya's little weapon isn't as obedient as we were led to believe!"

"So what? He still does her bidding. He's still godsdamned untouchable." Youtrin had found another glass and was well into the second bottle of wine.

"If he can disobey, he is not what we thought him to be." Sereth could see the machinations whirling behind Neera's sharp eyes. "If he can disobey, what else can he do? What else *could* he do?"

"He hasn't signed a blood contract!" Horice slapped the table again. "He could kill Mya!"

"Once again, so what? Where does this get us? Are you suggesting we walk up to him and say, 'Hey, we want you to kill your boss.'"

Neera levied an exasperated sneer at the Master Enforcer. "It may get us nowhere, Youtrin, but it's at least it's an avenue to follow, considering that our plan to convince her to destroy the ring has failed. It may provide us the opportunity to strike from within Mya's shield. We need to find out more about that weapon. Where does he go when he's not with Mya? Who does he live with?"

"None of those I've assigned to follow him have been able to keep up, let alone discover where he goes at night."

"We found him before," Youtrin shrugged his massive shoulders, "we can find him again."

"Mya found him."

"No, she didn't. One of my enforcers, Jingles Jarred, stumbled upon him by accident when the Grandfather had Mya coordinating the search for him. Jingles was following up on a protection racket blunder; one of my thugs and a few of his men had gone missing. Jingles was assigned to the retrieval team, too."

"Where?" Horice looked over his shoulder to Sereth. "You were assigned to work for Mya during that search, weren't you?"

"Yes, Master, but I wasn't in on the operation to retrieve the weapon. It was at an inn in Eastmarket. I don't know which one."

"Surely he wouldn't be stupid enough to go back to the same place." Patrice scowled at the notion.

"Find out the name of that inn from Jarred, and let's send some people into the area. Patrice, use your inquisitors; they blend in. Let's cast out a net and see what we catch." Neera rose from her chair in one fluid motion. The excitement of this new discovery had melted years away from her.

"And if we find him?" Youtrin asked.

"We look for a weakness. Something we can use. If her control over him is not complete, we may be able to exploit him for our own purposes. My fellow masters, we may win this one yet!"

Sereth grimaced when he realized that another trip to Hensen was in store. Whatever the man's interest in Lad and Mya was, this new development would certainly intrigue him.

CHAPTER XVII

Belief flushed through Lad as they stepped out of Youtrin's warehouse into the late-afternoon sunlight. The crisis had been averted. Mya had convinced the masters that cooperation was better than forging a new ring. Despite the concessions she had to make, it eased his mind to know that they had accepted her back into their ranks. It was unlikely now that a new security contingent would have to fight off any more assassination attempts.

Mya strode up the street, fast and silent, still angry at him, he assumed. But once they were out of sight of the warehouse, she whirled, grabbed his arm hard enough to hurt, and jerked him to a stop.

"Now! What's so damned important that you had to interrupt me in the middle of that catfight?"

I've got to tell her, he realized. *She needs to know the truth.*

"We have to talk, Mya, but not here. Every dock worker and teamster around here works for Youtrin." What he had to say to her could not be overheard by anyone in the guild.

Grudgingly, she released his arm and turned away. "Follow me."

She led him to the *Ebony Urn*, a little blackbrew shop on River Way. This late in the day, the place was virtually empty. Mya strode in and waved to the serving girl polishing the colorful tile table tops.

"Two brews and a nut pastry, please." Mya continued to the back of the place and picked the corner booth. She surprised him by claiming the corner seat, leaving Lad to sit with his back to the room. He couldn't watch for danger sitting like that. At his questioning glance, she said, "I've got to start looking out for myself now, don't I?"

Lad's eyes flicked around the café before he sat down. There appeared to be no threats here, but sitting with his back exposed to the open space instantly had his nerves singing like violin strings. He took a deep calming breath and said "You did a good job convincing them not to forge a new ring, Mya."

"What the hells did you *think* I was going to do?" Mya paused as the waitress arrived with two steaming mugs of blackbrew, sugar, cream, and her pastry. When the woman was out of earshot, she continued. "You *know* I don't want a new guildmaster. And it cost me almost a third of my Hunters to get them to back off. Who knows what it'll cost next time. But what do you care? You're *leaving*."

"Mya, you don't understand. They can *never* create a new guildmaster's ring. A new ring *cannot* be made! It's impossible!"

"What? What do you mean 'impossible'?" Suspicion narrowed her eyes. "The only reason a new ring couldn't be made is if—" Mya's face blanched, "—the old one wasn't destroyed!" Pushing her cup away, she leaned across the table, her voice a bare whisper, shaking with dread. "Where is it?"

"Safe."

"Bullshit!" She snatched his wrist so quickly that it actually surprised him. Her grip, no doubt panic-induced, pinched into his flesh. "Bring it to me, Lad!"

He pried her fingers from his arm. "No, Mya! I can't."

"Why the hells not? I *need* that ring!"

"You can't have it. But don't worry. When I leave Twailin, I'll go where they'll never find me, and you can rightfully claim ignorance, both of what I did and where I've gone. They saw you order me to destroy it. It's not your fault that I kept it instead. If they want proof, you can show them you don't wear it."

"They'll still think I'm behind it, Lad! For five years we've kept up the pretense that you're under magical control, that you can't disobey my orders. Even my *own* people believe that! In their minds, if the ring still exists, I must have ordered you not to destroy it. If you're gone, then I must have ordered you to take the ring away. They'll go to the Grandmaster, and if I can't produce a guildmaster's ring, I'm dead!"

Lad started to protest, then the accusation hit home. He'd always faulted Mya for her deceptions, and prided himself on keeping his word, but now their roles were reversed. He'd deceived her; she had trusted him to destroy the ring, and he hadn't. His caution, his attempt to protect himself, was coming back to haunt him. Now he *couldn't* give her the ring, and for his mistake, Mya would die.

"Give me the ring, Lad! You've *got* to!"

"I *can't.*"

Mya leveled a trembling finger at him. "You're not leaving until I get that ring. If you try, I'll have my Hunters follow you to the ends of the earth."

Lad's ire rose at her threat. "Good *luck* with that! None of the others have been able to follow me."

Her face fell like he'd slapped her. "What others? Who's following you?"

Mya's sudden confusion was so open it took Lad aback.

"People try to follow me almost every night when I leave the *Cockerel.* I assumed at least some of them were your Hunters, that you sent them as part of their training. That's why I thought, last night..." His voice trailed off as she shook her head. There were no tells here, no evasions or lies.

"I haven't told anyone to follow you, Lad. Why would I?" She narrowed her eyes again, and he could see her thoughts

hris A. Jackson

buzzing like a nest of hornets. "Something's wrong with this. There are more players in this game than seems possible."

"Who?"

"I have no idea, but since you're going to stick around until you decide to give me that ring, we've got plenty of time to find out." Mya's hand shook as she ripped off a bite from the pastry and washed it down with a great swallow of blackbrew. "Now, tell me every detail about last night's assassination attempt, right down to the color of the woman's dress."

Lad began his recitation, but his mind drifted. He knew Mya was right; even if he managed to elude her Hunters, they would find his family. In order to buy their freedom, there was a choice to be made, but he was not the person who had to make it.

𝒽𝔍𝓏◦𝓏𝓎𝓀

This is stupid, Jingles thought, scratching at the chafed spot under his arm. The hauberk he wore as part of his disguise— *Damn that inquisitor and her disguises to the Nine Hells*—was too large, and the iron cap on his head weighed a ton. His feet were already sore from only two hours of walking on the cobble streets, and his legs ached. The only good thing about wearing a City Guard uniform was the utter invisibility it offered; nobody glanced twice at a guardsman, and walking the same four blocks for hours drew no attention whatsoever. Unfortunately, he was likely to continue walking for many more hours before he slept. All because those fool masters thought there was a chance that Mya's weapon still haunted the same inn where they caught him the first time.

Nobody's that stupid. The first rule is never go back to the scene of the crime. But I've got to waste an entire night and get blisters on my feet just to prove it to the bosses!

Being summoned to an *emergency* meeting with all four masters on his night off hadn't helped his mood. The messenger hadn't even given him a chance to finish his supper. Youtrin's warehouse had teemed with more activity than a kicked ant's nest. They'd dressed him up like a city guardsman and sent him out on this wild-goose chase. He wasn't the only assassin out combing the streets, of course, but the thought didn't give him much comfort.

Jingles made his turn and started back down the street, his thumbs in his sword belt, his practiced stride casual and unfeignedly bored. He didn't know why real guardsmen did it, walking the same streets hour after hour, day after day, risking their lives for the pittance that the duke paid.

No wonder they're so easily bribed.

It was getting dark, and a lamplighter was working his way up the hill, his long, double-crooked pole over his shoulder. Jingles sauntered on, watching the poor sap stop at each lamp post, lift the tiny door with a practiced twist of his pole, light the wick inside, then close the door with another twist. In the morning he would walk the same route, extinguishing the lamps he'd lit only hours before. That job looked even more boring than a guardsman's.

The man tipped his hat in passing. "Merciful dry, ay?"

"Pray it lasts," Jingles agreed. The only thing that would make this drudgery less pleasant was rain. He passed the *Tap and Kettle's* gated yard for what felt like the thousandth time, and glanced inside. The stableman was at the barn door unharnessing a team from a merchant's wagon, while the merchant was being ushered through the open inn door. The golden glow of hearth and lamp looked all too inviting.

Perhaps I could stop in for supper, Jingles thought, continuing his stroll. *I am supposed to watch the place, and the chances of Mya's weapon showing up here are about the same as the Emperor of Tsing dropping by for tea and cakes!*

"Good evening, sir."

"Evening," Jingles said, reflexively touching the rim of his iron cap to the lanky young man passing by.

216

Bright hazel eyes met his for a heartbeat that seemed to last forever.

Gods, it's him!

Jingles was no inquisitor, no spy, but he had the presence of mind to keep his face blank and his gait relaxed. The weapon's physical appearance had changed—he was heavier, more muscled, with longer hair and better clothes—but his eyes, like twin chips of amber, had not.

Just keep walking! Don't look back! Look back, and you're dead!

A dozen strides later, he did glance back. The street was empty. The weapon must have gone through the inn's gates.

"Well, I'll be damned." Jingles increased his pace as he rounded a corner. If he got back to the South Docks District quickly, he might even get supper tonight.

✶⅃⅁℈⅃ℒ⅂ℌ

"So, we've decided to leave." Wiggen clutched Lad's hand and blinked back the tears as they faced the shocked faces of her family. Keeping the secret of their decision from her family all day had been one of the hardest things she'd ever done. Lad had come home early, but they had been busy with the dinner rush, and she'd had to wait even longer. Now, after stammering through a recitation of the events that had led to their decision, it seemed that everyone felt as badly as she did. Tears trickled down Josie's cheeks, and Forbish frowned so hard that his first chin receded into his second. Tika and Ponce were more vocal in their disapproval.

"You *can't* leave, Lad!"

"You're not done training us yet!"

"You promise to teach us that trick with the dagger!"

"Where will you go?"

"How will you live?"

217

"Hush, you two!" Josie sniffed and glared at the twins. "You'll wake the guests. And weren't you listening? They can't tell us where they're going. It'd be too dangerous, for them *and* us."

"Josie's right, I'm afraid." Lad gave the twins an encouraging smile. "We're not leaving quite yet. I can show you the dagger trick."

"Why delay?" Forbish asked, taking Josie's hand in his and giving it a comforting pat. "If there's danger, why not leave right now?"

Wiggen glanced at Lad. He'd been oddly reticent when he'd told her that they couldn't leave immediately. He had to help Mya get settled with new bodyguards, he'd claimed, but...there was something he wasn't saying. Usually so forthcoming, Lad had avoided her eyes, and several times she had turned to find him staring at her with a disconcerting expression. *It's something to do with Mya*, she thought, suspicious as always of the woman's motives.

"Lad has some things to wrap up before we go, but it shouldn't take long." She gave them a smile that she hoped looked more confident than it felt. "Don't worry. We'll be fine. We've saved every bit of money Lad's earned over the last five years. We've got plenty to open an inn of our own somewhere."

"Somewhere quiet, where Lissa can grow up safe." Lad's hopeful whisper eased her aching heart, and Wiggen squeezed his hand.

"But what about us?" Tika argued.

"Yeah. What are we going to do without you two?"

"We'll be able to contact you eventually," Wiggen promised. "Once things settle down, maybe in a year or so."

"A year?"

"That's forever!"

"Quiet, now. This is for the best." Forbish released Josie's hand and stepped forward to embrace his daughter. His thick arms felt good around her shoulders, comforting and safe.

218

Wiggen wished such a simple thing could really make her safe, but she knew better.

"I'm sorry, Father." She pressed her face into his shoulder, willing herself not to cry.

"Don't be sorry, Wiggen. Just find someplace safe."

If any safe place exists in this world. Wiggen wished desperately that there was another answer, but her heart belonged with Lad, and if he had to leave, then she and Lissa would leave with him. She just never thought that doing the right thing would make everyone she loved so miserable.

CHAPTER XVIII

"So, you've got your assignments." Mya checked the names of her four best senior journeymen off her list as she recapped their orders. "Kara, report to Neera at her estate in Barleycorn Heights. Simi, you're going to the Docks District to help Youtrin. Vic, you're with Patrice. I assume you know where her brothel is in West Crescent." That got a chuckle. "And lastly, Pictor, you've got Horice. His townhouse is in Eastmarket, near the river, but he works out of that armory on Ironmonger Street." She looked up at them. "And you all know what to look for."

"Yes, Miss Mya." Pictor was senior among them, and technically her second, though they had never gotten along very well. Ten years her senior, he obviously felt that he should be Master Hunter. He was good at his job, however, and loyal. "A thug with broken fingers on both hands, and anyone who's expert with a blowgun and poison."

"Right. Other than finding these two people, I don't want you to poke your noses into the other masters' business at all. You do as you're told, when and how you're told to do it. You all know your jobs. I'm relying on you to do them without having to come back to me for help, but if you or any of your people feel threatened, you let me know. Got it?"

"Yes, Miss Mya," they answered.

"All right. Report to the other masters first thing in the morning, and give them my regards. Go." She watched them file out. The loss of so many of her people, even temporarily, made her feel as exposed as a bug on a white tablecloth. Shaking off the uncomfortable sensation, she glared down at her empty blackbrew cup. She lifted the pot, but it was empty, too. "Gods, what time is it? Mika!"

The hulking door guard ducked in amidst the noise of the drinking and gaming patrons down the hall. "Yes, Miss?"

"How late is it?"

"Near midnight, I think, Miss."

"Where the hells is Dee?"

"Dunno, Miss. Want me to get him?"

"Have Paxal fetch him. And have him bring me another pot of blackbrew as well."

"Yes, Miss."

The door closed, and Mya blinked her tired eyes before returning to the papers in front of her. She pored over her lists, checking off items and circling others. She'd been over everything three times already, but directing her energy toward work calmed her nerves. After her discussion with Lad, she had sent him home early, still so angry that she had to fight the urge to slap him for being such an idiot.

He kept the godsdamned ring. He kept it for himself!

They'd gone over the details of Lad's stalkers, the assassination attempt, and the masters' meeting. Lad had mentioned Norwood's investigation, but Mya had managed to switch the subject. *She* knew Vonlith's death wasn't relevant to the rest of these baffling goings-on, and didn't want Lad digging into it any further than he apparently already had.

Damn it, Mya! Why did you have to kill him? He already had your money, for the gods' sake! He wasn't going to brag to his cronies about how he'd tattooed the Master Hunter of the Assassins Guild with magical runes. But she knew why she had done it. The reason was the same one it had always been.

Fear.

221

Vonlith had given her the magic, and as he had when Lad fought Saliez, he could take it away. Though it had only been a temporary suspension of the runes' powers, it had been enough to allow Lad to kill the Grandfather, and could be enough to allow someone to kill her. She would not tolerate anyone holding that kind of threat over her head.

The door opened without a knock. She knew instantly from the look on Paxal's face that something was wrong.

"What?"

"We've got a problem, Miss."

"With what?"

"Well, with Dee, but I think you'll want to see this."

"Dee?" She was up and around the table in a flash. "What's wrong with Dee? Is he all right?"

"Easier if you just come see, Miss Mya." He waved her through the door. Mika fell in behind them. "Third floor, south wing, third door on the left."

"I know." In fact, it was her old room.

Mya took the stairs two at a time with Mika close behind. Paxal was still one floor below, ascending as quickly as his old legs could climb, when she reached the third-floor landing. One glance down the hall told her something dire had occurred. Two of her Hunters guarded Dee's door with their hands on their weapons, their faces like stone. She forced herself to approach slowly, quelling the desire to burst in and find out what was wrong.

"Where's Dee?"

"Inside, Miss Mya." The guards stepped aside.

The smell of vomit and urine hit her as she opened the door. Dee sat nude on the edge of the bed. He didn't even look up when Mya walked in. His eyes never left the dead woman on the floor.

The barmaid, Moirin, lay equally nude in a contorted position near Dee's desk, a rumpled dress clutched in one hand. A pool of vomit stained the rug near her mouth, and a dark puddle of moisture attested to the fact that she had voided her bladder when she died. Red contusions encircled her throat like a necklace.

"I found them like this, Miss Mya."

Paxal stood behind her, breathing hard. Nodding, she drew her eyes from the spectacle of Moirin's body to see that the floor beyond the desk was strewn with letters. *Her* letters.

"Gods*damn*it!" Mya stepped around the corpse and peered down at one of the letters. It was addressed to her and still sealed, but other letters, already opened, along with reports and Dee's notes from their conversations, lay scattered about. Atop the desk, the metal coffer where Dee kept her correspondence sat with its lid open.

Mya's skin tingled with a sudden flood of anger, an urge to lash out surging through her. Now of all times, with the wolves at her door, something like this? *Dee,* she thought murderously, *what the hells have you done?*

Whirling toward the bed, she took in his frozen gaze, the saliva trailing from the corner of his mouth. Reaching for a dagger, she stepped toward the bed...and stopped. *No!* She clenched her fists and took a deep breath, forcing her heart to slow and her thoughts to calm. No, she couldn't kill Dee; that was something the Grandfather would have done. She was *not* the Grandfather. What she really needed from Dee was information.

"Dee? What happened here?"

Only a shallow sigh and a fleeting grimace told Mya that he had heard her. His blank stare, not to mention the fact that he hadn't even tried to cover himself, left her wondering if he was spelled, poisoned, or if his wits had simply fled.

Slowly she walked around the bed, examining every detail: clothing tossed aside, Dee's daggers on one night table, a bottle of wine and two glasses on the other. She sniffed each glass. Even her enhanced senses couldn't tell the two apart, but the heady aroma of the red wine would mask the odor of a subtle poison or potion. She sniffed the bottle, too, but learned nothing new. She walked back to face her assistant.

"Dee? I need you to answer me. What happened here?"

"I'm...sorry," he whispered.

"Sorry?" *You* will *be sorry*, she thought, then bit back her temper again. "Sorry for what, Dee? What happened?"

"She's...dead." He blinked and his face contorted into a mien of pain and regret.

"I see that she's dead, Dee. What happened? Did you kill her?"

"I...don't know." He swallowed and blinked again. "I didn't mean for her to die. She...she..." His voice trailed off to nothing.

"Damn it, Dee, I need to know what *happened* here!"

He didn't respond.

I don't have time for this shit! she thought. *I won't kill him, but a little righteous fury might knock some sense back into him.*

Mya whirled to the door and made a shooing motion. "Out! Everyone." Paxal opened his mouth to protest, but she silenced him with a glare. "I need to know what happened here, Pax, and I don't have time to screw around. Out!"

They all retreated. She closed and bolted the door.

Two long strides took her to the bed, and her open palm left a handprint on the side of Dee's face. She'd been careful with the blow; hard enough to get his attention, but not hard enough to break his neck. His head snapped around with the impact, but at least it diverted his attention from Moirin's corpse.

"Get up!"

An instant of panic registered in his eyes. "Mya! I..." He fumbled off the bed, clutching at the sheet to cover himself. "I'm sorry, Miss! I..." His eyes drifted toward Moirin's corpse, but Mya brought his attention back to her with another slap, not as hard as the first, but lightning quick.

"Look at me, not that whore!"

Dee stiffened and glared at her, his lip curling in a sneer. For a moment Mya thought he might strike her. Then she noticed his fingers twitching futilely on the sheet clutched in his hands. He *couldn't* strike her, couldn't even attempt to, preempted by the magic of the master's ring on her finger. That power, that feeling of utter dominance over someone else, made her want to vomit. She bit back the visceral reflex and focused on her assistant.

Dee might be angry with her, but he was more cognizant of what was going on. He was trembling now, and fear shone in his eyes; he knew that Mya could have him executed for allowing such a breach of security. Fortunately for Dee, she needed information more than she needed to see him dead.

"Tell me what happened here, Dee. How did she die?"

"I... Yes, Miss Mya. She took poison, I think."

"Poison? What do you mean? When?"

"When I caught her looking at your letters."

"Start from the beginning, Dee." Mya lowered her voice, trying to remain calm. If Moirin had been looking at her letters... "What happened?"

"We...um...have been seeing each other for some time, Miss Mya. She works...worked here. Her name was Moirin."

"Okay, that's a start. I know who she was and that you've been seeing her. There's no problem there. What happened this evening?"

"Well, she came up after her shift, when I was waiting for you to call for me." He looked suddenly embarrassed, and clutched the blanket a little closer. "We...um...had a little romp, then a glass of wine. I guess I fell asleep. When I woke, I saw her by the desk, peering down at your letters." He swallowed and cleared his throat. "I'd locked them up like always in that double-lock iron box you gave me, and the keys were still on the chain around my neck, but the box was open. I asked her what she was doing, and she jumped like she'd been stuck with a pin."

"I imagine she did. You caught her spying."

"Yes, Miss Mya. I jumped up and grabbed her wrist, and that magnifier fell to the floor." He pointed to a small glass disk not far from the woman's outstretched hand. "I picked it up and... Well, if you have a look through it at one of the letters, you'll know what I mean."

Mya retrieved the glass and held it at arms-length over a sealed envelope. Every word of the letter within sprang to clarity in the lens.

"Magic! She was reading my letters!" *The grandmaster's letter!* she realized with a flash of horror. *Gods, if she worked for one of the other masters... Horice? Is that why he tried to have me killed?* She thought back, but the timing seemed wrong. *Then who?*

"Yes, Mistress. I figured that as soon as I looked through the glass. Then I got angry. I...grabbed her by the throat." Dee's voice choked up and he blinked rapidly, shifting his gaze to the floor.

Mya followed his glance and took a closer look at the body. Under the stench of vomit and urine, she could detect the faint musk of the intimacy they'd shared. Dee, it seemed, had actually fallen for this woman. To discover that she was using him to spy, that she had betrayed him, then her suicide... Mya clenched her teeth against the sympathy that welled up from her gut.

"Go on, Dee. How did she die?"

"She wouldn't tell me who put her up to it, so I figured I'd bring her to you." His shoulders slumped, and he pointed to the crumpled dress. "I told her to get dressed, but she pulled something from a pocket and put it in her mouth. Then she fell and started shaking all over, like she was having some kind of fit. Before I could try to help her, she was dead."

"Gods*damn*it!" Mya began to pace, trying to think of all the correspondence that had passed over Dee's desk in recent weeks that could incriminate or condemn her. If this woman was a spy for the Royal Guard, she might as well walk up to Duke Mir and confess her sins. If she worked for one of the other Assassins

226

Guild masters, she might as well slit her own throat. But there was no way to know who Moirin had been working for. Unless...

"I'm sorry, Miss Mya."

"Sorry?" Mya stopped and glared at him. "You'll be more than *sorry* if you don't stop sniveling about a dead *spy* and put your head together, Dee! The only reason you're not just as dead as your former girlfriend is because I need your help."

"My help?"

"Yes, Dee, your help!" She recovered his trousers from beside the bed and flung them at him. "Now get dressed and start *thinking*, for the gods' sake! Neither of us is going to sleep until I know every bit of correspondence that passed through your hands since you've been seeing Moirin. Everything! You understand?"

"Yes, Miss Mya!" He struggled into his trousers and started collecting the fallen papers, averting his eyes as he stepped carefully over the body of the woman with whom he'd recently made love.

"You keep a log of my correspondence, don't you?"

"Of course, Miss Mya! A detailed log!"

"Good. Bring it down to my office. We've got a lot of work to do."

"Yes, Miss Mya!"

She strode to the door and flung it open. Paxal, Mika and the two Hunters stood close by; they had undoubtedly heard every word through the door.

"Blackbrew, Miss Mya?"

"You guessed it, Pax. Lots of it, and some food. I'm afraid Dee and I are in for a late night. She glanced back over her shoulder at Moirin's corpse. "We need to keep this quiet. Get rid of the body without a trace. She left immediately after her shift today, and nobody knows where she is. Got it?"

"I'll see to it myself, Miss Mya."

She looked at Paxal for a moment, realizing how much she relied on him. "And remind me to increase my own rent." She nodded to the two Hunters. "You two, help Pax, and keep this under wraps."

"Yes, Miss Mya."

"Good." She looked back again. Dee had finally managed to dress and gather his ledgers. "You ready, Dee?"

"Yes, Miss Mya."

"Come on then," she said as she looked him up and down, "and tuck in your shirt."

⸘ᘒⱦᕽᘒᘒᘓᒥ⸘

A tiny silver bell chimed next to Hensen's bed. His hand silenced it before it could ring a second time. The last thing he wanted was to disturb his bedmate; the poor fellow was simply exhausted. He pulled the cord that rang the bell on the other end to tell his assistant that he was awake, and slipped out of bed. Pulling on a robe, he shrugged the kinks out of his neck and shoulders. He was tired, but not exhausted, not by far. In fact, he felt *good*. His assistant knew to ring the bell only when something dire was afoot. Like a dog salivating at the scent of roasted meat, Hensen's nerves sang at the sound of that bell, banishing his desire for bed and sleep like nothing else.

Hensen's companion rolled over in his sleep, the white silk sheet clinging to his lithe, young body. Hensen bit his lip. *So beautiful...* He suppressed the desire to tug the sheet down just a tiny bit more, and eased away from the bed. He slipped out of his bedchamber without a sound. He was, after all, a thief at heart, if not one in practice much anymore.

Kiesha stood at the bottom of the third floor stairs, also garbed in a robe. Her tousled hair and sleepy eyes were a far cry from her tidy daytime appearance, but no less beautiful. Unfortunately, if her mien of annoyance was any indication, she didn't share his appreciation of late-night intrigue. But business was business; she wouldn't have woken him for something trivial.

"What's happened?"

"I'm sorry to wake you, sir, but Sereth is here. He insists on speaking with you personally. He wouldn't let me take a message."

"Very well. It must be important then. Lead on."

He followed her down to the first-floor parlor. Before Kiesha could open the ornate door, Hensen laid a hand on her forearm. "You disarmed him, didn't you?" A silk robe gave no protection, and all of a sudden he felt frightfully vulnerable.

Annoyance flashed in her eyes before she nodded. "Of *course*, sir."

"Of course you did. Proceed."

She swung open the door to reveal Sereth standing in the middle of the room, his boots muddying the priceless western rug. Overcoming his annoyance, Hensen ran his gaze over the spy, noting the subtle marks and creases where a sword and daggers were usually carried: at his side, in his boots, even strapped to his forearms. The man was a walking armory, and no doubt adept with every weapon he carried.

"Good evening, Sereth." Hensen strode past the spy to the sideboard and pulled out two snifters. From a crystal decanter, he poured a measure of brandy into each, then offered one to the assassin. "Here. You look like you could use a drink."

Sereth's jaw muscled tightened, his eyes narrowing at the snifter. "I didn't come here to socialize. I came here to tell you that things are coming to a head. The masters finally got Mya to attend a meeting, and forced a vote to forge a new guildmaster's ring. They hoped to scare her into destroying the old ring, rather than admit that she didn't actually have it destroyed years ago."

Hensen placed one of the snifters back onto the sideboard and swirled the other in his hand. He sniffed the heady bouquet, then sipped, letting the brandy's slow burn ease the fire of his flaring temper. When a master extended hospitality to an underling, the offer should at least be acknowledged with gratitude. He and Sereth were not friends, of course, but snubbing his act of generosity was blatantly rude. The slight made him angry, and when Hensen was angry, he was petulant.

"That's it? You woke me for *that*?"

"You *told* me to report immediately on any plots against Mya or her weapon. And no, that's *not* all. The masters offered to support Mya's bid for guildmaster, but she turned them down."

"She turned it down?" Sereth might be insubordinate, but his information was too intriguing to ignore. *The Grandmaster offers her the position of guildmaster, her fellow masters say they'll support her, and she still turns it down?* What sort of woman was she? Everything she did surprised him, which of course, made her interesting. "Did she say why?"

"She's convinced that appointing a new guildmaster would make them all slaves. They held the vote, but it deadlocked. But during the discussion, Master Inquisitor Patrice noticed something; Mya gave her weapon an order, and he disobeyed. No one thought he could do that. The masters think that if he can disobey, he might be able to do more. They're looking for some way to pressure him."

Hensen silently forgave Sereth his insolence. *So, Lad is his own man. He's not unconditionally bound to Mya.* What a revelation! All kinds of benefits might be derived from this new situation; it merited careful consideration. But first, he had to keep Lad alive. "How do they intend to pressure him, and what do they intend to pressure him to do?"

"They've discovered where he lives, so they've got people looking into his personal life. As to what they want him to do; kill Mya, probably."

"Do you think he can? Surely the magic prevents him from killing his master. She's the one who captured him. She bound him to a life of slavery! If it didn't, he'd have killed her years ago."

"They don't know how the magic controls him, or what motivates his actions."

Oh, but I do! Hensen thought, remembering Master Forbish's scar-faced daughter with the plump baby on her hip. "Interesting, indeed."

"What are you going to do?"

Hensen's eyes snapped to Sereth's. Why would he think Hensen would tell him his plans? *Surely he's not playing double agent.*

Raising his snifter in a toast, he smiled and said, "I'm going to sip brandy and *think* for a while, Sereth. You ought to try it some time. Now please go. Don't worry, we'll tell your wife you send her your love."

Sereth stiffened, then whirled away. Hensen watched him wrench open the door and stomp across the hall, Kiesha hurrying after him.

Dismissing Sereth from his thoughts, he paced for a while, enjoying the brandy and the ideas rambling around in his head. Once again, the sense of danger had brought his mind to razor sharpness. He ignored Kiesha when she returned from escorting their guest out. He paced and sipped and thought, until finally his thoughts congealed into a plan. Then he turned to her and smiled.

"Orders, sir?"

"Contact our operative at the *Golden Cockerel*. See if she can discover anything else about the Master Hunter's reluctance to take the guildmaster position."

"Yes, sir."

Hensen sipped his brandy, then noticed that she was still staring at him.

"Was there something else?"

"Sir, it's not my place, but this contract concerns me. How do we protect both Mya and Lad if the other masters set them against one another?"

"Yes, that is a paradox, isn't it? Frankly, I'm not sure we can, but we must be poised to try if need be." He shrugged. "And we must be prepared to cut our losses."

"Should we send a letter to Baron Patino?"

"No." He finished his brandy. "No, we might not like the answer. Better to apologize after the fact, I think. We'll see how this plays out."

"And if it comes down to saving one or the other of them?" she asked.

That was the real question, wasn't it? Lad or Mya? *Forget Baron Patino*, Hensen thought, *which one would be more valuable to* my *plans*? Mya, from all accounts, was a brilliant strategist and competent master who would undoubtedly strengthen the Assassins Guild, whatever her position. Lad, on the other hand, was apparently more than just a weapon. Who knew what he might do if his master was killed.

Such a lovely young man…and what a thief he would make!

Hensen decided. "If Lad chooses to kill Mya, do nothing. If Mya makes an obvious attempt on Lad's life, one that you think might actually succeed, kill her. But remember, his skills far exceed hers, so don't expose yourself unnecessarily."

"Yes, sir." Kiesha paused, her features thoughtful. "And the contract?"

"If the two come into conflict, we'll explain exactly what occurred and demand half of the final payment. It only seems right, since we will have fulfilled half of the contract."

"Do you think he'll pay it?"

"No, but since he may have eyes in our own organization, honesty, in this case, seems the best policy."

An involuntary snort of laughter, quite unladylike, escaped her. "Pardon me, sir, but that's a hell of a thing to hear you say."

"Yes, well, this is a hell of a situation." He waved her away and turned back to the sideboard for another brandy. It was going to be a long, thoughtful night, and despite his slumbering companion upstairs, Hensen could not imagine going back to bed.

CHAPTER XIX

We've got to figure out who was running Moirin."

Mya fought through the cobwebs in her mind, trying to stay focused. Lack of sleep weighed heavily on her. She had spent all of last night going through records with Dee, then grilling Paxal and several of her Hunters on everything they could remember about Moirin. Unfortunately, she had learned precious little. The night before had been just as sleepless. Every time she'd closed her eyes she'd pictured Lad and Wiggen making love, so she'd trained for hours in the hope that exhaustion would bring sleep. Unfortunately, her tattooed runes kept physical exhaustion at bay, but did nothing to relieve mental fatigue. She felt like she was being held together by nothing but blackbrew and magic.

"What about Dee?" Lad asked.

"Sleeping, finally. He was fine until I started asking him about Moirin, then he started shaking and saying he was sorry. He must have really been head over heels for her. I had Paxal slip him a sleeping tonic with a shot of whiskey and post someone to watch over him. I just hope when he wakes up, he's back to normal."

"You drugged him?" Lad cast a skeptical glance, but she just shrugged. She was too tired and too grateful he was here to argue.

Much to Mya's relief, Lad had arrived at his customary mid-morning hour. She had filled him in on the night's events as they made their usual rounds to the businesses under her purview, attempting to appear as if nothing untoward had occurred. She'd been bouncing ideas off of him in hopes that his fresher outlook might induce some answers. So far, it wasn't working.

"There's got to be some kind of connection here. It can't be coincidence." She ticked items off on her fingers. "Horice mounts an attack on us that's better organized, manned, and executed than any previous one. Moirin is reading my letters and spying on me through Dee. The masters all but *hand* me a guildmaster ring on a platter. Someone tries to murder you, and someone *else* saves your life. Not to mention that people have apparently been chasing you every night for years. How does it all relate?"

"One or more of the other masters could be behind all of it, except for someone saving my life. I don't see how keeping me alive would benefit any of them." Lad squinted up at the burgeoning clouds. The rains had not yet begun, but the deluge was coming. Yesterday's sunny weather had passed. "And let's not forget Vonlith's murder."

Mya rubbed her eyes. She knew Vonlith's death had no place in the equation, and she was sick of him yammering on about it. "Forget Vonlith! It has nothing to do with this!" She brushed her hair back and tried to think.

Lad stopped dead in the street and stared at her. When he spoke, his voice was hard and cold. "What aren't you telling me?"

Mya's heart pounded, and she knew that Lad could hear it, interpret its significance. *How could he know? Did Norwood tell him something to make him suspect me?*

"What do you mean?" She could never tell Lad that truth. Her murder of the runemage could well be the last straw. He'd leave...with the ring. And despite her threats to have him followed, he could easily kill anyone she sent. The crowds ebbed and flowed around them as people hurried to complete their errands before the rain started. "We can't talk here. Come on."

Three steps on she realized he wasn't following, but standing like a statue amongst the bustling humanity. Mya had to tell him her something.

If he wants a secret, I'll give him one!

"I haven't told anyone, but..." Mya stepped close and pitched her voice as low as she could, knowing he could hear her over the commotion of the busy street. "Last week I received a letter from the Grandmaster. Moirin had to have read it. That letter may very well have started this whole thing. It was an offer, Lad. He told me to forge a new guildmaster's ring and claim it for *myself.*"

Whatever Lad was expecting to hear, that wasn't it. His eyes widened in shock. "Really?"

"Really." She rubbed her eyes again. "I burned it."

"Why?"

She glared at him for a moment. "Because I don't *want* to be guildmaster!"

"You don't?" Confusion furrowed his brow. "But it would protect you from the other masters. They couldn't touch you. You'd be safe."

Mya just stared at him. "Being guildmaster wouldn't protect me from the Grandmaster; it would put me directly under his thumb! Did you think I was blowing smoke yesterday when I turned down Patrice's offer?" Her mind reeled. Did Lad really not understand her at all? Did he think all she wanted was power? A guildmaster's ring only put her that much closer to becoming the person she had abhorred most in the world, the Grandfather.

You're already halfway there, Mya, a little voice in her mind mocked as she pictured the runes lacing her flesh.

"If Patrice was running Moirin, she might have backed you because she knew the Grandmaster already made you the offer."

Mya shook her head. *At least his mind is off Vonlith!*

"Assigning a spy like Moirin to use sex to get close to my assistant would be Patrice's style, but it doesn't fit. She didn't back me until I convinced her that I really didn't want a new guildmaster. If any of the other masters actually *knew* that the Grandmaster sent that letter, they would have blocked any notion of forging a new ring. And none of this gets us any closer to finding out who saved your life."

Lad looked thoughtful. "The Grandmaster... Why wouldn't he just tell everyone that you're the new boss?"

"I don't know." The cobwebs were reasserting themselves in Mya's brain. She wished she could just *not think* for a while, lie down and sleep.

"How long does it take to forge a guildmaster's ring?"

"A while, I guess. Weeks. Why?"

"Because until it was forged, you'd be vulnerable."

The flame of an idea burned away all the cobwebs. "That's it! The letter said to forge a new ring, and *then* show the masters the letter! He must know that we're at each other's throats. He wanted to protect me, and the best way to protect me is to protect you! Lad, you're a genius!"

"Miss Mya!"

Lad whirled to scan the surrounding crowd, buildings, and rooftops, but Mya recognized the voice, and tapped his arm. "It's all right, Lad. Just a messenger."

A girl ran up, one hand clutching her side, her breath coming in gasps. She'd obviously been running hard.

"Miss Mya! Urgent message..." She held out a folded note.

Mya glanced over the short message, and felt like she'd been kicked in the gut. *Gods, no...* She crumpled the paper and looked into Lad's pale eyes. *Not his family.*

"What, Mya?" From his tone, she knew he could see the horror on her face. "What's happened?"

"There's trouble at the *Tap and Kettle*." She watched his pupils dilate, the tiny blood vessels around his eyes pulse red. His skin flushed with sudden heat, palpable from two feet away.

"Wiggen!"

"Lad! Wait!" She may as well have tried to stop the rain that had begun to patter down on the warm cobblestones. He was already gone, dashing through the crowd faster than any human being should be able to run.

𝒩𝒥𝓎𝒹𝓏𝓎

"Forbish!"

Wiggen's hands were deep in pie dough when Josie's cry came from the common room. The urgency in her stepmother's tone brought her eyes up to her father's in a flash of worry. Forbish put down his rolling pin and gave her a tense smile.

"Probably just—"

Josie burst into the kitchen, her face red. "Trouble, Forbish. There's a bunch of bravos in the courtyard."

"By the gods, I'll—" Forbish took up his biggest cleaver, but Wiggen was already past him.

"No, Father. I'll go. Remember what Lad told us to do if something like this happened. Bolt the kitchen door and stay here." She nodded to the crib in the taproom off the kitchen where Lissa was finally napping. "Watch over Lissa. Josie, get the customers and the help upstairs, then close and bar the common room shutters."

"Be careful, Wiggen! What if they're…"

She didn't hear the rest; she was already across the common room to the front door, her heart pounding in her throat. Tika stood there, one hand holding open the heavy oak door, the other grasping the two hardwood staves that they kept propped by the coatrack. Past him, in the courtyard, she could see Ponce standing with his back to a coach. Four big men wielding swords surrounded him. Wiggen stopped short, blinded by a vision from the past: men with swords and knives, blood and screams, her brother Tam dead on these very front steps…

Not this time!

238

Chris A. Jackson

"Go, Tika! Help Ponce, then both of you get back in here. I've got the door!" Wiggin reached though the hanging cloaks to the back of the coatrack and found the sheathed dagger that hung there. Wrapping her fingers around the cold hilt, she tucked her hand and the weapon under her apron.

"Right." Tika grinned maliciously and strode across the porch, a staff grasped casually in each hand. "Is there a problem, gentlemen?"

Wiggen braced herself in the doorway and watched two of the men turn at Tika's question. The other two kept Ponce backed up against the coach at sword point. The driver of the coach stayed in his seat, hands on the reins, staring at the spectacle with wide eyes.

"Flippin' right there's a problem." The apparent leader of the men flourished his blade and squared off at the bottom of the stairs. "Unpaid taxes."

"You're the duke's tax collectors, then?" Tika stopped four steps from the bottom and planted the two staves on the step below his feet. "You don't *look* like the duke's men, and I think our taxes are all paid up."

The man just grinned at him. "No we ain't the duke's men, and you best put up those toothpicks of yours before I stick 'em where the sun don't shine."

"That sounds uncomfortable, but if you really want to try…" Tika lifted one of the staves until its tip hovered a hand's-breadth under the leader's nose. "I don't think they'll both fit up your arse, though, so you might ask one of your friends if they'd like to—"

"Why you little…" The man tried to knock the staff aside with his blade, but Tika was already moving.

The young man planted the tip of his second staff on the next step down and vaulted over the two men. Landing in a crouch, he brought both staves whistling around low behind him. The leader had quick enough reflexes to parry, but his partner did not, and the hardwood cracked against his knee.

Weapon of Blood

The instant Tika vaulted, the tips of the two swords facing Ponce dipped, the attention of their wielders drawn to the threat. Ponce dropped into a roll and lashed out with a foot, sweeping the legs of his nearest opponent out from under him. He stood just as the man's backside met the cobblestones, and one of Tika's two staves slapped into his hand. The twins turned back to back, both grinning like fiends.

"I don't think these fellows are tax collectors at all, Tika," Ponce tapped the butt of his staff against the cobblestones.

"Neither do I, Ponce." Tika tapped his own staff. "Did you have lunch?"

"Yes. Lovely meal."

"Did you have the chicken? It was delightful."

"I had the lamb. A delicious shank with rice and beans."

"Excellent! Good nutrition is so important, don't you agree?"

"I do!"

How can they joke? Wiggen knew the twins enjoyed bantering during their practice, but this was real. *Gods help them if they don't understand that.* Her hand fluttered to her scarred cheek. *Gods help us all!*

The two young men flourished their staves, and the hardwood shafts met to each side and over their heads—clack-clack-clack—too fast for Wiggen to follow.

"I'm gonna break that stick over your head, you bloody little peasant!" The leader spat and nodded to his men, who spaced themselves evenly around the twins.

"Driver," Ponce said casually, "you may want to move your coach."

"Bloody right!" The reins cracked, and the coach lurched into motion.

As one, the twins struck. Wiggen gasped; the staves seemed to vanish they moved so fast. But the four swordsmen, having been deceived once, were ready. Steel met wood, and wood parried steel in a cadence faster than the horses' hooves on stone as the coach rumbled away. The twins whirled around each other, one low, the other high, staves whistling through the air. Ponce spun under a sweeping blade stroke and lashed out a foot to trip one opponent, while Tika's staff met with another's forearm hard enough to crack bone, sending the man's sword clashing to the ground.

The swordsmen, however, were obviously not novices. One raked his blade down the length of Tika's staff to slash the young man's knuckles. Another ignored a high feint and parried low against Ponce's sweeping foot.

Wiggen gasped as blood flecked the cobblestones, her throat tightening with worry. Tika and Ponce were no strangers to fights, she knew, but she didn't think street scuffles compared with facing trained swordsmen.

"You all right, brother?" Tika asked, whirling and rolling over his sibling's bent shoulders.

"Sauce for the goose, brother!" Ponce took the opening presented by Tika's roll to bring his staff up between the legs of another opponent. With an impact that sounded like a meat tenderizer pounding steak, the swordsman crumpled.

The odds were now even, and Wiggen caught her breath. Though both Tika and Ponce had been injured, neither wound looked serious and they had cut their number of foes in half. She allowed herself a brief smile.

A shadow fell from the eaves of the porch to land right in front of her.

The man's sudden appearance caught Wiggen completely off guard. Unlike the thugs attacking Tika and Ponce, he was dressed in dark clothes, a loosely draped cloth concealing the lower half of his face. He drew forth a long, curved knife and a sap. Fear surged up from Wiggen's stomach in a nauseating wave.

A little fear is good, but you can't let it paralyze you.

Lad's lessons steadied her. This was what he had always feared, but this was also what he'd prepared them for. She

241

clutched the dagger beneath her apron so tightly that the edge of her wedding ring cut into her finger, and thought, *Please...please let this work.*

Her attacker strode forward, sap raised to strike, dagger poised...and stopped barely a foot away. His eyes widened with confusion, then panic, as if a puppet master had just pulled his strings the wrong way.

Wiggen jerked the dagger free from its sheath and thrust it forward with all her strength.

Her assailant's panic transformed to shock. A ragged wheeze escaped his cloth-covered mouth, and his eyes rolled up.

Warmth flooded over Wiggen's hand, jolting her back to sensibility. Looking down, she saw the dagger's guard pressed against her attacker's stomach just below the sternum, the blade angled up, just as Lad had taught her. The hilt twitched with the last beat of the man's heart. He slid off the blade and crumpled the porch. Wiggen stood staring at the blood-drenched dagger still tight in her grip.

"Oh, gods," she mumbled, horrified at what she had done. She wanted to throw the bloody weapon away, but she knew she had to keep it. She had to do as Lad had taught her. *Be calm. Think. Be ready!*

A quick glance to the courtyard, however, and her panic faded to relief. Ponce and Tika stood their ground, bloodied but hale, as the thugs retreated through the gate. Only one was uninjured, the other three hobbled as fast as their wounds allowed. Wiggen relaxed; it was over.

"Forbish!"

The blood-curdling scream brought her around so fast that blood from the dagger in her hand flicked in an arc across the front door. The common room was empty save for Josie, who stood by the kitchen door, her face white as a sheet.

"Father!" Wiggen dashed to the kitchen, past her stunned stepmother. The kitchen door stood open, the frame splintered.

Forbish lay on the floor, blood pooling beneath a ragged gash on his temple. She dropped the dagger and went to him.

His breathing was steady. The wound was bleeding, but not badly. Wiggen felt a brief flush of pride when she saw that the cleaver in his hand was stained red. Whoever had attacked him had received a nasty cut in return.

"Josie, get me a damp cloth." Wiggen pressed her apron to the gash to stem the flow of blood, careful not to push too hard in case the skull beneath was cracked. Forbish moaned, and his hand clenched on the haft of his cleaver.

"Here!" Josie pressed a dripping washcloth into Wiggen's hand, and she applied it to his forehead.

Forbish's eyes fluttered open. "Wha—! Wiggen! What?" His hand came up with the cleaver. "Look out, they... Two of them!"

"It's all right, Father. They're gone. We fought them off."

"Wiggen!" Josie still sounded hysterical.

"Josie, he's going to be fine!" Wiggen turned to reassure her stepmother, but Josie wasn't even standing behind her any longer. She stood in the taproom beside the crib.

"Wiggen, Lissa's gone!"

The world darkened, shadows closing in around her. Lurching up, Wiggen stumbled to the taproom. She reached the crib and grabbed hold of the edge. Inside there were only blankets and pillows. Lissa, her sweet baby girl, was gone.

The room spun around her, and her knees gave way. The shadows descended. She couldn't breathe, couldn't think. A terrible, high-pitched keening reached her ears, and before she fell into the smothering darkness, she realized it was her own voice.

CHAPTER XX

Rain fell in sheets by the time Lad arrived at the gate to the *Tap and Kettle*. His headlong sprint through the city had left a trail of astonished onlookers in his wake, but he didn't care. The only thing that mattered was getting home to Wiggen and Lissa. In the courtyard, he spied a broken sword lying on the cobblestones, but it was the sight of Tika and Ponce manhandling a canvas-wrapped bundle down the front steps that brought him up short.

"No…" He stared at the bundle, his mind reeling. "No, it can't be…"

Guilt surged through him. *Why didn't we go? Just leave, run away.* The answer seemed ridiculous. *Loyalty? To Mya?* He lurched forward.

"Who?"

"One of *them*." Tika's voice was strange, as if he was about to be sick.

"Wiggen killed him." Ponce nodded to the front door where Josie was scrubbing at bloodstains. "You should go to her, Lad."

"She's not…" *Injured, lying in a pool of blood…* He didn't wait for an answer, but sprinted up the steps, past Josie, and through the door.

The common room was empty, so he went straight to the kitchen. Inside he gaped at the incongruous scene. Beside the table strewn with flour and dough and bowls of fresh berries ready to be made into pies, Forbish sat on a stool, his white

244

apron stained red with the blood that dripped down the side of his face. Wiggen stood over him with a needle and thread, finishing the last stitch in the gash. She looked up, and Lad saw her tear-streaked cheeks, but it was her eyes that paralyzed him. Never had he seen such pain and horror in their depths, even when a thug held a knife to her throat.

"Lad!" She dropped the needle and hurled herself at him, her face contorted in agony. Her arms encircled him, and she clutched him tight with her bloody hands. "Oh gods, Lad!"

He held her gently as she sobbed into his shoulder, rocking her in his arms. She was obviously in shock. Ponce had said that Wiggen killed a man. Taking a life was a horrific experience; *she* had taught him that. "Everything's all right, Wiggen. Everyone's alive and safe."

"No! It's not!" The cry from her throat was more animal than human. "They took her!"

Grasping her shoulders, he thrust Wiggen to arm's-length. "*What*?"

"Lissa! They took her!"

A visceral agony tore through Lad, worse than any physical pain he had ever endured, as if someone had flayed open his chest and wrenched out his heart.

"Who took her? When? How?"

"Lad! You're hurting me!"

Wiggen's cry snapped his rising panic. Realizing that his grip was nearly tight enough to break bones, he released her.

Think! Reason is always better than panic. Calm your mind. Remember!

Lad couldn't recall which of his instructors had taught him that lesson, but whoever it was had obviously never had their child kidnapped. How could he be calm when his soul was torn and bleeding? But he also recognized the truth in the lesson. To get Lissa back, he had to *think*.

Several deep breaths calmed his racing heart and stilled his mind, and finally he managed to regain a measure of control.

"Tell me exactly what happened."

"What happened?" Wiggen stared at him as if she didn't understand, hysteria edging her voice. "They came and took her. That's what happened!"

"Wiggen." He grasped her shoulders again, gently this time. "Calm your mind. I know it's hard, but I have to know every detail of what happened in order to get Lissa back. Take a deep breath and let your mind work."

Wiggen took a deep, shuddering breath and let it out slowly. "Okay. I was here in the kitchen…"

She told him everything she could remember of the thugs in the courtyard, their fight with Tika and Ponce, the man she killed.

"He just stood there," she said in a disbelieving tone, "like he'd hit a wall. And I… I killed him. He couldn't touch me, just like you said, and I just did it."

Lad looked into Wiggen's face. *It worked*, he thought gratefully, and for now, that was enough. Wiggen was alive. He lifted her hand and kissed the ring he had put on her finger on their wedding day. The lantern light glinted off of the gold-entwined circlet of obsidian.

"Lad?" she said hesitantly.

"You did what you had to do, Wiggen." He squeezed her hand gently. "What happened next?"

"The thugs ran away, Josie yelled, and I came in here."

Lad released Wiggen and turned to his father-in-law. "And what happened here, Forbish?"

The innkeeper shook his head slowly as he pressed a cloth to his wound. "I bolted the door, but they broke through. Two of them rushed in. I took a swipe at one," he nodded to a bloody cleaver on the meat block, "but the other whacked me upside the head, and everything went dark. Next thing, Wiggen's here and…"

"What did they look like?"

"Dark clothing, with scarves or something across their faces."

"You didn't send for the City Guard, did you?"

"Hells, no!" Forbish gave him an exasperated look. "Never helped before. But who do you think they were, Lad? "

"Assassins," he said, squeezing Wiggen's hand. They had never told Forbish about the ring she wore, and now wasn't the time to explain. "It had to be guild assassins."

"But why, Lad? Why would they take her?"

There was still plenty of hysteria in Wiggen's voice, but there was something else, too. She was angry, enraged that someone would take their child.

Well, she's not the only one.

Never in his life had Lad wanted so badly to kill someone. He'd vowed not to kill for Mya, but this was his family, his blood. Whoever had taken Lissa, or more accurately, those who had ordered the kidnapping, were on the top of that list. He knew it must have been the other masters.

All four of them? he wondered. *Mya?* She had threatened him when she found out he had the guildmaster's ring. Would she kidnap Lissa to ensure that she got it back? He thought of the look in her eyes after reading the message of trouble at the inn. There had been no guile there. *Or could this be another of her deceptions?* The thought felt like a dagger in the back.

"Lad?"

He looked up and gave Wiggen the obvious answer. "They took Lissa to control me."

No more, he thought murderously. *No one controls me!*

"Lad!" Josie burst into the kitchen, her face flushed. "Lad, there's a woman out front asking for you. She's skinny, red hair, dressed like a man. Tika and Ponce are on the porch with their sticks, but—"

"Mya!" With a surge of rage, Lad shot out of the kitchen. Assassins had kidnapped his daughter, and one way or another, it all centered on Mya.

𝒲𝓓𝓳𝓪𝓩𝔂

Rain trickled down Mya's neck as she exchanged glares with the two dour young men blocking her way into the *Tap and Kettle*. They were so alike that she could only tell them apart by the different bandages they wore. They held their staves like they knew how to use them, and the grim expressions on their faces brooked no argument. She'd never seen them before, but knew them from the descriptions in her Hunters' reports: the nephews, Tika and Ponce.

The front door slammed open, and Lad strode out of the inn. Relief washed over her at the sight of him; at least he was all right. His sodden clothes were plastered against his body, and his face was flushed.

Gods, he's beautiful. The thought emerging from the haze of her mental fatigue startled Mya, though she couldn't deny the truth of it.

"Mya! What are *you* doing here?"

His question stabbed her, so accusative, so angry. Before she could reply, three others followed him out of the inn. Again, she knew who they were, though they had never met. Fat Forbish the innkeeper, and his wife and former barmaid, Josie, were unmistakable. At the sight of Lad's scar-faced wife, Wiggen, Mya felt a gut-wrenching stab of jealousy.

Forget her! You're here to help Lad, she reminded herself. She answered him as dispassionately as she could. "Why do you think I'm here, Lad? I came to find out what happened."

"You mean you don't *know*?" Three strides brought him down the dozen stairs to stand before her. He was trembling, and she could feel the heat radiating from his body. "They took my *daughter*, that's what happened!"

Oh, dear gods! It was worse than Mya had expected, and he seemed to be blaming her. "Lad, I'm here to help. Tell me what happened."

248

"Why don't you ask your Hunters, Mya?" His hazel eyes shot a pointed glance over her shoulder at the Hunter who had just sidled up behind her.

Mya recognized the woman as the senior of the two who were assigned to watch the inn. "Shalla, report!"

"Yes, Miss Mya. Four swordsmen entered the courtyard through the gate, drew weapons, and started threatening the stableboy. The thugs were apparently a distraction to draw them out," she pointed to the twins, "while three others tried to gain access to the inn. I saw one attempt the front door, but he was killed on the porch, by her." She pointed to Wiggen.

Wiggen killed an assassin? The notion that the innkeeper's daughter could kill anything more dangerous than a dormouse struck Mya as ludicrous.

"Birdie was watching the back, and reported that the other two smashed through the side door. They came out about a minute later, one injured, the other carrying a bundle. They went up and over the cow shed and the wall behind it. I immediately sent Birdie to the *Cockerel* to get a message to you."

"They saw the whole thing! They watched, and didn't lift a finger to help!" Lad's voice dripped venom. He took another step forward, forcing her to back up. "Why didn't they *help*, Mya? Why didn't they stop them from taking my daughter?"

"They didn't help because their orders were to watch and report, Lad. You wanted it that way, remember? No interference." She turned to her Hunter. "Shalla, did you recognize any of them?"

"Yes. One of the thugs was an Enforcer." She turned and called out to another Hunter just emerging from the barn. "Birdie! Anything?"

The gangly youth trotted up to Mya and nodded. "The dead one's a Blade."

"You're the cause of this, Mya," Lad said as he once again stepped aggressively closer. "It's all about *you*!"

Mya waved off Shalla and Birdie, whose hands had dropped to their weapons. She'd never seen Lad like this, so emotional, so threatening. She knew she could defend herself, but if she had to fight Lad in front of her two Hunters, her secret would be out. Besides, she needed to speak to Lad alone. Keeping her eyes on Lad, Mya issued commands over her shoulder.

"Get back to the *Cockerel* and spread the word; we're at war with Horice and Youtrin, and probably the rest of the guild. Send secure messages to Pictor, Kara, Simi, and Vic. They're to drop whatever they're doing for the other masters and get back to headquarters *immediately*. Call everyone in; we've got to marshal our forces. All senior journeymen are to meet with me at the *Cockerel* in an hour. And send a clean-up team back with a cart for that body."

"Yes, Miss Mya!"

The two dashed off. The exchange, however, hadn't quelled Lad's temper.

"This is about *you*, Mya! You and your plots and plans, always grasping for more power to keep yourself safe! Well, what about my family? What did you do to keep *them* safe?"

"I didn't know the other masters would do this, Lad."

"How could you *not* know? You *think* like them. Why wouldn't you think about *this*, Mya? It's something you would have done, isn't it?"

Probably. She shrugged; there was no arguing the point. "A family is a weakness, Lad. I've told you that a hundred times."

"You're wrong, Mya. They're my life, my strength!" He glanced over his shoulder at them, then turned back to glare at her. "Is that what this is about? Were you so jealous of my happiness that you let someone destroy it?"

"Jealous?" A bark of laughter escaped her throat before she could stop it. A surge of anger at his accusation dampened her caution. She waved her hand at the group assembled on the porch. "Of *them*? They don't make you strong, Lad, they make you vulnerable. You think I should have known what would

250

happen here? What about you? What the hells did you *think* assassins would do? It's not *my* job to keep your family safe. It's *yours*."

His hand shot out.

The move was fast, but not so fast that she couldn't intervene. Mya's hand clamped down on his wrist before he could wrap his fingers around her throat. Surprise flashed in his eyes at the speed of her response and the strength of her grip. He twisted free and took a half-step back, scrutinizing her through the curtain of rain between them.

He struck with lightning speed, an open palm blurring through the rain toward her cheek.

Water misted in a halo as, again, she blocked the blow.

Now an expression of disbelief masked his face. His hands balled into fists at his sides, and his mouth hardened into a grim line.

"Lad, don't."

His attack came like an explosion, full-speed, full-force strikes that would have crushed the skull, snapped the spine, smashed the ribs, and pulped the heart of any normal human.

But Mya wasn't normal.

Magic flushed through her with a wave of heat, her runes igniting every nerve and muscle into action. The world cleared as if she had previously viewed it from behind a translucent veil. Mya could pick out every raindrop, every pore in Lad's skin, every drop of moisture on his lashes, and she reacted as her years of training had taught her.

Mya met each of Lad's attacks reflexively. She knew his fighting style, his dance of death, better than any other living soul. He'd taught it to her five years ago, and she had practiced it every day since.

A kick lashed out at her throat like a stroke of lighting, but she blocked, whirled, and swept aside the next blow, a clawing sweep of his fingers that would have raked through her ribs like a scythe through wheat. She bent back to dodge a fist that

251

buzzed through the raindrops like a swarm of hornets, and spun away from his next attack, sweeping his lashing foot aside. Lad spun also, her mirror, her shadow, and she knew his next move before it came. Her open palm met the strike with a report like a hammer on stone, a nimbus of misted water radiating out from the point of impact in a shockwave. Three more lighting punches, and she met each the same, her timing flawless. She glimpsed a fleeting opening in his defenses, feint or real, she didn't know, but she let it pass, pivoting and sliding out of his reach.

Don't kill him! the voice of her heart screamed to her mind. She could heal her wounds, but Lad could not. The force of his blows told her that he was truly trying to kill her. But try as he might, she would not—*could not*—kill him.

Mya fought defensively, blocking, twisting, and spinning out of reach time and time again, but little by little, his superiority showed. He was every bit as fast as she, and while she had trained for years, he had trained his entire lifetime. Fighting was as innate as breathing for Lad. She might have learned the dance, but he had choreographed it, and what he had made, he could change.

The pattern suddenly shifted, and Lad's next strike caught her off guard. Mya flung back her head to avoid the blow, but his fist brushed her cheek, the shockwave of compressed rain lashing across her face to blind her for an instant. She blocked the subsequent kick with her forearm and heard a bone crack with the impact. Spinning low, she swept his feet, but he used the momentum to flip in an impossible twisting flurry of kicks. Rain sprayed from him in a cloud, a fog of blurred motion.

Mya blocked two of the kicks with one arm, then spun to block his sweeping fist. It was only then that she realized it had been *her* bone she heard cracking. Her broken forearm met Lad's blow before she could pull back. Bone splintered and lanced through her flesh, shredding her wrappings and her shirt

252

in a spray of blood. She gaped for an instant at the shards of bone, the torn meat—her bones, her flesh—but no pain.

In her split-second of inattention, the edge of Lad's foot caught her cheekbone, and she felt the orbit of her eye disintegrate. Her vision went dark on one side.

A fleeting moment of panic surged through her. She was *hurt*! She should feel pain, should feel *something*! *He's going to kill me, and I'm not going to feel a thing!*

Yet even through the haze of panic, her training held true. Mya caught Lad's next kick in the crook of her unbroken arm and twisted inside his guard, slamming her elbow into his midriff.

Don't kill him!

At the last instant, she pulled most of the force of the blow. Her elbow met with his solar plexus, but didn't rupture any organs or snap his spine. The impact was, however, hard enough to stun someone not inured to pain. She spun away.

Lad crouched, gasping but poised, his piercing eyes fixed on her.

Mya glanced down with her good eye at the bloody bone sticking out through her torn sleeve, and her stomach flipped. She should be screaming in pain, but she felt nothing, and the lack of sensation made her want to retch. Unlike Lad, who had grown up with the magic blocking his pain and healing every wound, she had not. She knew pain, had felt bones break, had watched her own flesh part under a knife like water before the prow of a ship, and felt the searing agony in its wake.

This isn't right...

She gritted her teeth against the imagined agony and straightened her arm, pulling hard to realign the bones. They snapped into place, and she watched as the cracked bone smoothed and the bloody muscles writhed together. Her skin pulled closed and puckered into a rapidly fading scar. Her runic tattoos glittered across her skin before the enchanted wrappings sealed themselves, enveloping her once again in her secretive cocoon.

Mya heard Lad's gasp, and knew he'd seen her secret, but she couldn't pay attention to him right now. She felt the bones of her cheek realigning, and reached up to feel something dangling from the void of her shattered eye socket. Round and wet, knew what it was. Swallowing a surge of nausea, a visceral swell of wrongness—*Not human... Monster...*—she popped her eye back into the healing socket. By the time she blinked twice, she could see again.

"What have you done?" Lad's tone mirrored her horror.

"What?" Mya squared her shoulders and met his scorn with her own. "Don't you *dare* judge me! All I did was protect myself."

"You've made yourself into *him*! You've made yourself into the Grandfather!"

"I saw a weapon to wield and I took it." She felt a stab of conscience. This was why she hadn't told him. He didn't understand. He was right, but he was also wrong about her. He didn't know her. Not really.

"You murdered Vonlith," he breathed, "just to protect your secret."

Mya glanced over her shoulder toward the figures huddled on the inn's porch. She and Lad were far enough away for the rain to obscure their voices. Noticing her glance, Lad rose from his crouch and circled until he stood between her and his family.

"Vonlith was a threat to me. He could suspend my magic, just like he did when you killed the Grandfather. I ended that threat."

"You make it sound so simple! So easy! *Logical* even!" He wiped blood from the back of his hand, and she saw the wound where her broken bones had lacerated him. "He saved your life, both our lives, and you thanked him by putting a dagger in his brain!"

"How can you feel compassion for the man who was ready to make you a slave for the Grandfather?" She pointed to the tattoos they both knew marked his torso. "He would have made you a murderer again. He only saved us to keep my dagger out of his heart."

"So you murdered an innocent man."

"*Innocent?*" She laughed a ragged peal at his naïveté. "*Nobody's* innocent, Lad. We're all guilty of something. I'm an assassin; murder is my business. But you! Telling yourself you're a husband and father is just foolish! It only makes you vulnerable and puts *them* in danger. Don't deny what you truly are!"

"I am *not* like you, Mya." The pain in his voice told her she'd struck a telling blow.

"You're more like me than you are like them!" She shot another glance at the cowering people on the porch, reveled in the fear on their faces. *Damn right, you should fear me!* "You tell yourself you love them, but all that does is put you *and* them at risk. You blame assassins for taking your daughter, when it's *you* who's to blame!"

"You're *wrong*, Mya!" His tone changed. His voice was fuller now, more confident, stronger. "You think my family makes me weak, but you're wrong. They make me strong. They make me *human*. Without them, I'm nothing but a weapon. Without them, I'm like you."

He's more human than I am. The thought staggered Mya, blinded her for an instant, but she denied it. "I'm not a weapon, Lad. I *wield* the weapons."

"Tell yourself the truth for *once*, Mya. Has not loving anyone made you safe? Has it made you whole?" His scornful gaze raked her from head to foot, hurting her like no blow or blade ever could. "Has betraying me made you feel like a real person?"

"I *didn't* betray you, Lad." He didn't understand her. Or wouldn't. "Why would I? I *need* you."

He waved a hand dismissively. "Like you said, you've got your weapons. You're safe now. You don't need me."

"I..." *Love him? Do I? Can I?*

Mya knew the answer, but clenched her teeth against the words she couldn't say, and thanked the rain for hiding her tears. Glancing over his shoulder, she saw his family watching Lad with fear, pain...and love, plain on their faces. He had more in them than she would ever have from anyone. *That's what I want. That's what I need.* But she couldn't tell him, not now. "I need someone I can *trust*, Lad. A friend."

"You've already lost that, Mya."

"Have I?" Mya looked into his eyes, those eyes like chips of mica framed in white, and her soul shuddered. He was right; she had lost his friendship. But there might be a way she could get it back, get *him* back. "I may have lost your trust, Lad, but you've lost something, too. And if you want her back, you need my help."

Lad sneered at her and flexed his hands, as if imagining them around her throat. "You offer to help me get my daughter back? Why should you care about *my* family?"

She flinched as his words struck her. *Family...*

Mya recalled the day she walked out of her mother's home for the last time. She looked down at her hands. The blood was still there. There wasn't enough rain in the world to wash it away.

Murderer!

She deserved it.

She was your mother! Your family!

She hurt me...too much. What was I supposed to do, die for her?

Yes.

NO. She didn't love me!

But you loved her!

Mya looked at the pain and loss in Lad's eyes and she realized what she had done. She *should* have known—*had*

256

known—that they would go after his family, and she'd done nothing. She'd allowed her enemies to destroy his family because she couldn't have one. Unconsciously perhaps, but that was no excuse. He was right.

"Why should I care? Because you're *right* about me, Lad," she whispered. "You're right about what matters. Family. Love. Things I've never had and never will."

There it was. The truth. She nodded again over his shoulder at the people who loved him, the people who hated her, feared her. A pit of longing opened up in her heart, and for once, she didn't deny it.

"I thought strength and speed would protect me, but they haven't. Not from what's important, from what really matters. Not from what can really hurt me." She reached down and ripped the wrappings away from her forearm, displaying the black runes etched into her flesh, bearing her soul to the weeping sky. "Power is a lie, Lad. It makes you feel safe, but it doesn't *make* you safe." She let the torn wrappings fall, and they slithered back into place like dark serpents. "It only makes you a slave to the power. That's why I burned the Grandmaster's letter. That's why I want to help you get your daughter back."

"I don't trust you, Mya."

"Then don't, but I'm the only one who can do this for you, Lad." Mya smiled then, the whole situation striking a chord of irony in her cynical mind. "You said it yourself. I think like them. I know them. I know what they'll do."

"How do you know?"

She laughed derisively. "Because I know what *I* would do."

"I don't need your help, Mya. I don't want it." Turning his back on her, he walked away.

His denial struck her yet another blow.

"You can't do it alone, Lad!" she shouted at his back, wiping the tears and rain from her face. "You need me!"

Still he walked away, climbing the steps to his family, his loved ones.

257

"Godsdamnit, I'm going to help you whether you want me to or not!" she vowed, but all she got in response was the slam of the door.

CHAPTER XXI

T his is all Mya's fault and she says she wants to *help*!" Wiggen paced in front of the fireplace, her anger growing with every turn she made. "Why didn't you kill her, Lad?"

Lad couldn't believe Wiggen's venomous question. His sweet wife, the woman who taught him that killing was wrong, was now out for blood. Startled, he jerked his hand as Josie finished stitching his wound. Josie flinched and shied away, and he sighed inwardly. She had been fearful of him since witnessing his fight with Mya, and he couldn't blame her.

He considered Wiggen's question. In fact, in his rage he *had* been trying to kill Mya, and only her elbow to his midriff had stopped him. That blow could have killed him, would have killed him if she had wanted it to. Then the shock of seeing the dark tattoos etched on Mya's pale skin... In hindsight, he should have suspected—her evasions about Vonlith's death, the ease with which she killed the two assassins, her feeble excuse of training—but this was *Mya*. She had reviled the Grandfather, and now she was following in his path. Is that why she fought tooth and nail to avoid becoming the next guildmaster? Was she afraid that putting a guildmaster's ring on her finger would complete the transformation? But as wrong as Mya might have been in her actions, she was right about one thing.

"I couldn't kill her, Wiggen," he said. "We *might* need her help."

Wiggen stopped pacing and stared at Lad, a look of utter shock on her face. "You want to ask *her* for help?"

"It's not a matter of what I want, Wiggen, it's a matter of what we might have to do to get Lissa back. I didn't anticipate this. I didn't anticipate a lot of things. But Mya knows how the other masters think. She might be the only—"

"It's *her* fault they took Lissa!" she protested. "If you didn't work for Mya, this wouldn't have happened. If Mya hadn't angered the other masters, this wouldn't have happened. You told me that, Lad! She brought this on herself, and *we're* the ones paying for her mistakes."

The accusation in Wiggen's tone lashed him, though he knew it was directed toward Mya. *This is my fault. I've got to make it right.*

"Supper!" Forbish announced, backing through the swinging kitchen door with a huge tray in his hands. The food had been intended for the guests, but after the attack, the innkeeper had refunded their money and urged them to find other lodgings. Needless to say, all had been eager to go.

"I swear to all the Gods of Light, all he ever thinks about is food!" Josie finished wrapping Lad's hand and gathered up her supplies.

"We've all got our jobs. Mine is making sure everyone stays fed." Forbish placed the heavy tray on the table, then lifted a huge pitcher and started filling tankards. "I thought everyone could use a spot of ale, too. I drew a pot for us." He held one out to Wiggen.

"No, thank you, Father." She crossed her arms, her face hard. "And I'm not hungry."

The front door opened, and Tika and Ponce entered, dripping and dour.

"Two codgers with a cart came and took the dead assassin," Tika said.

"We locked and barred the gate behind them," Ponce added.

Chris A. Jackson

Tika reached for a tankard and passed it to his brother, then took one for himself. The twins had been uncharacteristically quiet since Lad's fight with Mya, obeying the orders given them without their usual banter.

They've learned what they're up against, and that this isn't a game.

"You gotta eat, Wig." Forbish began filling plates and passing them out.

"I said, I'm not hungry!" Wiggen turned away and resumed pacing.

Normally, the aroma of Forbish's wonderful cooking would stimulate Lad's appetite, but right now it held no delight. He knew he needed food, however, and dutifully began to eat. "Thank you, Forbish. You're right. We do have to eat. We've got a lot to do, and we'll need the energy."

"What are we going to do?" Tika and Ponce asked together.

"Now, you two just keep quiet!" Josie scolded. "You shouldn't even be here! You don't need to be knowing about assassins and such. Just eat your suppers and mind your own business!"

"But this *is* our business."

"Ever since those thugs showed up."

"And if we have to fight more of those assassins, we'll—"

"Enough talk about fighting," Forbish interrupted, handing out more plates.

"You shouldn't have to fight them again. The people who took Lissa have what they want, a means to control me. Next, they'll send a messenger with demands. I need to—" Lad stopped, looking at the anxious faces around him. He knew what *he* wanted to do, but his decisions lately all seemed to turn bad. And though he wasn't used to consulting anyone before acting, this was his *family*. They all loved Lissa, and deserved a say in the decisions to be made. He rephrased his thought. "The question is, do I wait for them to act, or do I take the initiative?"

261

"What do you mean, take the initiative?" Wiggen stopped pacing, her voice now tinged with worry.

"I mean, instead of waiting for them to send us their demands, do I go to them and find out what they want?"

"That sounds dangerous." Forbish frowned and sat down, but he didn't start eating. "It'd be safer to wait here."

"Yes, it would be safer, but one thing I've learned from Mya is that when you negotiate with someone, you can't let them think you're afraid. If I sit here and wait, I'll look afraid."

"Do you even know where to find them?" Wiggen asked.

"The masters vary their meeting places. I'll go where the last meeting was held. I'm sure the inn's being watched, so if I make the trip slow and obvious, word will get back to them, and they'll be waiting for me."

"Walking into a lion's den." Forbish took a swallow of ale and shook his head.

"How can you even *think* of doing that?" Josie's face went pale. "Those people are murderers!"

And so am I, Lad thought, grateful that only Wiggen and Forbish knew of his original role in the Assassins Guild. If Josie and the twins knew how many people he had killed... "It's not as dangerous as it sounds. They don't want to hurt me. They want something from me. I just have to find out what it is."

"And give it to them." Wiggen's words were a declaration, not a question.

"That depends."

"Depends on what? Don't you think we should give them what they want to get Lissa back?"

"It depends on if I think they're really *going* to give Lissa back."

Wiggen blanched, and she reached back to steady herself on the mantel. "Do you think they *won't* give her back?"

The question hung like a blade ready to fall. Every eye in the room turned to Lad.

I don't know because I don't think like they do! Lad steeled his face against his roiling emotions. He'd let his anger get the better of him when he attacked Mya, and he couldn't let that happen again. It had been so much easier when his feelings had been magically suppressed: no fear, no anger, no guilt, no hate. *But no love either*, he reminded himself. And love was worth the pain of all the rest. For the sake of Wiggen and the rest of the family, he had to hide his misgivings. He had to show them he had a plan.

"They won't want to give up control over me. I may have to take her back, but to do that, I have to find out where they're keeping her, or get them to bring her to me. It won't be easy."

"And if they keep her to control you?"

"If they *don't* give Lissa back, I'll kill them all." Josie put her hand over her mouth at Lad's vow, but Wiggen just nodded, her look of rage cooling to resolve. "In fact, if they're stupid enough bring Lissa to me just as proof that she's alive, I may be able to take her back immediately. But the first step is to meet them on their own ground, and show that I'm not afraid of them."

"So, what can we do to help?" Forbish asked.

"Stay here and be safe," he said. "Close the inn for a few days, Forbish. Keep the doors and shutters barred unless one of you is outside doing chores, then Tika or Ponce should stand guard, one at the door, the other with whoever's outside. Everyone should be armed. I'd tell you all to pack up and go somewhere safe, but there is nowhere safe from the guild."

"We're not going anywhere, Lad. This is our home." Forbish took a draught from his tankard, and thumped it down on the table like a magistrate's gavel. "Nobody runs us out of our home!"

The twins grinned at each other, and even Josie seemed to relax.

Wiggen stepped in front of Lad. "I'm going with you."

Josie gasped, and Forbish started to protest, but Wiggen just looked steadily into her husband's eyes.

Lad clenched his fists under the table as fear gripped his gut. "No, Wiggen. You'd be a distraction. They might decide to take you as a second hostage. It's too dangerous."

"Too *dangerous?* You just said it *wasn't* dangerous."

"It's not dangerous for *me.* If something happens, I can defend myself. They—"

"—can't touch me." Wiggen held up her left hand, the guildmaster's ring glinting on her finger. "And if they try, I'll kill them! I'll kill every godsdamned assassin in Twailin to get Lissa back!"

"But they won't know that they can't attack you, Wiggen. And if they try, we'll be forced to fight." *Not just fight*, he thought. *We'll have to kill everyone in the room.*

"They took my baby." The razor edge of her voice brooked no argument. "I'm not asking you. I'm telling you! I'm going *with* you!"

Silence.

The twins looked nervous, and Josie looked scared, but Forbish looked at his daughter with eyes filled with cold, hard pride. There was no arguing with her, and Lad knew it. Besides, Wiggen was right; she was protected from attack, and had already proven that she could do what was necessary. If the masters were stupid enough to bring Lissa, he couldn't protect her and fight at the same time, but Wiggen could. That might work.

"All right, Wiggen, you're coming with me, but you've got to promise me not to do anything rash. We can't appear weak, but we've got to make them believe that they have us under their control, that we'll do whatever they want to get Lissa back."

"Even if we decide otherwise?"

"*Especially* if we decide otherwise."

"All right. I'll do whatever I have to get her back, Lad."

"I know. So will I." He picked up a plate and handed it to her. "Eat something, Wiggen. We should leave soon."

Wiggen took the plate and sat next to Lad. Together, they ate in silence. Though the food tasted like sawdust in Lad's mouth, he meticulously cleaned his plate. If he had to kill someone tonight, he'd need his strength.

Accounting must have been invented by a sadistic devil.

Hensen blinked to clear his vision, blurry from poring over columns of numbers in his ledger. Guild income and expenditures were complex in the extreme—from professional children beggars and pick-pockets to high-profile lenders of money to financially strapped nobles, from buying information for a heist to fencing the stolen goods—and rife with opportunities for his numerous underlings to skim profits. *He* had certainly skimmed a small fortune while he was in the ranks. Consequently, Hensen trusted no one but himself to do the final accounting. This was, without question, his least favorite aspect of his position.

He sneered at the irony of his life. He had learned bookkeeping early in his apprenticeship with the Thieves Guild, assuming that the numeric slog would end when he moved on to bigger and better things. The skills helped him pose as a moneylender for years, a wonderful cover for a thieving operative. But regardless of how high he rose or how interesting the projects, there were still books to be done. He would much rather be out fleecing the populace on a face-to-face basis. He'd especially enjoyed walking the streets, flanked by guards, click-clicking his black sword cane along the cobbles, watching people tip their hats and step out of his way.

So much better than this drudgery.

The knock at the door came as a welcome interruption. "Come in."

Weapon of Blood

Kiesha entered bearing a silver tray with a carafe and a single glass. The pale wine accented her golden gown and blonde hair perfectly, but her severe expression spoiled the image.

"Bad news?"

"It's not my place to judge what's good or bad, sir." She put down the tray and poured wine into his glass. "The Assassins Guild has made their move, just as Sereth said they would. They've kidnapped Lad's daughter."

"Hmm." Hensen accepted the glass from her and inhaled the wine's delicate bouquet. "No demands yet?"

"No sir, but it only happened a few hours ago. They'll probably let him sweat until morning."

"Does the Master Hunter know what's happened?" He sipped his wine and swished it across his tongue before swallowing. *Oak and honey, a hint of fruit and a pleasant aftertaste of apple.*

"Yes, sir. She came to the inn. They…" Her mouth pursed in a pensive moue, as if she was considering each word's potential danger. "They had a disagreement."

"A disagreement? Mya and Lad?"

"Yes, sir. It was raining hard, and I couldn't hear it all. Most of it didn't make much sense. I couldn't see into the courtyard without exposing myself, but their voices were definitely raised and angry. It may have even come to blows."

"They *fought*?" Hensen nearly dropped his wineglass.

"From what I heard, it could have been a fight, but Mya left with no sign of injury, so I must have been mistaken." She shrugged and bit her lip.

"Hmm." He put down the wine. "Well, write down all you can remember of their conversation. And contact Sereth to see if he knows where the child has been taken. Wherever that is, I want someone there. Surveillance only, but when this comes to a head, that child will be at the center of it. We have to be poised to keep Lad alive."

"And the Master Hunter as well, sir?"

"Of course, but focus on Lad."

"Yes, sir."

"What news from our operative at the *Golden Cockerel*? I imagine the place is like a kicked anthill about now."

"No news, sir. Our intermediary said she didn't arrive for their scheduled rendezvous."

"Didn't arrive?" Hairs rose on the back of Hensen's neck. "Where the hells is she?"

"We checked her apartment, and she's not there. No sign of a fight or intrusion."

Hensen frowned, then stopped himself. Wrinkles were so unsightly. "Any sign that she's been discovered?"

"No, sir. If she was discovered, she had orders not to allow herself to be interrogated."

"Yes, I *do* remember giving those orders." He once again stopped himself from frowning, and instead picked up his wineglass, swirling the vintage to watch the legs flow down the fine crystal. "We need to find out where she's gone, but we need to do so discreetly."

"Yes, sir."

"Anyone who works on this contract gets the same orders. Nobody's to be taken prisoner by the Assassins Guild. We can't let this come back to haunt us, my dear."

"Of *course*, sir."

The wagon creaked and clattered over the cobbles of the deserted streets as Lad flicked the reins to urge the cart horse along. The animal had balked at leaving its warm stall for the harness, and tried to turn into every stable yard they passed. Lad didn't blame it. The rain kept most people indoors.

But not everyone.

Weapon of Blood

Though his senses were impaired by the rain and the noise of the wagon, Lad knew they were being watched. He had counted on it. He just hoped that their progress from Eastmarket to the South Docks district had been slow enough and obvious enough to allow those who had kidnapped Lissa to assemble. He needed them all in one place.

Finally they pulled up outside the inconspicuous door of an inconspicuous warehouse in an inconspicuous neighborhood. Clasping Wiggen's hand, Lad helped her down from the wagon and led her toward the door. He could feel her shivering, and wondered if it was due to the chill of damp clothes, or if fear had finally overwhelmed her anger. His own tremors were of a higher pitch, vibrations of singing nerves, artifacts of his heightened tension.

At least, that was what he tried to convince himself.

No fear...

The door opened as they approached, and together they stepped into the dimly lit warehouse. Two armed thugs remained by the door, while another two escorted them without a word to the office where the masters met. The scuff of boots, thuds of heartbeats, rustle of fabric and leather, and the clinks of metal told Lad that at least a dozen assassins lurked in the shadows, ready to pounce if things went awry. He struggled against the murderous impulses that raged beneath his calm façade. *They took my child!* Violence was not an option as long as the assassins still had Lissa. But if they could just get the baby into Wiggen's arms, she would be safe. Then he'd be free to release the killer within him.

They stepped through the office door, and Lad assessed his adversaries.

Know your enemy's capabilities, strengths and weaknesses. Remember!

All four masters were there, which didn't really surprise him. Add in their bodyguards and the two thugs at the door. Ten against one. In the confined space of the office, where they

Chris A. Jackson

would get in each other's way, he could manage those odds, but that was not counting the assassins outside. If all Nine Hells broke loose, he'd have to kill them all quickly.

Neera first. Who knew what mayhem the alchemist could hurl with her potions and poisons. Best to rid himself of that unknown before he found out.

Then Horice. The Master Blade was highly skilled, and the sword at his hip, Lad knew, was enchanted, making him a candidate for quick elimination.

The enforcer or the inquisitor next? Brute force or cunning?

Lad decided on Patrice, not because she might be more dangerous than Youtrin, but because he believed the Master Enforcer to be more of a bully than a fighter. It wouldn't surprise Lad if Youtrin tried to take Wiggen as a shield. Of course, if he did, then the surprise would be on Youtrin.

"Welcome, Lad." Patrice rose and gracefully waved to the two empty chairs at the table. "How good of you to anticipate our desire to meet with you. And this must be your lovely wife. Both of you, please have a seat."

Lad tensed. Neera usually took the lead at meetings. Though demanding and outspoken, she was generally straightforward. Patrice, on the other hand, excelled at verbal sparring, tricking people into revealing what they didn't want to tell. Although Mya could hold her own against the Master Inquisitor, Lad felt ill at ease in this type of confrontation. He would have to be careful with every word.

Think like an assassin.

"We'll stand." He grasped Wiggen's hand tightly, drawing her close. "We want to see Lissa. Now."

"We need to discuss a few things first."

"No." *Show no weakness, no fear.*

"*What?*" Patrice looked at him as if he'd slapped her, then let her astonished gaze circuit the room. "What do you mean, 'No'?"

269

Lad drew upon his memories of a thousand meetings he had attended with Mya, some dangerous and some not, and tried to emulate her confidence, her stern demeanor, the cold menace she was so skilled at projecting.

"I mean that if you don't let us see our daughter this instant, I'll kill each and every one of you, right here, right now."

He watched them closely, and saw that his threat had the desired effect. Hints of fear rippled through them: Horice's hand twitched toward his sword, Neera's shoulder shifted as her hand settled beneath her robes, Youtrin's scowl deepened, his knuckles cracking under the table. Their reactions weren't surprising. The masters were unused to being threatened, and Lad knew that his reputation as a killer had preceded him. Only Patrice showed no response.

Wiggen squeezed his hand, the ring pressing his palm. She was ready. He squeezed her hand twice. *Not yet. Be patient.*

"You're not that foolish," Patrice countered. "Kill us, and your wife *and* child will die."

"And you'll be no less dead," Lad said.

"Cocky bastard!" Horice growled with a glare as sharp as any blade. "Let him see the brat."

"Very well." Patrice gestured to the two thugs at the door, and they moved to a canvas-covered shape in the corner of the room. Lad had noticed it when he entered—it hadn't been there during previous meetings—but didn't know what it was.

They removed the canvas to reveal an ornate, oval mirror in a free-standing frame. Patrice stepped over to it and touched several spots around the rim. Her reflection swirled and melted like dripping wax, the image finally resolving onto another place, a bare room with wooden walls that could have been any one of thousands in the city.

Lad's heart sank. Lissa wasn't here. The masters had outwitted him, abolishing any chance of him rescuing his daughter before he submitted to their demands.

"Kellik! Move into the view of the mirror and show our guests your charge," Patrice commanded.

A thickset woman clad in leathers moved into view, and in her arms she held a bundle of swaddling blankets. She smiled and tilted the bundle up.

"Lissa!" Wiggen surged toward the mirror, but Lad kept a grip on her hand and pulled her back.

"How do we know this is real?" He struggled to keep his eyes on the assassins instead of the squirming image of his daughter in the mirror. "It could be an illusion, a magical lie."

"Feel free to speak to her," Patrice offered, waving toward the mirror. "Doubtless she knows her own parents. She can see and hear us as well as we see and hear her."

This time, Lad allowed Wiggen to pull him to the mirror.

"Lissa? Lissa, baby. Momma's here." Wiggen choked with emotion.

The woman in the mirror held the babe up, and Lissa's little face came instantly alight with joy. She reached out her pudgy hands and emitted a squeal of delight.

"Oh, Lissa…" Wiggen reached her free hand toward the image of their daughter. Her fingertips brushed the glass, and the image immediately faded to a mundane reflection. Wiggen gasped and turned to glare at Patrice. "Bring her back!"

"We've given you a glimpse of your daughter as a token of our good faith. Now we will discuss the terms of our agreement, what you will do for us in exchange for the safe return of your child."

"Agreement?" Lad gave her a withering glare. "You *say* you'll return my daughter, but how can I trust you to keep your word?"

"What choice do you have?" the inquisitor countered, taking her seat. "The only thing you need to trust is that we *will* kill your child if you don't do as we ask. You need not trust us, only obey us."

"And if I refuse?"

271

"Then your child is dead."

"And you with her."

"And Lissa will be no less dead," Patrice said, using Lad's own logic against him.

Lad gritted his teeth. This was going all wrong! He had hoped to walk out of here with his daughter in his arms and the knowledge that the masters could never, ever hurt them again. That, however, was not to be.

"Lad!" Wiggen's free hand grasped the sleeve of his shirt. "It's *Lissa*! You have to do as they say!"

He looked into his wife's eyes and saw the same pain that he felt. They had planned to agree to the masters' demands as a ruse until they could determine what to do, but plans were one thing, reality another.

"What do you want?"

"We want you to kill Mya."

"Why not do it yourself?"

"Don't be coy. You know we can't attack someone wearing the guildmaster's ring. But *you* can, because you never signed a blood contract."

They think Mya wears the ring! Lad failed to mask his surprise.

Patrice smiled triumphantly. "Yes, we know the ring was not destroyed, just as we know you are not wholly bound by her orders. So kill her, and we will give you Lissa."

"I *can't*." Lad put everything he had into the lie, hoping they would believe him. His expertise was in physical conflict. Mya was the expert in deceit.

"Why not?" demanded Horice. Patrice shot him a glare at his outburst.

"The magic in me prevents it. The Grandfather ordered me to never harm her." The last part was true, even if the first wasn't. Lad hoped that no spy had witnessed his fight with Mya in the courtyard of the *Tap and Kettle*. "Mya's hold over me is not as strong as the Grandfather's was, but his original commands still bind me; I can't harm her."

To his astonishment, Horice turned to his bodyguard and asked, "Is that true, Sereth?"

"Mya *was* assigned to tend the weapon, sir. The Grandfather had to have granted her protection." The bodyguard's eyes shifted to Lad for an instant, then back. "He killed Master Targus. He would have killed Mya if he wasn't commanded not to."

"Then we have a problem." Patrice exchanged glances with her three colleagues, then turned back to Lad. "And your child's life hangs in the balance. What a pity."

"I think we can get around this," Neera said, her voice a harsh rasp. "You say you can't harm Mya, as commanded by the Grandfather, but..." her eyes glinted deep in their sockets, "did he ever command you not to *betray* her?"

Lad blinked. They were handing him a way out, though they didn't seem to realize it. In fact, from their surreptitious glances and tiny nods, this seemed to be an agreed-upon alternative. He answered immediately and truthfully. "No, he didn't."

Neera reached inside her cloak and pulled forth a tiny crystal tube. She placed it on the table and pushed it toward him with a vile yellow fingernail.

"Put the entire contents in her wine or blackbrew. It will induce unconsciousness, but will not harm or kill her. Bring her to us in bondage, and we will exchange your daughter for her."

Lad cocked his head as he picked up the vial, wary of some sly deception. "If you're lying, and this is actually poison, I won't be able to give it to her. The magic in me will prevent it." Dead, Mya would be of no use in bargaining for Lissa. They would have what they wanted from him with no incentive to return her. In fact, by keeping her, they would continue to control him.

"I'm telling you the truth," Neera said with a wizened smile.

Lad slipped the vial into a pocket; he had little choice. "Where and when?"

"Tomorrow night," Patrice said with a smile of satisfaction. "You know the courtyard behind the tenements east of Fiveway Fountain in West Crescent?"

"Yes."

"Midnight."

"All right." He squeezed Wiggen's hand, and they walked back out into the rain.

CHAPTER XXII

A silver coin clattered onto the desk top. "For the night."

The innkeeper looked up from his ledger at Sereth, and then at the giggling doxy on his arm. "Two for the whole night. We're a respectable establishment."

"Fine." Sereth knew he was being fleeced, but also knew that this was one of the few inns free from Assassins Guild eyes, and the coins would keep the man's mouth shut. He flipped another silver crown onto the table. "The sheets better be clean."

"Third floor, last door on the left." The innkeeper took the money and handed over a key. "And keep the noise down."

"Right." Sereth snatched up the key and pulled his companion toward the stairs. "Come on!"

She giggled and stumbled drunkenly. "Whoa, there! What's your rush, love? We've got all night!"

"I want to get my money's worth."

"All right, all right. Just keep your codpiece fixed."

She stumbled a few more times on their way to the third floor, and teetered unsteadily as he worked the key in the lock. When he closed the door behind them, however, locking it and throwing the bolt for good measure, her pretenses fell away.

"Did you find out where they're keeping the baby?" Kiesha went to the night table and took up a towel to dry her dripping hair. They'd both been drenched by the rain, but Sereth at least had a cloak. She was wet to the skin. It was her own fault. Kiesha had insisted on meeting away from Hensen's house.

275

Though she said it was for his own safety, he was pretty sure that his last late-night visit had scared the master thief. He'd let his temper get the better of him, and he was paying for it; banning him from the house also kept him from seeing his wife.

"No. The masters are keeping it under wraps. They're afraid that Lad might take one of us to question. They've assigned a team of journeymen to watch over her, but only that team and the masters know where. The only one of the team I know for sure is an Enforcer named Kellik." The inn's tiny room was stifling and malodorous. Sereth went to the window, opened the shutter, and lifted the frame for a little fresh air. "The masters are staying together at Youtrin's warehouse, surrounded by an army of bodyguards. They're running scared."

"They *should* be scared of him."

"Don't I know it," Sereth murmured. He remembered the string of impossible murders the Grandfather had orchestrated. The whole city knew of them, though Sereth was one of the few who knew who had committed them. The weapon...Lad. And the masters had taken his child. Sereth knew too well that feeling of helplessness, and the rage that accompanied it. He turned toward Kiesha. "When he and his wife walked into that—"

"He brought his *wife* to meet with the masters of the Assassins Guild?" The thief stared at him in disbelief.

"Yes. And that didn't stop him from threatening to kill them all if they didn't let him see his daughter." Sereth remembered thinking that Horice would shit his pants when that happened.

"Does he honestly believe that if he kills Mya, they'll hand his daughter back?"

Kiesha had finished drying her hair, and was now dabbing the water from her neck and décolletage. Her disguise as a low-priced prostitute was remarkably accurate, right down to ragged stockings and cheap shoes. A far cry from the glamorous gowns he'd seen her wearing at Hensen's. The sodden dress clung like a second skin to the curves of her body, the curves he'd seen revealed only a few days before. He opened the window a little more as the air in the room suddenly seemed even closer.

"I have no idea what he believes, but I don't think he's that stupid." He watched as Kiesha pulled back the coverlet and held the lamp low to inspect the sheets. Surprisingly, they looked clean. "And he's not going to kill Mya for them."

She put down the lamp and gave him a curious look. "He's not?"

"He says he can't, that the magic constrains his actions. The Grandfather ordered him not to hurt Mya, and the command still restrains him."

"Interesting." She sat on the bed and began unlacing her shoes. "So, if he can't kill Mya, what did they order him to do?"

"Drug her and bring her to them. She's wearing the guildmaster's ring, so they're going to use someone outside the guild to do the deed. Someone stupid enough to believe he'll get more than ten inches of steel in his back when it's done."

"That must be a short list of potentials." She finished with her second shoe and kicked them off into the corner. "When and where?"

Sereth swallowed hard. This was the moment he'd been both waiting for and dreading. Firming his resolve, he said, "I'll tell you after you release my wife."

"What?" An incredulous smirk spread across her face, as if she thought he was joking.

He wasn't.

"You heard me. I want her back. Now."

"That's not in our best interest, Sereth."

"I don't care about your best interest, Kiesha. I want my wife back."

"And you think one little bit of information is worth us losing you as a spy?" She laughed and pulled off her tattered stockings, draping them over the nightstand. "You're delusional."

His hand went to the dagger in his sleeve—one flick of the wrist, and he could bury it in her eye—but he knew she considered him no serious threat. If she died, so would his wife. She'd called his bluff, but he'd be damned if he'd play her games.

"Fine, then. Find them yourself." Sereth strode toward the door, but before he could reach the latch, she was past him, quick as a cat.

Kiesha leaned her back against the door and smiled. "Oh, come on, Sereth. You can't give up so easily." Without taking her eyes from his, she began unlacing the strings of her bodice. "Hensen won't let your wife go, but surely there's *something* else you want that I can give you."

His mind spun. "What are you doing?"

"I'm *negotiating*, Sereth." She slipped her arms out of the sleeves of the dress, then pushed the sodden clothing down to her hips. "Besides, it's pouring outside, and neither of our masters expect us back before morning."

"Not interested." Sereth turned away, hating the tremor in his voice. "I'm married, remember?"

"That's all right, Sereth. I know you're married. In fact, I talk to your wife regularly." He heard the wet fabric of her dress hit the floor and swallowed hard. "She's lonely, you know."

"She'd be a lot less lonely if you talked Hensen into letting her go." He glanced over his shoulder to see her hanging the dress on the coatrack beside the door. Her pale, moist skin glowed in the lamp light, the muscles beneath long and lithe. Sereth looked away. His wife wasn't the only one who was lonely. *Three years…*

"He won't do that, Sereth, and you know perfectly well why." He felt her approach, but refused to turn around. "You're *much* too valuable to him." Her hands reached over his shoulders to unclasp his cloak. "You've performed very well, and he's not about to let you go."

"So, is that what you're doing? Rewarding me for good behavior?"

"Is there something wrong with showing a little gratitude?" Her hands came around again and began to work on the buttons of his shirt.

"Yes, there's something wrong with it." Sereth grasped her wrists, but she pressed herself against his back, her damp skin cool through the cloth of his shirt. He felt her shiver. *It's been so long...* "Does your master pay *all* of his informants with your favors?"

Kiesha stiffened against his back for a moment before easing in again, but when she spoke, her voice sounded strained. "No, Sereth. This was my idea."

"Why?"

"Because I want to."

"But I don't."

"Yes, you do."

"No, I don't. My wife—"

"Your wife is safe and healthy." She pressed closer now, her breath warm in his ear. "And she will never, *ever* know."

Sereth's knees weakened and he closed his eyes. "She may never know, but I will."

"Yes, you will." She kissed the back of his neck. "Take a little pleasure in your work, Sereth. If you don't, it'll kill you."

No!

Sereth released Kiesha's wrists and turned to face her, glaring into her sultry gaze. If she and Hensen thought they could manipulate him this way, they were dead wrong. He loved his wife, and he wouldn't betray her for a quick tumble.

"Tomorrow night at midnight. A tenement courtyard in West Crescent, east of Fiveway Fountain." Gripping her shoulders hard, Sereth shoved Kiesha onto the bed. By the time she recovered, he'd flung open the window, slipped out into the rain, and descended to the street. He was a block away before he realized that he'd forgotten his cloak.

Weapon of Blood

𝒮𝒱𝒥𝓏𝒶𝒵𝓀

The *Golden Cockerel* buzzed like a hornet's nest struck with a well-aimed stone. The pretense of a simple drinking and gambling house had been cast aside; no pub was this busy so early in the morning. Stern-looking men and women came and went, their hands on prominently displayed weapons, and their eyes scrutinizing every passing cart, carriage, and pedestrian.

Lad mounted the steps with barely a glance at the two dour sentries stationed at the door. They knew him and, although their glares were hard, they let him pass without a word. He wondered for a moment why they didn't try to stop him, until he realized that Mya hadn't told anyone about their fight. *No one knows about her magic. She's kept it secret.* Well, in a few minutes, her secrets wouldn't matter.

The door swung open easily at his touch, and the woman stationed inside took her hand away from the dagger beneath her apron. Lad ignored her and crossed the busy common room. Though he kept his gaze straight ahead, he felt the eyes of the Hunters following him, and heard their whispers. Some blamed him for the war with other guild factions, resenting the vulnerability—his family—that the other masters had exploited. Most of them, however, despite Mya's claim that assassins didn't have families, had someone they held dear somewhere. And if this could happen to Lad, it could happen to them.

Either way, Lad didn't care.

Mika had acquired a companion of equal height, girth and demeanor, and they both stood guard at the door to Mya's office. Mika knocked and opened the door with an expressionless nod. Inside, Mya and a half-dozen senior journeymen looked up from the paper-strewn table.

"Lad!" Mya stared at him unbelievingly. "You're here."

He bit back an acerbic reply and said, "Yes. I'm here, Mya."

280

"Good." She flashed a little smile and motioned him forward. "We've made some progress overnight." She drew a large map of Twailin from beneath the pile of papers and laid it on top. "Have a look at this."

"I need to speak with you, Mya."

"About what?"

"I've learned something you need to know."

"What happened? Did they contact you?"

"I need to speak with you *alone*."

The Hunters bristled, offended at the implication that there were secrets between Lad and Mya too sensitive for their ears. He ignored them, focusing his attention on Mya. The suspicion that flashed across her eyes quickly faded to curiosity. His years of practiced naïveté had convinced her that he was incapable of a convincing deception. Now, with the vial of Neera's drug in the palm of his hand, he plotted against her and she couldn't see it.

"Take a break. Gods know we could all use a moment's distraction. I'm starting to see this damn map when my eyes are closed." Mya reached for her blackbrew cup and drained it in one long swallow. The Hunters stared at her dubiously, but she waved them off. "Go on, get out of here. Grab a meal, get some sleep, relax for an hour or so. We're not going anywhere yet, not until we have a plan."

The Hunters filed out, some muttering, others relieved at the prospect of a break. Mya reached for the blackbrew pot and refilled her cup. When the door closed, the pot clattered back onto the tray, and she looked at him with clear relief.

"I'm glad you came."

When performing a sleight of hand, a distraction is always wise. Remember!

In this case, the truth seemed the best distraction. "I went to them."

His admission widened her eyes and stopped her hand halfway to her cup. "You did? When?"

281

"Last night." He rounded the table. "You were right. We needed to know what they wanted from me. Wiggen and I took—"

"Wiggen? You took your *wife* to a meeting with *them*?"

"She insisted on going. We took the wagon to Youtrin's warehouse."

"And they were there? Who was it? All of them?" She cocked an eyebrow at him.

"I knew they'd be watching me, so we drove slowly on the main streets. It wasn't hard to figure out where we were headed. And yes, all four of them were there."

"That was…very clever, Lad." Mya reached for her cup again. "I wish you had told me. We could have taken them all right there." She lifted the cup.

Lad stepped closer, so their faces were only inches apart, his anger flaring, burning away any sympathy he might have felt for her. "You'd have gotten Lissa *killed*!"

"All right." The cup hovered over the map. "I admit, it would've been risky, but—"

"That's why I *didn't* tell you, Mya. They threaten *me*, and instead of trying to help, you see it as an opportunity to take them out and rid yourself of a problem." He grasped her wrist, and the cup trembled. "You say family and love are important, but you'll never change. You always look for the advantage, but the advantage for *you*, not anyone else."

"You're…" Mya stopped, her eyes fixed on his. He could smell the stale blackbrew on her breath, see the sleepless nights in the tiny blood vessels in her eyes, feel the tremor of fatigue through her wrist. "You're right, Lad."

He released his grip.

Mya put down her cup and rubbed her eyes wearily.

Now!

Although most of Lad's skills were in direct confrontation, he'd had some training in administering poisons. As he stepped back, he passed his hand over her cup, and the fine white crystals

282

cascaded down to vanish in the steaming brew. Before Mya opened her eyes again, he had capped the vial and slipped it into a pocket.

"I'm...trying, Lad, but I can't stop the way I think. I've been doing it too long. It's kept me alive. But you're right. I need to push my thoughts along the right track. To help you, not myself." Sighing, she dropped into her chair. "So, what did you learn? Do you know where they're keeping Lissa?"

"No, but she's alive. They showed her to us through a mirror. She recognized Wiggen."

"Okay, so what do they want?"

"They want me to kill you." Worry flashed over her face. "Don't worry, Mya. I'm not here to murder you. I told them I couldn't."

"And they *believed* you?" Her voice was incredulous, and her hand trembled as she reached again for the cup.

"I'm not very good at lying, so I explained that the Grandfather ordered me to never harm you, which is the truth, and that the magic still binds me to his command, which isn't. I offered to betray you instead."

Mya lifted the cup to her lips, nodding in approval as she sipped and swallowed. "You're learning to be quite deceptive, Lad. So, you offered to betray me. What do they want you to do?"

"Bring you to them." Lad watched her eyes for any sign that the drug might be working. Was one sip going to be enough? He had to keep her talking, keep her suspicions eased until she fell asleep. "They fear you, Mya. They think you wear the guildmaster's ring."

"Ha! There's a bit of irony." Mya sipped again and put down the half-empty cup. "So, you bring me to them, supposedly subdued. This could work to our advantage, Lad. Where and when?" She gestured to the map. "Show me."

"Here." Lad put his finger down in the center of the courtyard east of Fiveway Fountain. "Midnight tonight."

"Tonight?" She rubbed her eyes again. "Damn, that doesn't give us much time." She reached for the cup and downed the rest of it in one swallow, then squinted at the map. "That's Patrice's territory. She owns that whole block."

"She does?"

"Yes. Let's see, they'll have people in all the surrounding buildings with crossbows, and probably Blades and Enforcers spread out over a few blocks as well, but they'll focus on the courtyard, bring a bunch of people with them." She rubbed her eyes again and yawned. "Godsdamnit, I'm tired. Anyway, we should be able to...um...ambush them from..."

"No, Mya."

"What?" Mya looked up at him, and he could see by her dilating pupils that the drug had taken hold.

"It's too risky. You can't bring your Hunters in for an ambush. One mistake and they kill Lissa."

"Um...okay. What do you suggest?"

Lad watched her pupils widen with every word. Now all he had to do was make sure she didn't raise an alarm before she passed out. He had to distract her for a moment longer. The truth was distracting enough, so he kept it up.

"I think we should do exactly as they suggested, Mya. I should bring you to them just like they asked."

"Wha...what?" Her eyes cleared, then lost focus again. "No...I..." She sagged in her seat, and he caught her before she hit the floor.

"It's all right, Mya," he whispered into her fading consciousness. "It won't hurt. You've already seen to that."

Lad took the key from Mya's pocket before lifting her in his arms and carrying her to the fireplace. Inserting the key into the lock that she thought was her secret, he stood back while the hidden door opened. Quietly closing the door behind them, he carried her down the stairs. Though he'd never been down here, Lad knew she would have another way out. Someone as

284

controlled by fear as Mya was would never allow herself to be cornered with no escape route.

All he had to do was find it.

CHAPTER XXIII

It's like the heavens are crying, Wiggen thought as she looked up into the rain. *Maybe the gods know what's going to happen tonight.*

Lad nudged her out of her thoughts as he pulled the wagon to a creaky stop. "We're here, Wiggen. It's time." He vaulted from the seat and went to the back of the wagon.

"I know."

Though it was only the weight of her sodden skirts, Wiggen felt as if some heavy force dragged her down, slowing her motions, delaying the inevitable. By the time she alighted, Lad had lifted the canvas-wrapped bundle from the bed of the wagon and hoisted it over his shoulder. Wiggen heard a muffled curse and recalled the expression on Mya's face when they'd lowered the canvas hood over her head. She felt a pang of guilt, but pushed it aside. *We have to do this to get Lissa back! That's all that matters.*

Two men emerged from the shadows of a narrow alley between adjacent tenements. Wiggen stiffened in fear. Sidling over to Lad, she clutched his free hand in hers.

"Remember what I told you," he whispered.

"I remember. I'm ready." She felt the comforting weight of the naked dagger she'd sewn into the folds of her dress, and hoped her words were true. *Calm your mind. Focus on Lissa. No fear...no pain...no mercy.*

286

The tenements joined above the narrow, dark alley to form a tunnel, and as she and Lad passed between the armed men and into the gloom, Wiggen felt as if she was being swallowed by some great beast. Heavy footsteps echoed as their escort fell in behind them, but she refused to look back. *No fear...*

They emerged into a lamp-lit courtyard with a central well, two scraggly trees, and a few stone benches. But something was wrong. Though it was late, she would expect at least some lights to be on in the surrounding tenements, but every window was dark.

The cold hand of fear clutched the back of her neck. *They want no witnesses.*

The four masters awaited them in front of the well—Neera, Youtrin, Horice, and Patrice, each flanked by a bodyguard—the four monsters who had taken her baby. Unfortunately, the hatred burning in her for these creatures didn't make her fear them any less. And they had not come alone, for in the gloom outside the lamplight, around the entire periphery of the courtyard, she perceived a ring of assassins, their hands on sword hilts or holding crossbows, their eyes fixed on Wiggen and Lad. *So many...*

Lad squeezed her hand, then released her as they stopped near the middle of that deadly circle. He shrugged the burden off his shoulder, and it landed with a wet thump at his feet, splattering mud in all directions. A muffled curse escaped the hood.

"Where's Lissa?" Lad's voice sent a chill down Wiggen's spine. For years she'd associated his voice with love, comfort, and warmth, but now it raked through the rain as hard and cold as steel dragging on slate. Wiggen cringed at how different he was in the company of these assassins, no longer the loving father and husband she knew so well. He was different; like them, he was a killer.

"Show Mya to us first." The Master Inquisitor, Patrice, stepped forward, a rouged harlot sporting a smug smile.

"Fine." Lad lifted the canvas-bound Mya to her knees and tore away the hood.

"Bastard! You traitorous piece of shit!" Mya writhed against her bonds, spittle flying from her lips. "I'll *kill* you! I'll kill you all!"

Contemptuous laughter clattered through the rain, but Wiggen could hear true fear in it. The assassins thought Mya wore the guildmaster's ring, and that, if unbound, she could make good her promise of slaughter.

Mya blinked through the rain, taking in her surroundings, and her struggles ceased. "They'll betray you, Lad. Once I'm dead, they'll kill your daughter. You *know* you can't trust them!"

"Oh, and he can trust you?" Patrice took another step forward and sneered at her bound colleague. "A traitor to her own guild?"

"Enough!" Neera stepped forward. "Let's finish this business." She beckoned to someone behind her. "Lakhshim, it's time to earn your apprenticeship with the Assassins Guild." One wizened finger crooked toward Mya. "Kill her."

"Yes, Mistress Neera!" A swarthy young man of perhaps fifteen years strode to the fore. He pulled a long, keen dagger from his belt, his dark eyes fixed upon Mya.

"No." Lad stepped into his path.

Wiggen drew in a gasp through gritted teeth. She knew her husband's preternatural abilities. She had seen him in action. But now, standing amongst these men and women with swords and crossbows, all sly-eyed assassins ready to murder on command, Lad seemed no more than a peasant straight from the farm. Unarmed, his clothing simple, his feet bare, he appeared vulnerable to anyone who didn't know what he was.

And apparently, the boy did not know. He didn't stop, but growled at Lad, "Out of my way, you—"

Wiggen didn't even see Lad move. One moment, Lakhshim was striding forward, knife in hand, ready to kill, and the next moment, his arm was bent at an impossible angle. The dagger splashed to the muddy ground as the boy's scream tore through the night. Lad stood exactly where he had, unruffled by his lightning-fast strike.

"Nobody touches Mya until we see Lissa."

The boy collapsed to his knees, cradling his broken arm, his screams echoing off the tenement walls.

"Oh, shut up!" Horice drew a long rapier, took one step forward, and lunged. The tip of the sword pierced the boy's skull from back to front as easily as it would a ripe melon. He twisted the blade and the body jerked spasmodically. Yanking the rapier free, Horice wiped it clean and slipped it back into its scabbard in one easy motion.

Wiggen watched as the boy toppled into a twitching heap, his blood thickening the mud. Her whimper seemed loud in the sudden silence. They'd not been here five minutes, and already someone was dead. Her knees began to shake, and she was thankful they were hidden beneath her skirts. Was she wrong to have come? What could she do among people like this? Did they have any hope of getting Lissa back?

"Horice! That was…" Neera shook with apoplectic rage. "We *needed* him!"

The Master Blade shrugged and scowled, refusing to meet her caustic glare. "We couldn't have him drawing attention."

"You see, Lad?" Venom dripped from Mya's voice as she struggled against her bonds. "You see what they'll do to your pretty baby?"

"Shut up!"

Every eye in the courtyard turned to Wiggen, and it took her a moment to realize that it had been her voice crying out.

"Yes, do be quiet, dear Mya. We have no intention of betraying Lad. In fact," Patrice gestured toward the corner of the courtyard, and the woman they'd seen in the mirror strode forth, "here is your precious little bundle of joy, safe and sound."

"Lissa!" Wiggen managed one step before Lad's grip on her arm restrained her headlong rush into the midst of the assassins.

"Bring her here," Lad ordered. "Close enough that we can see she's safe."

"Go ahead, Kellik." Youtrin motioned the woman forward. "But be ready."

To Wiggen's horror, Kellik drew a long, curved knife. She came to within a few steps and propped the fussy babe up for them to see, then nestled the length of razor-edged steel across Lissa's chin.

"Lad..." Wiggen choked on her words.

"Calm, Wiggen," Lad said, his steady voice barely loud enough for her to hear.

For an outraged moment she wanted to tear away from his grasp. How could he be so calm? How could he stand to see their little girl threatened? She felt like screaming, like fainting. Then she felt the hand on her arm trembling like a plucked harp string, and the heat emanating from his body. Lad quivered like a tightly wound spring waiting for violent release. How he kept himself in check, she didn't know, but she did know that, if they wanted to get out of this alive with their daughter, she couldn't distract him with imprudent actions. She had to stick to their plan.

Calm. Wiggen tried to breathe deep to still her pounding heart, to rein in her terror, but the calming techniques Lad had taught her wouldn't work. Her breath caught in her throat, and she began to shake all over. It had been easier when the blade had been at her own throat, but Lissa...

"You see? Safe and sound." Patrice smiled again as she waved a hand toward the baby, but her eyes were cold, and her voice had taken on a steely ring. "But now, Lad, you've created a problem for us. Our deal was your child for the delivery of your master, but you knew that our intent was to kill her. By ruining our only available means of completing the task, you've extended your obligation."

"I didn't kill him." Lad pointed to Horice and glared. "He did."

"What was I supposed to do, pat the idiot on the shoulder?"

"Quiet, Horice!" Neera snapped.

"You don't order me!" Horice countered, his hand drifting to the hilt of his rapier.

Youtrin cracked his huge knuckles. "Didn't I *say* we needed a backup?"

"You see? They'll betray you!" Mya surged and thrashed against her bonds.

"The baby," Patrice raised her voice to be heard, "will remain in our possession, and you will stay here until we can—"

The bickering assaulted Wiggen's ears like the roar of a storm wind, but her eyes remained fixed upon the gleaming knife at Lissa's throat. She knew what she had to do, and could delay no longer.

"Shut up! All of you!" Wiggen wrenched her arm out of Lad's grasp and wiped the tears and rain from her eyes. "I'll do it!"

"You?" Patrice sounded skeptical, and Youtrin actually laughed, but Wiggen had already bent to pick up the dead boy's fallen dagger.

"You'll hand Lissa over when it's done! Say it!" The blade trembled in her grasp, rain dripping from its tip.

"Of course. Kill Mya and we'll hand over the child. That's all we want." Patrice's easy tone and casual smile made her assurance almost believable.

"Wiggen, I don't—"

"Shut *up*, Lad!" She turned on her husband, the naked blade between them. "I don't care! It's for Lissa!"

He nodded and stepped back, and Wiggen glared down at Mya, bound and kneeling like a lamb ready for slaughter. She stepped forward, her rain-slicked grip on the dagger's hilt so hard that her knuckles shone white.

"Wiggen. Don't." Mya looked up at her, her eyes no longer hate-filled, no longer blazing with spite. "You don't have to do this."

Wiggen considered all the pain this woman had brought to their family, all the sleepless nights Wiggen had endured waiting for Lad to come home, wondering if he lay dead in a gutter. How wonderful their lives would have been if not for Mya. *No mercy...*

"Yes, I do."

Wiggen grasped a handful of Mya's hair and slashed with the dagger, surprised at how easily the blade parted flesh. Fear flashed in Mya's eyes as a waterfall of crimson cascaded from her neck. Then her eyes rolled up and Wiggen released her grip on the assassin's hair.

Mya toppled forward into the mud.

It was over.

Wiggen dropped the dagger and turned to Kellick. "Now give her to me." She strode forward with her arms outstretched, ready to take Lissa, but the assassin stepped back, her eyes darting to the masters.

"Not yet, I'm afraid." Patrice's honey-sweet tone couldn't hide the triumph in her voice. "With Mya's death, Lad, you become a weapon without a master. A blade without a hand to wield it. We intend to be that hand."

Wiggen slumped. She'd hoped against hope that these people would uphold their end of the bargain and hand over Lissa. But, as Mya had aptly predicted, they'd been betrayed.

"I'm sorry, Wiggen."

Her hand drifted toward the dagger sewn into her dress as she turned to face her husband. The pain in his eyes grasped her heart like a vice. But for the first time since Lissa had been kidnapped, Wiggen's fear ebbed. She had insisted on taking her part in this, and here was where she had to be. A mother belonged with her family.

She smiled gently at Lad. "It's not your fault." Steeling her singing nerves, Wiggen turned to Kellick, looked her straight in the eye, and took a step forward. "Give me my daughter."

"Don't be ridiculous!" Patrice snapped. "Another step and Kellik will slit your baby's throat!"

"No. She won't." Wiggen ignored the masters and locked eyes with the woman who held Lissa's life in her hands. One more step forward, and she was nearly within arm's reach of Lissa. "Kill my baby, and Lad will slaughter everyone here. But *you*, Kellik," Wiggen punctuated her words with a thrust of her finger, "you will be the *first* to die. Give me my baby, and you live. Don't, and you die. *That's* the deal."

Kellik's eyes flicked beyond Wiggen to Lad, then back again. The woman's sneer faded to a grimace of fear. She, apparently, knew Lad's reputation. The blade at Lissa's throat wavered.

Wiggen's hopes soared. *So close!* She took a slow step forward and reached out her free hand toward Lissa. Her daughter caught sight of her then, and let out an insistent shriek.

"Oh, no, you don't!" Fast as a viper, Horice whipped his rapier free of its scabbard and lunged. Immediately, his arm drooped, the elbow slack, and the sword's tip dropped to the ground instead of plunging into Wiggen's chest. Confusion twisted his face, followed quickly by belligerence. "What the hells?"

For a moment, every eye snapped toward the Master Blade...except Wiggen's. She grasped the hilt of the dagger sewn into her dress and lunged forward with all her strength.

The long, narrow blade sliced easily through the material of Wiggen's dress, barely slowing as it pierced Kellik's leather vest. Wiggen felt it plunge hilt-deep into the flesh just below the sternum, angled up, just as Lad had taught her.

Kellik's eyes widened in surprise, and Wiggen used the instant to snatch the blade at her daughter's throat. Not until she saw the blood flowing between her fingers did she feel the pain, but she gritted her teeth against it. Though the dagger cut her, Kellik couldn't jerk the knife, couldn't slash or stab at her. The magic of the guildmaster's ring prevented any counterattack. As Kellik crumpled to her knees, Wiggen released her grip on both weapons and caught Lissa in her arms.

"Grab her!" No honey dripped from the Master Inquisitor's words now as Patrice stepped back toward her bodyguard. "Now!"

As she turned from Kellik, Wiggen spied Youtrin lunging for her. His steps faltered as if he had been caught in an invisible net. The veins in his thick neck bulged as he tried, and failed, to reach out and grab her.

"Hells, just kill the bitch!" Horice shouted as he straightened from his lunge, raising the tip of his rapier out of the mud.

Nothing happened. Every assassin in the courtyard tensed, but not a single crossbow fired, not a single sword lifted to strike.

Wiggen gathered Lissa close to her body. The ring would protect her, and she would protect her child. Then she caught Horice staring at her, or rather, staring at her left hand as it clutched Lissa's blanket.

"The ring! She's wearing the godsdamned guildmaster's ring!"

"Wiggen, go!"

With Lad's voice urging her on, Wiggen raced across the courtyard as all Nine Hells broke loose behind her.

With every eye on Wiggen, Lad struck.

No mercy…

Horice stood only three long strides away, but the Master Blade's reflexes had been honed by decades of murder. The long blade swept in a perfect arc of rune-etched steel to intercept Lad's leap.

Lad twisted like a corkscrew around the weapon's path, losing only an inch of hair from his head as it swept past. Then his feet cracked together, snapping the assassin's forearm like a stick of kindling. Horice's nerveless fingers loosed the hilt, and the blade flipped end over end.

Lad landed in a spinning crouch and reached out. The wire-wrapped hilt of the enchanted sword smacked into his palm...and writhed in his grasp. The hilt melded into his grip as if it had been made for him, the ornate basket guard and crosspiece constricting into a simple round guard. The blade thickened and curved into that of a katana, the weapon he knew best.

The change nearly threw Lad off, but he recovered as he spun on the ball of one foot and swept the blade around in a flat arc. Enchanted steel passed through Horice's middle with little resistance, snicking through his spine like a scythe through a blade of grass. The Master Blade fell in two, his voice rising in a horrible wail of panic as he clutched at his spilled entrails.

The other masters were slower to react, but not by much. Neera flung a spray of poisoned glass shards, and Youtrin whipped a hand axe at Lad with an underhand pitch. Patrice hastened her retreat, shoving her bodyguard forward.

Lad flipped backward, easily evading the twirling axe, and splashed back down after the storm of poisoned shards had passed beneath him. He spared a glance toward the tunnel to the street, and breathed easier to see Wiggen ducking unhindered into the darkness. All attention centered on him, just as they had planned.

His concern for his family cost him, however. At a flicker of movement in the corner of his eye, Lad twisted away, snapping the sword up to parry, but too late. The whirling axe scored a line of pain across his shoulder. The blade had apparently arced in flight like a boomerang, then hurtled back for a second pass before the haft smacked precisely into Youtrin's meaty palm.

The Master Enforcer grinned as he drew a second axe from his belt.

"No one else has to die tonight."

Lad's proclamation elicited derisive laughter from Youtrin and a silent sneer from Neera as they and their bodyguards stood their ground. Patrice's bodyguard looked ridiculously vulnerable in her low-cut dress, but the snarl on her face did her more credit than the worried look on the Master Inquisitor's. One other, Horice's bodyguard—*Sereth*—glanced at his fallen master, then at Lad, and backed away, his face strangely blank.

"I disagree." Youtrin grinned and nodded toward the assassins encircling the courtyard, their crossbows aimed at Lad. Some of them still looked baffled at being unable to shoot Wiggen, but they quickly brought their weapons to bear. "You're quick, but not that quick. Kill him!"

More than a dozen crossbows began firing a ragged volley. In that split second, Lad despaired. He might have been able to evade the swarm of deadly missiles if they'd all flown at once, but the staggered fire thwarted the effectiveness of a displacement maneuver. He couldn't dodge them all. He needed help, and there was only one place it could come from. He wondered if it would come too late.

But as the bolts took flight, Mya exploded up from her brief death in a storm of blood, mud, shredded canvas, and flashing daggers. She deflected six bolts that would have pierced Lad, and two more plunged into her flesh as she intercepted their flight. The others Lad managed to deflect or evade before he landed back to back with Mya in the bloody mire.

Lad couldn't suppress a feral grin at the astonished looks on their opponent's faces. These assassins knew death better than anyone, and they'd watched Mya die. But they hadn't known her secret. Though bloody, the death stroke had not immediately stopped her heart, and the wound had healed in moments. Mya had been right; they needed her help, but he'd been surprised when she had readily agreed to their grisly plan. And not only agreed, but praised him for the scheme.

"Finally," she'd said, "you're thinking like an assassin!"

He heard the snick of her dagger severing the head of a bolt that protruded from her stomach, and the wet sound of the shaft being pulled free. Another snick, and the one from her leg splashed to the muddy ground.

"How…" Youtrin gaped in shocked puzzlement.

All around them, assassins stared wide-eyed. Several looked panicked, but most had been in the guild for too many years to be fazed by facing two foes instead of one, even if one had seemingly risen from the dead. But Lad kept his gaze on the masters; they were the truly dangerous ones here.

"Neera first," he whispered too soft for anyone but Mya to hear.

"I need to get close," she whispered in return, "but I'll need help."

He reached back with his free hand to grasp the belt of her trousers. "Now!"

Lad lunged forward as he felt her leap, and flung her straight at the alchemist with every ounce of his strength. Unfortunately, Mya's flat trajectory was predictable, and Youtrin's axes reached her before she could put a dagger in Neera's eye. She parried one, but the other struck under her the arm, the head buried in her ribcage. The impact deflected her, and her dagger stroke only scored Neera's cheek.

Lad charged.

Youtrin and his bodyguard stepped in front of Neera, whose own bodyguard inexplicably fell face-down in the mud, his poisoned darts still in his hands. The Master Enforcer caught the axe that Mya had deflected, and drew a hooked dagger. Crossbows fired, but only a few; Lad and Mya were too close to the masters for a clean shot. Instead, he heard the splashing footfalls of charging assassins. He deflected two bolts and one shuriken, but another bolt found him, lodging deep in his thigh.

Ignoring the pain, he slashed at Youtrin, satisfied as he felt the katana snap the hooked dagger and cleave sinew and bone, flaying open the Master Enforcer's massive chest. On his back swing, Lad sent the charging bodyguard's head flying out into the rain.

Beyond Neera, he saw Mya roll to her feet, and heard the crack of ribs as she removed Youtrin's axe from her chest. She would heal, he knew, but how fast? Mya had already lost a lot of blood when Wiggen slit her throat. Lad knew from experience that blood loss would weaken her, even though her wounds healed.

Bloody spittle darkened Youtrin's chin, his breath a ragged, wet gurgle, but still he kept coming. As Lad dodged the sweep of his axe, he heard two more crossbows fire. He managed to deflect one bolt as he swept the blade around and split Youtrin's thick skull just above his jutting brows, but the second bolt lodged in his shoulder. Knocked off balance, Lad fell to one knee in the mud. He envied Mya her magical pain block as agony lanced through him. Forcing the pain aside, he sprang away to prevent Youtrin's corpse from falling atop him and pinning him in the mire.

Steps away, Patrice's bodyguard fell to a stroke of Mya's stolen axe. Unfortunately, the distraction gave the Master Alchemist the opportunity to reach into her robe. A ball of green glass appeared in the old woman's hand, and she flung it down at Lad's feet.

Lad lunged for small sphere, the bolt in his shoulder grating against bone as he flung out his free hand. He caught it as he would a falling egg, knowing that death awaited him inside that glass ball. He tucked into a protective roll, grimacing as the bolt in his shoulder snapped off against the ground, and hurled the glass sphere at the assassins rushing him from behind. The ball ruptured against the leader's chest, a cloud of green vapor exploding forth to envelop several of Lad's foes. Flesh melted from bone in a runny mass of liquefied meat wherever the mist touched them.

Through the screams and hissing rain, Lad heard a strangled gasp. He hoped it was Neera choking on her own blood, but a glance dashed his hopes. The Master Alchemist was backing away from the battle, a bottle clutched in her hand. She looked down at the dark glass vessel, her ancient features pale with fear as she popped the cork and quaffed the potion. Still he heard the sound of choking breaths. Whipping around, he spied Mya standing over the corpse of Patrice's bodyguard, one hand tearing at a serrated silver chain that constricted around her neck. Patrice clutched the other end of the chain, her painted features contorted in a rictus grin of vengeance.

Mya clawed at the throttling chain, gasping for breath, and slashing ineffectually at it with Youtrin's stolen axe, but she could not break free. It was killing her.

I've got to help her. There was no way Lad could fend off all the attackers alone. But as he prepared to leap to Mya's aid, the charging assassins fell on them both.

Lad parried and slashed, kicked and punched, struggling to reach Mya. Though impeded by his arrow wounds, his strength sapped by pain, no blade touched him.

A glance showed him that Mya fared far worse. She had managed to lay Patrice flat on her back, the axe blade embedded between the Master Inquisitor's kohled eyes, but still the chain writhed and coiled around her neck. Mya fought to breathe, bloody fingers wedged between the chain's serrated links and her throat. She met the onslaught of assassins with her last dagger, drawn hastily from her boot, and many well-placed kicks, but she was surrounded, and blades scored her flesh. She couldn't take much more of this before she was too weak to fight. And once she was down, they could kill her.

Lad slashed through his ring of adversaries and leapt to help Mya.

Two of the assassins facing her fell before they knew he was on them. As another turned toward him, Mya's dagger flicked out too fast for anyone but Lad to see. The assassin fell twitching to the ground, his brain disconnected from his spine. But Mya still couldn't breathe. Her face had darkened, her mouth gaping for air. Lad slashed the writhing end of the chain, severing the handle from the rest, but the chain still constricted her neck, sawing into her flesh like it was striving to cut off her head. Her face darkened further, her eyes bulging from their sockets.

"Mya! Hold still!"

Desperate to draw breath, she complied as best she could, deflecting two sword strokes with her dagger while she stood rock steady. Her eyes bulged even further, however, when Lad slashed at her neck with the enchanted blade.

The katana severed the chain binding her throat. It also cut a half-inch furrow in the muscle of her neck, but that razor-thin wound sealed in seconds. The chain fell in pieces at her feet.

"Thanks," Mya gasped as she flicked a fallen sword up to her free hand with her toe. Once again, they stood back to back.

Lad took a deep, steadying breath—*No pain...*—and assessed their opponents. More than a dozen assassins still stood against them, but twice that number lay dead or maimed. Not ten feet away, Neera thrashed on the ground, her yellow fingernails digging deep into the mud, her back arched, and her face contorted in a grimace. Lad wondered if the Master Alchemist had taken Moirin's way out, poisoning herself to prevent capture. He didn't care; as long as she was dead, his family would be safe. He turned back to the surviving assassins.

"Your masters are dead! Leave us, and we'll spare your lives!"

"We will?" Mya nudged him in the back, and he could hear her malicious grin. "Why?"

"Because they can't beat us, and they know it."

300

The assassins exchanged worried glances, some looking to the senior journeymen, others to their fallen masters. They eased back a step...two steps. Several at the outskirts of the crowd turned and bolted, then the rest fled, some quickly, some backing slowly, only breaking into a run at the last moment.

"You okay?" Mya dropped the sword and touched her hand gently to Lad's shoulder above the splintered arrow.

"No, I really don't think I—"

A tearing, hacking cough interrupted him. Lad and Mya turned to the pile of thrashing robes where Master Alchemist Neera had lain. What stood up from the robes wasn't Neera. In fact, it wasn't even human.

Chapter XXIV

"W" ell, *damn*!" Mya stared as the thing heaved up.

It stood half again as tall as Lad, and was twice as broad, with massively muscled arms and legs. The silk robes that had clothed Neera tore as the creature straightened, but it wasn't just its size that shredded the cloth. Its entire body was armored with scales, each bearing an inch-long barb. One backhanded swipe would rip the skin right off a human being.

"What...is it?"

Mya heard more disgust than fear in Lad's voice, which helped to boost her own flagging courage. She felt no pain, but the fatigue of blood loss lay on her like a wet blanket, pulling her down.

"Neera, I think." She swallowed hard as the creature reached up one clawed hand to rip away the last clinging vestiges of Neera's face. A vaguely reptilian visage glared at them, eyes like yellow coals burning beneath a jutting brow. Scaled lips drew back from a broad mouth that sported far too many teeth. They both backed away as the monstrosity stepped forward. Mya dropped the sword, and jerked Youtrin's axe from Patrice's corpse. "We could run."

"We could, but if it *is* Neera..." Lad paused, "...she has to die. She knows Wiggen wears the guildmaster's ring. If she tells the Grandmaster, my family will never be safe."

"I thought you'd say something like that."

The creature took another six-foot stride forward, eying first Lad, then Mya, as if deciding which of them it should eat first. They both stepped back again.

"Well, staring at each other won't solve anything." Mya threw the axe with all her strength, right at its head.

The blade glanced off its armored brow, whirled in an arc and ricocheted off the scales of its shoulder before returning to Mya's grasp. The creature had made no effort to dodge, but neither impact had penetrated its armor.

With a hiss like rain on a tile roof, its mouth gaped, a basketful of daggers. Beneath the forked tongue, Mya glimpsed two fleshy pits that swelled and opened. She shoved Lad away as a spray of yellow liquid jetted forth. The reflexive action struck her as ironic; for the last five years, Lad had been saving *her* from attacks. But the fact was, she could heal and Lad couldn't. And she stood a much better chance of surviving this fight if he was alive to fight beside her. She was thinking like an assassin.

At least, that was what she told herself as acid splashed across her legs.

The noisome stench of burning flesh, *her* burning flesh, sent a surge of panic through her. She backed away from the creature and glanced down. The legs of her trousers had melted away in a cloud of noxious vapor. Unfortunately, the magical wrappings, her armor of anonymity, had finally betrayed her. The acid-soaked cloth burned, knitted back together, and burned again, each time searing her flesh anew. In the brief gaps of the writhing cloth, she saw her blistering skin. The magic renewed it, pink and soft, and still etched with runes. Fear ripped through her, for she knew that if too many of her runes were destroyed before they could heal her and reform, the magic would fail.

Mya slashed frantically at the wrappings with her dagger, peeling them away bit by bit with her fingers before they could knit back together. Her hands blistered, healed, and blistered again. The dagger smoldered as acid pitted the fine steel, and still she slashed, ripped and threw away the acid-soaked cloth. Finally, the saturated wrappings were gone. The flesh on her legs healed, and the runes reformed, shimmering in the streaming rain, their magic intact. She allowed herself a breath of relief.

"Mya!"

Lad's shout brought her eyes up to see a massive, scaly arm sweeping toward her.

Mya had just enough time to turn and take the impact on her shoulder and back. Barbs like a wall of thorns ripped into her. The force of the blow snapped her head back, and she felt the muscles of her neck tear in a painless but nauseating sensation. Bones cracked, and she wondered why the scenery tumbled past in a spinning swirl. A brick wall flashed across her sight, and Mya's vision went suddenly dark.

𝔴𝔍𝔥𝔞𝔷𝔥

Lad heard Mya hit the wall of the tenement building with a sickening crunch. He didn't dare look to see how she was, for the Neera-creature had turned its full attention to him.

It lunged, its mouth gaping and clawed hands grasping. It was fast for such a large creature, but not fast enough to seize him. Lad spun away and slashed at a wrist as thick as his thigh. The katana skittered along the armored hide, shearing the spines off a half-dozen scales, but didn't penetrate into the flesh beneath. Ducking under a sweeping backhand, he leapt to slash at its face. The creature jerked back, and the blade scored a line in the fine scales of its cheek. Blood as black as midnight flowed from the gash, and the flat, reptilian head snapped around to glare at him. Lad landed in a crouch, stumbling at the pain from the crossbow bolt still protruding from his thigh.

This isn't working.

He circled to buy time, favoring his injured leg, every moment weakening him further with trauma and blood loss. He had to end this fight quickly, but how, if he couldn't hack through the scales? He searched his memory for a lesson and came up with nothing. He'd been trained to fight people, not a monster like this. *Got to find a way to get through its armor.*

Armor... *When fighting an armored opponent, seek the joints between plates with the point of a weapon or apply blunt force to vital areas. Remember!*

Lad considered his options. Blunt force wouldn't work; he would only tear himself to pieces if he tried to kick or punch those thorny plates. He had Horice's sword, but the creature didn't have any joints in its armor. If he thrust at the right angle, the blade might slip between the scales, but it could become jammed between them, and he would lose the weapon. He edged to his left, and the creature's gaze followed him, its yellow eyes narrowed.

That's it! Lad smiled grimly as he focused on his targets. The creature might be armored, but if he blinded it, he might be able to kill it.

He dodged another grasping hand and slashed at the fingers. Again the blade chipped off a couple of the spurs from its knuckles, but did no real damage. Lad backed away, but his heel found one of the dead assassins. He turned his stumble into a short backward flip into the midst of the corpses and snatched up an abandoned weapon. Feinting to his left to draw the creature's attention, he flipped the heavy, leaf-bladed dagger in his hand and threw.

One of the yellow eyes went dark.

The beast's half-hiss, half-scream, shattered the rain-soaked night as it yanked the dagger out of its ruined eye. The toothy maw gaped, spewing acid in a broad arc, but Lad was already tumbling out of the way. A cloud of noxious fumes rose behind him as the corpses of the fallen assassins hissed and smoked. Lad looked around wildly, searching for something else to throw, and spied a crossbow bolt. He had just wrapped his fingers around the short wooden arrow when a deep rending noise snapped his attention back to his foe.

The creature had ripped one of the stunted trees right out of the ground. Holding the root end, it brandished the tree like a huge leafy club and advanced. As it cocked the tree back for a swing, Lad took aim and hurled the bolt at its remaining eye. A last-instant twitch of the creature's head sent the arrow ricocheting off into the dark. Lad prepared to dodge the sweeping blow of the tree, but realized that he had mistaken its attack. Instead of using the tree like a club, it flung it straight at him.

Lad leapt, but the raking limbs caught him like a huge net. He hacked a swath through the foliage as he fell, but landed hard, pinned for a moment beneath the densely packed branches. He thrashed to free himself, but the limbs bent rather than breaking. A huge foot came down on the trunk of the tree, pressing hard to pin him to the soggy ground. Cold mud rose around Lad as he slashed at the encumbering limbs, to no avail. Droplets of acid hissed in the rain as the toothy maw snapped forward, as quick as a striking snake. Lad plunged the katana toward the soft tissues at the back of the throat, but the creature twisted its neck, and the blade punctured its cheek instead of its spine. Teeth grated on steel as the jaws closed.

The enchanted blade snapped off near the guard.

The creature flung its head, spitting blood and shattered steel as the sword's hilt writhed in Lad's hand, morphing through a hundred different forms as the magic died. He flung the useless thing away and struggled to free himself, agony lancing through his leg as the crossbow bolt in his thigh caught on a limb. A huge clawed hand reached down for him. He couldn't evade it, couldn't dodge, and couldn't break free. He grasped the hand by finger and thumb to keep the claws at bay, but the creature's strength could not be resisted. Finger-long claws plucked at his throat.

A flash of movement caught his eye just before one of the thick stone benches crashed down on the Neera-creature's skull. Blood and pulped gray matter gushed from its ruined eye socket.

Lad rolled to evade the falling corpse, pain lancing thorough his leg as the crossbow bolt snapped off. A stifled cry escaped his lips as the heavy body crashed down onto the tangle of limbs and foliage. Pushing himself up slowly, he eased out of the pressing branches, every wound screaming for attention.

A slim hand grasped his arm and lifted him up, steadying him on shaky legs. Mya looked like a tattered scarecrow, her shredded wrappings hanging in rags. The tattoos on her legs, shoulder and one arm shone dark in the glistening rain, unveiled for the world to see.

"You okay?"

"No." He looked around the corpse-strewn courtyard, his eyes drawn to the narrow tunnel through which his wife and daughter had fled. "But I will be."

He brushed off her helping hand and stumbled toward the dark passage. "Wiggen!"

His heart leapt in his chest as his wife emerged from her hiding place. Wiggen was soaked and shivering, but she was alive, and clutched Lissa to her breast. Lad could have sobbed with relief. It was over. The masters were dead, and his family was safe.

Wiggen's eyes took in his injuries, the blood, and her face paled.

"Oh, gods! Lad!" She hurried forward, but then stumbled to a stop. Her eyes widened, and a startled expression crossed her face. "Lad? I don't..." She took one more staggering step and fell to her knees.

"Wiggen?" Lad lunged forward to catch her, his pain forgotten. He clutched her, then caught Lissa as her arms went slack. "Wiggen! What—"

"I...can't feel..." she gasped in panic. "Lad, I..." Her eyes lost focus, and one last sigh escaped her lips.

"Wiggen!" Lad clutched her close with one arm. He was vaguely aware of Lissa wriggling in his grasp, crying as the rain pattered onto her little face. Wiggen's heart fluttered against his chest like the wings of a caged sparrow. "No, Wiggen. Please. Don't..."

Wiggen's tremulous heartbeats slowed...then ceased. Her head dropped back, her beautiful eyes staring sightless up into the weeping sky.

"NO!"

Lad didn't know if he actually voiced his scream, but it echoed raucously in his mind, a cavern of confusion and pain. Wiggen couldn't be dead. If anyone died, it should have been him. He was the weapon...the killer...the assassin. Not her. Wiggen was just an innkeeper's daughter, a wife, a mother, a lover, a friend...

The pain of his wounds vanished in a sea of anguish as a thousand memories rushed over him. Wiggen with her eyes closed, tenderly cupping a sparrow in her hands. Wiggen in the kitchen, humming as she prepared oatcakes. Wiggen lying beside him in bed, smiling sleepily in the candlelight, the sweat of their lovemaking beaded on her breasts.

Nevermore...

Eventually, Lissa's cries penetrated the fog of loss that obscured Lad's mind, and he slowly recalled himself. He looked to his child, but even his relief that she was safe and sound couldn't allay his grief.

I must care for her, he thought numbly. *Wiggen would want that.*

Gently, Lad eased his wife to the sodden ground. As he pulled back his hand, however, his fingertip brushed something hard in her back, and he plucked it out. A chill that had nothing to do with the rain washed over him as he stared at the small dart that had been lodged deep in her flesh. The metal shaft was black, fletched with a tiny tuft of black feathers, its tip beveled and hollow.

308

He stared at his dead wife, then at the dart in his hand. Like a smoldering bonfire rekindled, rage ignited in his heart. Someone, somehow, had murdered Wiggen. Lad lurched to his feet. He had thought his fight was over, but now he knew it was just beginning.

$\mathscr{W} \mathbb{J}^{\mathcal{P}} \sim \mathfrak{d} \mathbb{Z} \mathcal{H}$

"Lad! What—"

Mya stared down uncomprehending at Wiggen, or rather, Wiggen's corpse, Lad's wretched cry ringing in her ears. *What the hells happened?*

Lad evidently had not heard her. He just stood there, staring down at his dead wife, the squalling babe held limply in one arm.

"Lad!" She touched his arm, and when he still didn't respond, she grabbed him by the wrist. Despite the chill rain, it felt as if his skin was burning. "Lad! Come on! All this noise is bound to attract the City Guard. We've got to go!"

Lad turned blank eyes toward her, his gaze as dead as his wife. "They murdered her." He held out a small dart, bloody rainwater pooling in his palm around the tiny cylinder of black metal.

Confusion clouded her thoughts. "They *couldn't* have! She's wearing the guildmaster's ring!" There was no time to discuss this now. She tugged on his wrist. "Come on! We've got to go!"

"The ring…" His eyes snapped to needle sharpness. "Here! Take Lissa." He thrust the crying babe into her arms.

"I don't—"

"*Take her!*" The sudden murder in his eyes brought her up short, and she took the child, holding her close to block the rain. The crying eased, and Lissa opened her eyes—*eyes like his*—and looked up into Mya's face.

Lad dropped to his knees beside Wiggen's body, leaning over her. He took her hands in his, kissed them gently, then slipped the guildmaster's ring off her finger. For a long moment he just knelt there, looking at the ring. Finally he spoke.

"They murdered my wife, Mya. They must have hired someone outside the guild. I'm going to find them, and I'm going to kill them. But I need your help. I need the *guild's* help."

"There *is* no guild, Lad. Look around!" She waved a hand at the litter of bodies in the morass of churned mud and blood. "It's destroyed. *We* destroyed it."

"No," he said firmly. "We killed *some* of them, but there are more. As long as there's a guildmaster, there's a guild."

Mya shook her head. *What is he talking about?* "There *is* no guildmaster, Lad. Hells, I'm the only *master* left! There's just—" She choked on her words as Lad raised his hands. "*No!*"

He slipped the guildmaster's ring onto his finger.

Mya froze as Lad stared at her, his luminous eyes glowing in the gloom. In that moment, she could count every raindrop that fell between them, as if they took an eternity to descend from heaven to earth. The sight of the gold and obsidian ring on his finger stabbed through her. All the fighting, all the killing, everything she'd done to prevent this, and here she was, a slave once again. She looked into his eyes, but she no longer saw the man she knew, the man she loved. Lad was gone; only the weapon remained. She could do nothing but obey.

Lad lifted Lissa from Mya's arms and nodded toward the tangle of corpses. "Take the other masters' rings."

"Why?"

"*Take them!* We'll need to appoint new masters from the surviving journeymen."

"But—"

Lad's voice grated between clenched teeth, low and dangerous, as he leaned toward her. "I'm the new guildmaster, and your life is mine to spend! Now get the other rings, or I swear, I'll kill you right here!"

310

My life...his to spend, she thought, swallowing the bile that flooded her throat.

Mya splashed through the mud and recovered the other four masters' rings. The creature that had been Neera had melted in the rain, the scaly horror dissolving away to reveal the corpse of a shriveled old woman. When she returned to him, Lad handed his daughter back to her and gathered Wiggen into his arms.

"Where to?"

"I'm taking Wiggen home." He turned away from her, starting toward one of the tunnels out of the courtyard. "And you're coming with me."

"Yes...Master." Mya fell in behind Lad, and they vanished into the gloom of Twailin's rain-soaked night.

Chapter XXV

"Looks like a band of ogres came through here." Sergeant Tamir toed the hilt of a broken sword, then stumbled back when it slowly shifted from a rapier to a broadsword. "What the hells?"

"Careful, Tam." Norwood steadied Tamir as the sergeant's heel struck the corpse of a man who had been neatly cut in half. "Try not to fall on the evidence."

"Yes, sir."

Norwood concurred with the sergeant's assessment of the scene. Corpses were strewn everywhere, some slashed, some twisted, some crushed, and some little more than smoldering puddles of liquefied flesh. Most bore weapons, which he would expect given the violence of the scene, but others confused him. One woman was dressed like a high-priced courtesan, but sported a deep wound between her eyes. Another, a wrinkled old woman with a crushed skull, wasn't dressed at all. Norwood maneuvered around an uprooted tree, trying to put together a reasonable scenario that fit the evidence.

Yawning, he wondered what time it was. Probably another three hours until daylight. It had been well after midnight when he received an urgent summons from the captain of the City Guard. A terse note explained that there had been a battle near Fiveway Fountain, and that Norwood and his Royal Guard should come immediately. He had nearly had the messenger arrested for waking him with an obvious prank—the thought of a battle taking place in Twailin seemed ludicrous—but now that he had seen it, the evidence that this had indeed been a battle was hard to refute.

"How many, Captain?" he asked his City Guard counterpart.

"Hard to say exactly, but our best count's around thirty or so." The captain indicated one of the puddles of remains slowly being incorporated into the courtyard mud by the rain. "Going to have to count bones to figure out if that was one or two."

"I know this one, Captain," said a city guardsman, pointing at a corpse with a deep chest wound and the top of his skull sheared away. "His name's Youtrin. He's head of the Bargeman's Guild."

"A guildmaster?" Norwood's pulse quickened as he thought, *Not only more violence, but now we've got city leaders being killed. The duke will have my head!* He stepped over two more bodies and looked down at the face frozen by death in a snarl. The hands of the body still clutched the hilt of a shattered knife and a hand axe. "Looks like he was more than just a guildmaster if he was involved in this. He certainly doesn't look like an innocent bystander."

"What's a guildmaster doing at this time of night in this part of the city, sir?" Tamir's question was rhetorical, but it started Norwood thinking.

"Guild war," he murmured, remembering his late-night visitor's claim. Five years ago he would have laughed at the thought of an upright citizen being involved with the Assassins Guild, but the experience with Saliez had taught him differently. "I wonder who won."

Tamir, the only one close enough to have heard his captain's musings, looked skeptical, but refrained from commenting.

"Well, we'd best get started, Tamir, but be careful. Send for Master Woefler to examine the scene for evidence of magic." He poked the broken blade that had distressed his sergeant with the toe of his boot. The hilt shifted from a broad cross to an ornate basket guard right before their eyes. "Like that."

313

"Right, sir. Come on, people! Work in from the edges, one body at a time. Everything gets bagged and tagged. It may be muddy as a pigsty, but that's no excuse for missing evidence!"

As Tamir directed his men, Norwood stepped out of the way. The bodies would be taken to the City Guard headquarters for identification, if there was enough left to identify. Somehow, he didn't think many family members would be coming forth to claim loved ones.

"Knew things were coming to a head, but I didn't think it'd end up like this."

Norwood turned to the City Guard captain. "End up? You think this is the end of it?"

"Maybe not, but with so many dead, I don't know how many more would be left to carry on. Somebody must have won here, and whoever lost, lost big."

"I hope you're right, Captain." Norwood looked around at the bodies again and wondered if his mysterious visitor lay among them. Since he had never seen the man's face, there was no way to know. "We've obviously got some higher-ups involved here. Maybe without their leaders, the violence will ease off. But what the hell am I going to report to Duke Mir?"

"I don't envy you that job." The City Guard captain nodded farewell and picked his way through the carnage, gathering his men and leaving the Royal Guard to their grisly job.

"Captain!" Tamir called, waving him over. The sergeant had an incongruous grin on his face, one that sent a shiver of worry up Norwood's spine.

"What, Sergeant?"

"You're gonna *love* this, sir." He knelt beside the corpse of a young man and pointed to a dark speck on his neck. "That look familiar?"

"What the..." Norwood knelt, oblivious to the bloody mire soaking his trousers. The dark speck did look familiar. He grasped the tuft of feathers and drew a black dart from the dead man's neck. "Well, I'll be a..."

314

"Yes, sir." Tamir held out an evidence bottle. "Don't need a wizard to tell me it's the same as that other one."

"Right." Norwood dropped the dart into the bottle. "But have Woefler check the poison to make sure. Keep an eye out for any more." He examined the body and noted the lack of other injuries. "Pay particular attention to the bodies that aren't hacked up."

"Yes, sir." Tamir pocketed the evidence bottle and continued his work.

"Too many questions," Norwood muttered, scowling down as if he could get the answers from the dead man's eyes.

𝒶𝒹𝓏𝒶𝒹𝓏

Kiesha placed the matte-black metal tube snugly into its velvet-lined case, and ran her fingers over the neat row of black darts, each tucked into its own recessed nook. A half-dozen nooks were empty; the night had been eventful. She frowned.

So much death...

Pulling a dart from its nook, she pressed her fingertip against the hollowed point. She barely felt the tip pierce her skin. Blood welled from her finger, and she licked the crimson drop with a flick of her tongue. The dart she'd picked wasn't envenomed, of course.

Maybe it should be.

A knock at the door startled her. She hadn't heard footsteps, but in this house that wasn't unusual. She reinserted the dart into its nook, closed the case, and turned to the door.

"Come in."

The latch turned and Hensen walked in, resplendent as always, his embroidered jacket fairly glowing in the lamplight. That he was still dressed meant he'd waited up to learn the outcome of the evening's events, and Kiesha's heart dropped. She'd hoped to put off her report until morning. She was wet, cold, and...disheartened. The physical discomforts she could ignore, but rarely had a job affected her thus. All she wanted right now was a warm bath, a large brandy, and the oblivion of sleep.

"I didn't hear you come in."

She shrugged. "You taught me well. I'll have a detailed report for you in the morning, sir, but—"

"I want the highlights now. Are Mya and Lad still alive?"

"Yes, sir."

"And the other masters?"

"All dead, sir."

"Ahhh!" One of Hensen's plucked eyebrows arched, and Kiesha wondered vaguely if she should warn him about wrinkling his brow. "The confusion of succession should provide us with a unique opportunity to further advance our interests into Assassins Guild territory. How were the Hunters able to overcome all the other factions?"

Kiesha sighed before answering. She really didn't want to go into details tonight.

"They didn't, sir. Mya and Lad killed the masters, and many of their underlings as well. Lad had delivered her in bondage, but it was a ruse. They fought together. I killed a few assassins whom I believed might harm our charges. The rest fled."

"They killed *how* many?" Hensen's tone was part curiosity, part skepticism. Kiesha didn't blame him. If she hadn't seen it, she wouldn't believe it herself.

"I didn't count, sir. Two dozen at least."

"*What?*"

"Mya is…" She hesitated, wondering how to tell him what she'd seen. This was why she preferred written reports; it gave her time to think things through. "She's not what we thought, sir. She moved like Lad. As fast and as deadly as he is, but with one exception: every wound she took healed instantly."

"Magic! Gods, she must have some kind of magical enhancement. The guildmaster's ring doesn't bestow that kind of power."

"No, sir, but, in fact, Mya wasn't wearing the ring."

"What?" Hensen couldn't hide his surprise. "Sereth told us she did!"

Kiesha wished he would just go away and leave her in peace. This was not how she wanted to tell the story, piecemeal in response to his peppered questions. She was too tired to organize her thoughts.

"Sereth told us what the masters thought, but they were wrong. As it turned out, Lad's wife, Wiggen, actually wore the ring. She used it to protect herself and the baby."

"What do you mean, 'wore it'? She doesn't any longer? How can that be?"

He doesn't miss a trick, Kiesha thought bitterly.

"She's dead, sir. The battle had just ended when a figure ran out of the tunnel right below me. I thought she was another assassin." She paused and gave him a regretful look. "I reacted prematurely."

Hensen stared at her, and Kiesha was unnerved by the hint of fear in his eyes.

"Did Lad see you?"

"No, sir! I left immediately. All the other assassins were already dead or had fled. If he saw me…"

"He would have killed you." He sighed and shook his head. "We're in a very delicate position here, Kiesha. You did well to ensure that Mya and Lad weren't killed—at least we've earned our full contract—but you were careless. If Lad tries to find out who killed his wife... Well, we must ensure that he doesn't."

"I'm sorry, Father."

Hensen stiffened as if he'd been knifed. He slammed shut the door and strode over to Kiesha, the muscles of his jaw writhing under the skin. "I told you *never* to call me that! You don't know who's listening, even here!"

"I…I'm sorry. It slipped." She fixed her eyes on his shoes, properly abashed. "It won't happen again, sir."

"See that it doesn't!" He raised his hand and she flinched, expecting a blow. Instead, he took her chin between his thumb and forefinger, and tilted her eyes up to his. "If they find out you're my daughter, they'll use you to get to me, just as the Assassins Guild used Lad's daughter to get to him. Weapons of blood are the deadliest of all, my dear. Do you understand?"

"I understand, sir."

"Good. Get some sleep. We'll talk in the morning."

"Yes, sir."

As the door shut behind him, Kiesha sank down on her bed. Hensen would never know her lie. She'd known exactly who had dashed out of that tunnel. In fact, she'd been waiting for Wiggen to expose herself. With the ring on Wiggen's finger, no one else could be appointed Twailin guildmaster. She was sure the Grandmaster would be pleased with her decision.

Her decision to kill an innocent woman.

In the silence of her bedroom, Kiesha clapped her hands to her ears. More than the blood and the horrific deaths she had witnessed tonight, more even than killing Wiggen, one thing wracked her. It had chased her across the rooftops as she fled through the streets of Twailin, and pursued her into her home. It still rang in her mind. She wondered if she'd ever be free of Lad's heart-wrenching howl of grief as he mourned his dead wife.

⚡ ⅃ℑↄ ᗞ ℤⱨ

The morning sun glinted off the slab of polished marble that marked Wiggen's grave, and blossoms from the overhanging plum tree garnished the mound of newly overturned earth. A sparrow sang out the end of the rainy season, and Lad cocked his head to listen.

Wiggen so loved the birds.

They had buried Wiggen in the little plot behind the inn, out of sight of the main courtyard. She was not alone; her mother, brother, and Forbish's father all lay here. His wife would forever be surrounded by the family she cherished. The priest they'd paid to say the blessing was long gone, but those who loved Wiggen remained, silent and thoughtful, devastated by her loss.

Fathers, lovers, friends, cousins...

Forbish stood at the head of the grave, his arm tight around Josie's shoulder. They both wept openly. The twins stood like sentries on either side of the fresh mound, their cheeks streaked with tears.

At the foot of the grave, Lissa fussed in Lad's arms, and he rocked her, murmuring meaningless words of comfort. Meaningless, because nothing could comfort a child who would never know her mother. For Lad, also, there was no comfort, no peace, no solace...no Wiggen. He felt as empty as a hollow gourd, lifeless and cold. The only heat within him was the smoldering hatred for the people who had killed his wife.

I'll find them and I'll kill them. All of them. No mercy...

Lissa wiggled again, snuggling her warm body against his chest, her tiny fist clenched in the laces of his shirt. As he hugged her closer, the guildmaster's ring glinted on his finger. He'd donned the ring in a moment of grief and rage, determined to avenge his wife's death. However, for that moment, he had forgotten that he was also a father.

Lad looked down into Lissa's eyes and he realized that he wasn't completely empty. His heart ached with love for his daughter, ached with the pain of what he must do. He caressed the smooth skin of her plump cheek, and she smiled up at him. Wiggen's smile, his eyes, a wisp of hair the color of honey... *Remember!*

His heart broke anew.

The killer within him had been released, and there was no way to put it back. Not until he had avenged Wiggen's death. And a killer could not be a father. Lad strode to the head of the grave and placed Lissa into her grandfather's arms.

"Please...take care of her." His voice caught on the lump in his throat, and his eyes burned as he brushed Lissa's gossamer hair with his fingertips. He resisted the urge to snatch her back and run to where no one would ever find them. "I can't be her father anymore."

"What?" Forbish's face, already red from crying, now flushed darker. "You're leaving her? Us? Just like that?"

"I'm sorry." Lad had repeated those words countless times in the past two days, but he knew it would never be enough. This was all his fault. The family had said time and again that they didn't blame him, that they loved him, and maybe it was true, but it didn't change the facts. "I can't stay here. It's too dangerous for Lissa...for all of you."

"You're going after them, aren't you?" Tika asked, his voice thick with pent-up rage.

"We could help you!" Ponce offered, wiping away his tears.

"No. You have to stay here. Be Lissa's uncles. Protect her. Protect the family." He fixed them with a meaningful stare. "Do that for me. Please."

The twins nodded and looked down.

"I'll send money by courier," he told Forbish, but the innkeeper shook his head.

"I don't want money, Lad. I want you to stay and be a father to Lissa. She needs you!"

"I know, but I can't...do what I have to do and be her father at the same time." Lad looked at his daughter again, and the lump in his throat threatened to overwhelm him. He swallowed it and shook his head. "Maybe someday when this is all over I'll be able to come back, but not until it's done."

Josie burst into tears. Forbish just stared at him.

"I'm sorry." He knew his sorrow would never be enough.

Lad wrenched himself away from his daughter, his family, everything in the world that he loved. Quickly, so as not to lose his courage, he strode through the inn gates, out into the city. His ill-healed leg and shoulder stabbed him with every step, but he refused to let the pain show in his gait. It was only right that the pain of his wounds embodied the pain of his soul.

No pain…no fear…no mercy…

ᚴᛩᚢᛃᛰᚨᛇᛰ

Four rings of purest obsidian lay upon the table in the back room of the *Golden Cockerel*. Before each ring stood a senior journeyman, one from each of the four masterless factions: Inquisitors, Blades, Enforcers, and Alchemists. Mya stood at the end of the table, the only remaining master. She fingered her own ring behind her back as she gauged each of her soon-to-be peers. They cast more than a few nervous glances at her, which was understandable. Rumors about her were flying through the guild. Her secret was out. She dismissed their interest and shifted her gaze to the man behind the table.

Lad sat in Mya's chair, a sheaf of papers before him. He eyed the potential masters, his pupils shimmering in the lamplight, hard and pitiless.

He's changed, she thought. *So different.*

"Journeyman Alchemist Enola, pick up the ring before you," he ordered.

"Yes, Master." The trembling woman stepped forward and picked up the ring.

No trouble there, Mya thought. *She's been terrified of Neera for so long, she's the perfect slave already.*

"You're now Master Alchemist Enola. Put on the ring."

"Thank you, Master." She slipped the ring onto her finger and backed up a step.

"According to our sources, Neera's body has not been identified, so you'll take over her apothecary shop, posing as her niece. Your aunt has been called away, and you're running her business for her until she returns. When news of her death arrives in a few months, you'll inherit the business." He lifted a stack of papers from the pile and dropped it before her. "All the documentation you need is there. Do you have any questions?"

"No, Master." She picked up the papers and tucked them under her arm.

"Good." He turned to the next in line.

The new Master Inquisitor, a young dandy named Bemrin, was known for his glib tongue and persuasive manner. He had quickly climbed the ranks to become Patrice's second-in-command. He accepted his ring with a bow, a grin, and a flourish, none of which seemed to impress Lad in the slightest.

Cocky bastard, Mya thought. *Thinks he can charm the spots off a leopard. He'll learn soon enough.*

"You'll have to open your own place, since Patrice's body was identified and her businesses confiscated by the Duke. We'll buy them back through intermediaries as they become available. For now, we've purchased an inn in West Crescent that you'll use as your base of operations." Lad dropped another pile of papers in front of Bemrin. "*The Laughing Fox*. Do you know it?"

"Of course, Master."

"Good. Journeyman Sereth." Lad turned his eyes to the Journeyman Blade. Sereth returned the stare with barely discernible trepidation. "You were Horice's bodyguard."

"I was, Master."

"Yet, when I attacked him, you didn't move to intervene. Why?"

"Honestly, Master, you struck so fast I couldn't intervene. Afterward, I saw no use in giving up my life in an ineffective attempt to avenge Horice's death. My job wasn't revenge." Sereth shrugged. "Besides, Horice was an idiot."

Mya raised an eyebrow at that. *The truth*, she thought. *That's an original approach.*

Lad cocked an eyebrow as if considering the Blade's words. "If my life was in danger, would you risk yours to save it?"

"I'm not sworn to protect you, Master, only to serve you. By guild law, my life is yours to spend. If you order me to fall on my sword, I'll do it, right here, right now. If you order me to step between you and something lethal, the answer is the same. But, frankly, I don't see how I can protect you better than you can protect yourself."

Again Lad paused, but he finally seemed satisfied. "Pick up your ring."

"Thank you, Master."

Curious… Mya thought, noting that Sereth slipped the ring onto the smallest finger of his left hand, foregoing the traditional position on the third finger of the left hand, though he wore no other ring there.

"You'll have to open your own base of operations, Sereth. Horice was well known. The guild will fund any reasonable expense. Is there a problem with that?"

"None, Master."

"Good." Lad turned to the last of the four, none other than Jingles Jarred. "Jarred, you're familiar with my former place of residence, are you not?"

"I am, Master." The Enforcer's wrist twitched and a musical chime sounded.

"Do you think you can enforce a secure area around the *Tap and Kettle*?"

"Secure from what, Master?"

"From everything. You'll let no racketeers, thugs, or thieves from our or any other organization near the inn."

"I can do that, Master. I can't keep the Royal Guard off their doorstep, but I can keep 'em safe from the likes of us."

"Make sure you do. Take up your ring and put it on."

"Thank you, Master." Jingles snatched up the ring and thrust it on his finger, as if afraid Lad might rescind the order if he delayed.

Another cocky bastard, Mya thought, *but one who knows how to follow orders.*

"All right, then. You're all the masters of your factions." Lad placed his palms on the table and pushed himself up from the chair. "I'm your new guildmaster. I'll be unlike your previous one, if any of you remember the Grandfather."

Mya saw Sereth and Jingles twitch. They both had known the Grandfather all too well.

"I'm also going to make some drastic changes in the way this guild operates."

The new masters shifted uncomfortably at the pronouncement. Mya fought to remain still, wondering what changes were in store. Lad hadn't spoken with her of his plans, keeping her at arm's length as he established his control over the guild.

"As of today, we're doing away with our protection racketeering. It's brutal, inefficient, and fosters too much animosity. Costs in bribes to the City Guard nearly exceed revenues, and hatred from the general populace hurts profits elsewhere. Instead, we'll provide *real* protection from the Thieves Guild racketeers who've been trying to move into our territories."

"Will we charge for the protection, Master?" Jingles asked, obviously taken aback by the orders.

"If the business is in our territory, no. If we're approached by a business outside our territory, we'll negotiate rates. Is there a problem, Jingles?"

"No problem, Master, but it'll hurt revenues."

"What we lose in protection monies should be made up with increased revenues from our other businesses. When business owners feel safe, they feel free to expand. Prostitution, gambling, information gathering, hunting, and contract killings will all continue as before, but everything will be approved by me personally. The distribution of black lotus and other illicit substances are controlled by the Thieves Guild, and we will *not* be pushing into those areas. If they try to take over or shake down businesses in our territories, we'll respond appropriately, but again, those responses will be approved by me and me alone. Is that understood?"

The masters all nodded and muttered, "Yes, Master."

"Good. One last item." Lad paused and fixed them all with a hard, cold stare that shivered Mya's spine. "You'll cooperate between divisions, or I'll find new masters to replace you. Is that clear?"

The nodding this time was more vigorous, their assurances clear and precise.

"May I ask a question...Master?"

Lad's eyes snapped to Mya's, and he cocked his head at her, a gesture she hadn't seen in days. She missed the old Lad. "Ask."

She chose her words carefully, wary of offending him in front of the new masters. "The changes you plan to implement are unprecedented. There may be repercussions. What news do you wish to send to the Grandmaster?"

"Send a message that the Twailin guild has a new guildmaster. That's all he needs to know. If he gets his cut, there won't be any repercussions."

"Very good, Master," she said aloud, though she thought, *You're not thinking like an assassin, Lad. There will most certainly be repercussions.* Despite her foreboding, she couldn't help but be thankful that it wouldn't be *her* facing the Grandmaster.

Lad raked them all with his gaze. "I'll conduct business out of the *Golden Cockerel* until I find a place of my own to work from. As our first order of business, we're going to find out who murdered my wife."

The new masters stared at Lad in shock, their discomfort plain to see. Knowing Lad, Mya had suspected that this order was coming, and had already started her own investigation, but she understood the consternation of the others. As a rule, guild resources were not used to conduct personal business, and this was *very* personal business.

325

This won't go over well with the rank and file either, she thought, watching shock evolve into resentment on the four masters' faces.

Though new to their jobs, they had been guild members for many more years than Lad. In their eyes, he was a tool—wielded first by the Grandfather, then by Mya—not a peer who had progressed up through the ranks of the guild by means of skill and effort. Lad was lethal, of that there was no doubt, but he was not a proper guild assassin. And now he presumed to be their master.

Lad seemed not to notice anything amiss with his subordinates, and continued with his directives. "I'll pass on information and orders as needed. Otherwise, you know your jobs. Do them. Cooperate with each other, and execute my commands. If I find that any of you are plotting behind my back, skimming funds, or flouting my orders, you'll never see the blade that ends your life. Do you understand?"

"Yes, Master," they said.

"Good. Now go to work. Mya, stay here. I need to talk to you."

"Yes, Master." She stood quietly while the others filed out.

After the door closed, Lad sat and poured himself a cup of blackbrew. Someone else might not have noticed, but Mya saw the faint tremor in the hand that held the pot, and wondered if he'd slept since Wiggen's death. She longed to say something, a comforting word, but knew it would only earn her grief.

The Lad she knew—the man who had walked beside her for five years, who talked and argued with her, who risked his life every day for her—didn't live behind those hard eyes. This stone-cold guildmaster she didn't know at all...and she was his slave. Mya suppressed a shiver of the kind of fear she hadn't experienced since she last stood before the Grandfather.

Lad took his time, sipping blackbrew and perusing the documents laid out in front of him, before addressing her. "What do you think of the new masters?"

Mya remembered asking him similar questions after innumerable meetings, but dared not remind him. "Sereth is the best of them, though he'll work in his own best interest. Jingles will do his job. Enola fears you enough to never cross you. Bemrin might be a problem; he's too full of himself."

"That's just about what I thought." Lad fell silent, staring down at the papers on the table.

Mya tried not to fidget. Finally he spoke.

"I need to ask you a question, Mya, and I want you to answer truthfully."

"Of course. You can ask me anything."

He looked at her, locking her with his gaze as he rose and walked around the table, stopping only when their faces were barely a hand's-breadth apart, so close she could feel the heat of his body, smell his scent. Mya struggled to control her breathing and still her nerves.

"Did you have anything to do with Wiggen's death?"

Terror ripped through her.

Never could she let him know that she had, indeed, wondered over the years whether, if Wiggen died, he might turn to Mya for comfort. This was not the Lad she loved. This Lad would kill her in an instant if he suspected her of having anything to do with Wiggen's death. And with the guildmaster's ring on his finger, even her magic wouldn't save her. His pitiless eyes studied her like a bug under a magnifying glass, and the death lurking within them would be hers if she answered wrong.

Mya swallowed her fear and met his gaze unwaveringly. "I did not. Why would I do that?"

"I remembered your offer to help me with my...marital problems, and it occurred to me that you might think that if Wiggen was dead, you could get what you wanted."

Mya gaped. She remembered her offer all too well, and now realized that Lad thought all she ever wanted was casual sex. *He has no idea how I feel about him.* For an instant, she considered telling him, but knew the admission could end her life. Instead, she adopted the cynical air that substituted for emotion and said, "And run the risk of you finding out what I'd done? I'm not stupid, Lad."

"No, you're not."

Mya thought she saw a flicker of relief in his eyes before he turned away and began to pace, limping ever-so-slightly. She knew his wounds must be killing him; she'd been there when they cut out the crossbow bolts. She'd suggested that a healing potion would ease his pain, and he'd told her to shut up.

"If I ever find out that you were involved, I'll personally remove every single one of your tattoos, and we'll see how well their magic protects you. Do you understand?"

She'd never heard a threat like that from him, but one look at his face told her that he was serious. Deadly serious. "I understand, but…"

"But what?" He pinned her with his eyes. Though still hard, Mya saw a hint of something more there. *Pain. Guilt. Loss. Need?*

"But…if you need someone, I'm here for you." She knew it was the wrong thing to say as soon as the words left her lips.

Lad's reaction struck like a bolt of lightning.

"The only person I *need*, Mya, is the person who killed my wife! There will never be anything between us but business, so get used to it. You work for me. You do as I say. Your life is mine to spend! Do you *get* that?"

"Yes." Mya dropped her gaze, kicking herself for her own stupid sentimentality. She was a slave and an assassin. Slaves couldn't afford sentiment. Assassins didn't love. "My life is yours to spend…Master."

EPILOGUE

Crimson robes swirled in the morning sunlight streaming through the high, gilded windows. The two bodyguards standing beside the breakfast table tensed, but their charge waved a hand in a casual dismissal. Hoseph approached, bowed low, and waited.

The Grandmaster took a bite of kippered herring and washed it down with steaming blackbrew. "You bring news?"

"I do, Master." Trepidation shadowed Hoseph's eyes. "The Twailin guild has been reorganized. They have a new guildmaster and four new masters."

"*Four* new masters?" The Grandmaster raised an eyebrow and put down his cup. "What in the Nine Hells happened, Hoseph?"

"Grandmaster, it seems that the original guildmaster's ring was never destroyed after Saliez's death. The other masters discovered this, accused Mya of deception, and went to war. They lost."

"And Master Hunter Mya won?" In a flash, he understood. "She wore the ring all along? Ha! No wonder she beat them."

"Not exactly, Grandmaster. Master Hunter Mya did not wear the guildmaster's ring. Her bodyguard wears it."

"The *weapon* wears the ring? How can that be? Did Mya order him to put it on? Is she running the guild by proxy?"

"It's possible, but that doesn't seem to be the case. All our sources tell us that the weapon is not constrained by his original

329

enchantments as everyone surmised." Hoseph shrugged. "In fact, he seems to be much more human that we'd been led to believe. He evidently has free will, emotions, and even a family."

"A family?"

Hoseph nodded. "It's rather complicated, Grandmaster. The masters kidnapped the weapon's daughter in an attempt to persuade him to betray Mya. The plan backfired. By all accounts, Master Hunter Mya and the weapon slaughtered the four masters and a number of their underlings to rescue the child. Our Thieves Guild operative was watching, and discovered that the weapon's *wife* wore the guildmaster's ring. She made a judgment call and killed the woman, knowing your desire to have Mya as Twailin guildmaster."

"But Mya didn't put it on."

"No," Hoseph conceded. "Apparently the weapon claimed it for himself."

"Well!" The Grandmaster picked up his blackbrew and sipped. "At least that eliminates the threat of him not being bound by a blood contract. He can't touch me now."

"Yes, Master, but he's acting...strangely."

The Grandmaster frowned. "Strangely how?"

"He's eliminated the guild's protection racketeering entirely, and is hiring out his Enforcers as security to whoever desires it. It's difficult to see what these changes may bring in the future, but our revenue collectors will be making their rounds in a few weeks, and we'll be able to make a preliminary assessment then."

"Hmph." He picked up his cup and downed the contents. "Well, if revenues are up, we'll allow him to continue his experiment. Send him a letter requesting that he attend to me at his earliest convenience, my standard meeting with a new guildmaster."

Hoseph hesitated, and the Grandmaster snapped, "What's wrong?"

"There may be a problem."

"With what?"

"With the new guildmaster. He seeks to discover who murdered his wife."

As the Grandmaster's grasped Hoseph's implication, the blackbrew suddenly felt like acid in his stomach. "And if he discovers who did it, the trail could lead back to us...to me."

"Yes, Grandmaster."

This did not bode well.

"We must strive to make sure that doesn't happen. Even though he wears a guildmaster's ring, there are other ways he might be dangerous."

"My thoughts exactly, Grandmaster."

"In fact, make that your highest priority. Use whatever resources you deem necessary, but keep him from tracing anything back to me, even if it means eliminating our operatives in Tsing. And delay our meeting until we have more information about him and can assess the threat he might pose. Two months, say."

Hoseph nodded his assent. "Yes, Grandmaster."

"Good. Now let me finish my breakfast in peace."

"Your servant, Grandmaster." Hoseph bowed low and turned to leave.

A thought occurred to the Grandmaster, and he raised a forestalling finger. "One question."

Hoseph turned back and bowed again. "Yes, Grandmaster?"

"Does this new guildmaster have a name?"

"Of a sort. He calls himself Lad."

"Lad?" *Curious*, he thought, wondering how that came about. It didn't really matter. "How difficult would it be to eliminate him?"

"Many have tried, and all have failed."

"Well, see if any of his newly appointed masters might be susceptible to corruption. We need eyes in that camp. They can't harm him, but they might be able to provide the opportunity for another."

"Yes, Grandmaster."

Crimson robes swirled again as Hoseph bowed and took his leave. The Grandmaster turned back to his breakfast, but found his appetite gone. Instead, a rank taste fouled his mouth. Impatiently, he plucked the crystal goblet from the table and swallowed the last of the tangy juice. Absently snapping to his servants for a refill, Tynean Tsing II, Emperor of Tsing, leaned back and gazed at the ring of obsidian and gold on his finger, murder, as always, foremost on his mind.

About the Author

Chris A. Jackson fell in love with the sea the first time he set eyes on those majestic rolling waves. He spent summers working on his father's fishing boat in Oregon as a youth. After moving to Florida, he permanently moved aboard a 45-foot sailboat with his wife, Anne. Trained as a marine biologist, he became sidetracked by a career in biomedical research, but regained his heart and soul in 2009 when he and Anne left the dock to sail and write fulltime.

With his nautical background, writing a pirate novel seemed inevitable for Chris. Years on the ocean allow Chris to write of the sea from knowledge and experience, and he draws his characters from the salty mariners he has met both asea and ashore. The first three Scimitar Seas Novels—*Scimitar Moon*, *Scimitar Sun* and *Scimitar's Heir*—won sequential Gold Medals in the *ForeWord Reviews* Book of the Year Awards for 2009, 2010 and 2011. *Scimitar War* was released in 2012. An all-new pirate novel based in the Pathfinder® world of Golarion was released from Paizo Publishing in April 2013.

Weapon of Flesh also won a national award, taking home a USA BookNews, BestBooks 2005 medal for Best Fantasy/Science Fiction novel.

Preview Chris' novels, download audiobooks, and read his writing blog at www.jaxbooks.com. You can also follow Chris' cruising adventures at www.sailmrmac.blogspot.com.

Novels by Chris A. Jackson

From Jaxbooks
A Soul for Tsing
Deathmask

The Weapon of Flesh Trilogy
Weapon of Flesh
Weapon of Blood
Weapon of Vengeance (Summer 2014)

The Cornerstones Trilogy
(with Anne L. McMillen-Jackson)
Zellohar
Nekdukarr
Jundag

The Cheese Runners Trilogy (novellas)
Cheese Runners
Cheese Rustlers
Cheese Lords

From Dragon Moon Press
Scimitar Seas Novels
Scimitar Moon
Scimitar Sun
Scimitar's Heir
Scimitar War

From Paizo Publishing
Pirate's Honor

JAXBOOKS.COM

CPSIA information can be obtained
at www.ICGtesting.com
Printed in the USA
LVHW081322071019
633420LV00012B/398/P